OTHER TITLES BY RISS M. NEILSON

A Love Like the Sun

Praise for *The Bridge Back to You*

"Riss M. Neilson writes tender, vibrant, breath-stealing romance."

—Emily Henry, #1 *New York Times* bestselling author of *Great Big Beautiful Life*

"Riss writes the emotionally rich and chest-achingly romantic stories of my dreams."

—Tarah DeWitt, *USA Today* bestselling author of *Left of Forever*

"A tender story of second chances and new beginnings! *The Bridge Back to You* is a love letter to food, friendship, first love, forgiveness, and finding your home. Riss M. Neilson writes sexy, evocative, emotional prose with dimensional characters who feel like you can walk past them on the street. Full of nuance and layers of representation from multicultural families, single parenthood, and endometriosis, this love story has it all. You'll be laughing, swooning, and tearing up until the last page. Perfect for fans of *The Bear*, Carmello and Olivia can 'Yes, chef' their way into any hearts!"

—Danica Nava, *USA Today* bestselling author of *Love Is a War Song*

"*The Bridge Back to You* is a delicious story about love, second chances, and the magic of a kitchen that feels like home. Riss M. Neilson's newest novel made me hungry in every sense of the word."

—Ali Rosen, bestselling author of *Unlikely Story*

"Lush, aching prose; relatable, tender characters; and chemistry that burns off the page—Riss writes the type of stories that epitomize why the world loves romance. Her characters grab you, hold you, and take up permanent residence in your heart, making it impossible to not feel hope."

—Betty Corrello, author of *32 Days in May*

Praise for *A Love Like the Sun*

"Unabashedly swoony, angsty, and pining." —NPR

"A deep and sizzling slow burn." —*The Boston Globe*

"Dazzling, tender, and romantic, *A Love Like the Sun* is a beautiful story about taking risks, being brave, and letting the people who know us best love us fully. I adored this friends-to-lovers romance!"

—Carley Fortune, #1 *New York Times* bestselling author of *One Golden Summer*

"[A] poetic, sexy, and intimate portrait of falling in love. . . . Neilson's prose is as warm and effortless as the love story that unfolded, and just as compelling. A stunning read."

—Jessica Joyce, *USA Today* bestselling author of *The Ex Vows*

The Bridge Back to You

RISS M. NEILSON

BERKLEY ROMANCE
NEW YORK

BERKLEY ROMANCE
Published by Berkley
An imprint of Penguin Random House LLC
1745 Broadway, New York, NY 10019
penguinrandomhouse.com

Book design by Jenni Surasky
Interior art: Flowers © Suwi19/Shutterstock

Library of Congress Cataloging-in-Publication Data

Names: Neilson, Riss M. author
Title: The bridge back to you / Riss M. Neilson.
Description: First edition. | New York: Berkley Romance, 2026.
Identifiers: LCCN 2025027731 (print) | LCCN 2025027732 (ebook) |
ISBN 9780593640517 trade paperback | ISBN 9780593640524 ebook
Subjects: LCGFT: Romance fiction | Fiction | Novels
Classification: LCC PS3614.E44326 B75 2026 (print) |
LCC PS3614.E44326 (ebook)
LC record available at https://lccn.loc.gov/2025027731
LC ebook record available at https://lccn.loc.gov/2025027732

First Edition: March 2026

Printed in the United States of America
2nd Printing

The authorized representative in the EU for product safety and compliance is Penguin Random House Ireland, Morrison Chambers, 32 Nassau Street, Dublin D02 YH68, Ireland, https://eu-contact.penguin.ie.

For the lover girls who know exactly what they want
and never settle for less.

And for anyone searching for a place to belong.

Chapter 1

Olivia

Now

THE CAKE IS HEART-SHAPED TO MARK AN IMPORTANT DAY of my life, with intricate pink-frosted flowers I'll never forget, and the words *You're Divorced Bitch* written in bold red letters.

When I blow out the candles, a chorus of hollers and even a dramatic hallelujah rings through the kitchen. The music kicks up, a glass is shoved into my hand, and my friend Denise orders me to drink my first shot of tequila as a "meant to be free" woman.

I appreciate that she hasn't said it too many times throughout the course of the celebration she surprised me with. Especially because everyone else here is more her friend than mine. A year ago, I told her I was going to marry Michael, and she cackled like it was a joke. Even my therapist said, "Olive, I'm afraid your ADHD is showing. If your friends wanted to jump off a bridge, would you jump with them?" To which I replied: "It would be my idea in the first place," and she responded with: "Exactly."

Needless to say, I jumped into marriage anyway. In hindsight, it could've been because I began receiving wedding invitations more frequently than birthday invites, but more importantly, I felt like there was something missing in my life: a partner I could live it with. And to be fair to myself, Michael was a great boyfriend for a solid six months. He was older than me, worked hard as a lawyer to match my drive, and said he loved that I traveled for work. He'd be busy, I'd be busy. What more could I ask for than someone who could fit so seamlessly into my lifestyle?

Unfortunately, after we eloped, he wasn't the person I thought he was. Suddenly, he was pressuring me for kids he'd said he didn't want and complaining about things he used to "admire" about me—like the number of stamps I was collecting on my passport and my "crazy" schedule. And sure, maybe I should've started working less so I could love on him a little more, but truthfully, somewhere down the line, I had a gut-wrenching realization that I never had the urge to come home to him after I was gone for a while. All this to say, I think we were pieces of entirely different puzzles, and whatever we were missing, we wouldn't get it from each other.

So here I am, sliding in to sit beside Denise in the white limo she rented for this occasion. She decorated it with streamers and a *Newly Divorced* banner and made sure it was big enough to fit the seven of us. We have a full itinerary, but first on their list: a male strip club. Truth is, a man dancing in my face wearing a blue thong isn't my idea of a good time, but I'm down to see if my mind might be changed today.

Except, my phone rings right as Denise holds the door of the strip club open for me, saying, "Time to see some thangs jiggle and wiggle."

My belly drops. A breath gets caught in my throat. I stare at the name in the same kind of shock I'd feel if someone just said I made a bad cheesecake. "Oh," I whisper.

Denise peers over at my screen, says, "Shit. Oh wow," in her raspy voice.

"I know," I say, and the other girls ask to get in on *the know* too.

"Don't pick it up," Denise demands. "Exes aren't allowed in your atmosphere today."

But after the fourth ring, I can feel my strength slipping. If I don't pick up, this particular ex probably won't answer my call tomorrow, and he might not ever call me again.

Curiosity consumes me, but there's also something else there.

A pull in my chest that I've never been able to ignore when it comes to *him*.

Denise's eyes widen when I place the phone to my ear.

I shift my attention to my shoes. "Hello?"

There's silence for a second. Then a low voice that haunts my dreams. "Olivia?"

He asks like he's not sure if he has the right number, and I remember that even though he hasn't changed his, he's never called my new one. "Carmello?" I say.

He sighs, short and soft, like he's relieved he doesn't have to look for me. Goose bumps break over my arms. It's been a decade since I've heard his voice over the phone. Ten years since he's sighed for me. Time has made his voice deeper, sleepier, but still distinctively *his*.

"You busy? Sounds like you're at a party. I can call you back," he says.

And suddenly on this fine Sunday, I'm the equivalent of the sweat-drop smile emoji, realizing the door to the strip club is still open, the speakers inside playing the song "My Neck, My Back" at the part about butt cracks. I take a step backward and can feel Denise's gaze, accusatory and laser sharp as I turn and begin walking down the block.

When I find privacy, I say, "It's not a party, it's . . ." Then I pause, remembering I don't need to explain myself to this man, to any man now that the judge signed a decree. Besides, *I'm at a strip club at 3 p.m. on a Sunday* sounds no better. "I can talk. What's up?"

I can't imagine why he's calling. We broke up ten autumns ago while the leaves were starting to crisp so they would fall, but now the branches above my head are bare save for the buds beginning to grow. I lean against the skinny tree trunk, hoping it'll support my weight while I calm my racing heart.

Carmello Rodriguez. Calling two days after my divorce was finalized.

Like some sick joke from the universe.

"How are you?" he says, and that muscle in my chest beats harder. Is he . . . missing me? The thought is laughable, another thing I can't fathom, but I still think it before he exhales again. This one is from some deep place in his stomach, and it makes mine flip. "Actually, I don't have time for small talk. I have to cook for dinner deliveries."

I ignore the sting below my breastbone. Carmello is a chef like I am, so I get the rush, but not the irritation in his tone that he should have contained. "Why are you calling me, Carmello?" I ask, pushing off the tree to pace the pavement. My own irritation bubbling to the surface.

Maybe Denise was right about not letting ex-boyfriends ruin the day.

"My mom's updated will was . . . discovered," he says, voice suddenly flat and airtight. As if there's not an emotion about *her* he wants to expose to me. His mom passed away from breast cancer six months ago. Someone posted the date for the funeral on their restaurant's social media pages, and I remember panicking when I saw it days later. I was working for a client overseas and didn't make it back to the States in time, but I couldn't bring myself to call Carmello to say how sorry I was. And with each day that went by, it became harder to pick up the phone, not knowing how to explain why I didn't call right away, not wanting to ask why he didn't call me and knowing I'd ask anyway, ridiculous as those expectations may have been. He didn't owe me anything, but when I first heard, I felt something sharp knowing Celia never told me her cancer had come back. We'd stayed in touch, even though I was no longer dating her son. The guilt of not being there, and the hurt of wondering if she didn't want me to be, has haunted me every day since. And sometimes Carmello isn't the only Rodriguez I hear when I dream at night.

I press my back into the tree again. I'm not sure where this conversation is going, but now's my chance for me to use my voice to say: "I'm so sorry that I . . ."

"Olivia," he cuts in, and I don't blame him for not wanting my condolences. In the past, his mom was like family to me, and there's no excuse for the bare minimum—I'd eventually decided on—of me sending a bouquet of her favorite flowers with a handwritten apology, detailing the first time she taught me something in the kitchen and how much it meant to me. I didn't have his address, so I sent it to the restaurant with my new number scrawled at the bottom, telling myself if he wanted to talk to me, he'd call. I wondered for months if he'd read my note; now I assume it's how he got my number. "You . . . you're . . ." He pauses, struggling to get words out. Then: "You're in the will."

I'm surprised by what he says but distracted by how he says it. He clearly doesn't want to be having this conversation, and I wonder why he didn't just give my number to the executor.

Nothing Celia left me could be so important that he'd call me himself, I think.

But it is. It is. It is.

Because while I watch the group I'm with coming up the block, calling out about how sexy the strippers are, saying, "Get over here and get you a lap dance, girl," my ex-boyfriend Carmello is telling me that his mother left her cherished restaurant to the both of us.

The world spins and the tree supporting me suddenly feels like a string. I struggle to keep steady while six women fast approach me. Denise is now wearing a necklace with little dicks strung around the beads, the balls swinging and bumping together against her brown skin.

I turn away from them and blow out a breath, count each heartbeat that pounds in my ear. "As in . . . she left it for you *and* me?" I whisper.

"Yes," Carmello says. A dry laugh. His worst nightmare come true. An old dream of mine making my body tingle. "Apparently, *we* are the co-owners of *my* restaurant."

Chapter 2

Carmello

Now

IT'S BEEN THREE DAYS SINCE I RECEIVED A SCHEDULED EMAIL from my dead mother. There was a one-line note inside that said: *For Carmello, this isn't a draft.* Underneath was a pdf file of her last will and testament, signed with two witnesses, dated five months before her death, declaring a quarter of the restaurant go to Olivia Jones.

A prank. That's what I thought this shit show was. In her lifetime, my mother Celia Rodriguez might have been better known by many for Celia's Place. The Filipino American–inspired restaurant she opened as a single mom with a toddler. The one that was still thriving months before she passed away. The one that we were equal partners in. A legacy she said she was honored to leave to me. Entirely to me, she'd implied. Not 75 percent to me and 25 percent to Olivia, of all people.

But Celia was also known as a woman that liked to play tricks. Once she called to tell me the building had been broken into, then was mad at me for being mad at her for "a joke." Her favorite holiday was Halloween. She'd dress as Michael Myers at the restaurant and scare children. She *would* be the person to type up a will, make it look official, and leave it somewhere for me to find in order to get a good laugh in the afterlife. But the will is legit. None of this is a joke.

Olivia Jones, who used to be *my* Olivia, a woman who became someone I don't want to know, owns a piece of a place that should only belong to me.

I'm zoning out about things I've tried to forget, and don't notice that I'm burning the ground beef in the pan until Paula walks into the kitchen at Celia's and says, "Carmello, you're burning the beef."

"Shit," I hiss, and make quick work to save the meat with a spatula.

Paula leans her hip against the stove. If anyone can tell I've hardly slept in forty-eight hours, it's her. She looks paler than she usually does too. "Debra told me that table nine wants to know what's taking so long," she says, "and the fridge started leaking again in the back room."

"Their order is almost ready, and I'll put some towels down on the floor in front of the fridge for now," I say, trying to keep my voice steady. A complaining customer I can deal with, but one more malfunction or surprise this week might send me over the edge.

Paula's worked at this restaurant as a baker and even the occasional waitress for twenty years, and she's got the tone to prove it. I can tell she wants to talk shit about my temporary solution, but she bites her tongue. "Have you spoken to Olivia about signing her shares over?"

"I did," I say, and my brain decides to relive the conversation from yesterday again. Olivia's voice. Low and breathy, a bit huskier than when we were younger. Hearing her say my name that first time. And . . . that bullshit apology she tried to give me.

A short laugh slips from my mouth now as I'm reminded that my mother left a piece of her biggest accomplishment to someone who didn't even attend her funeral.

I pull a fresh batch of lumpia from the pot, trying to keep my hands from trembling.

"What did she say?" Paula asks.

"She said she wouldn't sign anything over to me. When I asked why the hell not, she said she was at a strip club and she'd call me back. Then, she never did."

It's Paula's turn to laugh. "Well . . . isn't that something."

She only sounds a little surprised, and I'm sure it's because she's thinking what I'm thinking. Olivia Jones might have gotten older, but that doesn't mean she has grown up.

I check my watch and blow out a breath. "I need to leave to get Teddy before my meeting. Most of the food is prepped. You sure you can handle everything while I'm gone?"

The longest lag time during a day at the restaurant is between lunch and dinner, which usually works out perfectly for me to pick my son up from school. But our line cook quit last week, and it's made it harder on my sous-chef Steven. Paula's usually done baking for the day by noon, so she offered to be an extra set of hands in the kitchen until I hire someone. But I worry about her being back here. With hot things. She's more accident-prone than my six-year-old.

She takes the tongs from me and jumps to avoid the popping oil after adding more egg rolls to the frying pot. I flinch by proxy. "I'll be fine," she says. "Bring Teddy to see me after the appointment? I miss his little face. And don't worry. Steven's here to help me, if anything."

When Steven grimaces and mutters something in Tagalog, I pray they don't bump heads like they did last week. He's plating pancit bihon, and the glistening noodles studded with brightly colored vegetables remind me that I haven't had a chance to eat in hours. Not that I've had much of an appetite since that phone call with Olivia anyway. While I wash my hands, I try not to watch Paula at the stove, but she's standing so close to it and memories make my chest tighten. She's had random incidents involving fire while baking in the other kitchens.

"Can you at least roll down your sleeves?" I ask when the oil pops at her again.

"I never sued your mother for any accidents on the job, and I'll never sue you either."

"That inspires confidence," I say, and she waves me away.

WHEN I OPEN THE BACK SEAT DOOR, TEDDY SMILES AND MY chest warms at the sight of his missing middle teeth, pointy canines cradling a gummy gap. "Come on, Sharp Tooth," I say, smiling back. I wish I were bringing him to do something fun after school, but instead I'll have to watch my energy in this meeting so it doesn't make him anxious.

He grabs his iPad off the seat beside him and jumps out of the car, sticking the landing. My son's not a man of many words. While other kids at his school are shoving one another off the playground slide and screaming at the top of their lungs, Teddy's sitting on a swing playing games on his tablet. At four years old, he could count to one hundred but would only do it at home. At five, a therapist told me and his mother that his selective mutism is another indicator of early anxiety. He speaks to me a lot, but the best way to tell how he's feeling is still by reading his expressions. The look on his face tells me he missed me, and it doesn't matter where we go as long as we're together. I reach for his small hand and realize how much I needed to see him today. How easily he calms my own racing heart when he gives my hand a little squeeze.

My watch lights up with a text from Rachael, a girl I've gone on a couple dates with, and I make a mental note to text her back when I can think straight.

As soon as we enter the lawyer's office, Teddy lets go of my hand and runs over to his grandpa. My father is sitting in a chair with a straight back and an even straighter face, and I watch his frustration melt away when he stands to pick up his grandson. My throat thickens at the sight of them. Even though my parents separated when I was three years old, they stayed friends, so I never really felt like I was missing anything. It didn't work out between me and Teddy's mother, Daniela, but I had a good example of what healthy co-parenting can look like.

I can tell my father feels my mother's absence when he kisses the top of Teddy's head the way she used to.

It's a different story once we're in the meeting. Carlos Sanchez might be soft with his grandson, Teddy, but when his lawyer leads the conversation of options to "get rid of Olivia" with liquidating the restaurant, he can't contain himself.

"Don't play us with that bullshit, Greggor. My son has put blood, sweat, and tears into this restaurant. He's already a partner. That girl worked there when she was a kid for three years. Tell me what the hell you're going to do to make this whole thing go away."

Greg adjusts the tie at his neck nervously and folds his hands together. My father was born in the Dominican Republic, and he worked hard in America for years until he officially became a citizen. Before he retired, he did something in big tech for corporate that I never could quite wrap my brain around, but I think it involved drilling into people to get what he wanted. When he insisted he come to this meeting, I didn't fight him on it. I knew I needed someone like him in my corner, but I don't think it's making a difference today.

"Pa," I say, nodding my head toward Teddy, whose headphones are turned all the way up, but he's glancing from his game to my father with worry in his eyes.

My father mumbles an apology, then sits back in his chair, letting me lead the conversation. "If Olivia refuses to sign her shares to me," I say, "can't I contest the will?"

"You could," Greg says. "But the only thing that might work in this case is proving that your mother wasn't of sound mind. Because she updated it only months before she died, you could argue lack of capacity in court. But it could take years. It'll be a grueling battle."

"Celia was still sharp as a razor," my father says, and I can hear the fondness in his voice. The admiration. He might be willing to fight this with me, but he wouldn't want to dishonor my mother's name like that. And neither do I.

"What else do you suggest?" I ask Greg.

"Buy Ms. Jones out." He shrugs like it's simple. "Olivia only has 25 percent of the shares. You have 75 percent. You're already the majority shareholder. It will be a huge hit up front, but likely less than the legal fees for a battle in court you'd probably lose. It's the best option, in my opinion."

Two years ago, my mother made me an equal partner, giving

me half of Celia's Place. She did it in an elaborate way, surprising me with a party at the restaurant when I thought we were just meeting to go over the books. All of our family was there, our friends; Teddy was wearing a T-shirt with a photo of us from the very first time I brought him to the restaurant.

She said she was proud to call me her son.

My father exhales sharply, and I know his pulse is racing as fast as mine hearing this. The restaurant is doing well, but not well enough that I can buy Olivia out and avoid going into debt.

Greg's secretary comes into the room and tells him there's someone important on the phone. "If you'll excuse me, gentlemen," he says, then leaves us alone.

My father finally meets my eyes across the table, leaning forward on his elbows. "Email her and set up a meeting to buy her out. I'll help with whatever I can. Let's get this over with."

"I'm not sure she'd want the money," I say, speaking from my gut. "She wasn't like that."

"You don't have a clue who that girl is anymore," he says.

Teddy taps my arm, shows me he won his race against Bowser. He's been losing this specific race for the past week; the level is tough even for me to beat. I tell him he did a good job and ruffle his hair, and my father watches us for a moment before speaking again. "And Olivia doesn't know who you are anymore either," he says. "But I do. You're your mother's son. A fighter. She didn't give up when she couldn't get out of bed anymore; she used that last amount of fuel to put trust in you that you'd keep her legacy going. She told me that herself." My chest swells. I swallow and meet his gaze. "We might never know why she did this. But I refuse to believe it was because she didn't believe in *you*. Do whatever it takes to clean up this mess."

The words hit on something sensitive. Why Olivia, I don't know. But I have been wondering if my mom thought I wasn't strong enough to carry it all myself.

Good enough to keep the customers coming back.

I nod, the backs of my eyes burning. "I'll set up the meeting."

Chapter 3

Olivia

Now

YOU'D THINK THIS MAN WAS USING A BUTTER KNIFE the way he's fighting for his life to carve our steak. It's a shredded mess, and he's grinning like he's going to impress me. It's our first date, so I might've been impressed had he asked me before he made the reservation. I could've told him I worked at this restaurant years ago, and I would've chosen somewhere else. Still, it might've been fine if he didn't want to be "a gentleman and order for us." I can't tell if he doesn't have the money for separate meals or if he thought sharing an eight-ounce would be sexy.

I'm starving, but when he lifts his fork into the air to offer me a bite, I shake my head and sip my wine, wishing away the bad taste in my mouth. Once he's finished with our plate, he says, "You didn't miss out on much. My mom makes better steak."

"I bet she does," I say with a small smile. When I told him I was a private chef, he said, "My mom cooks for people too. Yeah, she sells plates on Fridays," in a way that felt like he was disregarding what I actually do. But had this date been on the right track, I might've said, "Let's ditch this spot, and I'll sit in the car while you pick up a plate of her food for us instead."

He calls the waiter over and orders dessert while I text Denise under the table.

SOS. Call me and say you're having an emergency. Get me out of here.

You're so picky.

The way he sawed into the steak was giving serial killer. And he just ordered dessert for the both of us without asking what I wanted.

What did he order?

The cheesecake, girl.

At Bethola's? Oh hell no. It's the size of my pinky and tastes sour.

I can't believe you told me to shave my pussy for this.

He's sexy, so I was hoping that you'd finally get some tonight. You're probably drier than a desert down there. I'll call you in a few minutes.

When I click out of the conversation, I look up to see that he's on his phone too. Smiling at a video. Denise was right; he is a good-looking man. Clean-shaven, knows what colors to wear to compliment his taupe skin. He seemed promising, especially after I had to report a stranger on Hinge who was demanding that I walk barefoot all day so he could suck my dirty toes. And to be fair to my date, I should've canceled to digest the big news. I've been on edge since I talked to Carmello yesterday. My therapist insisted I was being avoidant, and I can't stand it when she's right.

While waiting for Denise's call, I down the rest of my drink in one tilt and scroll to Carmello's text message from earlier. It's jarring to see his name on my screen, and I haven't been able to bring myself to open it, but my thumb hovers over it now.

"Excuse me," someone says, and I jump slightly before staring up at the man who came to our table. He's smiling in a shy, starstruck way that tells me where this is going. "I'm sorry to interrupt, but you're Olivia Jones, right?" When I nod, he continues. "You probably don't remember me. I was hired as a prep chef weeks before you left for a different restaurant. But you were a badass in the kitchen, and I learned so much from you in that short time. The boss man was absolutely crushed to lose you."

My date makes a small, choked sound, and I wonder if our steak went down the wrong pipe. I stick my hand out, give the chef a strong shake and some compliments on the meal. He tells me he's interested in becoming a private chef like I am now, and while the conversation is flowing, I can feel the burn of my date's stare. The chef must feel it too because he glances toward my date and says, "I'm sorry if I've been rude. Just excited.

But I'll let you two get back to your evening. The meal is on us tonight."

"It was *truly* not an interruption," I say.

When he leaves, I finally meet my date's eyes. For a moment, I think he might look intimidated, but then he smirks. "You didn't say you were a big deal like that." He's now looking at me like I'm the dessert, and I don't think I can wait for Denise to call. "We should've ordered more wine."

I tilt my head and give him a sorry smile. "I'm sure they'd cover it if you want to stay and have another glass or two, but it's time for me to get going."

WHEN I WAS TWELVE, MY PARENTS TOOK A PICTURE OF ME IN front of the WELCOME TO VIRGINIA sign and asked, *What beauty do you think you'll find in this state?* I said jellyfish, thinking about our short-term rental by the beach. But asking me this was their way to keep me excited as we hopped from state to state. I'd already been in two elementary schools that year, and I wasn't unhappy about it.

Two years prior, the house I had lived in since birth burned down in a tragic wildfire, propelling the trajectory of my parents taking their environmental advocacy very seriously. Luckily, we'd been able to evacuate quickly and no one was seriously injured, besides a burn to my hand. *Now we don't have anything tying us here,* my mom said when we stared at the rubble that was once our home. But I wasn't familiar with the term nomad until one of my new teachers called us that with judgy eyes. Still, I thought it was special that my parents wanted me to see the world with them while they fought for it. So I simply shrugged, knowing in a few months I'd probably never see him again. Little did I know how much this constantly shifting lifestyle would shape every relationship I ever had.

It's what I'm thinking about while sitting on my couch and staring at a photo of my parents in Madrid, kissing by a giant water fountain. Looks like you're not the most popular Jones anymore, sweetheart, my dad wrote when he tagged me in an article about the two of them working with citizens to protect the pyramids in Egypt from being climbed illegally.

They're proud of me and my popularity in the culinary industry, but while they travel for human rights, I travel to cook. *We'll accept it, as long as you're happy,* they've said.

Four years ago, I was hired as a head chef at a Michelin-starred restaurant in Houston. It was my dream job in theory, but it was demanding on my body and I found the environment stifling for my personality too. I was busy in ways that weren't fulfilling, longing for interaction with customers and staff members that was hard to come by. But I'd only been there for eight months and was trying to stick it out. After spending the six previous years cooking in different restaurants all over the U.S., I knew I was close to a time when my talent wouldn't win out over my questionable résumé, longevity being one of the indicators of a good work ethic and all that.

So, when a wealthy regular at the restaurant asked if I was interested in being his private chef, I jumped at the opportunity. He'd pay way more than I was making, we'd travel overseas for his job in finance so I'd get to see more of the world, and it'd be gentler on my body. As a woman with endometriosis, the latter would be greatly appreciated. In addition, the work would come in spurts and I'd get to keep a home base in Houston. I'd met Denise at the restaurant here, and even though I'd made friends with people around the world, she felt like my first *close friend* in a long time. My client base has grown since then and my life has been filled with unexpected adventures. It never feels like I live the same day twice. I used to say to my parents, *How could I* not *be happy?*

But the confirmation is harder to give now.

Each time I turn the key to my loft and find it empty, my ex-husband Michael's words ring in my head. *You're never going to have a real home. You don't want one.* When he first said it, I resented him, thinking the truth was I just didn't want a home with *him.* But now I know the truth is a little grayer than I thought. When I filed for divorce, my mom asked if there was anything I'd miss about him, and I realized I wasn't around enough and hardly knew him.

He was never the man for me, but I am thinking of him as I look at the heart of Houston through my floor-to-ceiling windows. Maybe it's because my couch is stiff, and I'm not here enough to break it in. Maybe it's because Denise pulled me only into the outer edge of her friend group, but I haven't nurtured any of those relationships enough to become part of the center. And I'm realizing that in my absence, Denise has made a life with the people she has here and should prioritize. When I'm in town, she can't just drop everything to come watch a movie with me, and she shouldn't have to. But when we had brunch a couple of months ago, she asked me a question that felt like a close friend might already know the answer to: *Is there anyone you're smitten with?* Since then, I've had the urge to pull her closer, but I'm not sure the feeling is mutual. She never did end up calling to bail me out of my date. And now I'm thinking of two things simultaneously: I tried to cure this loneliness by settling down with anyone who seemed promising, and I've only felt "smitten" once in my life.

Carmello Rodriguez's face flashes through my mind, and I have to tell myself that he's not twenty anymore. How I imagine him is not how he looks now.

I think of the photo of my parents, hearts in their smiles, love in their eyes. They're happy doing what they do, and that used to make me feel like Michael was wrong. "I do have a home," I told him before I asked for a divorce. *All you need is yourself, your pounding heart, and to listen to that feeling in your gut,* Mom used to say when she'd pull out the map to show me the cities she and my dad were considering next. I know I am my own home. But even though I can't picture my parents ever settling somewhere, I know they're happy because they're together.

When Carmello called me yesterday, I had a twisting feeling in my gut that told me refusing to sign over my shares was the right move. Since then, I've wracked my brain for a sensible reason why his mom would leave me part of her restaurant. The facts: I left Providence at nineteen, and Celia and I kept in contact over emails, sharing recipes and updates. But we hardly reminisced about my time working for her at Celia's Place, even though food holds memories and some of my most memorable were rushing to bite into one of her perfectly crisped lumpia right after she fried them and trying not to burn my tongue, or stirring a pot of arroz caldo that smelled strongly of ginger alongside her in the restaurant.

The last time she and I talked was five months before she died. That email was different from others. She asked if we could hop on a call because she needed advice on how to revamp the restaurant. I was excited she wanted my opinion on anything at all, but I was also busy. When I sent her my availability, she said she'd get back to me, then she never did. I had guessed she changed her mind on talking to me about it, and I didn't want to push.

This updated will situation could have been a slipup on her part. But two other theories are circulating in my brain:

1. There might be something Carmello still needs help with at the restaurant, but Celia knew he'd never accept mine without her forcing his hand a little.
2. Maybe this is her way of getting the two of us to see each other again. She always was a bit of a meddler.

Which is exactly why sensible me and dreamy me are battling for dominance.

With the latter whispering: *It sounds like fate, something tethering you back to Providence and him.* And what had I shaped my whole life around, but following the shifting winds, seeking out my own destiny?

It's why I curl up on the couch and open Carmello's text thread, trying to steady my hands and calm my racing heart by taking deep breaths before reading it.

Olivia,
Hope all is well. Writing to you because I'm wondering if we could set up a virtual meeting to discuss you signing over your shares. I have a couple of propositions for you that could benefit us both.
Warm regards, Carmello

I snort while rereading his fancy little outro. Is this an email or a text message? Warm regards, my ass. If someone else read this, they'd never be able to tell that this man used to enjoy having his head between my thighs. I chew my cheek while I quickly type up a reply.

Good evening, Carmello,
I'd love to hear these propositions of yours, and I may have some of my own. I'm not simply signing my shares away. But . . . if we put our heads together, I'm sure we can reach an agreement that we both feel good about.
We used to come up with the best recipes together when we were kids :)
Tell me when you're free.
Love, Olivia

I send the email-coded text message, and a rush of adrenaline washes over me, knowing it'll get under his skin. Wishing that I could see his face when he reads it. Thinking he'll probably simmer for a long while before he thinks of a smart reply.

But I'm wrong.

Bubbles appear on my screen straightaway, and I can't bear to keep the chat open while he writes back. I throw my phone down for a second and stick my face in a pillow. When I finally glance at my screen again, his reply is waiting for me.

I exhale and click on the text message. Then promptly roll my damn eyes.

Great. Sending a link to my calendar of the available times I have this week and next. I truly appreciate your cooperation.
Best,
Carmello

I stare at my phone until the words turn my thoughts petty. I could tell him we'll talk when I'm ready, have him wondering if it'll be never. But it *has* to be soon. I have no choice but to deal with this. I'm between jobs now, but days before my divorce was finalized and Carmello's life-changing call, I was asked to move with one of my favorite clients, who has work to do in Japan. I'll be contracted to cook for her for a year, which is a long time and far away from my life in Houston just when I'm starting to feel like I might really need to dig in on the relationships I've built here, but the money is great, and I've never been to Tokyo. She has some other things to sort out first, and I still have six weeks to commit before she looks for another private chef.

Now that dreamy voice in me whispers, *What if there's a different path? What if this is the world's way of saying there's something still waiting for me in Providence?*

So, I choose the 5:30 p.m. appointment slot on Carmello's calendar for tomorrow.

Chapter 4

Carmello

Now

I LOWER THE BURNER ON THE STOVE SO THE SINIGANG CAN slow cook while I'm in my meeting and realize my hands are shaking. Sometimes the tangy smell of the tamarind calms me down, but not today. Olivia's text messages from last night are still working my nerves, and now I have to face her for the first time in a decade. The kitchen door swings open, and Steven stands there scanning me from head to toe for the first time in our working relationship. He's five years older than me, and sometimes when I tell him what to do in the kitchen I get the feeling he wishes I'd shut the hell up. But I ignore his passive-aggressive tendencies because he's the best assistant chef I've ever worked with, and he's Filipino American so he's more familiar with the food than anyone else I could've hired.

He points his nose to my pot of sinigang. "It smells extra sour. Did you add too much tamarind? I'm not trying to hear any complaints from customers today." I shoot him a look and he takes pity on me. "Whatever. But uh . . . there's a girl sitting at the bar waiting for you."

I realize I never texted Rachael back yesterday. "Did she tell you her name?"

"Nope. Just said she has something to talk to you about."

I twist the knob to lower the burner to the right level three times before I'm satisfied to walk to the door and see who it is, but then my alarm goes off.

"Can you tell her I'm not here?" I ask. "I've got a meeting in two minutes."

Steven's eyebrows meet in the middle. Then he mutters, "Got it, *boss* man," before exiting the way he came. When I close the door to my office and sit down, I wonder whether I should apologize for sending him back out there, especially with a lie. I feel even worse after a few minutes because Olivia hasn't signed on for our Zoom meeting, so I really could've done it myself. Old feelings resurface, and my brain jumps to an instant replay of all the random times she was proven unreliable. Why'd I even attempt to . . .

Suddenly, her name loads on my computer screen, and while her video is still black, I straighten my spine. My stomach clenches. I can't lie, I've checked out her Instagram a time or two, but I never thought I'd see her again face-to-face. When the video clicks into focus, there she is with her long hair dyed a rich shade of blond since the last time I internet stalked her. The color complements her golden-brown skin. She's wearing one chain around her neck with a small heart dangling from it, honey-colored eyes bright as they focus on me, full mouth lifting into a smirk. She was gorgeous when we were younger, but she's grown even more stunning with age.

I'd never wish bad on anyone, but that she looks like *this* is unfair.

"Hello, Carmello," she says. "You're late for our meeting."

"Uh . . . Come again?"

"I said you're late."

And then I hear it, an echo, the sound of familiar music filling her space. She adjusts her camera, and the warm orange walls behind her make me suck in a sharp breath. I blink and run a hand over my face, but she's still staring back at me.

"Where . . ." An exhale. A beat. "Where are you, Olivia?" With the pendant lights that I handpicked hanging above her head, the question sounds stupid out loud. But there's a slight chance that she's somewhere in the world at a place that looks similar to *my* place.

The slightest chance. Which she squashes with a radiant smile.

"I'm sitting at the bar in *our* restaurant," she says. "But I heard you're not here."

Chapter 5

BEEF KARE-KARE

Carmello

Fourteen years ago

A SAVORY, TRADITIONAL FILIPINO STEW MADE WITH PEAnut butter to give the sauce a nut-heavy flavor. My mom used to take extra care while cooking it for customers at the restaurant. Making sure the beef was perfectly tender and the green beans were crisp. Because of the oxtail, it was the most expensive dish on the menu. And that's what the girl who sat down at a table up front for the eighth day in a row ordered. It was a Tuesday at 2:30 p.m. I remember because I rushed into Celia's Place straight from school and noticed that she wasn't even carrying a backpack.

In the kitchen while my mom was at the stove, I couldn't help but be curious about the girl. Paula looked at me and smiled. "Her parents are doing some kind of clean water work here in Providence. They aren't planning on staying for long, so she hasn't been enrolled in school yet. Why? You think she's cute?"

"No," I said, confused about why Paula would jump to that

conclusion. "I think she's weird. Do you see how long she studies the menu? And she keeps you at the table forever."

Paula grabbed the girl's order from my mom. "For a kid, she's pretty easy to talk to."

BACK OUT AT THE FRONT-OF-HOUSE WHILE I WAS BUSSING tables, I watched as the girl picked at the beef in her kare-kare with a fork and stared at it so seriously I wasn't surprised when she called Paula over about it. I wondered if she was trying to do some activism of her own by criticizing the food my mom just made to her face.

But Paula didn't ask why, just said, "The chef's busy, kid."

"I can wait here until she's free. It'll be quick, I promise," the girl said.

"I'll see what I can do," Paula said before going back to the kitchen.

I shook my head and laughed. The girl glanced up, narrowed her eyes, and said, "You're looking at me like I have two antennae."

I knew I could get in trouble if I interacted with customers the way I was about to interact with this one, but I'd had the type of week where I cared a little less about consequences. "Kind of audacious of you to ask to directly complain to the chef right after a busy lunch hour," I said, and I swear she smirked a little.

"Who said I'm going to complain?"

I had a rebuttal on my tongue, but my mom cut our conversation short by walking out of the kitchen wearing her apron and hat, thick black hair spilling out the sides.

"How may I help you?" she asked the girl.

I slowly cleared a table close to them, hoping the girl's cheeks were burning from embarrassment after what I said. But then she surprised me by asking: "Do you think you can tell me the recipe for this kare-kare? I, uh . . . I've been trying to make it at home to surprise my dad. He's mixed Filipino and Italian, but he doesn't cook . . . like, at all. He burned ramen noodles the other day. And my mom is Cape Verdean . . . but doesn't cook anything anymore." A slight frown formed on her mouth, and I suddenly felt more curious about her. "Anyway, whenever we have access to a kitchen, it's just me in there doing my best. And your food . . . It's so good. But this is probably the last time I can eat here for a while since I spent all my savings already."

I wasn't sure if my mom looked impressed or annoyed. As the only chef at the time, she was constantly fighting against the clock. "I love that you cook for your parents," she said, "but I don't share my recipes with customers. They've been in my family for generations, and that's what makes this place special."

"Oh. Yeah, sorry. I should've thought of that," the girl said. Then: "What about a job? Is the owner here hiring?"

The way my mom tilted her head told me that she found this girl just as entertaining as I did. We'd have something besides my "attitude" to talk about on the ride home later.

"I am the owner," my mom said, "but we're overstaffed right now."

The girl caught my eyes again before she said, "I've heard I'm audacious. So I have to say . . . my parents just told me we'll be in Providence for longer than they thought, *but* you won't have to hire me permanently, if that helps. And I'll do anything. I'll clean the tables. Throw out trash. You could even pay me in free meals"—she wiggled her brows—"possibly with a recipe I promise I'll forever keep secret."

My mother actually laughed. "What about child labor laws?"

"No one has to know," the girl said, then pointed at me. "And I promise I can bus tables faster than him."

My mom's gaze flicked to me, then back to the girl. "I'm sure you could. He hates being out here."

I glanced away, a fresh spark of annoyance rising in my body. I did hate bussing tables, but mostly because I felt like I should be doing something else. I was sixteen and didn't play football for my high school or go out with my friends to the arcade at Providence Place Mall or spend hours making out with some girl at a park. I was at Celia's every day instead. I'd been helping my mother at her restaurant since I was a kid, and she'd never said that thing about child labor laws to me. But sacrificing my teen years at Celia's wouldn't feel like that if I was the one making the kare-kare. I loved to cook, I was already very good at it, but my mom only let me cook with her when she *desperately* needed me.

I realized then that maybe the girl and I had something in common.

"How old are you?" my mom asked her.

"Fifteen. No work experience, but I do have papers."

"When can you start?"

"Today?"

"What's your name?"

"Olivia Jones."

"I'm Celia Rodriguez," my mom said. "The bad table busser over there is my son, Carmello. He'll get you a shirt and show you around. I have to get back to the kitchen."

Olivia's eyes bloomed wide. "Oh," she said. "I'm sorry for the insult."

My mother smiled slightly and said, "I know my son," then walked away.

Olivia's cheeks were kissed pink when I stood in front of her with a stack of dishes. From here, I could see that her eyes were the color of honey in the sunlight. She'd talked about being mixed-race. We had that in common with about 6 percent of the population in Providence. But she had an amalgamation of features that I normally didn't see come together in a person.

Still, they seemed to fit all the same.

"Hi," she said. "So . . . I guess I work here now."

"You do," I said, handing her the stack of dishes, "and you're already a better table busser than I am, apparently."

She smiled, possibly guilt ridden, while holding the porcelain to her chest. And when she silently followed me into the kitchen for the first time, I thought maybe she was a little cute.

Chapter 6

Olivia

Now

I'M QUITE LITERALLY BUZZING. I'VE BEEN SKYDIVING IN MONtreal. I ate at the Disfrutar in Barcelona—with their experimental tasting menu—and even got to see their kitchen. I once swam with bull sharks, though admittedly, I'd never do that shit again. But there was something extra satisfying about seeing Carmello flustered over Zoom. I don't think I've ever felt *this* tingly. I take a long sip of my Bloody Mary, savoring the taste while trying to bring a balance to my body and the muscle beating frantically below my breastbone. And right as I risk eating the contents of my drink, Carmello walks out of the kitchen. He's wide-eyed at the sight of me chomping on a dripping pickle, and I imagine that I too must look like a man-eater—with this much audacity.

If my heart was beating fast before, it's in dangerous territory now.

Thankfully, he gets stopped by an older woman at a table a few feet away and I have time to wipe tomato juice from my mouth and throw a mint in there for good measure before studying him.

Carmello's wavy hair is a little longer than it was when we were younger, faded on the sides, black with a healthy shine, and looks the kind of soft you'd want to run your fingers through. He smiles at the story the woman is telling him, and I find myself smiling too. It was always contagious back then, straight from the braces that his mom worked extra to afford, but more than that there's something about the way it spreads to every feature on his face. Real and hearty: Carmello smiles the way a hug feels. But it isn't just warm now; his full lips are complemented by a low, crisply shaped beard. Sexy.

And suddenly I can picture him going viral for shaving a steak on social media. He'd do it the smoothest way. Women going crazy in the comments. I wish I were a steak. Not my husband asking why this song keeps playing. Cute way to propose.

Carmello's *that* type of fine. And I shouldn't be noticing.

I shift focus to my surroundings. Celia mentioned needing a revamp in her email, so I was expecting to see walls still the color of fried chickpeas, framed photos from Rodriguez family adventures, customers laughing with people they love, and wooden tables with antique legs. But instead it looks like a designer did their thing. The brick wall in the back has been restored and brings an edgy vibe to the space. There's recessed lighting and glass pendants intricately designed in the shape of orbs hanging from the ceiling. The chairs and booths look sleek, and the bar I'm sitting at was not here before, but it currently spans the left side of the restaurant. The music is fun, the servers seem attentive, and it's somehow stayed cozy the way it was before. Not exactly like someone's mom might come out from the kitchen in their apron and hug you because they're so happy to see your face anymore, but I can still feel Celia's energy lingering. The restaurant still has the same savory smell that comes from Filipino food. It's still a place that'd make it easy to lose track of time while talking with a friend about your latest dating catastrophe.

Maybe sensible me was wrong about Celia's reasons. Maybe Carmello doesn't need any help at all. My throat goes dry. I reach for my glass and throw back the last of my Bloody Mary.

When I slam it back down, Carmello's close form startles me. I knock over a saltshaker. He doesn't even flinch. "Oh, hi." I laugh, that adrenaline I felt since booking my flight evaporating like water on a hot pan. Carmello just stares at me, not a hint of pleasure on his face to see mine after all these years. But then his eyes flick to my mouth, lingering there in a way that makes warmth spread through my belly. Is he . . . checking me out?

He clears his throat, the tattoo close to it catching my attention too. Then, in the flattest voice a man ever did muster, says, "There's tomato juice on your chin."

Okay. Yeah, that makes more sense.

"Um . . . thanks," I say, and wipe my face with a napkin while Carmello pulls up a barstool to sit down beside me. I turn to him with a smile. "No hug?" I ask. It's a joke to break the ice, but he shakes his head like I just insulted him. My stomach has yet to stop squeezing.

"Why are you here, Olivia?" The question isn't kind, but he seems calm, like me being close enough to touch has no effect on his body.

"You wanted to negotiate," I say.

"I asked for a Zoom meeting."

I stand up, take my chair, and put it behind the bar.

When I sit back down, Carmello blinks in confusion. "Now we can pretend we're doing this over the internet," I say, gesturing to the way we're seated across from each other. Giving him a little wave, fixing my hair like the camera is in front of me. "Hi again."

Forget laughter, there's not so much as a twitch in the corner of his mouth. His mood for me is drier than boxed potatoes. Meanwhile, my body does all the things while he stares. Finding him unfazed here drives me crazy. Maybe it's because of how long it took me to stop counting the miles between us. Looking at maps, tracing my fingers over the states from little Rhode Island to wherever I was in the world. Checking my cell phone for messages that never came, hoping that he'd tell me to come back, that he needed me here. But I broke his heart, and that broke mine.

When we were kids, it took a while to crack his shell. And once I did, we weren't quick friends. He was slow to warm to me emotionally before he was all in. But the physical pull we both felt was undeniable. A chemistry that was hard to control. It wasn't only sexual, it was the comfort of holding hands, the intimacy of a hug, our elbows pressed when we were cooking side by side. And I can feel that pull like it never left, finding myself fighting not to lean over the counter just to put my face closer to his. But I wonder if it's one-sided now.

He plays with his beard, and I try not to watch. Don't dare let my eyes wander to his neck and the tattoos stretching up from under his shirt collar. "You haven't been *here* in a decade."

"Quick math," I say. "You must've missed me."

"Olivia." Hearing my name in his mouth triggers my brain to remember a time when he would've said "O" instead. Other people call me Olive, but Carmello called me O. Especially when he was being firm. "You know what I'm asking. Why are you physically here? You haven't cared about this place since we were kids. If you ever did at all."

I suck in a breath. This is *his* mom's restaurant. And Celia didn't mention him much in emails, but I don't think Carmello has ever left. I know it means something to him. But how do I make him believe it means something to me too? It's *the* piece of my history that made me the chef I am today. I still make my sweet-and-sour sauce exactly how Celia taught me. When I'm feeling uninspired, it's memories of this place and this kitchen I draw from.

Carmello twists the cross ring on his pointer finger. Impatient. He doesn't even give me a chance to deny his claims. "How much do you want? I'll buy you out."

"Straight to that, huh?" I ask. "Would that not bankrupt the business?"

If so, there's no tell on his face. "I emailed you the books yesterday to discuss a financial agreement. I'm guessing you didn't read them, but you should know that before my mom passed away, she made me a partner, which means I'm the majority shareholder between us with my . . ."

"Seventy-five percent of the shares," I say with a sigh. "I can do math too, Carmello. And I read some of what you sent me, but not all of it. Regardless, I don't want money."

Of course, I knew he might think so, but hearing him say it out loud makes me certain that no part of him is thinking of our wild situation the way I am. I don't want to still be a monster in his story. I'm not purposely trying to confuse him or keep him guessing, but I can't just tell him that I have six weeks to accept or decline a job offer, and there's a part of me that needs to make sure what I'm missing from my life isn't *him*. Pitching the idea of us seeing if there's anything between us anymore—to a man who looks like he couldn't care less whether I permanently moved to the moon, let alone Tokyo—feels crazy.

He stares at me good and long. Memories flash of the first time we ever spoke. Carmello's gaze heavy on me while he bussed tables. The buzz in the air when we went back and forth. I wasn't used to being challenged like that. I think I liked it a little too much.

"I refuse to believe you want the responsibility that comes with owning a restaurant," he says, and I blink back to now, realizing I'm not sure I want that either. Getting myself to Providence only brings me to step one: Do I want him? Does he want me? I haven't even crossed the bridge of what a relationship would physically look like if both of those answers were yes.

"Truthfully, I'm still in shock about all of this and I don't know what I want yet," I say, "but I came here to find out. I just need . . . some time. I need to get to know this place again. You don't even have to give me any cuts of the profit while I'm here."

His demeanor continues to deteriorate. He leans back on his barstool, tone shifting slightly but enough to elicit attention from customers close by. "Are you going to treat this like another nomadic journey? This is my life, Olivia. This was my mom's life."

"And she wanted me here," I say. "There had to be a reason she gave me half of her shares."

"Did you know?" He swallows hard. "Did you ask her for this?"

I flinch at the reality that he thinks I'd do something like that. "Of course I didn't."

He tilts his head, examining me. "So you weren't keeping in touch with her?"

I wasn't sure if Celia told him about our emails, but now I know she didn't mention them. I feel a rush to defend myself with a lie, thinking he won't believe the truth, but instead I calmly say, "I didn't coerce her to give me her shares, Carmello. I wouldn't."

I think this might make Carmello feel worse because his laugh is bitter, and when he opens his mouth, I brace for whatever he's going to say next. But then the extroverted bartender that took my order earlier walks out from the back room with bottles to restock, shifting his gaze from my obnoxious position in his space to his boss. He's a white man named Bobby with a thick country accent, and he chuckles a little. "Well isn't this a sight to see."

I know it's a joke after we cut it up, laughing about the extra-extra pickles I asked for in my Bloody Mary. But suddenly it's like I'm seeing myself on video, and the playback is pretty rough. "Sorry I'm behind the bar, Bobby," I say, "but I own this place too, and thought being across from Carmello here might make the conversation easier."

His forehead creases in surprise and he looks to Carmello for confirmation. My ex-boyfriend narrows his eyes. He's fuming, and I realize he might not have told anyone yet.

Bobby puts the bottles on the counter, and then says, "No worries from me. But uh . . . I think I forgot something in the room over there." He jerks his thumb behind him, gives us a nervous smile, then walks backward until he's out of sight.

Carmello checks his watch. He doesn't even look at me when he says: "This conversation is over. You can see yourself out."

With his earlier composure, I wondered if this situation was just maddening to him because no one else should own this restaurant, and I'm not making it easy to fix that. But there's venom in his voice for the first time. And all I can think about are the words of Nobel Peace Prize–winning writer Elie Wiesel: *The opposite of love is not hate, it's indifference.*

Carmello doesn't feel indifferent toward me, I realize with a jolt. And if he hates me, even just a little, it means there's a chance of something more between us.

"I'll be here tomorrow," I say, catching his eyes, "so you're not surprised again."

"How kind of you to let me know, Olivia," he says. Then heads back toward the kitchen.

But on my way out, I recognize someone else across the room.

Veronica's hair is styled into a pixie cut that frames her small face. She has a pen tucked behind her ear, even though she's taking an order by memory. I had no idea she worked here. When she shifts in my direction, I wonder if she'll even remember which appetizer her customers ordered.

"Olive?" she asks, face morphing from surprise to possible . . . delight?

Chapter 7

Olivia

Now

ONCE A CLIENT ASKED ME WHAT MY MEAL OF CHOICE would be to break awkward tension, and I answered *a seafood boil.* Cap't Loui on Atwells Avenue is spacious, with three rooms and string lights draped from the ceilings. The bathroom has a classy mouthwash dispenser, and the waitstaff roll down the boil bags for guests with smiles on their faces. But halfway into our meal, I'm hoping this isn't the one time my icebreaker theory is proven wrong. We've been tiptoeing around the conversation, talking like acquaintances who are stuck in the same place with no clear escape. While we're knuckles deep in our boil bags, Cap't Loui spicy sauce dripping from gloved fingers, Veronica says, "I'm so glad you wanted to come here."

When I ran into her at the restaurant earlier, I asked if we could have dinner this week to catch up, and she told me that she was free after her shift ended.

"Me too. The Yelp reviewers weren't lying about the garlic noodles," I say.

They're in fact phenomenal, and even with my super-sense taste buds I can't nail down all the flavors. But I'm sure as hell gonna try to recreate them from memory.

Veronica laughs. "My friends pester the waitstaff here for the secret recipe. But I always remember my tita saying she only shared hers with intention or with her loved ones."

At the mention of Celia, I feel warm knowing she was still sharing recipes with me despite our distance. But I suck on a shrimp, trying to stop my brain from latching on to "my friends" like it wants to. Veronica Rodriguez was *my* best friend in high school. We'd have our schedules switched so we were in the same class. We were the *cover for me, please* kind of besties, anxious to talk to each other after we'd done something wild or incredibly stupid. When I first left Rhode Island, we promised to stay friends, but there was a Carmello-shaped wall between us. She's his cousin, and even though she and I were closer, it was clear she was upset with me. Soon our phone calls became "too busy" texts, then before I knew it, we were staying in touch thanks to Facebook.

You're one of those people who acts like no time has passed, and sometimes that's a good thing, but sometimes it's weird, Denise once said, and now I'm realizing what she meant.

The energy between me and Veronica isn't sharp like it was with Carmello, but it's careful. We're walking on eggshells, and the Sagittarius in me can only deal for so long before . . .

"Fuck," I say, when Veronica cracks a crab leg and the juice squirts me in the eye.

She's all, "I'm sorry, so sorry," while wiping my stinging eyeball with the cleaner side of her dirty napkin and suddenly we're laughing and standing to hug each other again. This time, a real one, our soiled plastic bibs rubbing together, my gloved hands accidentally brushing her hair and sending us into another fit of giggles because now there's garlic in it and we both smell.

"So much for us staying clean," I say when we pull back.

She shrugs. "I think maybe I missed your crazy ass, Olive."

"I missed you too, Vero," I say.

And just like that the seafood-boil-bag theory is proven true yet again.

UPDATES FROM THE LAST DECADE POUR OUT OF US. STARTing, of course, with our love lives. Veronica isn't the only person I know who's in an open relationship. When you travel as a chef the way I do, you'll hear and *see* a lot of different types of relationships: swingers, couples that have systems with more rules and boundaries than a sanitary kitchen as detailed by the CDC, and even bold-faced cheating. But she is the first person who tells me straightaway she's not sure how long she can keep it up for. "I'm normally not the jealous type," she says.

"Well, I'd hope not," I joke.

But her main man has another woman and this time it bothers her, though she can't figure out why. "She's sweet, respectful, she even sent me chocolate strawberries the other day."

I arch an eyebrow. "Does she have a thing for you too? Desire to make it a poly situation? Or you think she's trying too hard?"

Veronica pulls the tail of her lobster out of its shell and triple dunks it in the boil-bag sauce. At this rate, we're trying to savor whatever we have left, and I'm thankful that my endo symptoms aren't flaring up. I can enjoy this without feeling sick. "Hm," she says. "I'm really not sure. And Matthew's been regular with me.

No differences in his behavior that I can pin down. Just a feeling. But enough about that . . . tell me about you."

"Divorced," I say, and Veronica gasps. I haven't made the announcement on my social media yet. Mostly because I was hoping people would forget I was married altogether.

"I knew it was fishy that you hadn't posted him in a while."

"I hardly posted him when things were good."

"That was also fishy," she says.

"Yeah, well. It's over. And honestly, that relationship isn't important enough to talk about, so let's move on from it."

Veronica looks like she wants to disagree, but she peels her last shrimp and says, "So you're single?"

"And dating in what feels like a cesspool," I say. "Are the guys as awful here as they are everywhere else in the world?"

"Why? Do you plan on staying long enough to find out?" she asks. "I know about the co-owner situation. Kinda weird that you're sorta like my boss. For now."

I shift uncomfortably after that tack-on. "Kinda weird that Carmello's your boss," I say. "You despised the thought of waiting on tables for Celia. Said you weren't a people person."

She exhales. "Yeah, well . . . I'm working on being better at that. And honestly, I . . . started helping out when my aunt got really sick, then I just never left. I like it there."

"I get that," I say. "It's a great atmosphere. And I was only there for a bit today, but it somehow still has her energy." Veronica nods, but there's this look on her face that tells me she might ask why I wasn't at the funeral. I avert my eyes and clear my throat. "To answer your question, I'm sure your cousin is praying I sign my shares over to him and book a flight tomorrow, but I honestly don't know how long I'll be here. Just depends on what happens, I guess."

"I see," she says. "So are you going to jump in and start cooking with Carmello, then?"

I can't tell if she's being sarcastic. "That's the plan," I say.

A small smile forms on her face. "You're still as impulsive as I remember."

"Is that a good thing?"

"It's a *you* thing," she says right before the waitress walks over and gives us our funnel fries. They're crunchy, drizzled with chocolate, and topped with ice cream. Delicious. Mid-bite, Vero eyes me. "Did it give you butterflies to see Carmello again?"

I feel a flush creep over my chest, wondering how to answer. "There were some feelings in my stomach, but I don't think they were butterflies," I say.

"Gas?"

"Possibly."

She laughs and takes a shrimp tail from our tin trash bucket, throws it at me. "Liar."

"Hey!" I flick her with funnel fry ice cream and our waitress walks over to put our check on the table between us, an amused look on her face. Yeah, this place is great.

"You don't have to deny that you're still attracted to him. Not to me anyway."

The stubble along his jaw comes back to me. That short, bitable beard. The way he stared with those nearly black irises. The tattoos running down his neck and hiding under his shirt, peeking out from under the sleeve several inches below his wrist: giving me a sense of no skin left untouched on his right arm. The fabric pulled tight from his muscles, his biceps bulging through when he stood from his seat. I'm not sure I've ever found clothed forearms so sexy.

"I won't deny attraction," I say finally. "I'd sound dumb. I have eyes."

Vero sighs. "Do you think my crazy aunt is playing matchmaker from the grave?"

This question feels ripped from my brain and catches me off guard. When I choke on a chewed funnel fry, Veronica pushes my glass of water in front of me, watches closely while I take a sip. Once I'm half-collected, I say, "Do *you* think that's what's happening here?"

"Does it matter either way?" she says.

It matters, but I won't push her for an answer. I take one more funnel fry, not wanting to overdo it and risk the pain of being bloated later because of fried foods. "You used to think I was silly for believing in signs," I say. "But that's still me, and I can't help wondering . . ."

"I don't think you're silly," she cuts in. "But he was a mess when you left, Olive. Zeke and I spent entirely too long trying to put him back together."

I want to ask how her brother is doing, but if this is how she feels, I can't imagine how Ezekiel feels about me. "I didn't know it would hurt Carmello like it did," I say, and consider telling her about the day I decided to leave. But I don't think defending myself will ease the worry on her face, so I leave it there.

"I'm not going to tell you what to do with Mello," she says, "you're both grown, but maybe tell him what your plan is before you get sick of small-city living and leave again?"

"What if I never get sick of it?" I say. "What if I decide to stay forever?"

Even saying the words out loud makes me slightly uncomfortable. I shift in my seat, unsure of myself and what the hell I'm actually doing here while I wait for her to respond.

After a moment, she shrugs and says, "Then I'm quitting. How weird would it be if you were really my boss?"

"Is it not weird that Carmello is?"

"Yeah, but I can clap back at him when he's being annoying," she says.

"What if I said you could clap back at me when it makes sense?"

She considers with a small laugh, but her tone is serious when she says, "Maybe we should quit talking in hypotheticals. We both know the entire scenario is too far-fetched."

I chew my lip. Carmello isn't the only one I've hurt here. "Vero," I say, reaching across the table and covering her hand with mine. "I'm sorry I didn't tell you I was leaving before I did. I realize that I never said the words back then. I hope you'll forgive me for that too."

"We were kids, Olive," she says. "I already have. But . . . I still feel like I know you. And if you came to see if my cousin is the one who got away, good luck finding out. That man guards his heart like a fortress now."

A second passes, maybe six. "So . . . he's single?" I say.

Vero shakes her head at me, but I think maybe I can see the smile hiding. "Yeah, Olive. He's single. But you do know he's a dad, right?

"Is he still caught up with the mother of his son?" I ask. "Something messy?"

Celia didn't tell me much about Carmello over the years, but she did share the news that she'd be a grandma. That was years ago, but I still remember how tight it made my chest hearing that Carmello was having a baby, how sure I was that it was the push I needed to move on. Some of the other updates involved Celia's grandson, Theodore. *My Teddy Bear,* she called him. Then last year, after I told Celia I got married, she mentioned meeting Teddy's potential stepfather and how good of a guy he was, giving me confirmation that Carmello wasn't with Teddy's mother, but it's been a while now.

"No," Vero says. "Carmello is far from messy. He's not with Daniela at all. But he's a good man, Olive. A good father."

I smile, but I feel some tension between us. "I wouldn't expect any less of him," I say.

She shifts her eyes away from me, takes a sip of her soda, then changes the subject.

Chapter 8

Carmello

Now

I'M ALREADY DRAGGING MYSELF OUT OF BED WHEN MY alarm goes off at four forty-five in the morning. My daily routine consists of saying a gratitude prayer, splashing cold water on my face, brushing my teeth, and throwing on sneakers for a five-mile run before anyone else in my neighborhood turns on a light. With my loud mind and worries for the future, structure has always helped me function, but it's been especially important since my mom died and my share of work at the restaurant more than doubled.

Which is why I should've never let my cousin Zeke convince me to start dating again. Rachael texts during my run with a video of the band Empty Hour performing on tour: a subtle reminder that we have a date next week. When my mom found out her cancer came back, I stopped dating. But after months of grieving, Zeke sounded like he had a point when he said I can't burn my life away with work and sadness. Except now that I have to deal with this Olivia catastrophe, I think he was wrong, but I don't have the heart to tell Rachael that right now the thought of going to the concert is giving me anxiety. It's not her fault all of this happened in the middle of us getting to know each other.

I'm tired today, feeling fatigue in my bones. I walk the last half mile because my shins hurt and I know I need a good night's sleep soon or my life will go off track. But last night I had insomnia after seeing Olivia in person. It took everything in me to stay level-headed during that conversation, and I'm not sure I can keep cool if I see her again today.

Back at home, I rush to open the fridge and start on my smoothie, but I'm stuck looking at the only thing hanging on it: my mom's memorial card. She picked her picture before she died, saying, "Don't let me look ugly on the photo that is going to define my life after I'm gone. And you can't forget to add my favorite quote." I stare at her beautiful face now, and I'm happy I let her pick the photo. It was from the day she closed Celia's Place early so we could meet up with our family at Easton's Beach in Newport. She'd been fresh from telling my little cousins a scary story, her eyes had that sun spark, her mouth was still curled from a laugh.

My gaze flicks to the quote at the bottom of the memorial card, and I remember how I almost gave up on getting it to fit. There wasn't enough space to sum up how big of a person Celia Rodriguez was and what she left behind, but after it was done, I was happy to see it there.

A day without laughter is a day wasted.

—CHARLIE CHAPLIN

An image of Olivia pulling the stool to the other side of the bar and sitting across from me with an irritating smirk crosses my mind. I inhale. Exhale. Repeat.

"What are you up to, Ma?" I ask and open the fridge.

IT'S CHAOS IN THE KITCHEN. ONLY 7 A.M. AND THE FULL-TIME staff is surrounding me, throwing out questions quicker than I can answer. "Are you losing the restaurant? Should we start looking for other jobs?" Bobby asks. His Deep South accent always sounds like it has a smile in it and somehow that makes his serious question sound less so.

"Or are we just going to have another person here ordering us around?" Steven asks, with a look on his face that says if my answer is yes, he might consider walking out right now.

"I don't think that would be bad," says Debra. "More people to talk to around here."

"You already talk enough for the entire establishment," mutters Steven.

"I agree with Debra," Bobby says. "And babyyy is that woman easy on the eyes."

"You're a mess, Bob," says Paula.

But his words make Olivia's face . . . and her curves spring up in my mind. She's not reliable enough to be my partner in business, but clearly knowing that is not enough to stop me from remembering how much I used to know about her body too.

I swallow and say, "I know you're all anxious, but all I can tell you right now is I'm not losing the restaurant, and you don't have to look for another job."

For a second, Debra visibly relaxes, but then the kitchen door swings open, and it sends her out of her skin. "Oh, Veronica. It's just you rushing in like usual."

"Who'd you think it was? The boogeyman?" Veronica is snarky and miserable in the morning, though she'll probably apologize to Debra for it later. She looks at me and a small smile forms. "Worse than the boogeyman?"

"Olivia's not here yet," I say. "Which tells me there's a 50 percent chance she realized there's an itch she wants to scratch somewhere else more. Unless you know differently, Vero?"

Veronica's head snaps over to Bobby. "You snitched that I went out with her, Robert?"

Bobby lets out a laugh, using his hands to feign innocence. "Come on now, Veronica. I was just making conversation by the coffee maker."

"All right everybody," I say. "Enough bullshitting. Let's get this day started."

The door swings open again. And there she is: my own personal horror story.

Olivia has her hair pinned up, she's wearing an off-the-shoulder white shirt revealing defined clavicles and cream-colored slacks that hug her thick thighs.

She's got three boxes of pastries from Seven Stars Bakery.

"Yes, let's get to it," she says to *my* team, "and these should help."

Everyone looks at her, then back to me, faces ranging from amused to apologetic, but either way they're going to partake in Olivia's bribery. After they thank her and grab their pastries, they all scatter off to where they're currently supposed to be. Except Steven; for once he seems happy to be sharing a space with me. He whistles while walking over to his station, not even pretending he doesn't find this whole thing entertaining. But I decided as soon as I saw Olivia that she'd get absolutely nothing from me. I don't have the energy to spar with her today.

She moves a little closer. "Should we talk? Maybe someplace more private later tonight? You wouldn't happen to like eating seafood out of a bag, would you?"

I snort and check my watch. The fresh produce delivery should be arriving any moment, but I haven't had the chance to go to my office for a second of privacy like I do every morning. I release a breath and go to the sink to scrub my hands clean, feeling thrown off by Olivia already.

"Okay, then," she says, glancing around. "So, where do we start for the day?"

When I don't answer, she rolls her eyes and turns to Steven. "Need help with prep?"

"Oh nah, woman." Steven shakes his head. "You're not going to make my day here any harder than it is by putting me in the middle of whatever mess y'all got going on."

Olivia doesn't know about Steven's dramatic sarcasm. She shifts to face me with a wide-eyed expression, and I know she's wondering if the working conditions here are fucked. But I don't need to defend myself as a boss to her, so I leave to wait for the delivery out front, hoping she'll find something to do other than suffocate me.

THE DAY GOES BY IN A BLUR, THE WAY IT USUALLY DOES, AND here I am with a mop in hand, staring at the staff schedule for the month on the wall, wondering how to fix it without overworking anyone. Steven's always a huge help getting the orders out on time, but without a station chef, we've been falling behind. No customers complained today, but I hate knowing they waited. It didn't help that I spent so much time on inventory: ordering new supplies, checking on the food stock levels, and figuring out how to optimize all of it for profit. This is, by far, my least favorite part of the job. As organized as I am, just knowing how many things need my attention overwhelms me. Sometimes I have this voice in my head repeating: *one wrong move and everything you have here will fall apart*. When my mom was alive, she handled the bulk of the office work because she enjoyed solving workplace puzzles.

If she were here, she'd be able to figure out the gaps with no problem.

"Signing out," Bobby says when he walks into the kitchen. He's usually the last staff member here besides Steven, and I'm always grateful he gives me a rundown on everything I didn't see. He leans against the counter. "Your ex-girlfriend got a motor on her."

I wring out the wet mop, glad that it didn't take much to get the grease off the floor today. I'm ready to close the kitchen, see my son, and get to sleep. "Did she distract Vero on her shift?"

"She does talk a lot," he says, "but I meant she was cleaning just about everything she could. Started with the bathrooms out front, wiped down chairs at the bar, now she's got a ladder out and she's cleaning the air vents on the ceiling."

It was a busy day, but I wondered why I barely saw her. Now I know.

"Determined girl," Bobby says. "But she's also short, so she can't reach the vents all the way and she made the dust wet. It was barely noticeable before, but now they just look grimy. Know what I'm saying? I would stay to help her, but I'm late to meet my guys for beers and trivia."

I grind my teeth and glance over at Steven, who just finished washing his hands. He shoots me a look that says if I ask him to do anything else, he'll bug out.

I'm supposed to go see Teddy and still have to look over tomorrow's menu again, but I sigh and say, "Thanks for letting me know, Bobby. I'll handle it."

OLIVIA IS STILL ON THE LADDER BY THE TIME I'M DONE. DID she drag that heavy metal thing up the basement stairs herself? She's frustrated, a rag in hand, trying to rub out the mess she made, and making it worse. I try not to stare at her small waist, and I definitely have to rip my eyes from her ass in those slacks.

"Please don't insult me," she says when she sees me coming.

I glance up at her and say, "You can stop now. I'll do it."

She mumbles something under her breath but hangs the rag on a rung and starts making her way down. When she reaches the last step, the ladder shakes. I move to steady it, but she's already lost her footing, stumbling a little. And then my hand is on her soft hip, steadying her too. She takes a sharp breath and I have to catch mine. The physical contact sends a warm feeling through my center. We're close enough for me to see new beauty marks on her neck and smell the jasmine on her skin. She's sweating through her shirt, and I think I find her sexier than I did yesterday when the only work she did was getting on my nerves. I remove my hand and back away. Last I heard, she was married, and besides, I refuse to get caught up by what it feels like to touch her again.

When she turns around, she searches my face. I avert my eyes and climb the ladder. She stands there for a few seconds, watching me. Then says, "I was just trying to help."

"I know you were," I say because I'm not an asshole. From what Bobby told me, she did a lot today that needed to be done, but that doesn't excuse her being here and pulling me out of my normal routine. I glance down at the time on my watch, my chest tightening slightly. I try to make it to say good night to my boy a few times a week and pray over him before sleep. Because of Olivia, I might have to text his iPad. "But now I'm going to be too late to see my son before he goes to bed because I have to finish what you started," I tell her.

She blows out a breath, frown deepening. "I'm truly sorry for that. I didn't know."

When I don't respond, she leaves to wash her hands behind the bar, then throws her bag over her shoulder and heads to the door. "I promise I'm not trying to make life hard for you, Carmello," she says. "I'm proud of everything you have here. I can't believe how good this place is doing in your mom's absence. She'd be so proud too." The words hit and soften something inside of me. Even though I was my mom's partner before she died and it felt like she finally appreciated my input on things, this was still her place. And it's been a lot of work adhering to what Celia's was like before she left it forever. But my body tenses again when Olivia finishes with: "All I'm saying is, I'm here and I can help if I know what you need help with. When you're ready to ask, let me know."

I let her walk out without telling her I don't plan on asking her for help with anything. There's no way I'm giving her any reason to think this is really her restaurant or the satisfaction of knowing I need help with it.

Chapter 9

Olivia

Now

FOR THREE DAYS, I TRY NOT TO GET IN CARMELLO'S WAY. IT doesn't feel good to know that I took time from him and his son. I don't want to do anything that'll cause that to happen again, so I mostly distract myself from the itch to get in the kitchen by getting to know some of the staff at the front-of-house. Carmello has curated quite the cast of characters. There's Debra. The hostess with naturally rosy cheeks, who talks to every customer like they're besties. Yesterday, I heard her offering someone a haircut out of her house. Once, she did the Heimlich maneuver when someone's kid choked on a piece of steak. There's Rebecca, the runner. I caught her putting petroleum jelly on her teeth. "My uh . . . sister's a cheerleader and she said this will help me smile at customers," she told me. Bobby and Veronica were born on the same day, dubbing themselves zodiac twins. Veronica laughs more around him than anyone else here, including me. I'm trying not to be in my head, but she seems to be keeping her distance since our dinner date. It was going great until I asked if her cousin was single. In hindsight, I'm not sure that even matters anymore.

Once a day, I creep by Carmello to go down to the kitchen in the finished basement to bullshit with Paula and try her pastries. Yesterday, she slipped me a slice of Steven's tiramisu cheesecake and told me Steven might make the perfect grumpy to someone's sunshine. But his personality and proximity to Carmello present barriers for me to learn anything more than that.

They're sometimes a disorganized bunch, there's definitely fussing, but they also seem to mesh well with one another. And right now, I don't exactly fit in. I wonder if it seems like I'm hovering to study them for mistakes. Just like it always felt like I was listening in on conversations not meant for me when Denise planned a girls' night in Houston that I finally could attend.

I LEAVE THE RESTAURANT EARLY, ANXIOUS TO DO SOMETHING besides sit around there, and head to Oakland Cemetery adjacent to Roger Williams Park. The sun is starting to set in the sky, and I'm standing outside of the gates trying to force myself to face *her*.

"Get it together, Olivia," I mutter to myself, then push open the black metal gate.

The graveyard is quiet in the way they often are. There's no one else here but me, and it feels eerie to look for the right name while I'm alone, making sure I don't step on the hallowed ground above corpses. Luckily, Celia Rodriguez is easy to find. Her headstone is white and weathered-looking, made of rock that seems to have mostly been retired for this type of thing. It's dome-shaped on top, etched with her name in bold capital letters underneath an intricate design that features skulls. I take it in, and then I laugh. Something that bubbles right out of me knowing a gothic tombstone that looks like it'd been handpicked in the late 1800s was exactly what Celia probably wanted. I squat low, touch the fresh flowers in a vase beside her, admire how clean her space is, and imagine how many people come to visit her.

And then I sit in the dirt, as close as I can get. "Why'd you do this, Celia?" I ask.

Memories hit me one by one. When she taught me how to gut and clean the inside of a rock crab, when she let me cook with her on a slow day, how she kept letting me until I was always at her left in the kitchen. The last time I hugged her and it almost felt like she knew that it would be exactly that. *Mahal kita, Olivia,* she said into my hair.

"But did you really love me this much?" I say out loud, tears pricking the backs of my eyes. I suck in a breath, blink them away, and Celia never answers me.

So, I skim the small patch of grass at my side and tell her what I haven't told her since my last email. About the new kitchens I've been in and the dishes I still haven't mastered. I show her some funny videos and read her memes that remind me of her, and I say, "On the outside, it looks different, but your restaurant *feels* like it did when I was here. It's inexplicably inviting, and everyone who eats there seems comfortable. But . . . *I'm* not comfortable right now, Celia. Was this only a slipup?"

The wind blows and the flower vase falls on its side. I pick it up, but most of the water is gone. I glance at Celia's headstone. "Yeah, you're right. You were more careful than that. It'd make more sense as a prank, but apparently the will is legit. So, I guess I'm asking for a sign as to why I'm here. You know how I feel about signs, Celia. Are you matchmaking, or do you think Carmello needed help with something? Maybe you wouldn't mind coming to haunt him? Soften him up some? Because regardless of your reason, there's no way I can stay in this city if he's giving me the silent treatment and not wanting me in the kitchen. I'm going stir-crazy without cooking. You know?"

I stand and shake the dirt off my pants, but then I read Celia's tombstone again. The years between birth and death are too close together, and I find myself sitting back down.

"But I can stay right *here* with you a little longer."

Chapter 10

Carmello

Now

"HAT OR NO HAT, TEDDY?"

"Hat," my son says, then pops the pastelito back in his mouth.

It's only 8 a.m. on a Sunday, and some other kid might be eating cereal, but all Teddy wants lately is my homemade chicken-and-cheese pastelitos or plain white rice. Never together. Daniela's been stressed because he won't eat school lunch, and she worries teachers will start talking shit if we keep packing his lunch bag the way we've had to.

My blue nose pit bull One Piece sits beside Teddy, begging for a bite with pouty eyes, and I know if I turn my back long enough my son will slip him a little.

But I keep an eye on them in the mirror. "Okay. Hat stays, sneakers go."

Teddy lets out a huff and I can't blame the kid. I've switched outfits a few times already, and I can only hope his annoyance means my indecisiveness won't influence him to give his mother a hard time with his school clothes tomorrow.

"That was ridiculous of me," I say, in the hopes of detering him just in case.

But I do feel ridiculous. I'm only going to work in the kitchen. Usually, that means black cargos, a long-sleeved black tee, and whatever sneakers are closest to the door. But since Olivia's here, I'm conscious of stains on my shirt or smelling like sweat after a day in the hot kitchen. Because whenever she passes by, I'm hit with a rich, seductive smell. Each time I see her I try not to notice the unobstructed view of her skin while she wears those square-neckline shirts.

I don't *need* to look good for her, but who wants to look bad seeing their ex?

I justify this feeling by telling myself she won't be here much longer. My dad was right. I don't know Olivia anymore. But some things still seem true. She doesn't want money. Icing her out hasn't worked because she hasn't left. So . . . this morning I had an epiphany. On my eighteenth birthday, Olivia and I sat outside of Celia's and she asked what I wished for. I told her I wanted to own a restaurant of my own. But while I was having visions of us doing it together, she wondered if it might get boring after a while. I told her my mother never seemed bored, and she said, "Well, I just don't know if I want to be locked in like that."

From what I've overheard at the restaurant, she's now a private chef with multiple clients, and that suits her. She's never wanted to be stuck. And that might be the thing I can count on to not have changed at all. Once she realizes what it actually means to own a restaurant, she won't want it. Especially not with me. But

I don't think it'll be enough for her to realize on her own that she'll have responsibilities; I'll have to give them to her. When she starts feeling trapped, she'll be on her way, leaving her shares in my name so there's nothing keeping her from traveling the globe. And then I can pretend none of this ever happened.

"One Pieeeeece," Teddy says, stretching the name with a giggle. He falls back on the bed while his favorite friend licks the crumbs from his face. And even though One Piece has never hurt a soul, the voice in my head says, *What if he accidentally nips Teddy's skin even a little?*

I try to shake the thought off, knowing the worry is unwarranted, wondering where the hell it came from, but while Teddy is playfully pushing One Piece away, I can't help telling them: "Be easy, boys."

DANIELA'S UNLOADING GROCERIES FROM HER TRUNK WHEN I pull up with our son. Since I take him overnight on Saturdays, she can go to the supermarket alone on Sundays. We usually catch her right when she arrives back at her house. Like last week, I tell her to bring Teddy inside. She reaches for his hand, and I grab the grocery bags.

While Teddy's in his room, we discuss our schedules and put food away. Because Daniela does real estate, her in-office hours are the only predictable part of her week. Over the years, we've developed a good routine for our busy lives, but sometimes she goes on vacations with her friends out of state while I take care of Teddy full-time. I'm always happy to see her go; she works so hard and naturally does more of the parenting than me: he has a room at my house but he lives with her. Still, with everything going on right now, the vacation to the Bahamas she has in a couple of weeks slipped my mind, and she can tell by the look on my face.

"What's wrong? Did you forget?" She's not quick to overwhelm, but she cares deeply, and I don't want to explain how I was blindsided by my mother's meddling. She'll ask questions that I don't have answers for right now. Besides, I have my own feelings about Olivia being around Teddy that I've yet to unpack. These past few days, he hasn't been to the restaurant, and I can have my dad take him if something random crops up so he doesn't have to be there until Olivia's gone.

"I did," I admit. "But there's plenty of time before then. Everything's okay. It's fine."

"Are you sure? Because I can look for a babysitter. A week is a lot and . . ."

I reach to squeeze her shoulder. "I've got him. Don't worry," I say because Teddy doesn't respond well to strangers, and honestly, I don't feel comfortable with anyone we don't know watching him overnight anyway. I smile. "He'll get to hang at the restaurant a lot."

She sighs in relief. "His favorite place with his favorite person."

"A win for the both of us," I say. "Don't forget to bring us good souvenirs though."

She smiles, then scans me head to toe. "Do you have a breakfast date, Mello?"

"No. I'm going to work," I say, stomach squeezing. "Why do you ask that?"

"You look really nice. Date kind of nice," she says. "I like it."

Daniela and I had casual sex only twice, and one of those times accidentally led to Teddy's conception. Turns out, it was the best "mistake" I've ever made. We tried to date while Daniela was pregnant, but agreed there wasn't the lasting kind of chemistry, and we shouldn't force a relationship because we were having a baby. I like to think we've flourished as parents because of our decision to be friends. Some people think it's weird that we're as close as we are, and my biggest fear is that a future partner of hers will want us to change that. She's been dating her boyfriend, Connor, for a couple of years now, and so far he's had no issues with it, but we'll see how he feels if they take any next steps.

"Just going to Celia's, but thanks for the compliment," I say.

"I should've figured," she replies with an embarrassed little smile. "It's just I heard from a friend that you've been seeing this girl named Rachael who I went to high school with and . . ."

She trails off, and I hang her bananas on their stand. This is one of those moments when Rhode Island feels its size. Everyone seems to know everyone. But I'm surprised Rachael is telling people about us. "It's not serious. We haven't been seeing each other for long," I say.

"Oh okay," she says, and a flash of something I can't discern passes over her face.

I hope she's not worried that I'd have a random woman around our son. Daniela and I agreed years ago to talk to each other if either of us wanted to bring someone new around Teddy. Meanwhile, I'm also not going to tell her that I might be seeing Olivia again today, which is far from a date.

And Olivia Jones isn't new. And she won't be around Teddy. No issues there.

* * *

LAUGHTER. BOLD, LOUD, OBNOXIOUS LAUGHTER. THAT'S what I hear as soon as I enter Celia's.

It gives my nervous system a twenty-second head start before I see her. But I'm not prepared enough. Olivia Jones has her hair out today; it's swinging at the same time as her hips while she shows Paula how to dance salsa. At the sight of me, she startles before a nervous giggle escapes. But she doesn't stop dancing. I pry my eyes away from her body and shove my hands in my pockets. She's thicker in places that have me imagining things I shouldn't imagine. And I really need to get this girl on a plane to wherever the hell she's going next.

"Good morning, Carmello," she says.

"Olivia," I say. "Paula." I squint.

Paula gives me a guilty look. "You said you'd teach me but you're always so busy."

"Well, it's a good thing Olivia's here," I say, then head to the kitchen.

I'M CHECKING THE TEMPERATURE OF THE REFRIGERATORS when Olivia walks in. It's one thing to see her at the front-of-house but having her back here while the kitchen's empty sends an unexpected jolt through me. The first time we ever touched was in this kitchen. I learned what her tongue tasted like a few feet from where she's standing now. And when she tugs her bottom lip with her teeth, I hate wondering if she's remembering the same thing.

Her eyes dart away, and she says, "I'm still here," in her smooth, low-pitched voice.

"Sixth day in a row," I say.

"Don't sound so happy about it."

"I'm not going to pretend that I am," I tell her. "But . . . I can't waste time dwelling on it either. The restaurant opens in two hours. And *we* have work to do."

Her gaze snaps back to mine. She seems surprised but doesn't question it.

"What can I help with?"

"Check the freezers?"

"I can do that," she says.

"I sure hope so."

Olivia snorts, ties her hair up in a cute messy bun at the top of her head, and gets to work.

WHEN OUR FIRST BATCH OF ORDERS COMES, SHE STEPS RIGHT in beside me to look at the slips. I can't have her distracting us in the kitchen and think this could be a good opportunity to give her a task that might remind her how much of a drag restaurant ownership can be.

"Steven and I are cooking. But it would be great if you chopped onions," I say.

She's quiet for a second, then the corner of her mouth twitches. "Am I your prep cook?"

"We're down a station chef. If you insist on being in the kitchen, you have to work where you're needed," I say. "But I understand if you can't handle assisting after being a private chef who serves risotto on verandas in Italy."

"Careful, Carmello," she says, "you almost sound like you've been keeping tabs on me."

"More like everyone in here has a big mouth, including you," I reply. "You gonna chop the onions or not?"

"Sure, sure," she says, full on smirking now. "I'm really good at chopping things."

I turn toward the stove so she doesn't see me smile.

For the first time since we lost our prep cook, Steven starts singing to himself while he's seasoning meat, and I bet it's because Olivia's doing the *boring* work.

When she tells him how beautiful his voice is, he even sings a little louder.

A couple of hours later, a lunch customer orders pork monggo. In a staff meeting recently we discussed what changes we need to make to the menu, and it was voted to be taken off. It's our least popular dish but was my mom's favorite. And at this moment, I can't help remembering easy days, when she'd come home still energized from a long shift and tell me to gather the ingredients to make this dish for us. Now, I sauté onions, garlic, and cubed tomatoes before adding the pork to the pan and can almost hear her from across the room, *Make sure you're browning it well or you'll be missing some of the flavor when you add the mung beans.* I zone out, thinking of the last time I cooked this for her. She'd just gotten home from the hospital and was anxious to eat something "with taste." We sat on the couch, watching reruns of *The Simpsons*. She fell asleep, and I covered her with a blanket then took her bowl to the trash. She hardly touched it.

Someone's arm brushes against mine and brings me back to the present. Olivia's beside me, leaning over to look into the pan. "Do you still use your mom's original recipe?"

I pull away so that her skin is no longer touching my skin and my brain can return to functioning normally. "Aren't you supposed to be working on the vegetables?"

She points behind me, and I turn to see a generous mound of onions. Peppers beside them. All meticulously sliced. Screaming *this was done by a goddamn professional.* I grit my teeth when she asks, "Can I try it? I don't remember what her monggo tastes like."

"You can wash and peel potatoes," I say. There was a time when Olivia was sitting at our table back home, right across from my mom and me, eating this. But something about her intruding on my memory and wanting to taste it now makes me want to build a wall between us.

She gives me a look, then leaves. I heave out a breath, wondering if I've underestimated how hard it would be sharing a kitchen with her again. It isn't big enough for . . .

"Excuse me," she says, coming back with a spoon and cutting right in front of me to do whatever she wants. She takes a sip of the juice while I stew behind her.

Visible steam must be rising from my body because Steven whistles the way one does when there's a problem on the horizon but said whistler will only be observing it.

Olivia turns back to me, a satisfied look on her face. "It's delicious," she says. And when I don't respond, she tilts her head. "Can you teach me how to make it? I never learned this one."

"Why? So you can make it for the rich families you work for?"

She examines me further. "You're really upset I asked this. . . . Why?"

"My mom didn't give just anyone her favorite recipes," I say.

Olivia inhales sharply and takes a step back. A touch of guilt twists my stomach. After a second, she asks, "How many potatoes do you need?"

"As many as you can peel," I say.

OLIVIA DOES MORE THAN PROVIDE ME WITH THE MOST PERfectly peeled potatoes; she helps us plate dishes, organizes orders coming in so the kitchen runs more efficiently, and anticipates my needs like it's second nature. She sings with Steven, and he looks thrown off about it but doesn't stop. After lunch rush, I catch her laughing with the staff at the front-of-house while cleaning barstools with a smile on her face. Who is this person, happy to do any job, ready and willing to get her hands dirty? She washes her hands plenty between tasks, so I don't have to remind her or watch to make sure she does it well like I do with some of my staff. It's almost like she never left, the way she slots right in here. And even though she doesn't ask for other recipes or to cook the main courses with me, it seems normal to her when our hands reach for the same thing at the same time. There's no sign that she's unnerved by being close to me in these very strange circumstances, while we pretend they aren't strange at all. Meanwhile, as she wins over every member of my staff, I'm reconsidering my legal options. Who am I to know for certain that my mom was of sound mind and wasn't influenced by the spell that is Olivia Jones?

WHILE EVERYONE GETS READY TO LEAVE FOR THE DAY, I SIT IN my office trying to get a head start on tomorrow's work. Mentally listing off things I have to do. On that list is to text Rachael and check in, but when I reach for my phone, I see she's already texted me.

Hey! My friends rented a private room at Pasha and we're having a small party tonight. There's hookah. I'd love it if you came by and hung out for a little.

I reread the text three times. We've only gone on two dates, neither of us has professed to wanting anything serious, and she's already trying to introduce me to her friends?

I take a breath, trying to remember that everyone moves at different speeds. I won't shame her for wanting me around. I can't tonight, I text, but thank you for the offer. I'm about to send another message about seeing her at the concert in a few days, but she replies too quickly.

Are you ghosting me?

No. But I am going through some things, so I'm sorry if I've been slower to respond.

It's fine if you're busy 🙂

I stare at the text. The simple smiley face always seems a little passive-aggressive.

Okay, I reply. Have a good night.

Paula knocks on my open office door as I'm rereading the messages. "I have to get home to this wife of mine," she says. "But the fridge in the back room is acting up again."

"I'll handle it," I tell her. "Say hello to Gabby and tell her I'm sorry I've been keeping you here so late. Maybe I'll go over and teach her some salsa soon to make up for it."

Paula rolls her eyes at my Olivia dig. Then says, "Almost forgot how likable that girl is."

"If you get too attached again," I say, "you might be sad when she leaves."

"I'll be fine," Paula says. "Life is short. I take people as they come. One day at a time."

Chapter 11

Olivia

Now

THE ROOM IS DARK, SAVE FOR THE LIGHT COMING FROM the open fridge. But Carmello clears his throat so he doesn't startle me. I glance up to see him in the doorframe and wonder how long he's been watching me trying to mess with this raggedy fridge.

"Let me handle it," he says, taking a few steps into the room.

I stand up and grab some towels off the counter beside me. I'd already mopped all the water up earlier, but Paula said this has been their solution the past few weeks. I know the restaurant is doing well, but that doesn't mean the profit margin is great. Is Carmello keeping this busted beast for nostalgia? Because he doesn't want to spend on another one? Or because he has so much on his plate that ordering a new fridge is a task he puts off?

"It's no big deal," I say. "But I think this fridge is a hazard, sir. I was leaving and almost slipped on a gooey wet spot."

Carmello doesn't get defensive. He walks over, and I see that there are already towels tucked under his arm. He squats down too. Starts laying them right beside the ones I've already placed. "That could've been bad," he says. "I'm sorry."

"It's fine," I say. But now that he's close, giving me an apology I don't need, I realize I'm still sore about what he said earlier when I asked for his mom's recipe.

Neither of us speaks as we lay the last few towels. Besides the humming of this ancient metal thing in front of us, it's quiet. But when we both reach to tuck a towel under the fridge, our hands touch. My fingers are on top of his, and we're so close I can hear the change in his breathing. The affected sound sends pinpricks up my bare arms.

I have goose bumps even after he slowly moves away.

It was difficult to be in the kitchen with him and not feel chemistry. Each accidental touch sparked my nervous system. Years ago, we were magnetic, needing to be touching at all times. But we were also young, and we didn't explore *everything*. I zoned out a couple of times at the chopping counter while watching him work. He's grown now—with the body to prove it. Whenever he rolled his sleeves up and exposed the veins in those delicious forearms, I found myself wondering what I've been missing. And this is the first time since I've arrived here that there's been any indication that being close like this still fazes him too.

He stands and extends a hand for me.

I let him pull me up, a mix of feelings in my chest when he doesn't let go right away.

We're only several inches apart, and for a moment, neither of us moves. When his eyes flick to my lips, my belly aches with longing. In the past decade, I'd never felt a kiss that could rival Carmello's. Some nights I'd lie awake hating that I'd ever met him just for that. But I don't know what we would be like now. If it would still be as good. And I'm not sure I ever will. I came here hunting for a sign, but the only one I've gotten directly from him before this moment has been telling me to stop.

What is he telling me now?

He backs away like a warning rang through his body. Says, "Uh. Thank you."

It takes me a second to remember what we were doing back here, and he starts to walk away, but I stop him by saying his name. I watch his shoulders tense; he doesn't turn around. I can't help myself. "Do you really still hate me?" I whisper.

He pushes the fridge closed. The room goes darker, but I can see the frown on his face illuminated by the light in the hall. "I never did."

"You're acting like it," I say. "Giving me all the jobs you don't want to do like I'm not just as good of a chef as you. And . . ."

"Those are the jobs that a small restaurant owner does when we're short-staffed, Olivia," he says. "Steven and I have been doing them for weeks. Welcome to the team."

I sigh. "I can do them *and* more. I just want to be able to cook in *her* kitchen."

"Yeah, well, I don't want you here," he says.

I suck in a sharp breath and raise my chin, but my bottom lip is trembling when I say, "I didn't come here looking for some kind of journey, Carmello. I came here to figure out why your mom wanted this, and if there's something here for me. Because . . ."

"Because what, Olivia?" he asks when I trail off.

Maybe I'm delusional, but I swear his voice is softer now, so I gather the courage before I confess: "Because your mom and I *had* been keeping in contact through email. For a long time." His face falls. I give him a few seconds to let the news digest. I spend that time trying to calm my racing heart. "I'm sorry I didn't tell you the first day I came, but I didn't want you to think she was hiding anything from you, or that I made her give me half of her shares. She didn't even tell me she was sick." The tears gather in my throat and it's hard to keep them from my voice. "We hardly ever talked about me working here, and I wouldn't do that to you, Carmello."

He breaks eye contact and exhales. Time stretches and stretches.

Finally, he says, "I can understand why you didn't want to tell me that day, but I had a feeling I was missing something." There's defeat in his tone, and I don't know why it's there, but I hate that I'm the cause. He runs a hand over the side of his face like this conversation has given him a migraine, and I feel guilty that I'm relieved he knows. And maybe a little hopeful that he'll open up, let me in, and stop seeing me as an outsider, now that he knows the truth. "When did the emails start?" he asks.

"Three months after I left, she reached out just to ask if I was okay. The emails were sporadic at first, but then we started to check in monthly. A lot of times, it was silly: a video she thought I might like, reviews on scary movies. When I didn't hear from her for a few months, I just thought life got busy. I didn't know that you all were going through this."

Carmello considers my words quietly, head slightly bowed.

I wish I had direct access to his brain, his heart. I have no idea how he's feeling. I lean against the counter. My body suddenly heavy, the early tell of cramps starting to come on.

"In her last email," I say, needing to break the silence, "she mentioned wanting to brainstorm on revamping the restaurant. But when I tried to set up a call with her, she never responded.

Then I came here and saw the beautiful renovations, and I thought maybe she didn't need me for any ideas after all, because the two of you already figured it out."

His head snaps up like something I said hit him wrong. Like out of all the things I just told him, this surprises him the most.

"What is it?" I ask.

For a second, I think he'll tell me, but the fridge makes a choked sound. As if it, too, is shocked by this conversation. Water spills out in a gush, soaking the towels we just laid.

Carmello curses under his breath. "I need to deal with this mess," he says, pointing to the small pool starting to form at the fridge's side. "We'll talk more tomorrow, okay?"

"Okay," I say. "You need help?"

He shakes his head. "No, but . . . dinner rush until you leave?"

"Wait," I say, pulse picking up, "are you asking me to cook in *your* kitchen, Carmello?"

"In my mom's kitchen," he says, voice low, and my eyes burn a little.

"I'd love that," I say, backing out of the room slowly with a smile on my face. "Oh, and Carmello? Watch your step, the floor is wet."

His mouth curves up slightly. "See you tomorrow, Olivia."

When I walk out of the room, I have to catch my breath by the door. I feel so many things after talking to Carmello, but I'm also just a girl, and I can't help remembering the way his eyes flicked to my mouth, if only for a second.

I trace my lips, and then I leave.

Chapter 12

SURPRISES AND SPAGHETTI

Olivia

14 years ago

THE FIRST TIME I EVER OVERHEARD CELIA RODRIGUEZ mention me was a few months after I'd been hired. I was in the back room clocking in for my shift, and she said to Paula: "She talks too much, but she's hardworking. I think I'll let her learn to cook with Carmello."

I couldn't hide my smile when I peeked in. "I heard that," I said.

"And I knew you were there," said Celia, smiling back.

A WEEK LATER, I STOOD BESIDE CARMELLO, WATCHING AS HE seasoned meats for the following day's lunch menu. He was supposed to lock up, and everyone else was gone.

"Are you lonely or something?" he teased.

The question caught me off guard. "Why do you ask that?"

"You come early on weekends to do your homework at the two-seater table out front. You stay way past your shifts, including this one. And I just . . . have this feeling that maybe you don't want to go home," he said.

I shrugged, uncomfortable for a second. I hadn't really thought about it that way. "Well, my parents are doing amazing work in the city, but they're always gone. And the places we rent are never *home*. I'd much rather be here at the restaurant, anyway, waiting until you or Celia actually let me use a spatula, as promised. I have to say, I'm getting pretty impatient."

I said it hoping he'd laugh, but he just nodded. Sometimes he was so serious. Unless we were debating something back and forth, then his smirk was unrelenting.

"I could leave if you want to be alone though," I said, wondering if I was supposed to be taking a hint and hoping I wasn't.

He shook his head. Then gestured toward a pot on the counter with his pursed lips. His mom liked to point to things the same way. "Will you pass me that?"

I handed him the pot, and stayed to watch him fill it with water. Bring it to a boil on the burner. "I thought you were done for the night too," I said.

"My mom is home doing paperwork, and I know she probably won't feed herself tonight," he said. "So, I'm going to bring her dinner. Do you know how to make spaghetti?"

I tried not to grin because before this day he never said anything to me about his personal life. But I thought it was the cutest thing that he was taking care of his mom.

"I do," I said. "The only thing my dad taught me from his Italian momma."

"Well, do you want to learn how to make it the Dominican way?" Carmello asked, and he looked a bit shy about it. When I quickly said yes, he seemed to relax, and while he was sautéing the base for the sauce, he told me his dad might not be a chef but he's a good cook. "I've learned a thing or two from him and from my abuela too. And my mom was just saying how she misses my abuela's spaghetti."

"You're sweet," I said. He rolled his eyes, but I was grinning. "It's true! I feel like I'm in an alternate reality. Or like you've unveiled something to me. But is this your final form, Carmello Rodriguez? Or are you going to surprise me with other things? Are your layers like an onion? Or like lasagna?"

He smiled. "What's the difference, Olivia Jones?"

"One has more subtle layers than the other," I said. "Duh."

"I'm sweet, you're weird," he said. "Only one of us is surprised here."

"And yet, for some reason you don't want me to leave," I said. Then, I quickly realized it might've been the wrong thing. He averted his eyes and quietly started dicing more tomatoes I was sure he didn't need. My face was burning from embarrassment, wondering if he thought I was insinuating that he liked me. Was I? "I'm going to shut up now," I told him.

"I kinda like when you don't," he said.

My belly did a backflip. Wait. Was he flirting?

This was a temporary dilemma. I didn't know how to respond because I never flirted with boys in school before. They tried with me all the time, but it was rare that anyone got my attention. Besides, there wasn't a reason to, because I knew if I got attached to anyone it would be short-lived. But Carmello had caught my attention the first time we talked. He'd kept it ever since.

"So then I'll never shut up again," I said.

Carmello laughed. "You're the give an inch, take a mile type," he said. Then: “Not quite a spatula, but here.” He handed me his sauce spoon. “You finish.”

I was a little nervous to cook in front of him, but I gladly cut in, moving the sauce he started around the pan. “I think it needs more garlic,” I said after a few seconds because this flirting thing was hard, and I wanted him to stop staring at me. Even though I had no clue what I was talking about, Carmello didn’t argue, just got more garlic ready and tossed it in alongside the green peppers, salami, and onions. His directions were minimal and my nerves bubbled to the surface with him watching, so I turned up the burner on the stove, just to have something to do with my hands, not realizing how powerful it was.

The sauce popped and splattered everywhere, including my shirt.

“Shit, sorry. I should’ve warned you about how quickly it heats,” he said before sucking air through his teeth. “Oh damn, does that burn?”

I wasn’t sure what he meant until I saw sauce on my fingers. “Um . . .” I said. “Actually, no. I don’t have a lot of sensation in my left hand.” When his brows pulled together, I smiled so he wouldn’t think too much of it. “Touching a scorching doorknob can do that to a person, but at least the sauce didn’t sting when it got me.”

Weeks ago, he was in the room while I was telling Paula about the fire that set my parents on their unusual path, and though Carmello didn’t cut in to our conversation, he did make a face that let me know he was listening. He was making that same face again, and I had the urge to keep talking to try to kill the awkward feeling in my chest. I hated the thought of anyone pitying me for what happened. Luckily, I didn't have to speak because Carmello left me to walk over to the sink and wet a washcloth. And when he came back and gently took my left hand to clean the sauce himself, I forgot how to use words anyway. But when he reached out to brush the cloth softly against my cheek, I flinched slightly in surprise and he backed away from me fast.

"I'm sorry, you had sauce there and I . . . um." He bit down on his bottom lip. "I shouldn't have touched you without permission. That was . . ."

I didn't know how to flirt, but I wanted to learn, and I was a quick study. So . . . I took a step forward. Then another. "Do you like me, Carmello?" I asked, heart racing while anticipating his answer.

"You're a little annoying, sometimes," he said. "But yeah, O . . . I like you just fine."

I think he meant to say it in a friendly way, but I watched how hard he swallowed. How nervous he looked. I heard the nickname he called me for the first time. I decided I liked the way it sounded, and I liked *him* even more, and then my body was simply reacting. I went up on my tiptoes to kiss his lips. And it was instantly electric. I'd never kissed anyone before, but I already knew I'd be looking for that feeling in every kiss after it.

I wondered if Carmello felt it too. If he ever experienced adrenaline quite like that. If he kissed a lot of people before me and how mine measured up. He was silent, just staring after I pulled away. Then a smile tugged at his lips. He bent low and brushed his mouth over mine again. I went in for another right after he was done. This one more firm. The kind of kiss you can't pretend didn't happen. My whole body was fluttering. I had a hand on Carmello's chest; I could feel his heart beating fast too. When we broke apart, we were both breathing heavier.

"I don't know how long I'll be in Rhode Island," I blurted out, suddenly scared of what it meant that I wanted more conversation, more kisses, that I hoped for more of that with him.

Carmello wasn't a dumb boy. He knew this meant that we could kiss today, and if my parents told me it was time to pack up, I'd be gone tomorrow. But he still pushed curls from my face and said, "Okay."

And when our lips met again, we opened our mouths to try it with tongue.

Later that night, I went home with a full plate of Dominican spaghetti and a smile I couldn't hide from my parents.

Chapter 13

Olivia

Now

AT 7 A.M., I WATCH CARMELLO THROW OPEN THE DOOR to Celia's Place. His shoulders are tense; he scans the front-of-house with wide eyes. Sees Steven by the bar and releases a breath and a short laugh, says, "Shit, Steven. For a second, I thought there was a break-in because you never"—his face morphs from relief to confusion—"come in early unless you have to."

When I left Carmello mopping up fridge water last night, I dialed Paula's number and asked her to call Steven. Being the sous-chef, he has a key to Celia's Place in case he needs to open or close it when Carmello can't. And his exact words to Paula were: "Bro, I never come in early unless I have to." To which Paula reminded him that he owed her a favor. For what, I don't know. But the three of us arrived here an hour ago. Steven still had sleep in his eyes, and it looked like he'd been partying last night. When he unlocked the restaurant door, he glanced at me and said, "Carmello's going to be pissed. You better tell him this was all you." I reassured him that I could handle Mello.

Now, I clear my throat from where me and Paula are sitting in a booth across the room. Carmello stares at us, then shakes his head like he doesn't have the energy to question what the hell is going on here. We all watch him walk to the kitchen, and then we wait.

It doesn't take him long. The door is swinging open five minutes later and he's pointing a finger behind him. "Where the hell is my fridge?"

"You mean that big metal half-broken thing that's had more birthdays than me?" I say. "It's probably at the junkyard by now. I bribed these two to help me get rid of it."

"Olivia," he says. "You. Are not. Staying."

"Just thank me for the shiny new appliance and one less potential hazard at Celia's Place, then move on, Mello," I say.

He inhales loudly through his nose, mutters something that sounds like a thank-you, throws a sharp look at the three of us, and walks back into the kitchen.

"I already know how this day is going to go for me," Steven says before he downs an energy drink that has been referred to as diabetes in a can.

I HAD A SIMILAR THOUGHT TO STEVEN'S EARLIER, BUT SURprisingly, I think that the day is going much smoother than it was yesterday, and dare I say, Carmello looks relaxed. I swear I'm not trying to win his love with favors—that fridge really was a hazard, I just wanted to help—but every time someone compliments the new one, I shoot him a grin, which he doesn't groan at.

I'm patiently waiting for the dinner rush, happy to be dicing tomatoes in the meantime, when Veronica comes into the kitchen with a smirk on her face. She says something to Carmello that I can't hear. "What?" he asks. Something. Something. Whispers. And: "She wants to see you."

My ears perk up at that particular pronoun before those particular words.

Carmello grumbles something under his breath, then looks up at the clock on the wall, removes his apron, and turns to Steven. "It's almost time for me to go anyway," he says. "Can you take over from here? I've only got one order to fill."

I hurry to throw the diced tomatoes into a bowl, then step out from behind the chopping counter. "Me. Me. I can do it," I say.

"Don't you have to mince garlic for the . . ." he starts.

"Garlic finely minced, apples cored," I cut in. "Onions made me cry. Tomatoes diced like they've never been diced. Steven's busy. Put me in the game, Coach."

"We agreed to dinner rush," he says.

"But we didn't sign a contract," I point out.

I think he wants to smile. He takes his hat off, and I get the sudden urge to run my right hand over his hair and see how soft it feels. "Do you remember how to make pancit?" he asks.

"Don't insult me, Mello," I say. Food holds memories for me, and learning to make pancit from his mom, making the noodles just right, perfectly balancing the slight sweetness of the sauce, was one of my favorites.

Carmello's mouth falls slightly, and I wonder if it's my casual use of his nickname. "Don't do anything extra," he says. "Just like we used to make it. Okay?"

When he says *we*, I get flutters in my stomach, but I try not to show it.

"Got it, Boss," I say, and do a happy dance all the way to the stove.

He stands in front of the door for a few seconds, exhales, then pushes it open.

Veronica hurries to peek through the window. I glance at the pot in front of me, then rush to join her. Carmello's walking over to a table of three women in the back left corner of the room. One of them is waving at him. The flutters I felt have been replaced with a sharp sensation. Different from the cramps I had last night from my endometriosis trying to start up. This is . . . curiosity? Concern? Jealousy? A mix of all three?

"Who is that?" I ask quietly.

"Rachael," Veronica says after a moment. "Said she's a girl he's been seeing."

I have an instinct to look at Vero because her tone is tight, but I can't take my eyes off of her cousin heading toward that woman. That Rachael person I didn't know existed until now.

"I should've asked if he was actively dating instead of single," I say. "Do you think it's serious between them?"

"I don't know," Veronica says, "but she did bring her friends to meet him."

There's a knot in my throat as I stare. "She's pretty."

"She is," Vero agrees, then turns to me. "Are you feeling . . . insecure?"

"What? Hell no. Just a baddie recognizing another baddie."

From here, I can't tell if Rachael's white or a fair-skinned woman of color, but her makeup is on point and her long dark hair is laid. We don't look anything alike, but I wonder if Carmello has a personality type. Doesn't matter if I'm working alone in a client's kitchen, I enjoy getting dressed up and beating my face. Even my work clothes at Celia's Place are curated looks.

"Okay," Vero says, shifting her attention back to the window. "But maybe you should take *this* as a sign if you're still considering pursuing him."

She leaves the kitchen before I can respond, and I feel heavy about her passive-aggressive comment and the fact that Carmello might be getting serious with someone else. I've been taking him warming up to me being here as a sign that he might still feel something for me too. I swear there was a moment between us last night in the back room, but now there's a slight ache in my chest.

There's no doubt that I still have deep feelings for that man.

But I'm not going to force him to see me or try to ruin a relationship he's building.

When Steven slams a lid on a pot with emphasis, I snap back to focus. "Yo. You're burning the pancit," he says.

"Shit, shit," I say, rushing to the stove to fix the situation before Carmello smells it.

Chapter 14

Carmello

Now

THE COUPLE WHO COME IN EVERY MONDAY LIKE CLOCK-work to share saliva and eat off each other's plate isn't here, but Rachael is. I'm unnerved by her presence after our texts last night, but I try not to show it. No need to embarrass her.

"Me and my friends were in the area," she says, "and none of us have been here before, so we just figured what the hell."

I attempt a smile, but it's hard to get my mouth to move much in that direction.

For a second, there's something that looks like regret in her eyes. I'm sure she can see on my face that this isn't cool. But then her friend with the red hair and dark lip liner says, "We were going to go to Black Sheep for lunch and drag bingo, but this place is . . ."—she glances around—"nice." There's something in her tone that makes me think she wanted to say *boring* instead, but maybe that's my own insecurity because the kissing couple is absent today. Rachael's face is flushed now, and the blonde among them smiles at me nervously. “Anyway,” the redhead continues, “we devoured the egg rolls. So different. Your mom is an incredible cook.”

“Krista,” Rachael says, elbowing her friend. “I told you his mother passed away.”

The redhead is referring to the fact that the lumpia sampler plate is made with three different types of meat, instead of just the traditional pork, and an equal number of sauces, including the normal soy sauce and vinegar combo. I’m happy she likes the lumpia platter, but I’m annoyed with the way she assumed I wasn’t the one who made it because I look more Dominican than Filipino. I knew one day my mixed identity would be questioned now that my mom’s not here, but never did I imagine it would be in this context. And what Krista doesn’t know is that it was a fight for me to get that one new item on the menu and that it only happened after my mom made me a partner.

“It’s okay,” I reassure Rachael, then I tell Krista that I created that particular appetizer myself and thank her for the compliment.

Krista’s face falls slightly before she taps the seat between her and the third friend who’s been quietly checking me out. “Well, you are quite the cook, then,” she says. “Why don’t you sit with us and chat?”

I scratch the back of my neck, envisioning an interview I never asked for. “Actually, I can’t because . . .” but before I can explain, Krista cuts me off.

“Too busy in the kitchen?”

There’s a hint of insult in her tone, and I try to look unfazed by it, but she struck a chord that was already thin and fraying. “Actually,” I say, “I have to go pick up my son from school.”

Rachael's eyes widen slightly, even though she knows I have a child. "Right now?"

"Yup," I say.

"It's not something you can push back?" she asks like I just told her I have errands that can wait. She's not the first woman I've dated who's been weird when I have to be an actual parent to Teddy, and now I'm doubting she'll be the last.

"I can't," I say, "but even if I could, I wouldn't."

When we were young, Olivia always wanted to talk about superpowers. She said she'd want to be able to clone herself so she could be in two different places at the same time. I told her I'd want the ability to read minds. Right now, these three women are staring at me with different expressions, but I wouldn't pick that power. I couldn't care less what any of them thinks.

"Have a good day, ladies. Dessert is on me."

OUR FAVORITE ICE CREAM SPOT IN CRANSTON HAS BEEN IN business since I was a kid. It still has the same old sign, the words *Dairy Twirl* in red, a little worn from weather and time. But they're open earlier in the season this year, and they bought brand-new picnic tables. It seems like the wait time at the window has doubled. Even today, with a chill still in the air, the line stretches into the parking lot. The strange part: there's music coming from a Bluetooth speaker. We were here every week last summer, and they sure as hell weren't playing Drake songs.

While we wait in line, Teddy bobs his head to the beat and stares at the birds perched on a fence, waiting for someone to drop their chocolate cone. Once we reach the window, he says, "Look, Daddy," and points to a picture of new items added to their menu. The best part about Dairy Twirl is that it's classic. Sundaes and jimmies, soft serve, and "Two scoops or one?" There are a lot of ice cream spots in Rhode Island serving specialty flavors now, and I like that too, but it's comforting coming here and knowing exactly what we're going to get.

All of that is still here, but now there are doughboys, frozen s'mores, and mini pancakes to load up with toppings. "Do you want that?" I ask Teddy when he points to the pancakes.

"With rainbow sprinkles, please," he says, keeping that from his usual vanilla cone order.

ZEKE IS VERONICA'S OLDER BROTHER. HE USUALLY MEETS ME and Teddy at the park after ice cream, but today I asked him to come here first. Our mothers were sisters, pregnant at the same time, but I often feel like his elder. Doesn't help that he cracks jokes, calling me *grandpa* when I don't want to drink because of work in the morning. *Ole boring business owner ass,* he'll say.

He doesn't think I'm boring today. This is the most invested he's been in any of my stories. "You must've hit it right if she's showing up at your workplace with the squad," he says.

Nothing explicit was said, but Teddy often reads between the lines. "Watch your mouth."

Zeke doesn't give a wide-eyed *oops* face when I warn him, but he does give it when a big glob of his cotton candy ice cream drops from his cone to the picnic table in front of him.

He doesn't bother to wipe it away until I force him with a napkin in front of his face.

"How about you excuse *your* damn mouth, Gramps," he says

then pats my son's head. "Teddy's one of the boys, and he's distracted by this monstrosity you bought him anyway."

"As one of the boys, I don't want him speaking that way," I say. But Zeke's probably right about Teddy being distracted by enough ice cream to feed four kids. Until his attention is successfully caught when Zeke steals one of his pancakes without asking.

"Whatchu gonna do about it, Grandpa Junior?" Zeke says to him, and Teddy retaliates by twisting Zeke's ear until they're full-on wrestling. My son may be quiet, but he laughs with his whole belly. And sometimes my cousin is shameless, but he's the only other person in my life Teddy laughs like that with, so I like having him around.

When they're finished and Teddy gets back to eating his melted mess, Zeke's waiting for me to disappoint him. "I haven't even done that with Rachael," I say, talking about the sex.

"Wait, really? The girl's been throwing it at you since the first date."

"We've kissed," I say. "And after today, that's as far as we'll ever get."

When I left Celia's, I sent a text message telling Rachael it won't work out between us. That I think our personalities don't click. I wanted to give her a real explanation so she doesn't feel like I'm going to ghost, even if she doesn't seem like the type a man can easily ghost. But she said she understood, and I transferred her the tickets to the concert. Telling her she should bring one of her friends. I hope she doesn't take Krista.

Zeke sucks his teeth. "Man, listen . . . if someone as hot as she is offered for me to come upstairs to her apartment, I'd follow her with moving boxes."

"And then she'd call the cops," I say.

"Maybe," Zeke replies. "But it sounds like she's just as wild as me. It'd be a toss-up for which one of us would need a restraining order first."

"All right, let's pivot," I say. "There are kids around. People are staring."

"And their kids are currently listening to Drake," he says, pointing at the speaker.

I help Teddy clean his hands because he starts fidgeting like he's anxious about them being sticky. I can relate to the feeling. It's why I often opt for a cup instead of a cone.

"Shit. The music reminds me," I say. "What's your week looking like?"

Zeke smiles and says, "Got a food truck gig by the pedestrian bridge tomorrow, and I'm finally spinning a set at Black Sheep on Friday. They're letting me on with Slick Vic both days."

I try to ignore the tinge of bitterness I feel at the mention of Black Sheep, but it's tough when two weeks after my prep quit for "higher pay" elsewhere, I found out he's now working there. I can't blame him for needing more money than I can offer, but the Black Sheep bit sent me on a spiral. It's become one of the places to be in Providence these days, and it's also a blatant reminder among other reminders (like the redhead's comment) that maybe I should be concerned about my own restaurant, about how to make it into another hot spot in the city.

Still, Zeke's been trying to get a DJ gig at Black Sheep for a while, so I smile too.

"Happy for you, cousin," I say. "Check you out. Low Key now."

Low Key is a team of DJs that work at different locations in Rhode Island. Lately, most restaurants in the area are not only providing food but an atmosphere to encourage extended lingering. From hiring DJs for dance music during brunch to hosting drag bingo, Sunday Samosas, and trivia nights to accompany Wednesday fifty-cent wings. After 10 p.m., Black Sheep lowers the lights and treats it like their own little club. The culture shift is great for Zeke, who just became a DJ a year ago and is already getting some good gigs, but it might not be great for Celia's Place, which offers food without the frills.

Zeke shakes his head. "I'm not part of the team yet, but Slick Vic told me they're trying to juggle the increase in demands for DJs, so I'm hoping they like what I bring to Black Sheep."

"They will," I say, confident in his skills. Zeke's been good with music since we were kids. He's also been good at reading straight through me.

"Enough of that. What's up with you, bro? You seem heavy. Olivia on the brain?"

"Not in the way you think, Z," I say.

Then I tell him that two years ago I mentioned to my mom that we should brainstorm ideas for our own special night at the restaurant. She shot me down, arguing that profit margins were fine and that Celia's Place would do as well as it's always done long term. I got her to compromise on the major renovation to the front-of-house so that we could at least bring in more customers, but she was salty for so long about losing those ugly chickpea-colored walls. Then a week after we found out her breast cancer returned, she turned to me in the kitchen and said, "Let's do your idea. What is it?"

I asked if she was joking. She wasn't. She truly wanted to add something else to her plate and mine when she was sick again and we had to focus our extra energy on making sure she got the proper care team and whatever it took to fight the cancer. I told her she just felt guilty for shooting me down and now that she thought she was dying, she wanted to add it to a bucket list.

She told me I was just scared that she really was dying and I'd be on my own. I didn't want to talk about it anymore, so we never did, but I should've known she hadn't given up. My mom was the persistent type; the proof is in the fact that she was talking to Olivia for nearly a decade and I had no idea. Then last night by the fridge when Olivia told me about the timing of their last email exchange, there was a tingle in the back of my brain. Celia Rodriguez decided to email my ex-girlfriend to brainstorm ideas behind my back, and I'm pretty positive the only reason she didn't follow through with it was because she quickly realized she didn't want to put any more pressure on me. Her cancer was aggressive. She tried to work, but between treatments and rest, she barely could, and she'd worry out loud about me when I'd sit in the chair beside her bed after long days in the restaurant.

Zeke passes Teddy another napkin because my boy got chocolate syrup on his shirt, then shoots me a serious look. "Did you ask me to come for ice cream knowing I'm lactose intolerant but can't resist because you want to talk about your mom keeping this pen pal thing with Olivia from you?" he asks. "Or because you want to get your head out of your ass and finally honor her wishes that were your idea in the first place?"

"The latter," I tell him. Not wanting to give any attention to the sting of betrayal I first felt when Olivia told me they'd been emailing all these years and instead focus on the important part of the revelation: Olivia came here thinking my mom had unfinished business that she could help with. "Now that things are a little steadier again at Celia's Place, I think it's right to think about how it's going to do long term. Look at this damn ice cream shop playing Drake to attract people who want to chill here. If I don't keep up with the changing culture in Providence, Celia's Place might not survive. But without my mom here for it . . . I don't know, Zeke."

"You don't know what?"

"The thought of interacting with more people on a social night makes me want to crawl under a rock. That would have been her thing," I say.

A decade after Celia Rodriguez opened Celia's Place, it became an integral part of the Providence community. People come for birthdays, we cater weddings and baby showers, my mom was asked to be a godparent to a customer's child. The priest who baptized *me* still comes in for lunch. She might've given me the talent, but I'd be a liar if I said I want to hug customers and laugh with them instead of taking my breaks to sit in silence. But the food can only speak for itself if people are actually coming to the restaurant to eat it. Right now, that's not a problem, but earlier a voice in my brain insisted that the saliva-sharing couple were eating at a cool new spot instead of my restaurant.

"If you want change, you might have to be uncomfortable for a while," Zeke says.

"I know." I frown. "Got any ideas?"

"I'd say you can have me in there spinning a set every week," he says, "turn it into a party spot after hours, but your mom's flip-flop would descend from the sky and slap you good."

"Her flip-flop would have enough wingspan to slap us both," I say, and even Teddy laughs.

Neither of us needs confirmation to know that she wouldn't

have wanted that type of vibe at the restaurant. I'm sure it wouldn't have even been on the table if we had brainstormed.

"My sister told me she caught up with Olivia the other day," Zeke says. "That girl's well traveled inside restaurants and outside of them. She used to cook fancy dinners for rich people and shit. Imagine the vibes she's had to create? Ambience and all that. Bet that's why your mom specifically went to her to ask for advice."

"Yeah," I say. "I thought the same thing."

"So why the hell are you over here asking for my advice?"

"She replaced the fridge in the back room today, Zeke," I say.

"That thing from the eighteenth century? It's about time. Didn't the handle fall off last month?"

"I fixed it."

"With duct tape?" Zeke wrinkles his nose. "This is why I'm not gonna brainstorm with you. You hate change. I'm surprised you even want a social night. And you sound ungrateful too. Shit, if Olivia has money from being a fancy private chef and wants to replace appliances, that is not your problem."

I think of the emergency fund for the restaurant that my mom had been saving for years and refused to touch and how hard it's been for me to touch it either. Even for appliances that clearly need to be replaced. "I appreciate that she bought the fridge, and I won't deny it's going to be nice not to clean up that mess every day, but it will be a problem if she keeps investing in the restaurant like she's cementing a spot there."

Zeke leans closer with his elbows on the picnic table. "You scared she'll never leave?"

"Oh, she'll definitely leave," I say to Zeke right before Teddy's spoon drops and I hand him the extra one I had because I knew that would happen. "But that doesn't mean she won't randomly pop back in when she feels like it. If I ask for her opinion on how to make sure the restaurant thrives, she may never sign it over to me."

Zeke picks up the dirty plastic spoon from the ground and taps the table with it, tilting his head. "It's all making sense now. You know, I've wondered if you're stuck on Teddy's momma. But maybe it never worked with Daniela, just like it never works for your picky ass with the women you've been trying to date, because none of them are Olivia."

"I'm not picky," I say. "You've heard about my dates, Z."

"They've been bad, and this last girl definitely has issues with boundaries, but I still think you're picky. And that's fine because fate probably just brought back . . . your other half."

He says the last part in a sickly sweet mocking voice, and I'm damn near ready to take my son and go. His words make me remember a time when I couldn't imagine my life without Olivia and there wasn't a woman alive who could compare. Because she really did feel like my other half. Where she was a night owl, I loved the mornings. Where she was social, I liked my quiet. And that wasn't a bad thing because we balanced each other out. I craved her connection in ways I can't explain. But we were kids then, and I was a fool in love. It's been ten years, she's still her, and I'm still me. If I hate change, she loves it. If I want to try to fix something and make it last, she's comfortable with throwing it away and trying something new. Now I know for sure we're too different for anything that'll last. And that's not even considering the way she left me.

"You're bugging," I say. "And isn't Olivia married, anyway?"

"If this is your slick way of asking if Vero told me about Olivia's love life, she didn't," Zeke says. "But I think it's common sense that whatever Olivia had going on before isn't going on anymore. Assuming she's not a liar, don't you think her husband would be worried about her spending so much time with her ex-boyfriend? Because if my wife was in this weird-ass situation, I'd be sitting in a booth at the restaurant every day until she figured it out."

"Not everyone's like you, Zeke."

"And that's a shame," he says with a smile. "But come on, bro. I know you've thought this same thing too. Don't fucking lie to me."

My cousin gives Teddy another napkin. The mess is getting out of control. There are rainbow sprinkles in his curly hair and he's still trying to finish the ice cream.

"She doesn't wear a ring, but no one does in the kitchen," I say, scratching my eyebrow and trying to remember if she had one on when she came to meet me that first day. Except I'm distracted when a feeling shoots up my spine thinking of our hands touching on top of the towels yesterday. I blow out a breath. "And maybe I've thought something like it, yeah. She hasn't mentioned a husband once, but this is about the restaurant. Let's stop twisting it into something else."

Zeke raises both hands in the air. "If that's true and you're not just scared to have your little heart broken again, then consider what I'm saying. There's a scenario in which she's still married. That means she probably wouldn't be able to pop back in all the time. But regardless, it shouldn't hurt you to ask her for advice. You know she'll leave. Vero knows it too. Olivia's not going to keep your restaurant hostage and shackle herself. Don't even tell her the social night was originally your idea. Let her feel like she's helping with your mom's unfinished business. Give her a purpose. That'll probably get rid of her sooner than whatever you've been trying. And I think you already know this. Maybe you just needed me to say it."

Zeke's right. And anyway, my plan to drive her away with bottom-of-the-barrel restaurant tasks hasn't worked in the slightest—she's far too eager and helpful for that. But if she thinks she's fulfilling my mom's wishes . . . and if anyone has an idea that'll stand out among the things already being done in Providence, it's probably Olivia. When she was a teen she'd help my mom switch up the menu, rearrange seating, make sure the music was good. And I love being a chef. I love my mom. She led me to *my* purpose. I owe everything to her, and I owe it to myself to keep growing the place we both loved now that she's gone. An event night will cost me up front, but I do have the emergency fund and I could always put the money back once we see profit. And if there's any reason to work with Olivia, it's this. Both ideas make my chest tight, but I have to believe they'll be worth it.

"Teddy boy," my cousin says, "do you see that look on your dad's face?" Teddy stares at me, a smudge of ice cream on his chin. He nods. "That's the look of a man who's come to his senses. Now we can go play ball at the park and stop going back and forth with him."

I don't tell my cousin that part of the reason I don't want to give Olivia a reason to stay longer is because of my son. I'm not sure how I'll feel if I have to see them interact. I know there's nothing going on between me and Olivia. There won't be. But after Rachael being weird about Teddy today, I don't know how I'll react if Olivia is weird about him too. Especially because there was a time when I thought a future with her meant we'd have kids together.

Chapter 15

Olivia

Now

IT'S TUESDAY NIGHT AND AS SOON AS VANESSA THOMPSON sees me inside her shop, she shifts her gaze to the man counting the register and says, "See what I was trying to tell you, Lex? Wedding planning is getting to your head. I told you to flip the closed sign and lock the door."

"Oops," he says. "But the wedding planning isn't the reason, Vanessa. I just forgot."

"Yeah, because you're too busy being a bridezilla," Vanessa mutters, then turns to me.

She looks exactly how she does in videos and pictures. Striking, wearing a light pink pants suit with her graying hair in a slick ponytail. Her face card is immaculate. Smooth brown skin that is well cared for. She's exactly the type of person I'd want advice from about how to take care of mine. And that's why I'm inside of her shop . . . apparently after hours. When I first saw videos of Wildly Green circulating on the internet last year, I was desperate to visit, only to find out they were in Providence. What they offer here is a unique experience where they work with you to create natural products in-store for your skin and hair. When I left Celia's earlier, I could smell my hair as soon as the wind blew. It desperately needs to be washed. I've been in Providence for over a week but came unprepared. My therapist would tell me my ADHD is showing again, the way I didn't prepare for much of anything besides seeing if there were still sparks with Carmello. Now the man's probably getting serious with someone else, and I can't go another night neglecting this raggedy hair. But I might have to just hit the drugstore.

I walk backward toward the door. "This is on me. I should've checked the store hours."

"Honey," the woman says, "let's not take the blame for a man's mistake. Okay?"

Lex grumbles some words from across the room, and I try not to laugh.

"Okay," I say. "I'll come back tomorrow. Maybe you can help me find some products for this hair. Perhaps create a few."

Vanessa raises a perfectly crisp drawn-in eyebrow. "It looks pretty healthy to me. Especially for all the chemicals you must put in it to get it that color."

This time, I do laugh.

"I try to keep it strong because I like to blow out my curly hair sometimes too."

"I can see that," Vanessa says, examining my straightened hair. "But don't worry, I'm not too much of a natural hair snob, despite what people think coming in here. We've got the products for people who do both, so they're going to spend money regardless."

"I've heard, which is why I came here," I say. "But I need some tough truths to keep the curls healthy while I'm frying and dyeing it."

Lex snorts and calls out, "If you put it like that, she'll start acting like a snob."

"You hush, boy," Vanessa says, and I can't believe how comfortable I am inside of a store that's already closed. She goes behind the counter. Pulls something from under a shelf. "Here's a bag of samples. Looks to me like you're in need of a wash." I'm sure she can smell the grease and food on me from the kitchen because she wrinkles her nose. But at least she doesn't read me for filth out loud. "Try those for now until you make an appointment with my daughter for the Experience. Laniah's not here right now, but she usually does the evaluating. Lex will let you know what we have available this week."

"Are you sure?" I say. "It's late. I feel bad enough already."

"I got the schedule pulled up," Lex says, and even though I'm pretty sure he just doesn't want to hear Vanessa's mouth, I appreciate his warm smile.

CARMELLO CALLS WHILE I'M THROWING A PEPPERONI AND cheese Hot Pocket in the microwave. After cooking all day, it was between this and a PB&J. I glance at the time, my heart vibrating while his name dances on my screen. Yesterday when he came back to the restaurant after being gone a couple of hours, he was visibly happier than before he left. I wondered if that was from spending time with his son, or because his woman visited him at work. Then today, I kept catching him looking at me like he had something to say.

"Hello, Carmello," I say. "Are you calling to chew me out for how I made the longsilog? All I did was add extra garlic."

"No. Everything you cooked today was great," he says. "I called because I . . . uh . . ."

When Carmello Rodriguez trails off nervously, my brain lightning speeds a scenario in which he wants to spend time with me. That absurd thought stuns me into silence so that I'm just on the line waiting for him to say something entirely different that would make more sense.

Finally, he says, "That email my mom sent you to brainstorm ideas. That was something she and I talked about before she . . . well, because we uh . . . wanted to do something different with the restaurant, so I thought maybe you and I could talk about it instead. If you want to."

I respect how hard it must have been for him to ask me and don't want to leave him waiting so I say, "Of course, Carmello. I'd love to help in any way that I can." I sit on one of the stools and look up at the ceiling, silently asking Celia if this is my real sign. "I'm free now."

"All right," Carmello says, then he fills me in on the changes he's noticed in Providence while mentioning the places Zeke has been asked to DJ at lately. He tells me about Black Sheep: how at 10 p.m. sharp the bouncers start clearing the tables and moving them to the back in order to make room for a dance floor. They know how to seamlessly transition from a place to chill and eat to a place to party, and I imagine the adrenaline rush. They know their target audience, customers looking to eat in a cool place and move straight into a fun night out. Now I'm going to help Carmello find his. Because he's right, restaurants are evolving and Celia's Place has some room to grow. I feel a sense of relief now that I know what his mom wanted to talk about, and I realize how much it's haunted me to have to speculate since she's been gone.

When we're done with the housekeeping, I have an idea. "Thanks for trusting me with this, Mello. Let's go to the food truck event Zeke's DJing at tonight before it ends."

"Why would we do that?" Carmello asks. "It's an outdoor thing and . . ."

"And nothing," I say. "Don't question my methods. I want to see this new Providence vibe you're talking about for myself. And if we happen to have to switch up the menu with this social night idea, it'll be good to see just how creative people are getting out here, won't it?"

"But . . ."

"It's called recon, Carmello," I say. "And before you further protest, may I throw in the fact that it'll be a show of support for Zeke?" I glance at the microwave, wondering if I'll have to reheat my Hot Pocket. "Plus, I'm kinda hungry."

He's silent for a second. Then he sighs.

I smile, feeling accomplished, and send him a text. "That's the address of my Airbnb," I say. "I know the parking situation downtown is probably going to suck for this. Pick me up in an hour?" Carmello could refuse me altogether, say yes but tell me to take an Uber or to find parking on my own. But it'll be dark by the time we go, and I bet he's a gentleman, just like I remember. He grumbles out, "Fine," and hangs up without a goodbye.

I head to the shower to shave my legs and wash my hair with the products from Wildly Green. But then I turn back around to grab my Hot Pocket, because even though the thought of eating different things at food trucks makes me want to drool, I refuse to abandon it.

I KNOW A BATTLE FOR DOMINANCE WHEN I SEE ONE. CARmello shows up half an hour late without an apology, and I slide into his car with an unbothered smile. His eyes catch on me, the movements quick but visible as they sweep from my sideswept curly hair to my low neckline, lingering on the skirt sitting high on my bare thighs, which are pressed into his leather seat. He audibly releases a breath and shifts his gaze. My skin is several degrees warmer from it, but I try to remember that this man may already have another woman. When he puts the car into reverse, he extends his arm to the back of my seat. The scent of his cologne is intoxicating. Rich with citrus notes and cardamom. Suits him so well. The tattoo on his neck is clear for me to study. Light breaking through clouds. His mom's name scrawled there. I tell myself I might not be able to touch it, but I can admire it while he's this close. Just like I'm admiring his clean all-black attire and the concentration in his jaw while he drives.

He glances over at me. "What?"

"Nothing," I say. "You just . . . smell nice."

"So do you, Olivia," he says, and there's a hint of a smile on his mouth.

CARMELLO CIRCLES FOUNTAIN AND SURROUNDING STREETS twice before he asks if I want to get dropped at the entrance while he finds parking. "I don't mind a good walk," I insist, and he circles again until we finally find a spot several streets up College Hill.

When we get out of his car, he glances down at my feet, which are in six-inch stilettos. Eying them in a way that makes me wonder if he likes my French-manicured toes.

He meets my gaze, says, "The heels won't be a problem?"

"Why would they be?" I ask.

"I'll never forget what you said on our first date."

My belly feels like pan-melted butter. A warm ninety-seven degrees. "And what was that?" I ask.

"You loved how they looked with your outfit, but they were the devil's work," he says.

I laugh at the memory. "Well, I'm a woman now," I say.

"That doesn't automatically mean you like how it feels to wear heels," he says.

"It doesn't," I say, then speed walk to get in front of him like his words are a challenge. "But, contrary to your beliefs," I call over my shoulder, "I'm not the girl you used to know." He catches up to me, crosses over so he's the one walking street-side. Any decent man should do this, but I still find it sexy. I should check my calendar to see if I'm ovulating because this level of desire feels too far out of my control. Our eyes lock again. "Are you the same boy? Still scared of swimming in the ocean?"

"I was never scared of swimming in the ocean. I just . . . didn't like it," he says and I arch a brow. "All right. I was a little scared," he admits. "But I swim all the time now. Went to Newport every chance I got last summer."

"With Rachael?"

The question fell from my lips, and now my face burns because Carmello is staring as we wait at a crosswalk for the light to turn green.

I start to apologize for the intrusive question, but he shakes his head.

"Word gets around Celia's fast," he says. "Rachael is a girl I was seeing, but I'm not seeing her anymore." While he holds eye contact, I hope my body language seems unaffected by the news, but I feel like he can see everything I won't say. I feel like if he looks long enough my face will ask the questions I can't bring my mouth to. *Did you stop seeing her because I showed up? Now that I'm here, do you feel the connection crackling between us like a live wire? Are you thinking about what my lips feel like as we stand under the streetlights?*

"I hope you're okay with that," I say because I can't find other words.

I'm not surprised when he doesn't respond. He's never been an open book, and I doubt he'd admit to me about being hurt over a failed connection, but I am surprised when he tells me: "I learned how to swim so that I can teach my son. That's who I go with."

The confession fills me with dozens of questions but a single image: Carmello holding a little boy's hand as they enter the water. I'm curious about the relationship they have. What else do they do together for fun? Is Carmello teaching him to cook too?

It feels like an invitation to ask these things, but then he loops back around to what we were first talking about before I can. "Anyway. You might enjoy walking in heels now, but that doesn't mean it's not painful to do it on concrete for a quarter of a mile downhill."

"It's not comfortable, I'll tell you that," I say. "But I'm determined to be fine. Just like I was on our first date. Though, I'm surprised you remember what I said that day."

A delicious hit of dopamine runs the length of my spine with the way he's looking at me. And then he says: "I remember everything about my time with you, Olivia Jones."

Chapter 16

THE FOOD WE KEPT FORGETTING ON THE STOVE

Olivia

14 years ago

CARMELLO HAD HIS HAND TANGLED IN MY CURLS, MY LIPS were kiss-plumped, face flushed when we were caught by the deep freezers in the back room. I was shivering a little, goose bumps visible when his mom switched on the light.

"This is a business. My restaurant," said Celia. "Show some respect."

For days after that, I was too embarrassed to be in the kitchen. I couldn't even look Carmello in the eye. And I really didn't want to lose my job. When Carmello first asked me why I never seemed to want to go home, I wondered if he thought my parents were abusive or if I was unhappy with them. Neither of those things was true. But for the first time since my house burned down, I had a place that I kept wanting to come back to. At Celia Rodriguez's restaurant, Paula taught me to bake time-consuming things like pumpkin cheesecake. She talked to me about prom and glitter eyeshadow. Celia showed her love by letting me look through her family recipe books and answering my food-related questions even when she was busy. I started to dream about what it would be like to walk the stage with my new friend Veronica. And there was Carmello too. Of course there was. We were becoming real friends, and two days without talking to him was feeling like an eternity, but I didn't want to risk losing any of it.

I told my parents I was worried I'd get fired, and my mother said, "Maybe it's for the best. We can't take him with us when we go, and there will be other restaurants. Other passions and hobbies. When you're a teenager, everything feels like a crisis, but there are real crises we have to help with. These feelings will eventually pass."

It's what she said about everything since the fire. Pack light. Don't buy things you don't need. We won't be able to take them with us when we go. But I was convinced nowhere would be like Celia's. And no one would ever be Carmello. Still, I reminded myself of my mother's words when I went to work the next day. My feelings for him were growing too big, coming on too fast, and what the hell would I do when I had to leave? I had to save myself the heartache. So, I tried to seem detached, but Carmello wouldn't stop searching for me with his eyes. Halfway through the day, I realized our bodies were like magnets: it took force to go in the opposite direction as him.

When my shift was over, Celia asked to have a word with me and Carmello. I sat beside him on an upside-down milk carton, sure that a lecture would lead to me getting fired. But Celia folded her hands together and said, "If you're going to use my restaurant to . . . spend time together, do it right. None of that kissing while you work. Stop staring at each other. I'm sick of you two burning food. Your first date will be here. After hours on Saturday. Wear something nice. Both of you."

Neither I nor Carmello argued with her order, and I left the restaurant that day wondering if the person that might be hardest for me to detach from when I had to go would be Celia.

ON SATURDAY, I SHOWED UP AT CELIA'S PLACE WITH A BALL of nerves in my stomach, but the worst part was the heels. I always had an eye for fashion, but because I spent time with my parents protesting and helping people after hurricanes, my "packing light" consisted of comfort clothes and shoes. They also didn't make much money doing what they did for work, so I didn't want to ask them for a new dress. When I confessed to Veronica that I had a date with Carmello but nothing nice to wear, she said, "I can help you with that."

We had started talking months before when I ran into her at Celia's Place. I recognized her as the outspoken girl in my gym class, but it shocked me hearing that Celia was her aunt and Carmello was her cousin. That night, she taught me how to apply makeup for my face shape and let me roam through her closet, putting together an outfit that looked like something I'd saved on Pinterest. I felt so damn pretty looking in the mirror. Even though her heels were half a size too big, and I kept tripping on my way into Celia's Place, I thought it was worth it when Carmello looked at me with the kind of wide eyes that told me he thought I looked pretty too.

The boy was naturally quiet, but rarely was he speechless.

Celia made appetizers and Paula made the banana pudding.

The two of them decorated the restaurant with fresh flowers and color-changing lighting. There was sparkling water waiting for us inside of champagne glasses, and music was playing on a speaker.

"Have fun," Paula said to us. Celia gave us a nod and they left us alone.

And then we laughed and teased and talked. I smiled so much my cheeks hurt. Carmello asked questions other people were scared to—like what memories I had of my home before the fire. If I missed it there. What it felt like when I escaped but had to watch it burn to the ground.

I told him I remembered almost everything, including the color of my bed skirt and the smell of my mom's cooking still lingering in the house from that morning. I told him it felt like my world was turning to ash while it was happening. All of my dolls, books, clothes, gone. But I didn't watch it burn to the ground because I was in an ambulance, rushed to the hospital for the third-degree burn on my hand. *Kids are resilient,* they told my parents once I was feeling a little better, and I tried to remember how much worse it could've been.

Carmello listened quietly, and I loved that I knew him enough by then to know he didn't think I was talking too much. When the song on the radio changed, I asked him to teach me to dance salsa. He said he wasn't great at it, but if I wanted to learn he'd show me. So, I took his hand and tried my best, but he quickly noticed how horrible I was in heels.

"Do those hurt?" he asked, smiling a little.

"It's excruciating," I confessed. "I'm now convinced heels are the devil's work."

He laughed and led me to a chair. My stomach somersaulted

watching him get on one knee to gently help me out of them. Afterward, he spun me in silly circles all around the room.

But when Frank Ocean's "Thinkin Bout You" started to play, he pulled me into a slower dance, and I couldn't tell what he was thinking. My mind was racing, wondering what it meant that we were on a date with him staring into my eyes like that. He was a foot taller than me without the heels, and had to bend low to kiss my lips. It was the first time we had kissed since his mom caught us, and I missed the feeling so much. But when he broke away to raise my hand to his mouth so that he could place his lips to my scarred palm, I knew I'd eventually miss more than just his touch. I couldn't feel his kisses against my leathery skin, but my heart caught fire. My belly too. The tips of my toes. I was spinning inside but we were standing still.

That's when I realized there was one question I still hadn't answered. I wouldn't. Not that night. If I wasn't shy about my feelings for him at fifteen, I might've said that sometimes I missed my home, but I believed in fate. We wouldn't be dancing together if it didn't burn down.

Chapter 17

Carmello

Now

I TELL MYSELF CONCENTRATING ON OLIVIA JONES'S REACtion as we approach the event is just to help with the anxiety of heading to an area with so many people, but I'm a damn liar. I couldn't concentrate on something else if I tried. She's got that pull about her. At a safe distance, she is the prettiest tornado. But when she gasps a *this is going to be a good night* type of gasp as soon as she sees the pedestrian bridge, I wonder if I made the right decision coming here with her. Not only do I feel like *recon* could be done elsewhere, but I'm bothered by the fact that I enjoy seeing her eyes brighten as she takes in the bridge, and I can't be sucked into her. Not again.

I turn my attention to the bridge because it is beautiful. Spanning four hundred fifty feet across the Providence River, the two-level deck is made of Brazilian Ipe wood, as are the benches people are sitting on right now. Olivia tells me how much she loves the illuminated tables and then she quickly pushes past people to get to the middle of a bridge like she's racing me in her heels to get there. When she stops walking to lean against the railing and stare across the inky-looking water toward the lit downtown buildings in view, holding a hand to her chest, smiling and saying, "This might just be the best thing they ever did for Providence," I think thirty things at once. Like maybe she's right, but not when it's this crowded. Like maybe if things were different I'd bring her here for a sunset. And how small she looks right now—standing on this massive thing with people all around us—but how big of a person she makes herself just by squealing like there's no one else here while pointing to the ducks bobbing in the water before she's back to walking toward the other side of the bridge, saying, "Hurry up, Mello."

When we reach our first stop at La Fogata food truck, she claps her hands excitedly and gets on her tiptoes to see the menu over someone's head in line.

"I've never seen someone so anxious to be a critic," I say.

She plants her feet back on the pavement and says, "Pay attention to the space, not me."

"I'm not sure what I'm supposed to be looking for," I say. "I've been to one of these before. There are picnic tables, some grass sitters on our right side and music and more humans and trucks in which food is served out of windows."

"Are you being bougie, Mello? Are you too good for truck food? For this event?"

I hate that my name sounds so good when it comes from her mouth, especially when she's talking shit. "No. But I'm starting to wonder if you were just bored when I called you."

"Possibly," she says, batting her eyelashes with the cutest fucking face, and making me realize I need a drink. Luckily, the stand we're at serves beer along with their birria tacos.

Once we reach the window, Olivia orders a shrimp empanada and a Hot Cheeto Chicken Burrito, and I get a grilled steak sub and a beer.

"You're such a guy," she says, about my sandwich order and because I whipped out my card to pay. Then she points to something through the glass window. "Oooh, what is that?"

"Tornado Potato on a stick," says the woman taking our order.

"We'll take one of those too," I say, and I don't miss the way Olivia casually bumps her shoulder against my arm as we walk toward Poppin Minis to get some loaded donuts for dessert.

When we finally sit down at a free table, the grown woman in front of me happy-shimmies in her seat, and I feel my mouth twitch. "Did you see the way I secured us some extra donuts back there? I'm all ears in case you want to clap."

"Why would I do that?" I say. "I'm not surprised you're still a master at getting your way with those pouty lips."

She puffs out her bottom one. It's glossed and shiny. I try not to stare at it. "Guess I'll have to test it on you while I'm here."

"Good luck," I say, but she already has me weak with her sharp-winged eyes and . . .

"Ayoo."

My cousin's voice frees me from the torment of having a staring contest with Olivia Jones and not being able to break it by taking her big bottom lip between my teeth right now.

Zeke's wearing a fitted hat low on his face, but I can tell he's as shocked to see me as he is to see Olivia. "Olive? Cuzzo? What the hell are you doing here?"

Olivia shoots me a look, and I feel guilty that I haven't made it to any of his events lately. "We wanted to come for support and food of course," she says.

"We know you dragged his ass here, Olive," says Veronica, who pops out from behind her taller brother. "We just don't know how."

Olivia laughs at that shot at me, then stands to give Zeke a hug. He squeezes her like they haven't become strangers while I guzzle my beer. Wrestling with the memory of when we all went out for Olivia's nineteenth birthday. It was the last time the four of us were in the same space. But unlike then, Olivia hesitates to hug Vero. My cousin is equally awkward, patting Olivia on the back before letting go. I wonder what happened between bonding over a seafood boil bag and now. But then again, it is not my business. Celia's Place is. And all I have to focus on is working with Olivia on this social night and keeping my hands to myself, so that she leaves me and my restaurant intact when she goes back to her globe-trotting.

"I'm so excited to hear your set," Olivia tells Zeke. "How are you feeling?"

He runs his hand along the brim of his hat. "Always nervous before events. I'm sweaty as hell. Do I stink? I can't trust my sibby to tell me the truth."

Veronica sucks her teeth and puts her purse down on our table. "I wouldn't have you out here smelling like BO, Zeke. Stop being dumb."

He narrows his eyes, then turns back to Olivia expectantly. She laughs and leans in. "You're good," she says, and he smiles like he trusts her. "Let me just . . ." She fixes the collar on his jean jacket. "Okay. Now go kill it."

I lift my beer and Zeke smiles. Even though it's weird being with the three of them, I'm happy I'm here for him today. But when he heads to the platform stage to set up, I can't ignore the look Veronica gives me. She's asking with her eyes why the hell I'm with Olivia in a way that tells me if she had a say in the matter she wouldn't have approved. Olivia must get the same sense because she throws back her margarita like it's a shot, then starts shoveling food into her mouth.

Veronica slides into the seat next to Olivia and says, "I'm surprised you came here for Zeke's set, Mello," sarcasm punctuating every word. This girl won't ever let up. I'm technically her boss at the restaurant, but you'd never know it. Outside of that space? She's always on my neck about something. A year ago, she showed up at Celia's and got in my face after hearing from Zeke that my mom's cancer was progressing rapidly and I was struggling with the load at work. *You're my cousin. She's my tita. If you need help around here, open your mouth and say that.* Before I could form a comeback, she stomped away to get herself a work shirt and she's been there for me ever since. Just like she was there for me when Olivia left ten years ago and never came back. Sometimes this is how she shows it: "I haven't seen you step foot outside since my dad's sixtieth birthday party . . . two years ago."

"That's wild," Olivia says, stabbing a Tornado Potato slice with her fork.

"He's even worse with his social anxiety now than he was back then," Vero says. "If Carmello is with more than ten people at once in any circumstance, then it's a party. You should see the sweat glisten on his forehead when we pack into the kitchen for work meetings. Force him into a room with a bunch of people and he's counting down the minutes, but force him onto a dance floor when he's tipsy and suddenly he's doing bachata with someone's grandma for hours." She steals a big bite of my sandwich. I haven't even tasted it yet. With her mouth full, she continues to speak. About me. The quickest way for her to get on my nerves. I don't have siblings, but between her and Zeke I was never missing that kind of annoyance during childhood. "I know he doesn't have much free time these days, but since he's apparently dating women, where the hell does he bring them?"

I ignore my cousin completely and look at Olivia. "Can we just do what we came here for so I can head home?"

Olivia nods and pops a mini donut into her mouth. A second later, her sharp eyes open wide. "Oh, that's so damn good. Taste this first, please."

She passes me the plate and I shovel two donuts into my mouth. The mix of flavors hits just as quick. Surprisingly not too sweet. The texture on the outside is crunchy but the donut is perfectly soft in the center, which isn't true of even the better donuts I've tried in this state. The simple combination is delicious, and I'm wondering if Paula could add something similar to our dessert menu when Veronica glances between us.

"This makes more sense," she says. "You didn't come together on a date, or to support Zeke on a weekday when Carmello is usually knocked out by now. You came to see why these food truck events do so well."

"Very discerning, cuz," I say. "Absolutely not a date."

The confirmation relaxes her face. She even smiles at Olivia, who doesn't seem affected by what I said. "Are we switching up the menu?" she asks. "Because I vote yes. It's been the same for too long, and if I'm bored eating on lunch breaks, the customers must be too."

"Possibly," I say. "But mostly, we're talking through some ideas for a social night at the restaurant to keep the crowd coming and growing. The menu for that will be different."

"Finally," Veronica says. "Our clientele is aging. Definitely do something to bring in the younger folk." I blink at her, and she shrugs. "What? It's true. Pastor Lionel is pushing ninety."

She's right, but I'm thankful not to hear any more of her opinions when Zeke starts to play a song she loves and Olivia turns to her and says, "Let's go dance."

If there's something Vero can't resist, it's those words.

When the two of them get up to walk over toward the stage, I stay and sip on my beer, studying random things outside so that I don't study *her.* Olivia's always been a good dancer, got that natural rhythm, a quick learner too, but age has only made her better at it. I can almost see the countries she's been to whenever she isolates a different part of her body. The control she has over her hip muscles makes me envision her moving like that for me. And I need to stop staring because I'm getting . . .

My phone vibrates and when I see Teddy's name cut across the screen, I feel my pulse pick up. It's way past his bedtime. Why is he calling? I answer the phone but only hear some shuffling and whining. I call his name, again, once more. Then hang up and call him back. He doesn't answer. My mind races, horrible thoughts about what could be happening making my chest tight while I call Daniela. She answers on the fifth ring. Her voice groggy from sleep. I tell her Teddy called me and ask her to go check on him. When she does, she tells me that he was rolled on top of his iPad because he was watching a show before sleep, and my heart steadies to a slower beat. I tell her I'm sorry for making her get out of bed, and she tells me not to stress it. But when we hang up, my hands are shaking a little.

Daniela is such a good mom, but when small things like this happen I briefly wish I were there to check on Teddy myself. To make sure he gets to sleep safely and wakes up the same.

When I get up to throw out the trash, Olivia walks over and asks, "You okay?"

I nod. "Yeah. But I think I'm going to call it a night. Why don't you catch a ride home with Vero?"

She reaches for my hand, says, "How about you dance with us? Just one song?" Her fingers are warm and my body relaxes and fuck, she's pouting. "Come on, Carmello."

"That face isn't going to work on me," I say, but I'm suddenly grateful she came to distract me from my bad thoughts. Sometimes they hit hard, scary images that feel so real and possible it's like I'm drowning in them, and it takes everything in me just to breathe.

"I know you don't like me but don't let that get in the way of research," she says.

I laugh. This girl is something else. "Is that what you're going to call it?"

"What else would it be?" she says, and when she tugs me to follow, I can't fight anymore. And I can't keep my eyes from watching the way her ass bounces while she walks in front of me. At least she's married, so I know I have to keep my hands to myself. A little looking won't get me into too much trouble.

"Finally," Veronica screams over the music when we reach her. She's made some friends; one of them is dancing with a big turkey leg in her hand and the other looks like she's high off shrooms. When Beyoncé's version of "Before I Let Go" starts to play, people clap and form lines to do her rendition of the electric slide. Vero is a pro; we lose her to the front line.

I've never learned this version of the slide before and this time it's Olivia teaching me something. This song fills the outdoor space with serotonin, and when Olivia looks over at me and smiles, I'm smiling back. Feeling looser than I have in too long. But when the song switches, everyone rushes toward the center of the stage and *she's* pushed toward me. Somehow our middles are touching. My hands are at the small of her back. She hooks one arm around my neck while she sways to the beat. Her fingernails feel good against my skin. "Hi," she says.

"Hi," I reply, and my heart starts doing something funny with us pressed together.

I spent years fighting the feeling of missing her, but when her eyes flick to my mouth, I want to slide my hands down to where I know she's so fucking soft and tug her closer. Instead, I back away and say, "I need some air."

"We're outside," she tells me with a frown on her face.

"I know," I say, before reaching out to raise her chin, gripping her softly there, wanting to kiss that sad look off her mouth and knowing I can't. She closes her eyes from the physical contact, and I want to tell her I feel the pull too, but I keep my mouth shut.

"Okay, Carmello," she breathes out, then I let her go.

TWENTY MINUTES LATER, SHE FINDS ME SITTING ON A SIDEwalk up the street and drops down beside me. Our legs are touching slightly. I move over a few inches, and she sighs.

"Thought you might've left me here," she says.

"Doesn't matter how long it's been. You know *I'd* never leave without telling *you*."

I didn't mean to be petty using those words, but that's how they came out, and she winces like they stung. "Yeah. I know," she says.

"I meant it when I said I don't hate you," I say, wanting to ease the moment some.

"Are you sure about that?" she says, and I shift to look at her. "You're so hot and cold. I never know what I'm going to get. When we were dancing back there, you looked disgusted for a second. Sometimes you make the same face in the kitchen, but it's only so big in there, Carmello. It's not like I'm touching you on purpose."

"Are *you* sure about that, Olivia?"

She huffs out a short laugh. "You're serious?"

"I'm far from disgusted with you," I say. "But we can't ignore that time has passed. You can't just pick up where you left off with *me*. If you're grabbing my hand or we're leaning into each other after a dance, *I'm* going to think twice about it, and so should you." She pulls her gaze away. I don't take my eyes off of her. "I know I asked for help, but while you're here I need . . ."

"Some space?" she finishes.

"At least a foot between our bodies at all times, kind of space," I tell her, "because with you sitting so close I can smell lemon on your skin, hints of vanilla, the scent of blueberries in your curly hair." I swallow when she turns back to me. "Because when I moved away from you just now I had to stop myself from saying fuck it and pulling you toward me just to feel your thigh pressed into mine again. Because a lot has changed, but not everything has changed, O."

She takes a sharp breath. A beat of silence passes between us. Then . . . she smiles. "Are you saying you're still attracted to me, Rodriguez?"

I let all the air from my lungs. "Chemistry was never our problem, Jones."

She squeezes her thighs together, and I try to concentrate on her face instead of how good they look tonight. It's safer than finding the sweet changes in her body, but even under just a streetlight I can see her cheeks are flushed. And somehow that small show of affectedness is even more powerful. If I leaned over, I could kiss each one.

"No, it never was," she whispers.

I want to put my hand on her leg to stop it from shaking. "So, we're in agreement?" I say. "The pull is strong, but we can't give in to it. That'll be messy."

"Why would it be?"

"Why aren't you wearing your wedding ring, Olivia?" I counter.

"Because I don't have a husband," she says, arching her brow. "Is that what you've thought this whole time?"

"Did you not get married?" I ask. Heart thrumming, remembering how I felt when Vero told me. I had put Olivia out of my mind for so long, but that whole week my chest was sore.

"I did," she says now, "but I also got divorced."

"Oh," I say. *Shit*, I think, because dangerous thoughts come. Like how it wouldn't be bad if I found out how her mouth tastes now that I know she's single. I know she wants it too.

"I'm not even going to comment on you thinking I was trying to cheat with you," she says. "But now that we have the facts clear, what are your other reasons why we'd be messy?"

I feel like I should ask why she got married and divorced so quickly, but she's smirking with one side of her mouth, her eyes twinkling under the lights. The look teases me. It's like she's got a key to my body again. All she's gotta do is beckon me closer and I'll come.

But I need to take back control before I'm fully consumed by her. "The physical urges are still there," I say, "but I've moved on in other ways."

She blinks a few times, and I watch the fever in her eyes break. "Yeah, Mello," she says, shifting her body away. "We're in agreement. And . . ." She trails off for a moment. Then: "I'm actually going to Tokyo for a year soon, so you're right. We shouldn't be messy. I have a few weeks to help with the restaurant, then I'll leave. Okay?"

Her confession doesn't surprise me, but still there's a pit in my stomach all the same from the confirmation that she had already planned to leave. I'm not sure what this means about her shares of the restaurant, but I nod and give her a small smile. We're on safe ground for now; we can talk about serious business when we're back in the restaurant. "Wow. Tokyo. For work?"

She smiles a little too. "A client wants me to move with her there, and I think it'll be good to escape for a while."

I tell my wandering mind not to look for subtext behind her words. To focus on what she's telling me. She's leaving and she thinks it'll be good for her.

"That's really cool," I say. "I've heard great things about Japan. And listen, after what I said about us, if you don't want to help with the idea anymore, I promise it's okay."

"I want to," she says quickly. "For you and Celia. But for myself too. I know you might think differently, but I really do love the restaurant. It means something to me. It always has. It's where I realized that I want to do this chef thing forever. And I'd love to see it truly shine."

"All right, then," I say. "I appreciate your help. Thank you."

"Sure," she says, and looks down at her feet. Pushes some pebbles around on the pavement.

"What did you think about the event?" I ask to keep us from falling into silence. "Spark any ideas for Celia's Place?"

"The event was fun," she says, meeting my eyes. "And nothing solid yet, but it made me remember how happy people were to be around your mom. It was like she planted seeds in people's hearts. Always so much love in the room. I think that's what kept people coming back."

I watch a car pass us and wonder if I'll ever be able to replicate that feeling.

"Don't worry, Carmello," Olivia says. When we were young, it felt like she could read my mind, and it still does. "Your place has some of that feeling, even without your mom being there. Because you're like a magnet too." The words hit, and I have to stop myself from saying I feel the same way about her. "Now we just need to translate it into an idea," she continues. "But first, I should rest this brain. I had one shot too many from Vero's flask."

"All right," I say. "Let me get you home now."

"But Carmello? Can you go get the car?" she asks. "The pain from these heels is pretty excruciating right now, and I don't want to hear you say anything about that."

The memory of our very first dance tugs at my lips. "What if I said I could tell as I watched you wobble down the street toward me a few minutes ago?"

She elbows my side. Then rushes to say, "Sorry, sorry. No touching."

"I do want us to be intentional with that, but I think throwing elbows is fine," I say. "Your bony ones kinda hurt though."

"I'd kiss it better," she says, "but that'd break boundaries."

"Yeah," I say, but my eyes draw to her mouth. This time, she's the one to shift away.

"Earlier, when you called me O," she says quietly, "my heart felt . . . happy? It's been so long since you've called me that. And I just . . . Do you think we can ever be friends?"

"Maybe something like that," I say.

When she smiles the way she does, I realize I might've made a mistake admitting that we still have chemistry out loud. Acknowledging that something exists brings more attention to it, and I might've incited something that would have died out on its own.

Chapter 18

Olivia

Now

I'VE MASTERED THE LOOK OF UNAFFECTEDNESS, NEEDING A thick skin after cooking for different palates over the years, but I had to reel it in when Carmello looked at me as we sat on the sidewalk last night. All serious with those dark eyes. The veins in his neck contracting while he spoke. The tattoos at either side that I wanted to trace with my tongue.

Chemistry was never our problem, Jones.

I almost told him how dizzy I was with the desire for him to keep looking at me like that, to say my name over and over, to trail his fingers along my collarbone.

After he dropped me off and I got in bed, I was pulsing between my legs, sure that I'd see some nasty things when I fell asleep. But the dream was soft instead. We were teenagers again, and I was looking up at him wondering how dangerous it would be for my heart if I fell in love knowing I'd eventually have to leave. Now I'm realizing I was scared for myself, but I wasn't scared enough for Carmello back then. As a result, he built walls to protect himself from me, and I don't blame him, but I have a feeling his walls aren't strong enough. That if I press a little, we'll break the barrier and fall right into each other. I believe in fate, but I also believe in choice. Carmello made his. I not only want to respect it, but I want to consider both of our hearts this time. And as much as I want him, there's another part of me that yearns to get to know him again in a different way. To rekindle a friendship I made a mess of. If I let go of fantasies about a romantic future with him, being friends might just be possible.

I kick off the covers and grab my phone from the nightstand to send a text. My client reads it and replies with hearts and: **Weeks earlier than I expected you to answer and thank goodness because I was holding my breath hoping you'd say yes.**

Then I write an email to Celia that maybe she'll see in the afterlife:

Dearest Celia,

I asked for a sign, and I think I got one. Carmello wants me to help make some changes to the restaurant. I'm honored you still felt comfortable enough to talk things through with me, and that you thought to give me your shares. Whether that was for bucket list trickery, your last big laugh, or because you thought Carmello and I needed this, I'm happy you loved me. I love you too. Always. And I think Carmello and I might have a shot at being long-distance friends after this. I promise to be there for him whenever he needs it—just like you were there for me. But I've accepted a job that'll take me out of the States for quite some time. I'm going to Tokyo. Remember when we said we wished we could see it together? Promise to write to you plenty while I'm there.

<3 Olive

PS: I have an idea I'm not sure your son will like very much. I'm pretty persuasive though, and I think I'll be successful convincing him with the argument that my idea started with you.

My heart feels tender after I send it, but I'm relieved to have certainty about what to focus on while I'm here. And that won't be the urge to lick Carmello's jawline while he concentrates on whatever he's cooking. It certainly won't be the way his smile makes my stomach flutter. Or how he sucked his bottom lip and looked at me under the streetlights last night. I throw myself back onto the pillows with a sigh and run my hand over my T-shirt. My nipples are hard underneath. I pinch one between my thumb and index, roll it around and . . .

Feel a sudden twinge in my stomach. The first sharp sign of a cramp, and maybe one from the universe telling me to stop thirsting for this man.

My endo always acts up when I'm not watching what I eat, and I've definitely been overdoing it. As nice as it's been to be back in Rhode Island, it's hard to avoid cravings here. The small state offers more culturally diverse options for food in a one-mile radius than anywhere I've traveled to. I had Colombian cuisine from La Casona Restaurant the other day, feasting on fish and fried yucca. That same afternoon I ate a zeppole from D. Palmieri's Bakery. I've been tasting all the dishes I've missed at Celia's. Then there was the perfect meld of Mexican food flavors from La

Fogata truck and those fried donuts. I could've skipped that pepperoni and cheese Hot Pocket yesterday.

I feel myself sulking. Sometimes a girl just wants to indulge and throw back margaritas with her friend on a night out like she used to. But I guess it's back to being more careful.

I make a wish that the spasms will stop but I have a feeling it'll be one of those days.

WHEN MY SYMPTOMS START TO FLARE, SOMETIMES WALKING can help. It takes an hour to get to Celia's on foot. I concentrate on the warmth on my face from the sun beaming instead of the pain in my pelvis. As a further distraction, Denise sends me a sneaky picture from what looks like a café line. It's of my ex-husband—with his hand in the back pocket of someone else's jeans. She gives me about twenty seconds to digest what I'm seeing before she calls.

"Girl. Did you fucking see it?"

"You're short of breath," I say.

"Because I just ran out of that coffee shop," says Denise. "After your boy turned around and decided to make awkward small talk with me. Why are *you* short of breath?"

"I'm walking to work. Atwells Ave is kicking my ass. And he is not my boy anymore."

"You okay?" Denise asks. When I was first diagnosed with endometriosis through a discovery surgery years ago, we were new friends, but she still came to sit with me in the hospital. We made jokes about the food there, and she helped me get out of bed to pee.

"I'm fine. Just trying to avoid a bad flare," I say.

"Will telling you about Michael trigger some shit I shouldn't be triggering?" she asks.

I laugh a little. "Nothing you say about Michael could affect me that way."

"Even if I said he's having a baby?"

"Well, shit," I say, stopping short. "Wait. He told you this?"

"He didn't have to say a damn thing. His girl couldn't hide it if she wanted to," Denise says. "And she didn't. When he came to talk to me, she rubbed her big ole belly and said she's in her third trimester."

I try to catch my breath. "Oh. Oh wow. I don't even . . . Third trimester?"

"Yup. I did those same calculations in my head. Here you were waiting till the ink was dry on the divorce papers before you let anyone lay the pipe down and this man was already starting a family?" Denise kisses her teeth and takes a bite of whatever she ordered. She chews while she speaks. "At least he had the decency to look ashamed when I gave him a death stare."

I recenter myself. The sun on my face. The breeze at the back of my neck. Slow breathing. I wasn't in love with him. He has his own life to live. I have to keep putting one foot in front of the other. Only two blocks before I reach Celia's Place. I start walking again. "He has nothing to be ashamed of. He wanted kids. Now he'll have them."

"And I hope the first one is ugly," Denise says.

I snort. "Wishing bad on a baby, Dee? Foul even for you."

"I'm just cranky this morning," she says. "Men suck."

"Forget Michael. Tell me what's up with you," I say, trying to forget too.

"My husband said I gotta pump my own gas this morning, can you believe his ass?"

"I love you," I say. "And I love that you've got one of the good ones."

"He's annoying sometimes, but I got lucky," she says. "So will you."

"I hope so," I say right before I see Steven throwing trash in the dumpster outside of Celia's. "I have to go, Dee. Talk to you soon."

"Wait. Where exactly are you working right now? I thought you had some time off?"

"I thought I did too," I say.

"You're being cryptic," she says. Then gasps. "Atwells Ave. Isn't that in Providence?"

"The small city in Rhode Island that I said I'd never return to?" I say. "Yeah, possibly."

"Because you want the restaurant or because you want Carmello?"

I knew I shouldn't have told her why Carmello called. "Neither," I say.

"No wonder you couldn't care less about Michael," she accuses. "You're scheming on how to get back with a different ex."

"I am not scheming, Dee. I've officially let him go. But I'll call you later. Okay?"

"Don't forget the closure-sex. You need that, or the moving on isn't cemented," she says.

"I don't believe that, and I won't be spinning that block again," I say. "So please don't get your hopes up on hearing anything wild."

Steven whips his head in my direction, and when I get close enough to pass him, he sings a song with the phrase "spinning the block." Warmth cuts across my cheeks. I tell him to hush, and he shrugs before breaking down more cardboard boxes from this morning's produce order.

By the time I pull open the door to Celia's, my cramps have eased slightly, but I'm later than I intended to be. There's already a couple looking over the menu at a table up front and a little boy across the room. It'd be fairly normal to assume he's with the couple, that he's their kid, but somehow I know who he belongs to the moment I see him. The small boy fixes the chairs at one table and moves on to the next to adjust the vase there. He leans down to smell the fresh flowers, turning just enough for me to see the same curve to his nose. His hair has short ringlets at the nape of his neck. The shape of his face is . . .

He catches me staring and jumps back, knocking over the vase. The water spills on the tabletop, and for a second neither of us moves. But when he tears his eyes away to frown at the mess in front of him, my body goes on its own. I grab napkins from the bar and now I'm right in front of him. Trying to catch the water while it's slipping off the sides of the table.

His chest rises. Falls. He doesn't say a word.

"Hey, it's okay," I tell him. "It was an accident. I'm sorry I scared you."

Standing this close, I'm haunted by that face. His skin isn't as dark as his dad's but he's got the same yellow undertone. Long curly lashes. Eyes just like I've envisioned.

"Are you Teddy?" I ask.

The boy is silent for too many beats of my racing heart. I wonder if I'm wrong. Then, he nods. And I knew, I knew, I knew. But the confirmation hits differently. Carmello and I just spoke about him yesterday, but knowing he exists and seeing so with my own eyes alters my world for a second. I want to tell him he doesn't have to be afraid of me. That I loved his father like I've never loved anyone else. And since a part of him comes from Carmello, there's warmth already in my chest for him too.

"I'm Olivia," I say instead because that other thing is inappropriate as hell to say to a child, and a strange feeling—even for me. I pick up the vase. "Should I go get them more water?"

Teddy nods again, and while I do that at the sink behind the bar, he uses one of the napkins to pat the surface of the table so it's fully dry.

When I place the vase back down, Teddy points to the flowers.

"You want me to smell them?" I ask. Another nod. "Okay," I say, and lean in like he did earlier. When I pull back, the corners of his mouth lift, and God, does that smile span generations. I swallow, eyes stinging at the thought of Celia missing moments with her grandson.

She must have passed on her love of flowers because when Teddy speaks for the first time he says, "Hydrangeas." He turns around, points to another table. "Carnations." He shifts back to me, picks out a single flower with a long stem in the vase between us. "Gladiolus."

His pronunciation is perfect, and I'm impressed. "Did your grandma . . ." I start to say, but then a throat clears from behind me. Teddy's face lights up seeing his dad before I do.

There's a look on Carmello's face that I can't discern when I turn around.

"Hi," I breathe out, hoping I didn't break a boundary talking to his son.

"Hi," he says back, then glances around me. "Teddy, what did I tell you about staying with Steven? He told me he turned around to use the stove and you disappeared."

Teddy frowns and says, "Sorry, Daddy. I just wanted to help."

I can see the tension leave Carmello's face. He sighs. "It's okay, bud. Just next time, you've gotta be with someone out here. Okay? You scared me." When Teddy agrees, Carmello nods toward the kitchen. "Steven's making lumpia. You can go help him roll some if you want."

"I do," Teddy says, and his canines peek out when he gives a full-face grin. He walks over and leans his forehead against Carmello's stomach. Mine squeezes for a good reason watching them interact. I feel like this simple show of comfort might be able to tell me more about their relationship in twenty seconds than twenty minutes of explaining could do.

When Teddy puts his small body behind pulling the kitchen door open, I can't help but smile. He's so cute. "Go wash your hands first, little gremlin," we hear Steven call out.

And then I'm left alone with Carmello.

Chapter 19

Carmello

Now

WHEN I WALKED TO THE FRONT-OF-HOUSE TO GET Teddy after Steven said he'd wandered off, my heart was racing, picturing the worst things that could've happened to my kid. A voice in my head running through gruesome thoughts. And then my breath caught in my throat at the sight of him talking to Olivia. It took my body too long to calm down, even though he was clearly safe. But suddenly I had to process what I was seeing. Teddy takes a while to warm up to people, if he ever does at all. Now I realize this is partly why I've been protective about having them around each other. I had a feeling if he ever met Olivia he'd defrost fast. She has that effect on people.

She crosses one arm and holds her elbow. "He looks just like you," she says.

"I get that a lot," I say.

She tilts her head, squinting up at me. "He's sweeter though."

My mouth twitches at the corners. "I get that too."

"So . . . this is . . . kinda weird, right?" she asks. "Or is it . . . kinda not? I can't tell."

"It's a little weird," I say.

"I'm sorry if I made it that way. There was water and a vase and . . ."

"It's fine," I say. "You don't have to explain. I didn't think you two would run into each other today, but Teddy's recently figured out he can go to the school nurse to be sent home sick. We usually know it's not true, but we'll look like monsters to the school nurse if we don't go pick him up. And his mom is showing a house today, so it was my turn to get him."

"Oh," Olivia says, smiling. "A swindler."

"I swear he gets it from my mom," I say.

"I bet," Olivia says. "Remember that time she had us make sure every single fridge and freezer in this place was spotless, promising she'd let us cook for dinner rush if we didn't complain, and once we were finished, she laughed and said she didn't tell us *when* she'd let us cook for dinner rush."

"A core memory," I say. But I clock it when Olivia winces after she laughs, holding her stomach. "You good?" I ask, eyeing her.

She has her hair thrown into a messy bun, and she's wearing joggers. No makeup. No earrings. She smells good but I think it's just her soap.

"I'm fine," she tells me, but with her face slightly twisted, I'm not convinced. My mom used to say it's rude to ask a woman about "stomach stuff" more than once in case she's on her menstrual cycle and doesn't want to talk about it, so I leave it there. "Let me pivot us into something that'll possibly be less awkward," Olivia says.

"Which is?"

"I figured out how to translate the feeling of this space into something we can use. Before I tell you, I need you to prepare for the best thing you've ever heard that you'll also need to keep an extremely open mind about. Okay, Mello? As open as the sea. Accepting too," she says.

"You're scaring me," I say.

"Change is scary. But usually that means it's good."

I want to tell her I'm not sure that's true, but instead I say, "I'll be a lake."

"Good enough," she says. "Okay, so . . . a date night." She holds up her hands like she's prepared for an argument. "And before you say it's basic, that people go on restaurant dates all the time, I will counter you with: exactly. But the restaurants aren't specifically curated for people to get to know each other, to help people open up to someone special. So, what if we make a space for that? Whether for singles trying to see if they met a good match or for established partners looking to reignite their flame, we advertise it as date-night specific and . . ." She sighs as I stare. "Carmello, your eyes are glazing over. But we *just* talked about *our* first date last night. I know you remember the effort your mom and Paula put into it. They practically forced us to sit down and get to know each other. And the karaoke machine?"

"That was comical," I say.

"Yet your tone is flat in opposition to your words," she says.

"Because, Olivia. This idea is . . ."

"Different," she cuts in. "Think about how enticing it is to say we can give people their best chance on these dates. Half the battle is opening up, being vulnerable. We'll have games and tools to help people with that. I mean, you've been dating lately, so I'm sure you know what it's like to think you have something in common with someone only to realize you hate doing that shared hobby together because you don't mesh on the inside. Or the opposite: you think everything lines up, but you quickly realize you don't like spending time together. Speaking of quick, we could even offer speed dating." I raise my brows, and she says, "Don't knock it till you try it, Mello. It's fun."

"I don't know about speed dating," I say.

"But you think the regular date night idea is good?"

"I don't think it's bad," I say, "but I'm not sure it's the right one for me."

She pouts. Such a brat. "Why?"

"It's just not . . ."

When I trail off, she crosses her arms to her chest and inserts, "Masculine enough?"

"That's not it," I say. "But do I look like a matchmaker?"

"All you have to do is cook the food and have the spot. We'll ensure the team is in place to work out any kinks, but the customers will do most of the work on their own," she says. "And maybe we can offer packages for private dates to people who want to have the place all to themselves. That could be an opportunity to bring in big money."

The idea starts to settle in my brain, and I can almost see it. I'm still skeptical though. "But what if it doesn't?" I ask. "After a long day of cooking, I'm not trying to waste time on . . ."

She raises her pointer finger, almost touches my lips. I have the urge to press my mouth to her raised skin there. She smiles like she knows it. "I was thinking maybe you can do it after hours at the restaurant on Tuesdays, since you close early that day. And we can call the event Table for Twos-Days. Get it—like a table for two people? On Tuesday?"

We've always closed early on Mondays, but when my mom passed away I needed extra time off, especially so that I could make sure Teddy was getting my attention. Even though I don't want to give that up now, a few hours here for an event on a Tuesday night might make more sense than staying open even later than we already do on a different night.

"That name is a little corny," I say. "But I guess people love that stuff."

"It's cute." She grins. "And remember when you said my hair smells like blueberries?"

Memories of being close to her in the car last night come back, and I wet my lips. "Yup."

"I went to a place called Wildly Green. They have a service for finding the right products for your hair and skin."

"I know what they do," I say. "And I see your point. They're matchmaking, in a sense."

"Exactly," she says. "And I'll be leaving here early today for an appointment with them. I'll ask them for some time-management tips so we can make sure you're not overworking yourself on Tuesdays."

"Knowing you, you'll come back with a folder of their business accounts," I say.

She smirks. "So, is it a go?"

My watch beeps with the reminder I set to check on the chicken that's in the oven. "Let me think about it," I say.

"I'll give you until the end of the day," she says.

I blink at her. "Okay, boss."

She winks. And damn if it isn't sexy.

But when she starts to head to the kitchen, I realize she'll be in the same room as my son for hours today. "Olivia," I call, and she turns around. "What did Teddy say to you?"

"He told me the names of the flowers." She tilts her head. "Your mom taught him?"

"She taught him a lot of things," I say.

"Something we all have in common," Olivia says, then disappears through the door.

I TRIED NOT TO IMAGINE WHAT IT WOULD BE LIKE TO HAVE Olivia around Teddy. I just knew I never wanted to see it. And it was because of this: Teddy helping Steven, then gravitating toward Olivia. Playing on his iPad on an upside-down milk crate a couple of feet from where she's cooking. Every so often, she'll say something to him that I can't hear, and he'll give her a belly laugh like he does with Zeke. And each time she points at an object nearby (an oven mitt, tongs, paper towels), he'll hurry to go get it for her.

"Do you have any food allergies, kid?" I hear her ask him. He shakes his head. "Carmello," she calls, "is your son allergic to anything?"

I'm grateful she has the good sense to be safe rather than trust a six-year-old with that question, but if Teddy had allergies, he'd list them out in order of severity. I turn around to find them both staring at me. She's got a ladle held up and he's standing beside her, waiting.

"No," I say, "but he's not your taste-test dummy."

A flash of annoyance crosses her face. "He said he wants to try it," she tells me.

"Is that true, Teddy?" I ask because I want the confirmation that he keeps speaking to her. The boy knows how to use words; getting him to actively open his mouth to say them is the feat.

"The sinigang smells good, Dad," Teddy tells me.

The taste test happens. Teddy approves. Olivia smiles at him, then she slices me up with her eyes. Steven whistles like he knows what's going to happen before my phone dings.

If you don't want Teddy near me then tell him to sit by you, Olivia texts.

I never said I don't want him near you. It's fine, I reply.

All right. Well, stop acting strange. It's not my fault he likes me.

I glance up from my phone to meet her eyes. She holds the contact, unblinking. Then slides her phone back in her pocket. She doesn't care what I have to say in response, and I'm not sure I know what to say anyway. What the hell am I being weird about? She's my ex, but we've already established we're not crossing any lines. She's not in the running to be Teddy's stepmom. We're working together, and last night I told her we might be able to be friends. The more I think about her idea for a special night at the restaurant, the more I think it could work. I respect her, and I trust that she'd never hurt Teddy. But . . . after a string of women being weird about me having a son, Olivia hasn't been weird at all, and seeing them smile at each other makes a pit form in my stomach. I tell myself it's because Teddy had a hard time when my mom died. He's a smart kid, but he gets attached. And I don't want him getting attached to Olivia when she's leaving soon. Still, I know this is more about me getting attached to her being here than him.

I consider apologizing to Olivia over text right when Daniela's call flashes on my screen.

For a planner, I realize I've been living one moment at a time since Olivia arrived.

I definitely didn't prepare for the conversation I need to have with Daniela now.

Paula gives Teddy random things to take with him including a pack of gum she bought for herself but decides he needs instead, and a gift card someone got her for Dunkin' Donuts. Veronica tickles his armpit and tells him she'll take him to the movies soon, and while Olivia watches the whole thing, I wonder what she's thinking. I don't miss how he stares at her for a second—like he's trying to figure out which version of a goodbye he should give her. He decides on a wave, and my heart does a funny flip when a grin splits her face in response.

"Let's go, Teddy," I say, and wonder how quickly we can get Olivia's idea off the ground.

DANIELA'S LOOKING IN THE REARVIEW MIRROR OF HER CAR, fixing her hair before she sees us coming up from behind. When I get to her window, I compliment her on her new suit jacket, and I think she blushes. She's always dressed well, but I rarely see her wearing a full face of makeup. I triple-check that Teddy's seat belt is secure and help him adjust his headphones while he clicks into YouTube on his iPad. Daniela apologizes for not being able to get him from school, and I tell her she knows she doesn't have to. She smiles like I've said something out of the ordinary. And I note that she seems jittery. Like she just had double shots of espresso. She won't meet my eyes.

"Before I go," she says, "I want to tell you something."

"I need to tell you something too," I say.

"Really? Okay, you first, please."

"You sure?" I ask, and she nods. "All right, well, Olivia's here. At the restaurant."

Daniela's brows dip in a moment of confusion. "Your ex-girlfriend?"

"That's the one," I say, and finally explain to her the complicated situation I'm in, that we're still working out the details of the restaurant ownership, and that I didn't think I'd have to tell her about it because I thought Olivia would be out of town by now.

"So, why *are* you telling me?" Daniela says, shoulders suddenly straighter. "Are you getting back together? Is that why you broke up with Rachael?"

This conversation feels like it's going downhill, but I have no idea why.

"No," I say. "To both questions. And I don't know what you've heard at work, but Rachael and I were never together. I did tell her we won't be going on any more dates though."

Daniela releases a breath. "Good. Because I heard some crazy things about her, and I didn't know how to feel if you wanted to bring her around Teddy."

I don't ask what kinds of things because I don't have time to talk about someone I've already cut off and I have enough on my mind. "You don't have to worry about that," I say. "I'll never bring Teddy around anyone I don't trust. You should already know that."

"So you trust Olivia, then?" she asks.

"I do," I say. "But it's not like that between us. We're just doing business together. And I'm only telling you because there *is* a history there, and if she's not gone before your trip, Teddy might be around her again. I didn't want you to find out and feel uncomfortable or wonder if I was hiding anything. Maybe it's weird that I mentioned it, but I guess I wanted to show you some respect because you're my friend."

She considers what I'm saying for a second, but I know something is cooking in her head. She's tight-lipped when she says, "Okay. I appreciate that." She taps her steering wheel. "Well, I guess we'll see you later?"

"Wait," I say. "What did you want to tell me?"

"It was nothing," she says.

"Danny," I say. "What's wrong?"

She chews her cheek: a tell that she's nervous. "It's a coincidence that you told me about your ex," she says, "because Connor's now mine too. We broke up last month."

Damn. I wasn't expecting that. If anything, I would've made a bet that she'd tell me she and Connor were engaged or maybe that she'd be giving Teddy a sibling. I brought the man around my mom. He celebrated New Year's with us last year. And I can tell by the look on Daniela's face, he was the one who caused the breakup. I've been so stressed with the business, I didn't even notice something was off with her. "What the hell happened?"

"He cheated on me," she says, voice thick with the tears she's holding back. "It's fine. I'm healing. I just . . . thought you should know he won't be around anymore."

"Get out of the car," I say.

"What?"

"You heard me."

Teddy doesn't even look up from his screen when I pull his mom in for a hug.

"Carmello," she says against my shoulder. "I know you're busy. I'm okay, really."

She's right, it's busy in the restaurant right now. But even with a broken heart, she's still been taking such great care of our child. I need her to know she has every right to fall apart, and she can rely on me. When my mom died, I relied on her too. There are so many reasons to feel grief and this is one of them. So . . . I hold her close and let her cry. That's when I notice Teddy watching us with curious eyes. He smiles before locking back into his show.

When Daniela pulls away, she squeezes my arm. "Thank you, Carmello," she says. "For this. And for letting me know about Olivia." She gets back in the car, and I close her door.

Then I wait until their car disappears around the corner before heading back inside.

Chapter 20

Olivia

Now

I'M POPPING TWO IBUPROFENS INTO MY MOUTH WHEN CARmello walks into the back room. He grabs the water bottle off the counter, hands it to me, watches as I wash them down. He was outside for a while, and I tried my hardest not to wonder what he was talking about with Teddy's mom. Has he told her that I'm here? Would he? Does it matter? "What's up?" I say.

"I'm sorry about the way I was acting earlier," he says.

"Yeah? What was that? You and I were just joking over me talking to Teddy at the front-of-house then suddenly you were being weird," I say. "This that hot-and-cold thing again?"

Carmello shakes his head. "It's just . . . Teddy . . . he has anxiety and he's usually slow to interact with new people, so seeing him with you caught me off guard."

For a second I stress about what to say. What would a parent want to hear after telling someone they have a six-year-old with anxiety? But then I realize I shouldn't overthink it.

"It's all right," I say. "But if I'm going to be here for a while, I won't ignore him."

"I wouldn't want you to," he says. "And if you're going to be here for a while, I hope you don't want me to ignore it when you're not feeling well. I'm too stubborn for that."

He is, but the words are too tender for my heart. He's moved on and wants to stay that way, so I need to move on too. "Fine, but don't bother me too much about it. It's just stomach problems," I say, remembering that it was his mom's code for *don't ask any more questions.* He doesn't know about my endometriosis, and I don't want to explain right now.

Carmello examines me for a moment, and I know he wants to press, but I'm glad he doesn't.

"I'd have to envision it better," he says, "so maybe we try a small trial run of the date night? Get Zeke to help spread the word. He has a wedding to DJ this week. I'm sure there will be some people there searching for love or whatever."

That sends a jolt up my spine. I squeal and almost launch myself into his arms before controlling the urge. "I know you're nearly sick of me," I say, "but as proof of my good intentions: after I show you this can be a success, I'll sign my shares over and you'll be rid of me."

"Okay," he says. "But what are you getting out of helping me? Serotonin? Is it really just because you love this place? Because you think you owe it to my mother? I have to confess, she didn't even want to think about a social night years ago. It was my idea, and I think she messaged you to brainstorm because she felt bad about the dying bit."

The lighthearted way he says it is so Celia coded, but I know the man in front of me feels anything but light about what happened. I want to reach for him and have to stop myself after our physical distance agreement last night. "I think after I help you with this, I'll have Celia's blessing to move on from this place," I say, the words slipping from my mouth. But I don't take them back, and Carmello doesn't ask what I mean. "But you could cut me a check for the work I'm doing while I'm here if it helps ease your guilt over me helping you."

"I've already been putting money aside since you started cooking in the kitchen," he says.

"Slide it into my pocket before I leave," I say with a smile. "Okay?"

"Okay, O." He breathes out. "Just . . . thanks for everything."

"I'm just glad you said yes for date nights," I say, "because while you were bringing Teddy outside, I prepped everyone in the kitchen for the idea."

He sighs, but I can see his mouth curving up on one side. "Well, I guess that's one less thing I have to do today."

"See? We're such a good team already," I say.

THE DOOR IS PROPPED OPEN, AND THE SMELL OF COCOA butter is strong enough to pull in a person that was just passing by. But anyone who's like me will be extra enticed by the sound of someone singing Whitney Houston from inside. I know it's Vanessa Thompson's full voice I hear before I enter Wildly Green and see her swaying while whisking something up in a wooden bowl. The spot looks different in daylight during normal business hours. Modern with a colorful touch. Huge pots on the floor with plants and fresh herbs. Flowers everywhere. Customers are moving to the music while checking out products on the shelves like it's a record store instead. I'm taking notes with my business eye about what's making them so comfortable. When I spot teenagers giggling and trying to sneak pictures with their phones, I realize Issac Jordan is here.

Not every day do you see a man as famous as he is sweeping the floor. When Laniah walks out of a room behind him, he snatches her from around the waist, pulling her close. She laughs but doesn't resist his kisses. A while back, the two of them made headlines when they announced they were dating. Childhood best friends who finally gave in to their feelings for each other. I remember being swept up in their love story, giggling and kicking my feet whenever Issac mentioned her in a viral video.

They still seem very much in love, and that makes me long for a lot of things.

"You two stop that," Vanessa calls out. "There's a customer waiting."

Laniah bites her lip, hiding her face shyly against Issac's chest. He smiles sheepishly at me. They pull apart and he kisses her cheek, then moves toward the front of the store.

"Hi," she says as I walk toward her. "Sorry about that. Are you Olivia Jones?"

"Don't apologize," I say, and point to the mess at the top of my head. I couldn't bother fixing it this morning with my endo hitting hard. "Yes, and I could definitely use your help."

She gestures to the swivel chair in front of her and asks if she can touch my hair once I'm seated. "My mom told me you came in yesterday," she says as she examines my scalp. Her gorgeous wedding ring gleams in the sunlight, and I just got divorced but I still feel a tad dreamy looking at it. "She was right about your hair looking healthy. You take good care of it."

"Someone has to," I say. "But wait. Are y'all trying to lose money here or . . . ?"

"We just don't like to scam people," she says with a small laugh. "But I'm definitely sending you home with stock. Don't you worry."

I meet her eyes in the mirror. "So, are good ethics a crucial part of your business model?"

"Why do I feel like you've got some questions for me that don't involve hair care?" she asks, her tone playful.

I smile at her. "I can pay you a consulting fee."

"You remind me of my husband," she says. "Quippy and quick with it."

"Maybe that means we'd make good friends too," I say, and she doesn't deny it.

WHILE LANIAH TESTS DIFFERENT PRODUCTS IN MY HAIR, WE talk about the highs and lows of making Wildly Green an experience. When I tell her about wanting to make sure Carmello doesn't go past capacity with his workload, I think of Teddy's sweet face and the time they get to spend together the way the restaurant is set up now.

"He has a son," I say, "and he already does a lot by himself now that his own mom's not there to bear some of the weight."

"Well, my mom, Lex, and I definitely get overwhelmed, but we manage by anticipating the basic needs of our clients," Laniah says. "For example, we just recently started giving away those small bags of samples that people can try ahead of their appointments with me. It's helped a lot to see how they react to some of our more popular product mixes." She combs something through my hair then taps my shoulder excitedly. "Okay, what if the whole menu for date night is just sampler combos? Our clients talk to each other while they're here, people share their custom orders on social media too. The word of mouth through comparison has definitely helped build interest and generate profit. I think having small bites and desserts, charcuterie-board style, could be a talking point because people would be able to sample all the different foods you offer and talk to each other about what they like."

"And it'd definitely be less time-consuming than full-course meals," I say. She told me Issac is quick with it, but she came up with an idea within seconds that's giving me the good tingles. "You're brilliant. Definitely giving you a consulting fee."

"How about you buy some skin-care products and we call it even for today?" she says. When I agree, she starts massaging oil into my scalp. It feels so relaxing, something about it helps with the pressure in my stomach. She clears her throat. "And may I just say, as someone who is obsessed with food, but has restrictions because of my chronic illness, it would be nice to go to a restaurant where I might be able to have small bites of things I crave without worrying about how it'll affect me."

After she says it, she averts her gaze, and I wonder if she thought she said too much. Issac is open about his life on social media, but he calls her his hermit crab. I remember when I first learned about Laniah's chronic kidney disease from an article online and random people would comment on pictures of them saying their relationship was doomed to fail because of it. I'm happy to see it looks like they're thriving, and she feels safe enough to tell me this. And mostly, I understand exactly what she means.

"I didn't even consider that. I have endometriosis, so I have to watch what I eat too," I say. "I think a lot of people will appreciate this idea. And I appreciate you."

"Is that why you've been clutching at your stomach the whole time?" she asks. "Endo?"

"You noticed?" I say.

"You're in my chair," she says. "Is there anything I can do to make you feel better?"

I can tell she means it genuinely, but I say, "That's okay. You've been too kind already. I'll grab green tea after this and cuddle up for the night."

She shakes her head and calls Issac over. "Babe, would you mind grabbing us green tea at Schasteâ before they close?"

"Ginger cubes on the side?" he asks.

She gets on her tiptoes for a kiss. "Yes, please."

I feel like I'm spying on them during an indecent moment as I watch them tap kiss through the mirror. But it's mostly the way they look at each other. I haven't witnessed many long-lasting relationships in my life, but I think they have the kind of longevity my parents have. Issac looks at Laniah like she's the sun in his sky. I think maybe Carmello looked at me like that before too.

Chapter 21

Olivia

Now

FOR A WEEK, WE WORK WITH THE STAFF WHO WANT OVERtime pay to help with bringing the idea to life. No one's surprised that the money doesn't entice Steven to stay longer, so Carmello's responsible for figuring out what small plates he could serve. I leave this part up to him, not wanting to assume what would be feasible for him to do alone after I'm gone. Vero volunteers to be part of the trial date experience and says maybe they'll bring her partner's other woman along. The more the merrier, I tell her. She cuts her eyes and says it was just a joke. Since the food truck event, she's back to being distant with me, but at least she's invested in our idea. She has an eye for mood decor and knows how to thrift in order to stay on a budget, so she ropes Bobby into going around town with her to find things we need. Bobby hangs up the LED neon signs they get featuring sayings like **THIS MUST BE THE PLACE**. Zeke starts putting the word out about Table for Twos-Days, and we're already getting some interest for the real first night.

An unexpected highlight: Laniah Thompson met me for mocktails twice to help with financial questions, and we ended up talking about personal things. I'm finding comfort sharing my struggles with someone who also lives with a chronic illness, and I think she is too.

It's a Friday night and the restaurant is closed. Denise gave me a brilliant idea after she went to her friend Kathy's baby shower the other day. Kathy's an entrepreneur, and a marriage and family therapist. She's the owner of this card game called SinBobo that helps parents (soon-to-be, new, and seasoned) talk to each other about things that might otherwise be harder to bring up. "Would be dope if you had some cards at each table for the dates to get to know each other in a fun way," Denise said. And since then, I've been having Debra help me come up with cards for Celia's Place because she has a talent for getting people to open up about the most personal things. But she ditched me tonight to go meet her friends in Newport and have drinks on a dock by the water. I'm alone at the front-of-house at Celia's, sitting in a booth and jotting down possible questions to run by her, when Carmello finds me.

He picks up one of the stacks and says, "An astrology deck, huh?"

I search his sleepy face, noticing it's a relaxed look rather than drained—like he finished the work he has to do for the day and that weight off his shoulders has made it so he can rest.

"Debra and I thought it'd be good," I say, "even though most men seem put off by it."

"Not all men," he says with a shrug. "I think it could be interesting."

"It will help weed people out, that's for sure," I say.

Carmello was indifferent to astrology our first year together. He never agreed when I used to say common knowledge among astrologers was that our signs weren't a match, but he was also never upset when I compared us using the planets and stars. I'm a Sagittarius, he's a Taurus. As time went on, he picked up on the differences between our signs himself.

"Wasn't expecting anyone to still be here," he says.

"I wanted to finish this other deck tonight," I say, tapping the cards in front of me, "but I'm not sure the questions feel right, so I'll have to wait until Debra can go through them."

He surprises me by sitting down. Our feet are close under the table; I can feel the hum of energy that is his body near my body. Memories come of my leg draped over his when we took work breaks to do homework here. I pull back, cross my ankles. If he notices, he doesn't show it. We've been working so well together, laughing and talking and relying on each other in the kitchen, but I've made it a mission to avoid as many touches as possible while doing so, not just for him but for my sake too. Letting go requires discipline. The actions are easier to control with the brain than with the heart. I'm usually gone before he locks up for the day, so we haven't been alone like we are now. But I lost track of time tonight.

"We can go through them together," he says.

A warning bell rings in my head. "It's late," I say. "I should pack up so you can leave."

He scrubs at his eye with the back of his hand, the drowsiness coming quickly now that he's seated. "My father picked up Teddy from school today. They had a guys' day without me," he says with a smile. "They're bowling but they'll be coming soon so I can bring Teddy home."

The corners of my mouth curve too. It'd be nice to see Teddy. I haven't since the day I met him. But I also haven't seen Carmello's dad in a decade, and I'm not sure the man ever liked me much. He was strict about how Carmello was spending his time when he wasn't studying, in school, or working, which meant I was a distraction. The thought of running into him now makes me slightly uncomfortable.

But then Carmello reads off one of the cards: "What's the strongest animal you might be able to beat in a fight?" He looks at me, brows bunching together, tilting his head.

"Okay, so some of them are silly, but that's the point," I say. "Have to have lighthearted moments between the deeper stuff or the dates might become too heavy."

"You didn't answer the question," he says.

"I bet I could take on a lion," I say.

His eyes flick over the parts of my body he can see above the table and a flash of heat cuts across my chest, and I'm wondering if he's thinking about the parts he can't.

"Yeah," he says after a moment. "I could see that."

I snort and snatch the cards from him. "What's one thing you want to do before you die?"

After reading it out loud, I wonder if I should've picked a different question. I'm sure Celia had a bucket list and doubt she had time to accomplish all of it. But Carmello doesn't seem shaken by the card. He doesn't take too long to consider either. "I want to see the Philippines."

I'm not sure what I assumed about where he'd traveled, but I would have suspected he'd been with his mom a time or two since I've been gone. I know she didn't travel there much in the first fifteen years of his life—he was young and she had the business here to think about—but they always planned to go together. "I'm surprised you never went with your mom."

"She wanted to take a trip together before she died, but the cancer was progressing too fast and the long flight . . ." He pulls his eyes from me. "It just couldn't happen."

"I'm sorry," I say, ignoring the ache to reach across the table and squeeze his hand. "I've only been once for about a week when I was trying to hit a few of the countries in Southeast Asia in one trip, but it's stunning." I don't tell Carmello that it was also a little weird. My father is so far removed from his family and culture, I didn't get to meet up with any of my extended family while I was there. "I hope you'll get to see it one day. Your mom would want you to still."

He meets my gaze. Releases a frustrated breath and I'm not sure if I said something wrong, but then he says, "If I can get over my fear of flying, it'll be the first country I visit."

This confession catches me completely off guard. "Carmello Rodriguez," I say. "Are you telling me you've never been out of the country? Like at all?"

"Yes, Olivia Jones. That's what I'm saying." He opens his mouth to read the question off the card he just pulled from my hand, trying to change the subject.

I cut him off with a wave of my hand. "Nah-uh. Hold it right there."

He rolls his eyes. "It's not a big deal."

"It is," I say. "When did you become afraid of flying?"

"A long time ago," he says. When I give him a look, he sighs. "You're so unrelenting."

"Don't you adore that about me?" I ask.

"Sometimes," he says, so serious it warms my belly. He clears his throat and I swallow. “We had bad turbulence going to Chicago to visit my dad’s family the year before I met you. People were screaming and praying. A flight attendant fell in the aisle and got injured. My mom never wanted me to travel without her after that. And I was scared too. It took me years to get on a plane again. Then, for my twenty-first birthday, Zeke and I planned a trip to Miami. As you could imagine, he talked shit. ‘You’re a grown man, Mello. You’ll be good.’ It was a short flight. I figured it would be fine. Turns out planes can run out of gas in the air. Did you know that?”

I put my hand to my mouth, but he sees my shoulders shake with laughter. He narrows those pretty eyes at me. “I apologize for laughing,” I say, “it’s just . . . I travel so much. And it actually happens more than people know. It must’ve been scary to hear you had to make a pit stop for some gas though.” He nods and I think of how he knew that I wanted to go everywhere in the world. We’d planned to fly to different countries together once we saved up money from working. Was he going to face those fears for me and never say anything about it? “Did you ever get on one again?” I ask to distract from the fluttering feeling in my stomach.

He props his elbows on the table. “I had a couple of good trips after that. A short one to Virginia especially. Then four years ago, a bunch of us went to California. I got drunk on the plane after being told I had to give up control in order to relax and that this trip would prepare me for longer ones in the future. Thankfully, the six-hour flight was smooth. I slept through some of it. But on the way back to Rhode Island, we caught a storm. The plane couldn’t land. The pilot had to circle the airport. When he finally saw an opening to land, he made a surprise nosedive so we didn’t run out of gas. I thought I was having a heart attack on the way down. All I could think about was my one-year-old son. If I died, I'd miss his whole life, and he'd grow up without a father. I finally understood why my mom was so paranoid whenever either of us got on a plane. Everyone says it's a stupid fear, that the probabilities of a crash are slim, but it is what it is." He shrugs. "Anyway, let's move on from this one."

I don't want to move on. I thought I knew everything I could know about him back then. Turns out, there was something he was embarrassed to tell me. Some nights since our breakup, I'd lay awake and try to imagine his life, what cool things he'd done, if there was anything he regretted. I felt like a masochist because it hurt to know we'd keep making memories without each other. But with him across from me now, the energy between us feels more open than it has in so long, and I'm happy there are things to learn.

"We can move on, but it's not stupid," I say. "I can't imagine having a child and being scared like that. But I can empathize with fears. Even though my house burned down two decades ago, I still check that every Airbnb I stay at has proper fire safety. I'm careful cooking at home, and I've only just started regularly using candles again a few years ago. The probability of me being caught in a burning building twice is extremely low, but it is what it is."

He studies me, then says, "Do you still have bad dreams?"

"Rarely now," I say. "I've worked through a lot with therapy over the years, so I'd say things are getting better for me, and maybe they will for you too. The Philippines would be nice, but for now, I won't tease you about any fears."

"How magnanimous of you," he says, a smile on his face.

"I try to be a good ruler," I say, taking a small bow.

He laughs. "What's something you want to do before you die, my queen?"

The term of endearment from his mouth sends sexy images to my mind and a rush of heat between my thighs. "Get a tattoo," I say. "But . . ."

"You're still scared of needles?" he asks, and I remember telling him about being in the hospital after the fire. How much they poked and prodded me. How it was almost scarier than the actual fire at that age.

"I've had plenty of time and experience to get over that fear," I say, thinking of all the endometriosis testing over the years. "Supercharged ones that tattoo the skin? Not so much. But it's not the needles that scare me. I'm afraid of committing to something and regretting it later." He gives me a curious look, and I wonder if he's connecting it to some other ways I haven't committed. My therapist sure would. "I change my mind about getting one constantly, which is probably a product of my ADHD."

His tone is soft when he asks, "You ended up getting diagnosed?"

"I did," I say, thinking of how we'd joke about my impulsivity and forgetfulness, among other things.

"Has it helped now that you know?"

"I feel like it has," I say. "Recognizing patterns and having tools that can help with certain tendencies makes most of my days easier. And accepting that my brain might work a little differently makes me gentler on myself when I'm all over the place."

"Gentle is good," he says.

"Gentle is necessary," I agree. "Anyway . . . hit me with the question in your hand, sir."

He holds the card up and reads, "What's something you learned about yourself during a past relationship?"

I chuckle because the universe really wants to make this awkward. "This particular deck might be weird for us. Are you sure you don't want to try the astrology one?"

"Does what you learned have to do with our relationship, Olivia?"

"Actually," I say, blowing out a breath, "I was going to admit that when I first started dating Michael, I thought I would grow to want biological kids, but I'm not sure pregnancy is something I ever want to experience. What I do know is I don't want to feel forced to be someone that I'm not just because I'm in a relationship. Toward the end of our marriage, Michael liked to remind me that I wasn't meeting his new-to-me expectations. That being said, when I filed for divorce, I hoped we'd be able to be civil, maybe even friends eventually. Instead he laughed in my face and said hurtful things. I realized some of them were true, but I can't control what he feels or how he sees me. And I guess I have a hard time letting go of that control, but I'm working on it."

"What would you say to him if you were friends right now?" Carmello asks.

"I think I'd tell him congratulations because he's having a baby," I say.

Carmello's eyes bloom slightly. They're quick to settle into their normally narrow shape, but he still searches my face. "Were you in love with him?"

"That isn't a question on the cards," I say, shifting in my seat. "And isn't it your turn?"

He doesn't let up. "It's something I've been wondering since you said you got divorced."

My face flushes, but I try not to be delusional about why he's been wondering that. "I think I grew to love him," I finally say, "but I never fell in love with him, if that makes sense."

"It does," Carmello says. "Is that why you think it didn't work in the end?"

"No," I say. "There's more than one way to love someone. But I still think there has to be some sparks. I didn't have the urge to be close to *him*. Every time I went away for a work trip, I realized I didn't miss him. I don't think he missed me either. I think he just loved the idea of having someone. Maybe we were both lonely, because so did I. Too bad it ended the way it did."

The conversation is more raw than I was anticipating, and I'm not sure if I had to give Carmello that deep of an explanation. He looks so serious when he says, "So, you traumatized yourself ending things badly with me and now you want to be friends with all of your exes?"

"Is that what you're taking from this?" I ask.

"Sounds like your poor ego needs stroking after you break someone else's heart," he says.

I throw my pen cap at his chest, and he laughs. "I am a work in progress, sir."

"So am I," he says, twisting the cap between his fingers. "I learned something from our relationship that I've tried implementing over the years too."

"And what's that?"

"I could be better at it," he says, "but communication is important to me. I think that's why Daniela and I have a solid relationship. Whenever something feels off, especially with the way we each parent Teddy, we talk about it. I have an easier time processing things if I can talk them through. That goes for endings too."

"Ouch," I say. Putting a hand over my heart. "You're trying to wound me today."

"I promise I'm not," he says. "I'm just talking to you."

I have a momentary urge to tell him about why I left the way I did, but when I pull my bottom lip into my mouth, the way he tracks the movement makes other urges overcome that one. I snatch the cards from him, look down, and ask, "Is there a 'first time' experience you'd relive the same way all over again?"

I thought this question was innocent, picturing my first time skydiving, but I feel the heat in his stare before I even look up at him. There's something inviting in those dark eyes, and delusional thoughts come. Is he thinking of our first time together? Would he relive that moment with me now that we're older?

The air in the room feels charged while I wait. A little dangerous. Our legs are touching underneath the table, and I don't know when that happened, but it feels nice.

He slides his thumb along the stubble at the side of his jaw. "I'd say . . ."

A sudden knock against the glass door steals whatever he was going to confess from me.

While he goes to unlock the door, I take deep breaths and will my heart to stop stuttering.

Then, I stick that card into a random deck.

Chapter 22

Carmello

Now

MY SKIN IS STILL HOT. SOMETHING I SHOULD'VE ANTICIpated sitting so close to Olivia. She kept absentmindedly brushing her leg against mine while answering questions, and beneath the table I was already hard as hell, pressed against my pants and aching, before the flashbacks hit of our first time and the fantasies of what it'd be like if we did that now that we're more experienced.

I shut my eyes for a second, clear my head, and finally unlock the door. Teddy's got a stuffed animal the size of his body with him when he walks into Celia's. He leans his forehead against me, a quick hello, before he sees Olivia. She gives him a big smile, and he high-fives my dad before he heads over to her. My dad grumbles something about it under his breath, then offers Olivia a wave. She responds in kind, then fixes her attention on Teddy, gushing over his giant giraffe, before he tells her he beat my dad in bowling twice. My heart is in my throat watching them, and I can feel my father watching me.

I meet his eyes. "What is it?"

He nods toward the kitchen. "Let's talk."

I know by the look on his face what he wants to talk about: me and Olivia. Working late. The room dim. No one else around. When she first showed up, he said it was better to work on business deals in person anyway, but when I updated him that she was staying awhile to help with the event night, I could feel his temper radiating through the phone. He hasn't lectured me yet. Might as well get it over with. I lock the door to Celia's Place again and tell Teddy I'll be back in a second. He ignores me to read Olivia's cards.

My father walks all the way to my office for privacy. When I shut the door, his tone is calm, but his words come quickly. "Have you had paperwork drawn up with a lawyer for her to sign over her shares?"

I'm pretty sure if I drew up papers right now Olivia would have no issues signing them early. But it feels rude to rush when she's helping me, and there's something deeper there too. Every time I think of having a lawyer do it, my stomach squeezes. Something tells me to wait. I tell my father I haven't had the time but that I will soon, so this conversation doesn't go on longer than it must.

"But you have time to cozy up with her in a booth?" he says. There's a beat of silence between us. I feel like a teenager being reprimanded for not focusing on my future again. His hands tremble slightly when he runs them over his silver-gray hair. This situation has been stressing him more than I knew. "What if she changes her mind and wants to keep the shares after she helps see this event night of yours through?"

"She won't," I say.

"You really trust her with all of this?" he asks.

"If I trust her out there alone with my son, what do you think?" His face twists into something like a scowl. In both of my cultures, I was taught not to disrespect my elders. I sigh and say, "Lo siento, Pa. I'm just tired tonight. But you don't have to worry about Olivia."

"I'm more worried about you and your soft heart."

I grind my teeth together, trying to keep patient. "I know what I'm doing, Pa."

"Let's hope so," he says, lowering his voice. "I'd hate for you to get caught up in her pretty face and forget who she's always been. She's proven to be impulsive in the past. Don't count on her saying she's changed, get blindsided by feelings you might have for her, and forget this is about business. You've worked hard here since you were young." He releases a long exhale. "Anyway, let me say bye to my grandson before you take him home."

As I follow him to the front, I process the words I wished for him to say when I was a kid. Back then, he was convinced that I was making a mistake choosing a career path as a chef instead of one that'd make me more money. Now I realize his fear of me losing any control here is more than just the principle of it; it's because he's proud of me like he was proud of my mom. Something about that makes me a little less frustrated with the pressure he puts on me.

EVEN AFTER I LEAVE CELIA'S PLACE WITH MY POP'S WARNING about Olivia ringing in my head, my body feels like it's being pulled in her direction. I'm driving Teddy home, and I make an accidental left like I'm heading to the Airbnb she's renting instead. It's been comfortable talking with her this week, and her presence has been appreciated, but we haven't been physically close since we sat on Fountain Street after the food truck event. I know what I said to her about keeping our distance, but after sitting in the booth with her tonight, I wonder if I can control myself. The voice in my head keeps saying she'll be gone soon anyway, so what's the harm in being closer? I can't stop the intrusive thoughts until I pull up to Daniela's house and see her on the front porch, trying to reach the overhead light.

I've been meaning to change the bulb out but keep forgetting.

When we get out of the car, she squeezes Teddy and helps him name his giraffe. Then, she sends him inside to pick a movie for them to watch. When I'm done switching the bulb, I see how much the simple action lit up Daniela's face. She's self-sufficient in so many ways, and I'm sure she would've changed it herself with some determination, but I like helping in any way that I can. And now that Connor's not in the picture, I want to be able to anticipate some of the things I don't usually do but that might make her life a little easier.

We say good night to each other, but then Teddy pushes his face against the mesh bottom of the storm door. With his nose flattened, he oinks at us. "Daddy, movie night, please?"

I'm beat, and I'm sure One Piece is annoyed I'm not home by now, but I'll explain to him that his favorite human was giving me puppy eyes. Daniela looks excited by the thought too. We haven't done anything like this all together in a while. "Depends on what movie," I tease.

He enunciates, "*Mufasa*," like they do in the live-action version, and I wonder how much sugar my father gave him that he still has this much energy.

"We've watched it, like, seven times," I say. "But you know I can't resist that one."

A QUARTER THROUGH THE MOVIE, TEDDY FALLS ASLEEP CUDdled up near Daniela on the big couch, so I lift him from her arms and bring him to bed. He's a heavyweight sleeper, stays in the same position I lay him down in, still hugging his giraffe. His mouth is wide open and I'd tease him tomorrow about swallowing spiders while he sleeps, but knowing my boy it'd give him nightmares.

I kiss his head, say, "Stay safe, son," like I do every single day or it doesn't feel right.

When I go back to the living room, Daniela's folding the blanket on the couch. The room is darker with the TV off, but there's a light coming from the kitchen. While I'm standing by the door, I say, "He was exhausted. I'm surprised he lasted that long after the day he's had."

"I'm not," she says, picking up the popcorn bowl from the table and taking a few steps toward me. "He loves that movie, and he was happy that you were here watching it too. But I am surprised *you* lasted as long as you did. I saw you scrubbing at your eyes to keep awake."

"I'm tired as hell," I admit. "Might have to skip my run tomorrow and get an extra hour."

"You could . . . sleep here if you want," she says softly.

I start to laugh, thinking she's joking. We're friends, but we agreed early that we wouldn't cross *that* line while co-parenting, so we don't confuse Teddy or ourselves by introducing something that could become a habit. I've had plenty of late nights here where I've nodded off on the couch, but I've always woken up and taken my ass home.

"You're serious?" I ask.

She shrugs one shoulder. "It wouldn't be that big of a deal, would it?"

"I just . . . Where is this coming from?"

She hugs the popcorn bowl close to her chest, and there's that same nervous energy she had when she came to pick up Teddy from Celia's last week. Something tells me she had more on her mind that day than just wanting me to know Connor isn't in the picture.

"I've been thinking lately," she says, "and I feel like we're so good at this. Being a team. Taking care of Teddy together. And . . ." She trails off and tears her gaze away.

I scratch the back of my head, wondering how to approach this, but knowing I should speak the hard words for her. "And you're wondering if we should try a relationship?"

She meets my eyes again. I can tell she's embarrassed, and I don't want her to be. "Maybe we can be a real family. You know?"

"We already are a real family," I say, "but . . ."

She shakes her head and tries to smile. "I'm sorry. You're tired and I'm keeping you here with a silly idea that sounded better in my head."

"That's not the word I'd use to describe the idea, Daniela," I say. "You don't have to feel bad about bringing this to me. But I wonder if this is only because of the breakup with Connor."

She huffs out a breath, says, "Would it be bad if that put things into perspective for me?"

"No," I say, and struggle for the words I need to gently ease her into understanding.

"You've never thought of it, Carmello?" she says while I'm searching for them.

I see how this could quickly get sticky, but I always feel it's better not to sugarcoat things. This shouldn't be any different. "Not since we tried the first time and it didn't work," I tell her, and the words hit her in the chest. I watch it happen. For a second, I hate myself. Her heart has been sore, and I'm not trying to cause more harm by being honest. "I respect you, Daniela. I love that we've managed to give Teddy a family even without us being together, but when we called it quits years ago, I forced any thoughts of a traditional one out of my head."

"I understand," she says. "But what if you're able to shift perspectives now too?"

She sees the look on my face and bows her head. I want to hug her. Ease the unintentional hurt I'm causing. But I don't want to confuse her, so I choose to deepen the conversation instead. "Tell me what suddenly made me seem like an option for you? I'm not asking for my ego, by the way, but I'm warning you that it might accidentally become inflated."

This gets her to smile a little. She picks up her chin and says, "You're a great dad, you cook, you have your shit together, and you're good-looking."

"And you're all of those things, minus a good cook," I say.

She laughs and my chest loosens. "Exactly my point. You could be in this kitchen."

"But that's all it would be," I say. "Me checking off boxes. Nothing more."

"Why do you say that?"

"You didn't mention having feelings for me," I point out.

"Feelings can grow," she says. "We're getting older. Love doesn't have to look like it did in high school."

"No," I say, wondering if that's a slight against whatever she might think I have going on with Olivia, "and it probably shouldn't. But I don't think we should force a relationship just because we can check off boxes for each other, just because we're getting older."

"That's true, but how do you know we'll be forcing something if we've never *truly* tried? That's the question that's been on my mind. And honestly, I can imagine how easy it might be. Simple. A comfortable type of happiness," she says.

I think of Olivia mentioning how she believes there are many ways to love. And I know plenty of people who have grown to love. But Daniela and I have Teddy; I don't think we could go slow and find out if we can, if there will ever be a spark. It would be serious right away.

"But what if there's someone else that could make you feel something more than that?" I ask. She doesn't answer, so I press forward. "Are you worried you're going to be alone now?"

"If you haven't noticed," she says, "dating in Rhode Island feels pretty limited. My cousin's *current* boyfriend just swiped on my Tinder profile. And . . ."

"And what?"

"Even when you think you have a good one," she says, "they can prove you wrong."

"What if we decided to try and I proved you wrong?" I say.

She cocks an eyebrow. "We both know you're one of the good ones, Carmello. And you'd never hurt me like Connor did."

"How do you know that?"

"Because of Teddy," she says.

"Kids are so important," I say. "But I don't think we should choose each other because of Teddy. You're right, I would never cheat on you. But I couldn't promise that I'd feel things for you that I think we should all get to feel in our relationships. Maybe those feelings would grow, but I don't want that to be a goal. And what if we tried and it didn't work? We might hurt Teddy later. One of the things I appreciated about my parents calling it quits early was that I never had to be affected by the resentment of them sticking it out just for me. And I think they had more love for each other after they split. Their bond taught me co-parenting can work."

This is what gets her to break. Tears stream down her cheeks, droplets landing in the popcorn. "I thought Connor and I were crazy in love," she says. "I fell hard and he still hurt me. I don't know that I can trust feeling like that again. I don't even know if it's out there for me."

Even though I was young, I felt that way after Olivia left. I closed my heart up, protected myself for years, and I still move cautiously now. "I understand," I say. "And since I've been dating, I've been careful not to base everything on crazy-in-love feelings that might just be chemistry, but that doesn't mean we should settle. I do believe you can grow to love someone, but I think when that happens it's because you're naturally already heading in that direction too."

Her chin wobbles. "I don't want to end up alone."

I bridge our gap now, squeeze her shoulder and look her in the eyes. "I know," I say. "Neither do I. But we are still young. There's plenty of time for you to heal and get back out there. I don't think you should let what he did keep you from opening up to someone else."

She leans her forehead against my chest the way Teddy does, and for a brief flash I see a life here. Something easy with Daniela. Contentedness that I know could be possible. Having more kids. Growing a family. Being here every single night even after Teddy sleeps. A voice in my head says, *He'd be safer if you were here too. Maybe he'd have less anxiety. Maybe he wouldn't have bad dreams. Maybe you'd sleep a little easier too.* But I swallow and shake those thoughts away. Teddy is safe here with his mom, and I meant every word I just said to her.

I pull back and give her a serious face. "I was going to take the popcorn with me," I say, "but it might be too salty now that you cried in the bowl."

"Shut up," she says, laughter making her shoulders shake before she swats at her eyes.

WHEN I GET BACK IN THE CAR, I WATCH DANIELA SHUT THE front door and then I sit in her parking lot for a second. There's a small part of me still trying to turn her words over in my head, a voice asking if I shouldn't have been so quick to shoot her down. But then my phone buzzes. A text from Olivia. And I realize right away that it was the right thing to do when the notification makes *me* light up.

Hope this doesn't wake you, it says. **But I wanted to tell you it was really nice running through the questions with you. I think this is going to work.**

It takes me a moment to register the text. My heart instantly attaches the word *this* to *us*. Knowing there's still a spark and wondering if maybe there's something worth working for. She might not have been in love with Michael, but she was in love with me once. I know it because there's no way energy of that magnitude wasn't reciprocated. All of these feelings remind me of why I needed to shut Daniela down. Not for Olivia, but to be fair to me and to the mother of my child. I want to *feel* things for whoever I end up with. I want her to have that too.

I know I won't end up with Olivia, she'll be off to Japan before I know it, but despite myself, one thought still leads to the next, and I'm wondering what her bottom lip tastes like tonight. Shit, I'll even be happy with another conversation. It's stimulating talking to her. And I wouldn't mind a little more of that tonight, tired and all.

I fight myself so hard, but my body tells my brain to fall back.

I'm awake, I text. But she never reads it. She must've fallen asleep.

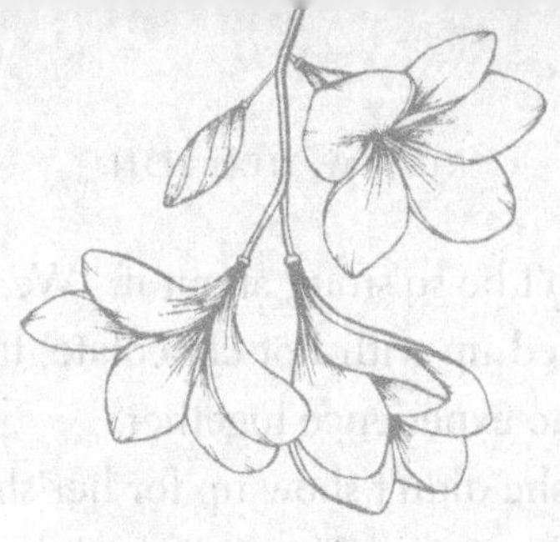

Chapter 23
UBE CAKE

Carmello

13 years ago

DEEP PURPLE WITH A WHITE CHOCOLATE CENTER. AN earthy aftertaste like sweet potato, slightly nutty, a hint of coconut. For Olivia's sixteenth birthday, my mom and Paula made her a cake that was perfect (not too sweet, low on the vanilla flavor, just the way we all liked it), and I saw tears sitting in the corners of her eyes when they surprised her with it.

"I haven't had a homemade cake since . . ." She trailed off, but I knew she meant the fire. She didn't mention it much, and I think that's because she was someone who felt it best to move on from things, but she did call me in the middle of the night whenever she'd wake up after a bad dream about it.

While she blew out her sixteen candles, I placed a hand at the small of her back.

That night, we went ice skating at the rink downtown. She'd been wanting to go for a while and was determined to be a pro right away. Each time she fell, I'd help her up and she'd roll her eyes and say, "Don't be so smug about it." We teased and kissed in the cold, warmed up with hot chocolate, talked about other things we wanted to experience together.

The next day, she didn't show up for her shift at Celia's. Her parents said she left at 6 a.m. They assumed she had an early shift at work. But her phone was going straight to voice mail, and it was the first time I ever felt like my heart wasn't in my body. Winter brought an early nightfall, and my mom paced the kitchen, cursing in Tagalog when she accidentally knocked over pots. My dad picked me up to search Providence, and by this point, her parents were worried too. They allowed her freedom to roam, but they'd never gone this long without hearing from her.

I finally got a call around 7 p.m. "Someone on the train was kind enough to let me borrow a charger," Olivia said, and I could hear the smile in her voice—still happy after chatting it up with this generous stranger. The relief came first. Swift. A long breath. Until she started explaining that she woke up with the sudden urge to see Boston, a birthday present for herself. Her phone was only on 25 percent because she forgot to put it on the charger the night before and then she forgot to bring the charger with her on her impromptu trip. She got caught up exploring museums, trying not to slip on patches of black ice, and hitting as many indie shops as she could find before her phone died. "I bought you *The Fellowship of the Ring* from Harvard Book Store."

That she thought of me like this on her last-minute trip made my stomach warm. Months before, I had told her I'd been wanting to read the series, but I never got around to it. "Thank you, O," I said. "But you didn't think to ask the staff to use a phone? Or maybe use the money from buying the book for a charger instead? Everyone was worried. I was . . . worried."

"I'm sorry, Mello," she said sweetly, trying to coax me out of whatever resentment I had started to feel. "Will you forgive me?"

How could I say I wouldn't? She was her own person, and I already knew the same things I liked about her sometimes drove me crazy. I could never stay mad at her for long and was desperate to see her. So, my mom and I went to wait at the train station, and I'll never forget my mom's sharp breath at the sight of her.

"I must've misread the schedule, Celia," Olivia said. "I swear I didn't know I was on it."

My mom wasn't very physically affectionate—she showed her love in other ways—but she surprised us both by pulling Olivia in for a hug. "I'm happy you're okay," she said, "but if you do another no-call no-show, I'll fire you."

Olivia's body stiffened, and I could see her taking serious note of my mom's warning. But I had a feeling my mom only said it out of fear that Olivia's impulsivity would frighten her again.

That night, Olivia's parents gave her a warning of their own. Though they seemed more interested in what she had captured on a disposable camera while sightseeing in Boston than in disciplining her. While they developed the film, Olivia and I sat in the back seat of their car, waiting in the Walgreens parking lot. And I couldn't help but ask, "Why didn't you wait for me to go to Boston with you?"

We had made plans to see the public library and to take a boat tour and to visit the Salem Witch Museum a month before, and I really wanted to understand her thought process.

"You just took time off from the restaurant to skate with me, Mello," she said. "I knew you wouldn't be able to take a whole day off anytime soon. And I got this crazy itch to get up and go—like Boston was calling to me. Do you ever feel like that?"

"Sometimes," I said, but I didn't know if it was exactly true. I had urges to try new hobbies, I wanted more time to read books like the one I was holding to my chest, and I even wanted to learn new ways of cooking. I had the desire to travel for sure. But it never felt like it'd eat at me if I didn't, and never did I feel rushed to get up and go somewhere else.

I realized then that Olivia was much more like her parents than like me.

She leaned forward and kissed my cheek. "Don't worry, Mello, we can go together soon. You'd love it there."

I was sure that I would, especially if we were together. But it was at that moment that I realized I'd have to be a little faster if I wanted to follow her. And I did want that, because while she was sitting beside me after one of the longest days of my life, her thigh pressing against my thigh, our fingers entwined, it felt like my heart had finally returned to my body.

Chapter 24

Olivia

Now

"SOMEONE'S OVERLY HAPPY THIS MORNING," STEVEN MUTters. He's throwing thinly sliced pork on the grill for Filipino barbecue, has a black hoodie over his head, and he hasn't sung all day. Where Carmello is pensive and quiet, sometimes quippy in the kitchen, this man's moods swing from sarcastic with a slice of joy to the definition of broody, I swear. But he's right. I'm buzzing. My body vibrating while I flash cook steak, the savory aroma hitting my stomach. I'm hungry *and* I haven't given myself time to sit still all day. For the past few days, really. As prep work for later, I'm reading the guys some questions from the cards because tonight we're putting my idea to the test.

"Maybe we should use the date night to match you with someone, Steven," I say with a wink. "You might be more pleasant to work with."

"Or consider this," Steven says, unfazed by my jab, "I might be worse."

"A test we shouldn't force on him, O," Carmello says, wiping sweat from his brow with his shirt. When he turns back to the burner, I smile big because he's been casually dropping my nickname. Little does he know that small show of closeness means so much to me. I'd missed his friendship more than I'd realized.

And there's something else making me vibrate today. I may have just thrown a jab at Steven, but I'm realizing that here, in this particular kitchen, with these two, I *feel* happy.

I pause, registering that feeling as *want.* Joy. An urge to keep doing what I'm doing right now.

But . . . Tokyo is waiting for me, it's the best choice for all of us, so I clear my throat and that thought from my mind.

"Okay, guys," I say. "What's your favorite thing about yourselves?"

"Are these going to be interviews or dates?" Steven asks.

"Listen, the cards are going to be available at the table to help encourage conversation. If the date is already going well then people don't have to use them. But, as a woman, if a man refused to use cards that had the potential to tell me if he's the man for me, then there wouldn't be a second date."

Carmello's eyes find mine across the room and a blush burns my cheeks as I think of him offering to run through the cards with me. I pull my eyes away and see Steven shrug.

"I know I can sing," he says, "but I'd say my humor."

"Some of us do love a man with a good deadpan, dry-ass humor," I say.

"Many of you," Steven says, mirroring my wink from earlier, though he's better at it.

I snort, though I can't help grinning too. This is going to be a good day, I can feel it in my bones. I place the cards down and put on gloves. "Carmello? Favorite thing about yourself. Now."

"Yes, sergeant, ma'am," he says. Then: "I . . . don't give up when I want something."

"True," I say. "Remember when your mom wouldn't let you make main courses? I don't think I've ever seen someone so determined to show why someone else should change their mind. I ate real good that week from the meals you made that she wouldn't send out."

"Yeah. But I guess I can consider that quality my least favorite thing about myself too," he says.

"For sure," says Steven. "Sometimes you say the same thing over and over and don't notice, or you do things repeatedly during our shifts, and a lot of times you . . ."

"Everyone has to have some sort of balance, Steven," I cut in, and begin marinating chicken thighs. What he's saying about Carmello isn't a lie; the man has his ticks and repetitive tendencies, but I feel defensive of him for a second. He's a great boss, and Steven's a great sous-chef, but he can be a jerk too. "And Carmello," I say, "your determination is probably why the restaurant is still thriving after all you've been through this past year."

Something softens in his expression at my acknowledgment. "Thanks for saying that, O."

Steven kisses his teeth like he's unaffected by my comment to him. "Am I really gonna have to suffer with you two going down yet another ex-lovers memory lane?"

FOR THE TRIAL DATE NIGHT, WE ONLY HAVE THREE COUPLES coming. It's not something we advertised, so there isn't a crowd when Laniah and Issac Jordan enter the restaurant.

Two nights ago, she invited me over and we sat on her front

porch with her friend Katrina. It was my first time meeting Kat, but we clicked like we'd known each other our whole lives. So, I wasn't that shocked when she shrugged her shoulders and said, "I've been talking to someone that has potential. Maybe he'd be down for a different type of first date. Lord knows I need to be able to weed these men out a little faster." But when Laniah jumped in with: "You know, Olivia. It could be good if you have a seasoned couple for this trial of yours. Two people who already have a great relationship and want to keep it that way," I was caught off guard. We'd been digging in on the deep stuff, and what we had in common was a bridge for comfort. It was something that told me we could have a real friendship, but it surprised me when her introverted self offered to bring her famous husband to a date that would be scrutinized later.

I'm still a little surprised to see Issac Jordan in the flesh. He thanks me and Debra for giving him something new to do with his wife and tells us to forgive him if we happen to see a man with an angry face and a shiny bald head in the parking lot.

"That'd be Bernie, my manager, prepared to run interference. Just ignore him."

Debra laughs nervously, then waits until Issac whisks Laniah away to their table before she whispers, "Did you hear the way he introduced himself? Like he doesn't have superfans. Like I'm not one of them. Like if he wasn't with his beautiful wife tonight I wouldn't . . ."

I gasp. "Debra! My jaw is on the floor, you frisky girl. You're married too."

She takes one last look at Issac and hums the way she did eating Paula's blueberry pie on her break earlier. "I'm gonna go give Bobby a hug before everyone else arrives."

There are still things I should focus on before the event starts, but I watch Debra make her way over to Carmello and Bobby by the bar. She wraps her arms around Bobby, and Carmello pats him on the back. I don't know what Bobby's going through, but I know he refused Carmello's offer to take PTO, insisting that being at work was a good distraction. Carmello says something to him now, and it's the first time I've heard Bobby's big laugh this week.

Suddenly, I realize that if I had to pick a favorite quality about Carmello, I wouldn't be able to. He shifts like he can feel my eyes on him, and when he smiles at me the way he does, butterflies beat a storm in my belly.

SO THAT I'M NOT *LOOKING* LIKE A CREEP, I CREEP BEHIND THE kitchen door. Staring through the glass, trying to get hints at what's going on during date night. The downside of Veronica not waiting tables for the trial is that we can't get any juicy details on what she might've overheard. The plus side? She seems like she's having a great time. She and her man have spent most of the date laughing at the card questions. They've hardly touched their food. I can't say the same about Laniah and Issac. The two of them can eat. We made sure to pull back on adding extra salt to the small bites menu so Laniah's not feeling sad about missing out on sodium-dense foods. But they've been feeding each other and sharing kisses over the table. The song switches to something with soul. Aretha Franklin's "I Say a Little Prayer." And Issac pulls Laniah out of her seat. They dance to the song like no one else is in the room, and a thought that may be an idea forms in the back of my mind. But something else takes precedence: my heart aches with want, and I know I won't settle until someone sees me that way again.

I'm swaying to the song when Steven comes over and says, "Zeke made a decent playlist, but isn't this song screaming old folk?" I cock an eyebrow up at him and Steven ignores me. "Who's that?" He taps his pointer finger against the glass door impatiently. "Her."

My eyes land on a willowy Katrina, long limbs and smooth russet-brown skin, stunning in red. "Laniah's best friend. Why?"

"Because she's cute," he says. "And she looks bored as hell with that dude."

His delivery is simple, but I'm confused because that hadn't been my assessment. I thought so far it seemed like her date was going well. Nothing overly exciting, and I don't think they broke the touch barrier since I've been spying, but they're using the cards, and she looks interested in how he's responding. "Why do you say that?" I ask Steven.

"Look at her body language," Steven says. "Her face is tight. The way she's leaning away from him probably means she's ready for the check and not because she wants to go home with him. Either his breath stinks or he's boring. I was trying to be nice by bringing up the latter first."

I look harder and realize he's right. All the signs are there, because for someone who talks a lot, Katrina seems to be saying very little compared to her date. And Steven's assessment feels proven when I watch her raise her phone and I wonder if she's sending an SOS text like I've done with Denise on dates.

"Now do you want to know what I see in your body language whenever Carmello's within twenty feet of you?" Steven asks.

"Shh . . ." I say, glancing behind me to make sure Carmello's still in the back room checking on the desserts in the fridge that Paula prepared this morning.

"Is that a no?" Steven asks.

"That's a hell no," I say. "And why do you care about Katrina? Gonna try to swoop in?"

"Shit. Possibly," he says, and then he's smirking. "Maybe I should take it as a sign that my plans for tonight fell through right before you got me to say yes to being here."

"Does that mean you'll be here Tuesday nights permanently?"

Even though I got him to agree to help out tonight, he hasn't promised he'd be available to help Carmello every week if this proves successful. I give him a hopeful face.

"I'll discuss that with Carmello in the future. If . . . I feel like it," he says.

"Fine," I mutter. "But where'd you learn to read body language like that?"

He shrugs. "My momma taught me. Didn't want to be raising a bad man then letting him loose on the streets."

"I love that, but did you just miss the lesson on general manners or . . . ?" He rolls his eyes, and I look back at Katrina through the window. "How do you read people so quickly?"

"Need to make quick deductions for my other job," he says.

I didn't even know he had another job. Where does he have the time, working so many hours at the restaurant? No wonder he's a grouch. "What's your other job?"

"I teach self-defense," he says, like it's nothing.

It's always so hard to know whether he's being truthful. "Really? Like at a studio?"

"Wouldn't you like to know," he says.

I call him childish, but he's too busy staring at Katrina to pay me any mind.

Finally, he says, "Maybe if you matched me with her, I'd consider being more pleasant."

Chapter 25

Olivia

Now

THE WHOLE THING IS TIMED TO LAST ABOUT TWO HOURS, but I feel like I've been holding my breath for twenty-odd years. I want to go up to each table and ask them to fill out a questionnaire, but I guess our trial couples need time to digest how the night went like it's the real thing. I still rush toward the door when I see Katrina and her date standing from their table though. While Debra's in the bathroom, I try to make myself seem busy by adjusting the things on her host stand. As Katrina's date passes me, he says good night, but she says, "Girl, thank you for this," with wide-eyed emphasis and a tone that confirms the date sucked like Steven said.

When they leave, I shift my gaze. Issac leans down to cup Laniah's face with his large hands, and the kiss is so sensual I have to look away. A hot feeling rushes through me. It's been a long time since I've been kissed like that. And once she's in the car, she texts: Olivia, this was perfect. We needed it more than we

knew. I think you've got something special going on here. Give you deets tomorrow, but my husband can't wait to get me home. 😉

That's the text I'm smiling at when Carmello comes up to the hostess stand with the server book, holding their check. "The man . . . left a two-thousand-dollar tip," he says. A stunned sound leaves my mouth. "Yup," Carmello says, handing it to me. "Here. You should have it."

I push the book back at him. "No. Why?"

"O, you did all of this. Call it a partial payment for your time here, if you want to."

"Mello, *we* did this," I say.

"But this idea wouldn't have come from me," he says, tone soft yet firm, "and I don't think anyone else could've pulled it off like you." I've been worried about how he was feeling while cooking for the sampler platters. He was concentrating and hardly spoke to me and Steven. At one point he left the comfort of the kitchen to check in with the couples about the food, and when he came back in, I swore his hands were shaky. "And abnormally big tip aside," he continues, "I want to move forward with this idea, so let me repay you somehow."

"That makes me so happy," I say. "And I agree with everything you said. I pulled it the hell together." He smiles at my confidence. "But Carmello, we both know this tip was probably intended for the entire staff tonight. Stop feeling so guilty for me. . . ."

"I agree," Vero cuts in, coming up from behind us. "The woman knows exactly what she's doing, Mello. If she wanted money, she'd have it by now. Plus, I'd like a cut of the tip, even though I'm not in work uniform tonight." The tension toward me is clear in her tone, but I still smile when Carmello sighs in defeat.

"Night," Veronica's boyfriend grumbles when he passes by her for the door, not bothering to say a word to me or Carmello before he leaves Celia's Place without her.

That's when I notice there are tears in her eyes she's struggling to hold on to.

Carmello's brows stitch together, noticing too. "You good, cuz?"

She sucks in a breath. "I'm fine. Let's recap."

"Are you sure?" I ask. "We can talk about the trial tomorrow."

She hops up onto the host stand like she's an expert in shaking sadness. "I'd prefer to do it tonight, because I'm calling out tomorrow. Take this as advance notice."

Carmello scoffs, but I can tell he's still worried about her while she gives us a rundown on everything she thought we could've done better, including more variety for the small bites and an extra hour for lingering. "Everything else was great," she says. "The music, the atmosphere, and especially the question cards." Her forehead creases, and she glances at her lap like she's reliving them. She hops down from the stand. "Anyway, I'd help you two with the cleanup, but that tip is only so big and I don't work for free." Carmello calls her annoying, then wraps her in a hug. "I said I'm fine, Mello. Stop being a helicopter human," she says, but I think she needed that hug. She grabs her purse just as Steven walks by and gives us a two-finger salute.

Once they're both gone, I ask, "Does Steven really teach self-defense?"

Carmello nods. "His family owns a Filipino martial arts studio in Cranston."

"Wow," I say, blinking at the knowledge. "That sounds like a very serious job."

"His grumpiness kinda makes sense now, doesn't it?"

"It kinda does," I say. Then I look around. "Well . . . I guess we're on our own here."

"You could go," Camello says. "It's not that much to clean up. I got it."

"Do you *want* me to go?" I ask.

"No," he says.

"So, I'll stay."

WHILE WE'RE CLEANING, I TELL CARMELLO THAT WATCHING Issac and Laniah dance made me realize how nice it must have been for them to have the place mostly to themselves. How I think we should make sure the events are intimate. With no more than five couples at a time, it'll feel exclusive too. People will have to book in advance for the limited slots each week.

"I think the exclusivity will make the restaurant more desirable in general, and it'll be a lot less work for you than opening up to max capacity," I say.

"I was thinking the same thing about keeping it small," he says. "I can definitely handle something like tonight every Tuesday, even without Steven. But I have been meaning to get the patio fixed up for a long time, and this might be the perfect reason to put fire under my ass. Could give us room for a couple more slots."

I tell him how perfect that would be, and while he's telling me his plans for it, images of an intimate night on a patio eating Carmello's food flood my mind and my heart aches. I won't be here to see it through. Opening night of Table for Twos-days is in a few weeks, but I should be flying back to Houston before then to prepare for the move to Japan.

"I don't think I've been this excited about anything in a minute," Carmello says. "But I do have one big concern considering whatever the hell happened with Veronica, and the way you said Katrina left. I'm not tryna be known as the owner of a spot where people break up."

"Damn, that'd definitely be a problem," I say. "I really wasn't expecting two out of three dates to go badly, but I should've realized it'd be a strong possibility. I'm glad you suggested a trial run. Celia's needs to be seen as a place where matchmaking happens. Not as a curse."

"How do we fix it?" Carmello says, and I try not to get hung up on the word *we*.

"I'll think about other details, but there's one glaring thing to consider. Everyone seemed to love the cards," I say, "but where there's good, there's potential for bad. The universal balance. Maybe the cards are prodding deeper conversation and causing people to know more than they can handle in such a short period of time. I can work to make them a little lighter."

"Okay," Carmello says. "I can help with them after hours, and maybe you can help me get more variety into the menu?"

"Wait," I say. "That might be the answer. What if the questions on the cards correspond with the small dishes menu? As people are picking their platters, they can choose what sorts of questions match the flavor profiles."

Carmello is quick to follow. "So if they choose a sweet dish, the questions match?"

"Yes," I say. "And if they choose spicy small dishes, the questions for that course are risky, spicy." Carmello's eyes flick across my face in a way that makes me remember us sitting down at the booth, talking about first times. My stomach warms the same way now. "It could be a good way to get dates to interact with the cards and the food at the same time."

"Sounds fun too," Carmello says. "Gives our guests more control over their own fate during their dates. Okay. I like this. Let's work on it together."

"Meaning, you cook and I taste test and match a question?"

"We can both cook," he says. "And both taste."

I bite my bottom lip. Why is he standing so close looking this good talking about tasting? How much harder will it be to leave Rhode Island in a couple of weeks if we have to ask each other spicy questions while cooking in close proximity . . . alone? While he's looking into my eyes like he is right now, I have the sudden urge to say something stupid to make the moment less intimate. We're going to be okay as friends, and I want that for us. So I smile and say, "But just for clarification, you want me to cook with you because I'm the better chef, right?"

"You have more experience cooking a variety of foods than I do as a chef," he says.

"That was close enough," I say.

He narrows his eyes. "You're smirking, which means you're going to be smug the whole time."

"Smug me or no me, take your pick."

He smiles, those white teeth so bright in this dimly lit space. "You," he says.

That single word sends a spark up my spine. Our eyes linger for a moment, then he shifts to survey the room. We've already put everything away, swept, mopped, and wiped down the tables. It was quicker working together than I thought it would be. "Looks like we're done."

The song switches from "Not Another Love Song" by Ella

Mai to "Unchained Melody" by the Righteous Brothers. Zeke sure did make an interesting playlist. "Except for the music. I'll go turn it off," I say, because he'll be able to read straight through me while *this* song is on. My mom played it on repeat in our van during our cross-country road trip when we moved here, and it was one of the songs I played over and over again when I missed Carmello after I left.

But when I start to go, he reaches for my wrist, shifting me back to face him. He pierces me with those dark eyes and doesn't let me go. I wonder if he can feel my pulse racing beneath his fingertips. "Let it run through," he says. "My mom . . . she listened to this song so much before she died." His confession triggers something in my brain, but it's the first time I've heard his voice crack while talking about her and that realization takes precedence. I know he misses her, and he's had no choice but to put one foot in front of the other every day, to keep moving. I'm sure it feels heavier than he'd ever let on. And suddenly I have a vision of a different life—one where I was here, sliding my hand into his while we waited for Celia at the doctor's office. Listening to her crack jokes on the way home, trying to lighten the mood for all of us, even though she was the one who was sick.

"I'm sorry that you lost her, Carmello. I'm so sorry," I say, my throat waterlogged.

"I'm sorry you lost her too," he says, and the words open something inside of my chest. Emotions and memories of Celia well up in me, and I can't blink the tears away fast enough. I won't tell Carmello that *I'm* crying because a couple of years ago, I sent Celia a video of me cooking for a client in Italy. This song was playing in the background and when she wrote back she asked me the name of it. And I'm not saying she was playing it before she died because she wished I was here to comfort her too, but maybe she missed me more than I knew.

When Carmello reaches out, I'm not sure what to expect, but then he brushes my wet cheek with the pad of his thumb and my whole body vibrates.

"I know what I said about touch, but is this okay, O?"

He can't see it but my heart is glowing. All of me aches. I miss him. "It is," I whisper.

He drops his warm hand from my face and pulls me into his arms. My belly dips at the suddenness of it, and my skin hums like hugging him is a brand-new feeling. But it's muscle memory the way our bodies fit. The way my cheek finds his chest and my arms hook around his back, the way he dips his head so that he can rest it in the crook of my neck. "And this?"

His shirt smells like fabric softener and my favorite foods. "This too."

"Good," he says, "because I really needed you."

The word choice hits for romantic reasons, but where I settle is somewhere deeper than that. It's in memories: him making Bobby feel better today, comforting Veronica knowing she needed it and wouldn't ask herself. Him, holding me through the night when we were young and I'd wake up drenched after a dream about the fire. A kind boy who grew up to be a kind man.

Someone who took care of his mom until the end and needs care in return.

I hug him closer, bury my face in his chest, rub his back, wishing I could take some of his pain in my hands. While the song runs in the background, we cry together like we haven't spent a decade apart. Earlier, I wanted to dance with someone, but I think my soul needed this more.

Chapter 26

Carmello

Now

I'M UNCOORDINATED THIS MORNING, CHECKING TEDDY'S backpack before I send him into school to make sure I packed his lunch while trying to do mental calculations of all this shit I gotta do today. Daniela went on her trip, so I have Teddy full-time. Moments like this remind me to never take her for granted. She does the majority of school mornings, which are harder than pickups in my opinion, with her own shit to get done. And her own . . . feelings.

I'm exhausted. Not just from the trial night, but from the no sleep that followed after hugging Olivia. I opened something between us and now I doubt I can close it. I can't stop thinking about her. My heart wants to be near her heart. And my body . . . Well, let's just say coming home to an empty bed after being reminded of the way she fit against me made me throb for her all night.

Why does she have to smell so damn good? Feel like *that*? Fuck.

Steven calls when I'm tying Teddy's shoelaces tighter. "Yo," he says, and if he's calling this early, I prepare myself for a problem at Celia's Place. Maybe equipment malfunction or that the produce order hasn't arrived, something stupid that might set us back for the day. But I'm not prepared enough. "You might want to come quick. There's a gas leak."

He says it so dryly, I think he's joking. "What? How do you know?"

"Me and Olivia both think it smells pretty damn obvious."

The moment he says her name I think of her confessing that she still has some fears after the fire. Then I notice Teddy watching me closely. I'm about to send him into school and I don't want my emotions to affect his day, so I try to keep my voice steady when I say, "I want you two out of the building immediately. Call the fire department. I'll be right there."

When I hang up, Teddy's staring up at me with those curious little eyes. His friends are calling his name at the playground attached to the school, but he's focused on my face, reading my body language like a pro at only six. Steven might not admit it, but he'd be proud.

"Fire department?" he repeats, a question I have to answer or he'll wonder. His therapist has taught us tactics like being in control of our emotions but not directly trying to control him with coddling through well-meaning deceit. It's been a struggle, but I'm working on it.

"There's no fire," I tell him, laying a hand on his shoulder. "But there is a problem at the restaurant that needs to be fixed. It's nothing for you to worry about, okay? I'll handle it."

He seems to accept this. "Okay, Daddy," he says. I tell him to be safe, kiss the top of his head, and send him off. But while I watch him walk toward his teacher, who's waiting by the door, instead of his friends who are taking their last turns down the slide, I pray he doesn't have a shitty day too.

THE ROAD NEAR CELIA'S PLACE IS BLOCKED OFF BY THREE fire trucks. More police cars are pulling up. An officer bangs on my glass door and tells me the road is closed.

"I'm the owner of the restaurant," I say.

He doesn't respond with words, just waves at where I'm allowed to park.

I expected Olivia to be in Celia's, asking the fire department questions, but Steven's the one inside with the firefighters. Olivia is sitting cross-legged against the brick of the building the way we used to when we'd take shift breaks as teenagers.

I know I should go inside first, figure out what the fuck is happening, but I crouch down in front of her instead. "You okay, O?"

Her arms are crossed over her stomach and one side of her mouth tugs into a smile. "The building for your business has a gas leak and you're asking me if I'm okay?" She sighs when she sees the look on my face. "I just had a headache already this morning, and was a little nauseous, so the gas smell hit me kinda hard. But that's all it is. Now hurry up inside and report back. I'm nosy as hell and have no idea what's going on in there."

THE REPORT I CAN GIVE HER: THERE ARE MORE BODIES IN THE kitchen than we'd ever want at any given time. Two firefighters are talking to an irritated-looking Steven, while four pull out appliances and test for leaks with their monitors. Steven sees me first. He snaps his fingers in a way that tells me he's ready to be done conversing for the entire day. "There's the owner." But before they can turn their questions on me, someone calls out from the basement.

My heart hammers with dread as the smell of gas gets stronger walking down the stairs. Paula's not in today, but she usually works forty hours a week in the kitchen down here. I haven't gotten a chance to do safety checks on appliances this month. If this wasn't her day off and she was down here . . . If there was a slow leak and she'd been ingesting gas for . . .

A firefighter cuts through the graphic thoughts plaguing my mind, and I inhale deeply.

"It's definitely coming from this room."

He's talking about the room with the furnace and the washer and dryer, not the kitchen, but my chest is still tight thinking Paula could've been here. "Furnace and appliances are clear though," a different firefighter says. Two more of them are pulling down tiles in the ceiling and pushing their monitors up to check the pipes.

"Okay. Got a little something," one of them says when the monitor starts beeping.

A RHODE ISLAND ENERGY INSPECTOR ARRIVES WITHIN TWENTY minutes to check the pipes himself and turn off access to the gas while I go outside to talk to the staff. Half of them are here now, gathered around Steven and Olivia. It's all a bunch of noise to my ears; my head is pounding. Everyone's eyes land on me and then it's a rush of questions I hardly have answers for. I wait until they calm down, then I tell them what I know: it's probably from a slow leak that has been gradually worsening for a while, maybe even an accidental gas line cut from when Celia's Place went under renovation. We couldn't smell it because gas doesn't usually produce a smell until the buildup gets bad. The firefighters and the gas company inspector come for safety measures, then they go, but because the building is old and there are so many interconnected pipes down there, they can't tell exactly where the leak is coming from. So, the one who has to fix the actual problem is a plumber. And neither the firefighters nor the gas inspector could give me a number to call for legal reasons. They did wish me luck finding a "cheap plumber" on Google though.

My temple throbs just thinking of searching through reviews to find one that is both affordable and will make sure it's safe for Paula to work down there. "We won't be opening Celia's today," I say. "You all can go home. I'll send an update tonight."

"This a paid day off?" asks Bobby. "Because a guy still needs a full check."

"Of course," I say, and a couple of them try to hide their relief from me before they all walk off together. While they're gossiping about it as they walk up the block to their cars, I release a long breath, trying not to run my mind ragged with unknown estimates of what this situation is going to cost me. The trial event didn't require me to dip into my mom's funds for the restaurant too much, but I know this will be different. I'll be lucky if there's still money left over to fix the patio. I sigh and pull up my phone, leaning against the building to look for plumbers in the area, and hear a small throat clear.

Olivia is here, just a few feet away. She must've turned back.

"When I said to go, that included you too," I say.

"You're not my boss," she says.

"I'm not letting you back in the building, O."

She lifts her brow, and I think she knows I like when she does that. "Why is that? Didn't they say it was safe while the gas was off?"

"They also said the plumber might have to do things that can make it a liability for me."

"Hm. I think it's because you're starting to care about me," she says with a playful smile, and I narrow my eyes. "Fine. I won't go inside, but I learned a lot about gas leaks working with my parents over the years doing restorations at old facilities, and I already found a plumber for you. They said they can be here in two hours." I open my mouth, but she shakes her head. "And yes, the reviews claim they're not too pricey *and* they follow all the safety protocols. I know you, Carmello. Now all you gotta do is have patience while we wait."

We've always worked so well together, able to make up for the other's weaknesses, but I don't know how to tell her it's a relief to have her here to take something like this off my shoulders. I smile and tilt my head, remembering her holding her stomach earlier.

"Are you hungry, O?"

Chapter 27

Carmello

Now

THE PEDESTRIAN BRIDGE ISN'T A FAR WALK FROM CELIA'S Place, but we take my truck there in case the plumber calls while we're gone. We picked up ginger scones and cheese sticks from Seven Stars Bakery, and we're lucky to find a free bench where we can eat on the lower deck. It's packed with runners, a big group is doing yoga in the grass at one end of the bridge, people are having picnics at the other. I can't count the number of dogs taking their morning walks here.

"The city has changed so much since I've been gone," Olivia says. "But this is my favorite change. I've never been here during the day before, but I have come a few nights since the food truck event. It's usually way less crowded than this."

She says it like she'd prefer it was night right now. "Isn't this more your vibe?" I ask.

"I don't always want to be social, Carmello. Sometimes the extrovert feels the need for peaceful moments like an introvert."

She squints her eyes. "Just like the introvert needs moments to go out and dance salsa."

"I see what you did there," I say. "And I'm ignoring it. At least until I get free time."

"We can get up and dance right now." She opens her arms wide. "Right here."

I put my coffee cup down. "Bet, let's go."

Her eyes sparkle with excited surprise, and I anticipate the feeling of her hands in mine, the smell of blueberries in her hair while we dance. I want to feel our bodies pressed together the way they were last night. She opens her mouth to say something, but then someone walks right by us with their poodle, and she squeals instead. Her attention stolen by a "pretty pampered princess."

"Oh, those are such nice kisses. Thank you," Olivia says to the poodle a minute later.

"I'm so sorry," the owner says. "Those shoes are so cute, and I've been wanting some for a while, so I know they're expensive. Here comes my girl slobbering all over them."

Olivia's face twists into an unreadable expression. Who knows how she'll reply. "Girl," she says, "I found these in Providence Place Mall on sale just two days ago for half off."

The woman gasps and asks from what store and the two of them start talking about everything from gold earring recommendations on Etsy to hair products they've tried at Wildly Green—while Pampered Princess the poodle licks all over Olivia.

And I sit here watching the one person I never thought would reenter my life remind me of one of the reasons I was devastated when she exited it.

When the woman walks away, Olivia shifts back to me. I note the joy on her face. She gets so much serotonin from simple human connection, and I realize I still get serotonin seeing her smile. "That curly-haired girl just reminded me," she says. "I want to meet your pitty, One Piece. Teddy told me all about your little baby that night your dad dropped him off at the restaurant."

Olivia breaks apart her ginger scone. She takes a small bite and moans out loud from the sweet taste. She always does that, and most times I can keep my mind from thinking of all the ways she might make that sound for me. Today is not one of those days. I wish we were alone here. I'd lick the crumbs off of her lips and taste the matcha on her tongue, if she'd let me. At this point, knowing she's leaving for Japan soon is the only thing keeping me in check.

I shift on the bench so she can't see it on my face or anywhere that's growing on my body. "One Piece is sixty-eight pounds of pure muscle," I say, "but does not know his body weight. Always wants to be held. So, definitely far from little, but he does think he's still a baby."

"That's perfect. He can sit on my lap," she says, and I have to bite my tongue to keep from telling her she can sit on mine. "How long have you had him?"

"I rescued him from the shelter a few months after Teddy was born," I say. "He was already beefy, but they estimated him to be about a year old. I wanted them to grow up together."

"Living vicariously through your son?" She smiles. "You always wanted a dog when we were kids." She takes another bite. There's that sound again. I inhale deeply through my nose. Sip my coffee. Hugging her last night felt right, felt good. I think we both needed it. But will my body give me a damn break? "Will you bring him by Celia's sometime?" she asks.

"I used to bring him in to work once in a while," I say, "but there were a couple of incidents with customers complaining about his breed. I don't want to have to kick someone out of Celia's for calling my boy a monster. So I have a dog walker go by my house every day to play with him and bring him out."

"Very understandable," she says. "But I'd protect him for a few hours."

I laugh and tell her I'll bring him by, but inside I'm wondering how realistic it is that she'll be here long enough for me to have a chance to keep my word. I watch her sip on her matcha latte and clear my throat. "You used to hate matcha, but maybe not more than almond milk," I say.

When we were eighteen, Olivia tried going vegan, but a week later she was whining, *Ugh, I miss cow's milk, and now our kisses taste like grass.*

"Yeah, well. Bodies change and, as a result, sometimes so do we," she says now.

There's weight behind those words but I get the feeling she doesn't want to talk about whatever's on her mind, so instead of pressing, I gesture to the cards in her lap.

"You ever going to read off a question?"

We agreed on the way here that even though we couldn't cook today, we could go over some questions and see which ones might pair with dishes we already know will be on the menu.

Her mouth twists up on one side. Eyes flicking to mine. "So bossy," she says.

I can't control the thoughts that follow. Me wondering if that's how she'd like me in bed.

I wet my bottom lip. "Just read the question, O."

She gives me a challenging stare, but then she backs down and splits the deck, pulls out a random card from between. I watch her eyes widen, then her full laugh does something to the muscle beating in my chest. I love the way she throws her head back and that it turns her cheeks pink in the process.

"I guess the universe really wants us to think about this question," she says.

"You're fucking with me." I grab the card from her and read it out loud. "Is there a 'first time' experience you'd relive the same way all over again?" I squint my eyes at her, but I'm smiling. "Did you plant this one here on purpose?"

"You think that little of me?" she teases. "Why would I do that?"

"Maybe because you already know my answer, but you want to hear me say it out loud."

She stops laughing in favor of sucking that big bottom lip into her mouth. I grind down on my molars watching her slowly release it. "We're supposed to be matching flavor profiles."

"Well, I think this one should be paired with a spicy dish because it's risky," I say.

"What about Bicol Express?" she says, choosing one of my favorite pork dishes. "Looks innocent, just like the question might be, but the chilies are surprising."

"That's perfect," I say.

"Now that we've decided," she says, "you should answer the question, so I don't have to assume."

A strand of her hair falls over her face and, before I can think better of it, I reach to brush it away. Her brows knit together, and her mouth visibly softens in surprise. But I hold her stare, still feeling the adrenaline rush at the hidden meaning behind her words. "We were young, and we didn't know what we were doing," I say, "but *our* first time together was . . . special. It's the only first of something I wouldn't mind reliving again the same way."

A beat passes. Then: "If you asked me that question, I might've answered the same way."

Heat flicks across my core from her words. God, what would it feel like to have her mouth against mine again? I've been silently asking myself that for weeks. If I'm honest, I've wondered for a decade. I've dreamed about her, ached for her touch. And now she's right here in front of me with her lips parted slightly like she knows I want to lean over and kiss her. It feels like a subtle invitation—that is taken away by the wind.

It carries her hair in the air and our napkins too.

We laugh and hurry to snatch them up before they fly off the bridge and into the water. After tossing our trash in the garbage, Olivia leans her elbows on the rail to look out over the Providence River.

"If I lived here," she says, "you'd always know where to find me."

The words sound wistful and they do a mix of things to my heart that I can't process right now. I swallow and check my watch. "We should get back soon for the plumber, but do you wanna go over some more questions while we walk across the bridge first?"

She smiles and says, "You sure?"

Her tone sounds like the extended version of her question is: *Are you sure you want to spend more time with me?* I want to tell her that whenever I see her heading into Celia's lately, I find myself hoping it's not the last time I'll get to see her do that. Weeks have gone by, but it's felt like seconds. I want more. I crave our conversations, and I love to hear her voice in the kitchen. That the start of this day was shitty, but whatever it's going to cost me won't hit as hard because I get to be here with her.

"Yeah," I say. "I'm sure."

Chapter 28

Olivia

Now

CARMELLO PARKS IN THE LOT BESIDE CELIA'S PLACE BUT doesn't turn off the engine. "Will you be difficult if I ask you to wait out here while I talk to the plumber?"

"I'm not one of your employees to keep safe, Carmello. I currently own the building too. I'd like to know how much the estimated repairs will cost. Plus, we both know I'm a better negotiator than you." I try to keep a straight face while I joke, but a smirk begs at my mouth. "Unless . . . there's another reason you'd like me to stay back."

"You're ridiculous." He shakes his head and gets out of the car, leans his elbows against the open window to talk to me. The sun catches the copper in his skin. I want to get on my knees and lean over to lick everywhere it touches. "You know I still care about you."

The admission has me kicking my feet and giggling on the inside, but I try to play it cool. "I wasn't so sure. But I guess I'll grant your request now that I know."

"What a tender heart," he says, and reaches into the car to cup my cheek.

The gesture was playful, but I find myself leaning into his touch. Craving the warmth of his large hand on my face. Feeling my skin heat beneath his fingertips.

I watch his throat while he swallows, and find myself whispering, "I would've stayed back anyway, because admittedly, my heart *is* a little tender."

He strokes my skin with his thumb, and like our minds are connected, replies, "It scared you some? That the building had a bad gas leak? Fire safety protocols, and all that."

"I uh . . . think it just caught me off guard," I say. "Yesterday was my first rough night in a while. Woke up drenched. Can't remember the dream, but I know it was about wildfires. My parents helped prepare me and a lot of other people for the potential of them, for the potential of all kinds of bad things happening to buildings and how to cope if you lose them. But . . . this is Celia's Place and nothing bad is ever supposed to happen to it. You know?"

Carmello releases a long breath, his heart synced with mine. When he lets me go and straightens out, I almost beg him not to leave. To keep touching me, if only for a little while.

"Yeah, O. I know exactly what you mean," he says.

My therapist has been teaching me how to recognize when I'm not acknowledging or expressing my feelings. But I still haven't wrapped my mind around her techniques on how to not move on quickly after I do that. "Well," I say, wanting to change the subject, "since I'm staying in the car, do I have permission to snoop? I'll be bored."

He sucks his teeth, and I take that as a yes.

Once he's in the restaurant, my eyes flick around his truck. A gorgeous black-on-black Ford F-150 Platinum SuperCrew. If I'm just a girl, he's just a guy. When he turned eighteen, his dad bought him a Toyota Camry. He called it his other baby and was at the car wash with it every other day. And even though he's a parent now, a business owner, when I run my finger along the dashboard it comes back clean. The leather looks so well taken care of, and I imagine him using the little free time he has vacuuming every crumb from Teddy eating in the back seat. If I paid for detailing twice a month, my car still wouldn't look like this. I open his middle console and at the sight of his lip balm and cologne, the memory of him sitting so close to me a minute ago comes back. I quickly close that compartment because the ache I feel between my thighs is already unrelenting enough without remembering his scent. Before last night, I had finally gotten a bit of control back while around him, but now I'm fantasizing about us finding a secluded parking lot and doing nasty things in his tinted truck.

I reach for his dashboard and the universe rewards me with a swift stop to the fantasy of straddling Carmello—anywhere. The only thing inside is a manual, a book with his registration and insurance, and a photo booth print. It's from Roger Williams Park Zoo during one of their dinosaur events. Teddy doesn't look much younger than he is right now. Maybe a year. With his mom and dad sandwiching him. There's nothing about the photos that feels romantic, but it's comfortable . . . intimate. Silly faces and big smiles. Vero told me that Daniela and Carmello co-parented closely, but I don't think I pictured that they'd look like a traditional family.

I'm not sure what the feelings are that are swirling in my stomach. But suddenly, my snooping feels sharp. I'm imagining that Carmello pulls this out and stares at it often, wishing Daniela was with him instead of her boyfriend. I put the photo strip back and shut the glove compartment, then realign myself. Even if Carmello cares about me again, it doesn't mean he wants to be with me . . . or we'd *fit* as people even if he did.

"You look . . . disappointed by your snooping," he says, and I startle at the sound of his voice. He's frowning when I find him in the window. "Damn. I'm sorry for scaring you."

I swallow and smooth down my hair. "It's fine. What'd the plumber say?"

He exhales and opens the truck door. Drops down beside me. "He can't give me the exact cost until after he's done with the work, but the good news is he's free today to take care of it. Said he'll call me when it's done tonight."

"I guess you have a real day off too," I say. "What will you do with it?"

He lets out a short laugh. "A real day off? I have paperwork to do, and I should save time by trying to figure out a few of the small dishes for the event night based on the cards that I already know exist in your decks. I can do both of those things at home, so there's no excuse."

"You're strict," I say, "but I guess you're right. Bosses don't always have the luxury of days off. I guess that means I'm coming with you to cook and figure out these cards."

I'm joking, I think, but Carmello grips his steering wheel and says, "All right, then."

My stomach does a somersault. He looks so serious but I ask him if he is anyway.

"I am," he says, "but if you were just fucking with me and you don't wanna come . . ." He trails off when his eyes drop to my mouth and he sees me chewing on my lip. I think we're both aware of what might happen today if I go with him. I compare the feeling of finding the photo strip in his dash to the energy between us while we sit here not even touching. For weeks, we've been slow burning like the couples in one of my favorite K-dramas, but I know how it'll go down if we're alone at his place. I weigh the risks and possible rewards. And I think Denise would say: *Aren't you curious? The worst that could happen is the dick is even better and you gotta leave it behind. You've done it once, you can do it again.*

He watches as I buckle my seat belt. "I do," I say, but he studies my face cautiously, so I know I have to sell it. "We'll get work done, and I did say I wanted to see One Piece."

"You did," Carmello says. "But his walker took him to a *doggy event* at a park, so it'll just be us." Without a slobbering seventy-pound pit bull in the apartment, there will be nothing but me and Carmello to keep ourselves in check. It makes me as nervous as it does excited. "Is that all right?"

I try to keep my voice from trembling. "Hurry up and drive, Carmello. I need to pee."

He laughs and reverses out of the parking lot. The song "What You Got" by Quail P starts playing on his Bluetooth, and I swear the sexual tension in this small space increases tenfold.

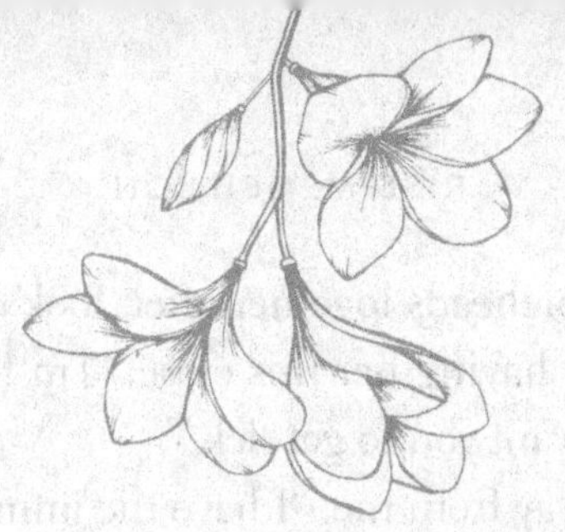

Chapter 29

CAREFULLY ASSORTED SNACKS

Carmello

12 years ago

SKITTLES. DILL PICKLE–FLAVORED SUNFLOWER SEEDS (Olivia's favorite). Cry Baby sour bubble gum. Lay's Wavy Original chips with French onion dip (my favorite). Spicy Nacho Doritos. Chili-roasted pistachios.

Olivia Jones was supposed to wait for the city bus to arrive at the top of her street and drop her off at the end of mine. But two hours before I was expecting her, my doorbell rang. It was only 8 a.m., I still had a towel wrapped around my waist after a shower, and there she was on my doorstep with this assortment of snacks for our day. It was the last Saturday we were ever supposed to have together, and she walked two miles in the snow because she wanted to stretch it as long as possible. There were snowflakes in her hair and her nose was pink from the cold.

I sighed and said, "What am I going to do with you, O?"

She shrugged, her puffer coat slick still. I could tell she was trying to keep from shivering. "Love me forever, I hope."

"Come here," I said, pulling her inside and kissing her temple.

We pressed our foreheads together after, took deep breaths. My heart ached more having her this close. "I'm happy you're here early, but I don't want you to get sick."

She pushed away from me. "I have the immune system of an ostrich."

I let out a short laugh. "Right," I said. "Let me go get dressed, so I can warm you up."

Her eyes flicked to my body like she hadn't noticed it was mostly bare before now and a blush crept across her face. I was turning eighteen in a few months, she'd just turned seventeen. Before this day we'd been to second base, made out in movie theaters. We liked to touch, but we weren't in a rush for sex. I could feel it then though, unspoken since we found out she was leaving but still making the energy between us thick. The air crackled with nerves and what-ifs. I know it was on both of our minds to have that first experience together before we never got the chance. But I wouldn't make her feel pressured for anything that she wasn't naturally ready for, and I didn't want her first time to feel forced. Not with anyone. And especially not with me.

"Please be quick," she said, something vulnerable in her voice. Like her heart was about to be split in two and she wanted to savor each second whole before the tear happened.

She had lived in Rhode Island for two years and thirteen days, much longer than any other state since her parents started their work as professional activists. But their job here had finally come to an end. They were needed in another city at the start of the week. She told me all of this so casually a couple of days before that I thought maybe she wasn't devastated the way I was. But standing a few feet from me right then, I could see the heaviness in her features.

Instead of leaving, I pulled her close, her cheek pressed into my bare skin, and I hoped she could feel the pulsing muscle in my chest.

"I'll be right back, O. I promise."

"I knew this day would come," she whispered. "I warned *you* not to fall in love."

She did. But when "any day now" turned to months and a month became a year, I stopped listening to her. I was in love and time would stretch to forever and she'd never leave.

"I don't know that I ever had a choice. You're you."

She pulled back just enough to look up into my eyes, and I saw tears gathered in hers. "And you're you. My sweet Carmello. My favorite friend." She was unable to keep her voice from cracking, but she did smile a little. "What am I going to do now that I didn't listen to my own warning?"

"Love me forever, I hope."

"Mm. I have a feeling that's exactly what's gonna happen." She pulled me down for a kiss and we paused there like we could still time and keep each other if we tried hard enough.

INSTEAD OF OUR NORMAL SATURDAY SHIFTS AT CELIA'S, WE spent this one curled up on the couch. We watched reruns of *The Simpsons* and talked about things we wanted to do in the near future. We were realistic kids, and I think we knew the likelihood of us doing those things together would be slim, so we didn't make any promises.

Evening came too quick. I was dreading the moment when my mom got home from work and I'd have to let Olivia go. She was sprawled out on top of me, our legs curled together, our stomachs rising and falling at the same pace like our breathing had synced, one of her hands dangling off the couch. My fingers were in her hair near the temple, rubbing slow circles there, and she was quiet for so long I thought she fell asleep. Already had the jokes in my head planned about her drooling on me. But she sat up suddenly, bracing herself with her palms flat against my chest, and gazed down at me. Some of my fantasies started like this, and I tried to stay as still as possible so she wouldn't feel anything growing between us. With her hair falling and covering us both, she said, "I'm really sad about one thing we won't be able to do together."

My heart began to race. I swallowed. "What's that?"

"Get tattoos," she said.

I laughed. "You're scared of needles."

She kissed me quick, said, "Quiet, Carmello."

"I'll be quiet if you keep doing that," I said.

She gave me one more. "I know what I said, but I've been secretly planning to make you hold my hand when I turned eighteen so we could do our first one together."

Something about the shy way she said it sent heat straight to my stomach. I pushed hair from her face. "Because you want one or because you want to share something with me?"

Her eyes flicked to my mouth, and I think we both became aware of all the places our bodies were touching. "Does it matter?" she asked quietly.

I moved my thumb along her jaw. "It matters."

"I'm not so sure it does," she said, then she pushed up off of me to go search through her bag at the other side of the room. I sat up and waited for her to surprise me. When she did it was with a handful of permanent markers. "Anyway, I thought maybe we could . . ." She trailed off and groaned dramatically. "Stop looking at me that way, Mello."

"Like you're cute for premeditating us giving each other fake tattoos?" I asked.

She cut her eyes. "Don't tease me."

"I'm not, O." I called her over with a nod of my head. "Come here. Sit back down."

It wasn't like her to care what people thought. To me, she was the type of person that put herself out there and said *Accept me as I am or try your best to ignore me.* But when she dropped down beside me on the couch, I could tell she was having a hard time trusting that I didn't think the idea was corny. So, I placed the markers between us and pointed to my forearm.

"Will you do mine first? I want it here."

I felt her relax then. "What do you want?"

"I've seen your drawing skills, so I'm thinking something really simple," I said.

She laughed and shoved my shoulder. "I'm not that bad. How about a dragon?"

"Oof. Just try your best, okay?"

She chewed her bottom lip to keep from grinning, then went to work. When she was finished, I had flowers floating up my forearm and realized they looked exactly like the ones my mom arranged in vases. Olivia was slightly allergic to pollen, so she stayed away from them.

"Is it too girlie?" she asked. "Because the dragon would've been tough."

I squeezed her thigh. "The pink-and-purple detailing is a little much, but I like it."

She smiled, then asked me to stand up before stretching herself out over the couch, lifting her shirt and lowering her pants to expose an area of her hip. I felt my core heat again. My hormones went crazy. "Your turn," she said. "I want a fox, right here."

"I don't get to pick it?" I asked.

She shook her head. "You're far better at drawing than I am, and . . . I don't know if I'll ever get a tattoo, for real."

I didn't ask her why she wanted a fox. I already knew how fascinated she'd become with them when her parents were doing work in the woods in Illinois. Particularly with their hunting habits and the fact that they were usually more solitary where other canines liked to live in packs. *Your spirit animal*, I'd usually tease. But this day, I just dropped to my knees beside her and took my time drawing her a red fox. Once it was finished, I smoothed my hand over the skin and placed a single kiss there. When I felt her shiver, I moved away and placed the cap back on the marker.

She looked down at it and a small startled sound came from her mouth. "If I ever get brave enough for a tattoo, this is exactly what I want." I smiled and started to pull down her shirt, but she put her hand over mine. "Take a picture for me. I want to be able to show the artist what it should look like."

It hit me hard then.

We were making real plans for a future without each other. I loved her. And I knew. I knew. I knew time would eventually pull us apart, but it wasn't supposed to hurt like this. And I wasn't supposed to be sad that she didn't mention coming back here for me one day or ask if I'd meet her wherever she was in the world for a tattoo when she turned eighteen. This was Olivia, and *the Joneses never made promises they couldn't keep.* That would be "unfair" in their line of work with people devastated all over the world from natural disasters and man-made ones too.

I tried not to let the feelings show on my face while I took the pictures for her.

She was happy, still lying on her back looking at them, and I thought about her going to another school and meeting someone else to get tattoos with. She's the one who brought up us being realistic and not making promises, and I knew part of her was excited to get back to traveling the world with her parents. When she first moved here, she'd swoon over it with Paula, saying *There's always another friend waiting, a place to love*. I knew I was the opposite. I didn't love very easily. Maybe because it felt like there wasn't a lot of room in my brain or my heart for how much space the people and places I did love took up. But I made myself concentrate on the moment, the way it felt watching her smile.

I turned around and leaned my back against the couch. Her hand fell over my shoulder, and I kissed each of her scarred fingertips.

She shifted on her side. Said, "I'll miss you, Mello."

Tears burned the backs of my eyes. "I'll miss you too, O."

She was quiet for a moment, then she sat up and leaned down to whisper in my ear. "The sun is setting," she said. "I have to leave soon. But I want my first time to be with you."

There was clarity and evenness in her tone. I believed it, but I still turned my head to search her face. "Are you sure?"

"I'm sure," she said.

AN HOUR LATER, MY MOM CAME HOME AND FOUND US FULLY clothed but cuddled on the couch. We were still floating after what we did. Small touches and sighs. My body was buzzing. I wanted to do it again. But it was time to pretend our day did not include sex, which was hard because my mom liked to make the kind of direct eye contact that felt like she was looking into your soul. I avoided her gaze as much as possible. Olivia was blushing but talking a mile a minute, and I was thankful that she was an expert at distracting without even meaning to.

We took her home that night, and my mom waited in the car while I said goodbye.

"Let's pretend this isn't the last time we're together in Providence. Okay?" Something about her choice of words sounded like she wanted to make a promise that we'd try to make it work, but all I said was, "Okay," because I knew she wouldn't, and I wanted to protect myself too. So when we kissed, I tried to catalog everything in case I never felt her in my arms again. From the way my fingertips felt while holding her face to her soft lips against mine. How cold it was, the dim light above her porch, how fast my heart was beating. Her forehead pressed against mine.

MY MOM WAS SILENT WHEN I FINALLY GOT IN THE CAR. I turned up the radio. Neither of us said a word to each other on the way home. But right when we parked, Olivia called me. I wondered if she forgot something at our house, or if maybe she wanted to say she loved me again.

"Carmello," she breathed, "we must've manifested something on my porch because your mom talked to my parents about letting me stay with you while I finish the school year. I'll get to graduate with Vero, and maybe we can all travel together after, but we don't have to say goodbye, Mello. I'm staying."

I turned to my mom, throat thick, thinking it was one of her tricks. But her mouth was set in a straight line. Did she really do this for me?

"Though I reserve the right to chicken out about a real tattoo when I turn eighteen," Olivia continued, laughing a little. I wondered if there was some hesitation in the sound, something uncertain hidden in her words. Was she truly happy to not go off with her parents for new adventures? She hadn't mentioned fighting with them about staying another year so she could graduate in Rhode Island and now here she was willing to separate from them to stay here for that. And for me.

Doubts circled my brain, but I couldn't bring myself to ask if this was what she really wanted because I might risk her rethinking her decision. I wanted her to stay. I was happy we'd get to have more firsts together, even if they weren't tattoos. That's what I told her before we hung up.

Afterward, my mom looked me dead in the eyes and said, "She'll sleep in the spare room. No more sex in my house."

Chapter 30

Olivia

Now

I'VE DEFINITELY MADE DEDUCTIONS BASED ON HOW MEN keep their cars before—only to find the dumpster fire that awaited at their apartment. I'm talking filthy with no toilet paper or hand soap in the bathroom type of living. But like his car, this particular man keeps his house clean. Simple things make me want to squeal—like knowing my socks will stay white when I leave my shoes at the door. It's bright in here from the big bay windows, homegrown basil and parsley sitting on the sills. Save for One Piece's toys scattered around the living room and Teddy's on the couch, it's not even what I'd qualify as messy. I can't say I'm that surprised. When we lived together at Celia's house, his room was more organized than mine. Still, ten years later, I didn't want to have expectations. But when I walk into his bedroom now, I decide that he tucks the corners of his sheets like they do in hotels without having to see them.

"It's exactly like I'd imagined," I say, turning to where he's leaning against the wall in the hallway. "And just so you know,

I'm not dirty by any means, but back at my apartment there are clothes I tossed around my room while deciding what to pack to come to Rhode Island."

"Some things never change," he teases. I'm still inside his room, just at the entrance, and something about the way he's examining me makes my body tingle extra with his bed at this proximity. "Were you trying to pick the perfect outfits because you wanted me to stare?"

Mmpf. I wasn't expecting us to go straight into flirting, but I can't say I'm disappointed.

"Did it work?" I ask.

"Well, I haven't been able to stop," he says. "Actually, when that woman with the dog was crushing on you this morning, calling you stunning, I wanted to jump in and agree."

I squint my eyes playfully. "Because you're crushing on me, Carmello?"

"How could I not be, Olivia?"

"I like it when you call me O," I say.

He smirks. "I know you do, Olivia."

Damn. He's so irritatingly fine.

The way he tugs on his chin hair tells me he's considering stripping my clothes off right here and now and my body is thankful for whatever shifted between us in the last twenty-four hours. But then he nods his head toward a door at his left. "That would be the bathroom."

ONCE I'M INSIDE AND THE DOOR IS LOCKED, I WASTE NO TIME. I pee like I'm in an Olympic race and use the wet wipes on top of the toilet paper holder. I showered this morning. I can still smell coconut on my skin from Laniah's handmade body butter, so should Carmello decide to lick any area between my legs today, I know I'm good. I wash my hands and roll some perfume oil behind my ear, in the crook of my neck, between my forearm and elbow. I use one of his floss sticks and gargle with his mouthwash. I glide ChapStick over my lips and fluff my curly hair: another reason to be thankful for Laniah—it's still shiny and soft, has a hint of lavender this time.

Three minutes later, I'm trying to catch my breath and look natural when I open the door.

Carmello's in the kitchen heating oil on a skillet. He pulls a marinated bowl of chicken from his fridge. Points to the cabinet beside me. "Can you grab me a cutting board?"

So we're really cooking, then.

My heart rate settles. Something I've learned about myself in therapy is that my impulsive nature might sometimes stem from the fear that I won't get to experience whatever I desire. But I tell myself that Carmello clearly wants me like I want him.

It might be even better in the bedroom if we go slow.

I open the cabinet and see six different cutting boards, reach up to grab one that looks exactly like the one he likes to use at Celia's. Even after what I just thought, I can feel his eyes on me from behind, and I hope he likes what he sees.

"What are we making?" I ask, letting my gaze track over the ingredients laid out on the counter. It doesn't look like anything we normally make at the restaurant.

He doesn't meet my eyes. The tightness of his jaw tells me he's deciding how to approach this conversation. Finally, he says, "I was going to make a small picadera."

That takes me by surprise. "For the event? A Dominican sample board?"

If he hadn't already washed his hands, this would be when he scratched the back of his neck: a nervous tick. I can tell he wants to. But contamination and Carmello don't exist in any kitchen. Despite his uncertainty, his voice is still steady and strong. "Well, more like a picadera with some Filipino finger foods thrown in. Possibly shrimp panara. I figured adding some fusion-style dishes to the menu could be good for the more serious questions, the ones that really make you dig deep and evaluate your feelings." He meets my eyes. "What do you think about that?"

I walk over and lean my back against the counter beside him so we're facing each other. "I think that sounds . . . perfect," I say, and watch some relief show in his features. "And with its savory flavor profile, I could definitely see a picadera going with a lot of the questions Debra and I came up with. But . . . can I ask why? Because I can only think of two reasons you'd want to incorporate foods from your other culture now that your mom's not here."

He starts peeling the plantains in front of him. "And what are they?"

I turn around to slice the ones he just peeled. "Maybe you want something at the restaurant that feels fully like you," I say. "It's your place now, and you shouldn't ever have to feel like only half of yourself comes through there. Dominican and Filipino fusion sounds delicious, it wouldn't be odd to find in Rhode Island, and it would complement the idea that date nights can bring different people together." A rush of excitement goes through my body at the prospect, and I hope he can hear it in my voice. When our elbows touch, we stay that way. "If that's your reason, I completely support it. But if it's because you don't feel secure serving only Filipino-inspired foods now that your mom is gone, well . . . I'd have to say that's bullshit. And if people judge you for that then they don't need to eat at your restaurant. If anyone knows the identity struggles that come with being mixed-race and living in America, it's me. I spent years in many states, combating the way I felt as a woman who never looked Black or Asian enough but definitely wasn't white passing . . . not anywhere in the world." He presses his arm into mine a little harder. "But Carmello, you are Filipino. And you are Dominican. You belong to that restaurant, and it belongs to you."

He inhales deeply, and my belly squeezes waiting for his response. After a few seconds, he reaches over to take the knife from me. A shiver shoots up my spine when he places it down. My body is unsure what to anticipate but knows something is coming.

Then, Carmello Rodriguez spins me around so that my back is against the counter again. He's in front of me now and a breath catches in my throat and my heart is thrumming. He tugs on my chin, tilts it for me to meet his eyes. His touch is firm, and with him towering above me, our bodies nearly pressed together, I can't think past how much I want him. Can he see it?

"Is this okay, O?" he asks, mirroring the words from last night.

"Yes," I whisper.

He moves his hand to the side of my face and bends low so that our mouths are touching only slightly. It feels like there's electric energy caught in the space between our lips.

"And this?" he asks, voice deeper, gruff. I shiver at the sound of a groan waiting in his throat.

"Carmello," I say, his name coming out like a plea.

He smirks. "I'm trying to be intentional here, Olivia."

I swallow and say, "Well, I want you to kiss me. Intentionally."

And when his lips finally meet mine, it lights up my insides, sends sparks up and down my skin. Something in me bursts, everything brightens. I can't believe I'm kissing Carmello. That this is how he's kissing me. So languid and sensual. As if he wants to savor me and this moment. Like he can't believe he gets to kiss me too and doesn't want to waste it on anything but a soft exploration. I've dreamt of us doing this. Fantasized about his fingers pressed to my face the way they are now and him shifting me where he wants me so that he can taste the desire on my tongue.

But the real thing, though tender, causes an explosion of sensations that I can't describe save for this:

Carmello's are the kinds of kisses that feel like firsts over and over again.

I'm floating. Moaning and reaching for him. When he answers by leaning into me, I can feel him hard against my stomach. Everything is muscle memory. Including how quickly *that* happens. My body sings right before he breaks the contact with a groan. We're both panting as we stare at each other. His eyes roam my face. He smiles and slides his thumb along my bottom lip.

"I had to do that," he says, then drops a kiss on my forehead.

When he lets me go, I'm a mess of feelings. I miss him already. I want more. My fingers shake as I touch my mouth, wishing to memorize this in a way that means I won't lose a single second of it to time.

And Carmello has the nerve to seem unaffected. He walks over to the stove with the cutting board to fry tostones like it didn't happen while I'm struggling to catch my breath.

Okay, so maybe we won't surpass the more make out–friendly K-dramas today, but of all of our kisses, that one had to be the most romantic.

Chapter 31

Olivia

Now

I'M STILL REELING FROM THAT KISS.

But with his back turned to me, Carmello says, "I want to feel fully like myself. Express all parts of me and cook food from the cultures I've been raised with. I love everything my mom has left to me, but I want to have something at Celia's that is mine too. That's part of the reason I'm thankful for you and your idea. My mom had . . . interesting tactics to get you here, but I think she knew exactly what she was doing." My heart is glowing when he looks over his shoulder and says, "How about you stop grinning and read off some questions that we could match with this while I cook for you?"

The way he says it is sexy, so I'm not opposed to letting him do all the cooking today. I grab the cards from my purse and hop up onto the counter to his left where we can see each other. After I read off the first three cards, I separate them out in their own piles: two sweet, one spicy. Finally, I find a deeper one that could go with the picadera.

"Tell me about a moment that changed your life."

He positions his body in such a way that when the oil surely pops, my legs will be safe, then flips the tostones over. "That one's good," he says and thinks about it for a moment before: "Um . . . I feel like most parents would say it was the moment their child was born, but I don't think the gravity of my new reality hit me right away. You know?"

I can't relate to having a child, but I can understand what he means. When I decided to travel the States alone, the reality that I was actually doing life without him caught up to me late and randomly. I nod my head in encouragement for him to keep going. Greedy for his answers. God, this is a good game. Gotta thank Denise again for the idea.

"When Teddy was about a month old, he came down with RSV," Carmello says. "A few days after he was diagnosed, Daniela called me crying in the middle of the night and said Teddy was struggling to get air." Carmello takes a breath like the memory is still hard to digest. He works on coating the chicken with egg and flour. I wait while he washes his hands again. When he walks back over, he looks more collected. "So I rushed over and saw what Daniela saw. Our boy was only ten pounds but he was breathing with his belly, a symptom the doctor told us to take as an emergency. When we got him to Hasbro Children's hospital, there was nothing we could do but wait. The nurses and doctors took good care of him there, but it was so scary to watch his little body fighting for the most basic part of life. He was only in the hospital for two days, but it was the longest forty-eight hours of my life. After he pulled through, I knew then that things would never be the same. There was someone I loved more than I loved myself, and I needed to watch him more closely than I had been doing before."

Carmello removes the plantains to fry the chicken and as soon as it hits the pan, a salty aroma fills the air. Greasy goodness. I'd normally start drooling by now, but tears are currently burning the backs of my eyes thinking of Carmello and a newborn Teddy and even Daniela.

"After your mom told me that you had a baby," I say, "I tried to imagine what you were like as a dad. Were you stern like your father was? How hands-on were you with him?"

He glances at me. "Am I anything like you imagined?"

I think of how worried he was the day Teddy disappeared on Steven to wander the front-of-house at Celia's Place, Vero joking that he's a helicopter human, and everything else I know about him so far. Then I say, "Even better," and when he smiles with his entire face, I feel something tug beneath my breastbone. "Do you want more kids?"

"No time soon," he says. "But yeah, I think I do."

Now that I've seen a recent picture of Daniela, it's easier to envision the parts of Carmello's life I wasn't here for. And there's a soreness knowing there are moments I may never have with him, even though we're back in each other's lives, but when he talks about being a dad, joy fills my chest too. I won't lie. I've had selfish nights when I hoped he was missing me like I was missing him, but I still used so many of my 11:11 wishes asking for him to be happy. I can see clearly that he has been.

A memory flashes across my mind of me and Celia checking the produce in the kitchen. She had just come back to work after her first battle with breast cancer. A bouquet of flowers arrived for her that morning. There was no note attached, and she cussed at me in Tagalog when I teased about them being from her secret man. "What? I just love how happy you look," I said. She lifted a carton of blueberries and set them aside because they weren't up to her beyond-perfect standards. "What would make me happier than anything is grandbabies." The wrinkles creased in her forehead, and she gave me her strictest tone. "Definitely not now, but eventually."

Carmello may have accidentally gotten Daniela pregnant, but I like to call it fate. If I would've stayed, one of us would've eventually felt forced to do what the other wanted just because we loved each other, and I know it probably wouldn't have been me. Carmello might not know the love he knows as a dad. Celia wouldn't have had any time to experience that kind of happiness either. And I think I feel some peace in knowing Carmello and I both got the chance to experience different types of joy without sacrificing what we wanted when we were young.

"Teddy's really special," I say to Carmello. "Last week, he wanted to help me with the questions." Carmello's eyebrows shoot up and I smile. "Don't worry, we stuck with the appropriate ones, but I remember him saying *What if this one hurts someone's feelings?* He was right, so I tossed that question out and thought to myself: Mello's son is more emotionally intelligent than most of the grown men I've met." It's Carmello's turn to laugh. A beautiful sound that kicks the natural pacemaker in my chest out of rhythm. "I'm so proud of you."

Carmello exhales. "You know, I never look for a clap on the back for doing normal things as a parent, but I'll admit, those words feel incredible coming from you."

I wink at him. "I can say them again if you want."

"Tell me a moment that changed your life instead."

When he takes the chicken out of the pan and puts it on a plate, I watch oil seep into the paper towel below. I want to devour them while scorching hot, taste grease on my tongue, but I should pace myself if we're going to eat a full plate soon, because the moment that changed my life most had many effects—one of them was on my relationship with food.

I tilt my head at Carmello. "Do you remember how I'd get really painful periods?"

He doesn't miss a beat. "You'd be laid out for days from the cramps. Always nauseous."

His tone causes me to remember the doubt in Michael's voice whenever I'd "complain" about being in pain. How hurt he'd look if I didn't want to have sex because of it. But Carmello isn't dismissive as he recalls the past, and I don't need further proof that his momma's spirit was well taken care of during her hard last days. In a big contrast from the heart-feelings, it also brings a flash of heat between my legs knowing he'd care for me in bed. I ignore that thought and tell him about a day working as a sous-chef at a Michelin-starred restaurant in Houston. The head chef was already barking at me for being slow and critiquing my dishes the whole afternoon, but when something sharp twisted in my pelvis, I doubled over. Nearly blacked out, the pain was so excruciating, and all I could hear was the sound of him fussing. *Someone check on what's wrong with this woman. We've got to get these orders out.*

Carmello's compassion and empathy are other traits I love about him. He doesn't get angry too often, but when he does, sometimes it's quick to shoot to the surface. His head snaps up from the stove, and I can see in his eyes that, if he were there, this chef would've been cussed the fuck out. He's not done cooking, but he shuts off the stove. The muscles in his jaw are tight before he lets out a long breath and walks backward until he's leaning against the counter opposite of mine. "Keep going," he says.

Oof. I'm not sure whether to pay attention to the tingles shooting through my body at his protectiveness, or how I suddenly feel exposed being in his direct eyeline.

I swallow and start twisting two strands of my hair together. Say, "I've never experienced labor, obviously, but the nurse said between me deeming it a nine on the pain scale and my body showing signs of that—it might've felt as bad to me as a contraction would." Carmello's eyes widen slightly, and I have a wandering thought of him holding Daniela's hand in the hospital. "Anyway, the six-hour wait in the emergency room was worth it because an ultrasound revealed scarring and cysts on my ovaries. It took about a year after that for a doctor to perform laparoscopic surgery and confirm that I suffer from endometriosis." Carmello's shoulder's fall considerably, and on instinct I want to look away so he can't study my eyes. I hold steady, but I do lighten my tone. "With the confirmation, I actually felt some relief knowing the symptoms weren't just in my head. But it meant I had to start drinking things that taste like grass if I wanted to consume as much caffeine as I do and that maybe I didn't want to work in a kitchen if it meant dealing with assholes like that. Besides, being a private chef can pay a whole lot better too."

"I've noticed things," Carmello says. "Particularly you not shoulder-checking me with a fork in hand to taste whatever I'm cooking at Celia's Place this past week." I smile and shrug one shoulder to my chin. His brows pinch together. "Stop looking cute when I'm trying to be serious."

"I can't help it," I say. "Serious is . . . boring."

"Is it?" he asks. "Or do you not want a spotlight on feeling sorry for yourself?"

I tap my nails to my chest. "Ouch. I am not feeling sorry for myself, I just want more control over my body. And I still hate matcha, and I want to devour your picadera because it already smells so good and fatty, but I gotta pick at it because I'm feeling better now but I'm supposed to be watching what I eat. Not most times—like regular people wanting to be healthy. Every. Single. Day. For the rest of my life, so that I get less agonizing episodes like the one last week. And that, sir, is not fair. So, yeah, maybe I do feel a little sorry for myself."

"Was that so hard to admit?"

"Yes," I say.

He runs a hand along his jaw. "You're pouting," he says.

I try to fix my face. "I'm just having a dramatic moment."

He examines me for a few more seconds and then pushes off of the counter. Once he's in front of me, he places both of his large hands on my legs, leans in so we're only inches apart. I have a tough time breathing with him this close, touching me where he's touching me, us eye to eye in a position that could quickly become compromising.

"I promise I wasn't judging," he says. "I was just taking notes, and I'm still trying to wrap my head around what it must be like as a chef. We try our own cooking constantly, and I wonder how hard it's been for you to do this type of work while knowing that eating certain foods can cause you considerable pain. And . . . I was also thinking about how you've been working hard at my restaurant without telling me."

"What were you gonna do about it if I did?" I say. "I don't

work *for* you. I took breaks when I really needed to. Was I supposed to ask for a heating pad and a massage like I did when we were younger?"

"If that's what would've helped," he says. "I'm here. You don't have to be so strong."

I want to tell him there were so many nights in the past ten years when I wished he was there so that I could fall apart.

"Stop being so sweet. It's making my heart do funny things," I admit.

He doesn't look surprised by the confession, and I wonder if his heart is doing funny things right now too. "Me, sweet? What about you? If you're just starting to feel fully better after the bad episode, why risk it being a taste tester for my fusion picadera? We can have someone else do th . . ." He stops mid-sentence, bites his lip. "You're pouting again."

"Because it would give me instant satisfaction to be your garbage disposal," I say.

There's a smile on his mouth after he sighs. "I'm never going to tell you how to protect yourself or not to whine about not being able to be a full-time taste tester. But I'm serious, O. You're safe here. You don't have to pretend with me. You don't have to suffer for my benefit."

"Because we're friends now?" I tease.

"Yeah . . . friends," he repeats, and usually it's so hard to know what he's thinking. Something about that has always thrilled me. Maybe it's because he has the ability to surprise me. Right now though, I'm pretty sure his tone is telling me he wants more than friendship. And the look in his eyes has me certain that he's suddenly hypnotized by our proximity. He leans in closer, mouth almost touching my ear, and says, "But I have a confession."

I brace myself against the counter with both of my hands. "What's that?"

My voice is raw with wanting. The hypnotism works both ways.

"When I was listening and taking notes," he says, inching his hands farther up my legs, "and I first noticed you pout, I didn't mean to say it out loud. But I was already feeling so many things for you, and after seeing your face like that"—I watch the muscles in his throat move and the tattoos on his neck contract as he swallows—"some of them weren't friendly."

"No?"

He shakes his head. His hands are so far up my thighs now. Another inch or two and he'd be able to feel how wet I am for him. "I thought, what can I do to make her make that face for me instead? If she wants instant satisfaction, what else can I offer?" He pulls back to watch me intently while his fingers slowly continue their exploration and his words cause heat to build like wildfire inside my body. "Maybe something with more lasting effects," he finishes, and I have to fight to keep my body from bucking to find friction against his fingers.

I swallow and lift my chin. "And have you arrived at any ideas, Mr. Rodriguez?"

"Yes," he says. "Would you like me to show you what they are, Jones?"

I blow out a breath, and then I beg: "Please."

Carmello's eyes darken considerably, but he still searches my face for a sign of uncertainty. When he finds none, he pulls my thighs apart like they belong to him and inserts his body between them. He tilts my head back, runs his nose along my neck, eliciting goose bumps as he groans. "You smell so fucking good. Lavender and lilacs. Sweet." His mouth finds the underside of my jaw, teasing with tentative touches of his lips. "Do you still like to be kissed here?"

I tug on the curls at the nape of his neck and pull a hissing sound through his teeth. "Carmello, if you don't put your mouth on me. Right. Now."

I feel him smile against my jaw before he rolls his tongue along the flesh there. Moves it down to my throat. Nips the skin with his teeth. The slight sting is instant dopamine. We were shy when we were younger, and our living conditions weren't ideal for explorative sex, but when our mouths meet again, I'm fully aware that we're starting something on his kitchen counter. He reaches under my shirt at the back to undo my bra with one hand, and I tug his bottom lip with my teeth.

"An expert at that now, I see."

He laughs. "Let me show you what else I've learned to do better."

My breasts ache in anticipation when he backs up a step to pull my shirt over my head. I let him explore me with his eyes, and I hope he can see how ready I am for whatever he wants to do to me, wherever he wants me. But he's such a tease, he palms both of my breasts slowly, working his thumbs over each of my areolas. Pinches my nipple. Does it again when a moan slips from my mouth. When he finally puts his lips on me, licking and sucking and encircling me so fully, the only thing I have to beg for is him not to stop. For a moment, memories of the past few weeks come back, and I thank the universe that one thing after the other has led us here. Carmello's tongue is lapping against my sensitive skin. He splits his attention so well. Using his hands to make sure one nipple isn't neglected for the next. And I don't know how I went a decade without his touch.

He softly scrapes his teeth along my areolas and he sucks and sucks and sucks. All while his eyes are closed: the way I've caught him savoring his favorite desserts. And I never want this to stop. But then he slides a hand between my thighs again, touching me where the warmth is pooling, and breaks away with a smile. "You're so wet, O. Jesus. Soaked. Aching and throbbing against my fingertips. I know just how to help you with that."

Then suddenly, he's hoisting me off the counter. I gasp in surprise but he hooks one arm firmly under my ass and says, "Don't worry, I got you."

Laughter fills the spaces between our kisses while he carries me to his room.

I'm on Carmello's bed with him hovering above me and my body tingling before he even comes down on top of me. The friction is instant. Even though we're separated by fabric, his length, thick and hard between my legs, provides the perfect pressure. As we kiss, desperate with our tongues, biting and sucking lips, he rolls his hips and rocks into me—our middles meeting in a way that will surely undo me. And when he moans against my mouth, I feel an intense satisfaction that he's making those sounds for me. He pulls back to kiss and lick along my collarbone and I dig my nails into his shoulder blades, and we grind and grind and grind. I want to slow down, I don't want to stop, but my body has been deprived and the edge is closer than I thought it was and suddenly I'm shuddering with his name on my lips.

I can feel Carmello throbbing, I can sense him smiling

against my neck. I'm grinning like we're young again and getting to do what we just did was the highlight of my day.

He lifts himself up to stare at my face. "You're happy," he says.

"Dry sex is criminally underrated, and you do it so well," I say, circling my hips to feel him still so hard it must hurt. "Are you happy?"

He leans down to kiss my mouth before he pushes into a sitting position to slide off my skirt. "I haven't heard you come for me in a decade. I'm going to taste you now and see if I can make it happen again," he says. "Does that sound like happiness to you?"

My stomach squeezes in excitement; there's this light energy in the room, almost as if we were always bound to be back here, focused in on each other, aching and wanting more. I bite my lip when he reaches for my waistband, but then the sound of his alarm pulls our attention to the time.

His phone is in the kitchen, but he shuts it off with his watch. He's not looking at me, but I know he has to pick his son up from school. I've noticed things about him too these past few weeks. Like how he sets an alarm ten minutes before he truly has to go. Then another one, just in case. The crazy part is that *I* hadn't realized how much time passed. That's definitely a newer feeling for me; usually my mind runs so much my body can't quite keep up.

Carmello takes a sharp breath, then comes over me again, lays his head between my breasts. We both throb. I want his tongue between my legs. I want to see him, to touch him and taste him, feel him slide inside of me. The orgasm was great, but my body aches to feel him fully.

I run my fingers through his hair and try to slow my breathing. "Your Teddy alarm," I say. I don't sound like myself; my voice is raspy—like I just had good sex or a cigarette. I don't smoke and I won't be getting the former. Not today, at least. But my heart is louder than my body. It's steady, soft, and warm. Beating for him the way it used to.

He lifts his head to look at me. "I'm sorry we have to stop," he says.

"It's okay," I say, then tug on his shirt for a kiss. Moan when he gives me one more. But I break the contact and cup his face when he tries for another. "As bad as I want you right now, if you left your son waiting at school to do nasty things with me, I'd be turned off with us both afterward." He smiles like he wasn't expecting me to say that, and I feel him starting to harden between us again. We groan in unison. God, what I wouldn't give to have the power to slow time. "But we should definitely reschedule as soon as physically possible."

He tilts his head. "So, you didn't take this particular interruption as a sign that maybe we shouldn't continue whatever it is we're doing?"

"No," I say quickly. A stutter below my breastbone. "Did you?"

Something flashes across his face before he kisses my forehead and pushes up off the bed. "I think maybe we should talk about what this means before we reschedule. Is that okay?"

I don't tell him that today *he's* easier for me to read. That I missed him, and I don't doubt he missed me anymore. That I'm happy we're having new moments together, but I'm not sure if we're aligned enough that they won't be our last.

I feel nerves gather in my throat knowing that a talk could bring clarity to that.

My heart is wide open, it's in his hands and he doesn't even know it.

"Maybe we should," I say, because I know he needs the communication to feel safe.

"Come here," he says, helping me off the bed to wrap me in his arms.

With my head against his chest, I can feel how nervous he is, so I close my eyes and enjoy every second while we're connected, just in case.

Chapter 32

Carmello

Now

TWO THOUSAND EIGHT HUNDRED DOLLARS. THAT'S HOW much I had to pay the plumbers from my mom's restaurant funds. I should be stressed about the holes they left in the ceiling getting to the pipes and the fact that they didn't clean up the debris in the basement, which means keeping the restaurant closed another day to clean up myself. But the gas leak is fixed; it's safe for Paula to be down there and to open when I'm done. And my mind takes that as permission to fixate on Olivia's face. Specifically when I'd looked up from sucking her breasts and seen her mouth shaped for the sweet sounds of her moans.

Hours later, I have to keep those images from getting me hard while with company.

My cousin came to my house to bring us dinner from Carolina's in Providence. Teddy's in the bathroom brushing his teeth now with One Piece on the floor at his feet.

Zeke grabs tostones from the plate on the counter. I forgot to put the picadera away earlier, and he's been picking at it since he got here. "Surprised you made this when you knew ahead of time I was bringing Teddy pastelitos and white rice, and you hardly eat fried foods."

I turn on the sink. "What are you getting at, Ezekiel?"

"Government name and everything. Yup. I knew you were strung tight for a reason." Zeke opens the fridge to pour himself a third glass of water, guzzling it in one go. The guy's thirst is excessive. I've been telling him to go get a blood test in case he has diabetes. After hearing of Olivia's endo, now I'm going to have to press him on it. "You made this for Olive, didn't you? It was her favorite kind of grease to help her get sober after we left the club."

My cousin knows me too well. Even though I wanted to pitch her the fusion-style menu idea, I made picadera specifically for her. Little did I know, fried foods were on her restrictions list. I'm happy the cards were an easy excuse for us to open up to each other again, but now I feel anxious to learn as much about her as I can. Including what she enjoys in bed these days. I just don't know if that's smart with her leaving for Japan soon.

I start washing dishes with my back turned to Zeke so he can't see my face when I admit: "Olivia was here earlier, and it was more than tap kisses at the door, but it didn't get too far."

Zeke puts his glass in the sink, expecting me to wash it, then hops on the counter beside me. "What do you consider far? Because Vero and I made a bet on when you'd crack for sex. Tell me you held out. I've got another week left. You know my sister doesn't play. She'll be at my door tonight with her palm up, expecting cash." A flash of me spreading Olivia's legs in this kitchen crosses my mind. Zeke must see the look on my face because he grimaces and hops right back off the counter. "You sexed her where I was sitting?" I raise both brows at *sexed* as a word choice, and he says, "I'm trying to be less vulgar around Teddy. Not because *you* think I should. I just realized he's getting older and needs good influences."

"Right," I say. "And don't worry, I think your money is safe and will continue to be."

He laughs. "I should be relieved, but man, what the hell is wrong with you?"

Before I can answer, Teddy comes back in the kitchen with his shadow dog trailing behind him. He tells us he's ready to watch the movie and Zeke says, "*Mufasa* again? No wonder you're starting to look like a baboon, you're watching it too much."

"Rafiki is a mandrill," Teddy says, then stomps on my cousin's foot with his huge sneaker-slippers. Zeke fakes hurt and One Piece starts to bark. Now the three of them are wrestling on my floor. When Teddy gives up, I tell him we'll be right in to watch the movie and One Piece lays a slobbery lick on Zeke's face, then follows my son back to the living room.

"You can barely walk in those things with your bony ankles," Zeke calls after him.

"And your ankles are disturbingly hairy," my son calls back.

"Kid's got a lot to say today," Zeke says, standing up. "Too bad he gotta wait." At his expectant look, I tell him to drop it. I hate for Teddy to think we don't care about him. "Stop being paranoid, he's probably buried in that damn iPad screen, playing Scrabble. Take a few seconds for yourself away from parenting to make it make sense *for me*, I'm begging you."

I blow out a breath, remembering how good it felt to grind against Olivia, the rush when she called out my name. "I had to leave to pick Teddy up from school when we were in the middle of . . . stuff."

"Oh," Zeke says. "Well, was Olivia an asshole about it or something?"

"Complete opposite. Which makes the whole thing, me and her, feel even more messy."

"Because you're going to fall in love with her again? Or because you already have?"

"I'm just feeling . . . a lot of things." I sigh. "It's like the more time I get with her, the more I want. I remember feeling like this before. But today, I had this crazy thought of telling her to come with me to pick Teddy up from school. Just so that I didn't have to be without her."

"Sheesh. That *is* messy." Zeke grabs popcorn from my cabinet and throws a bag in the microwave. "But all right, let's be realistic. You're scared if you have sex with her again it'll make it harder when she leaves, but I think the scarier part is that if you don't, you'll be feening, and she'll be good. On the next flight to San Francisco or wherever the hell she's going . . ."

"Tokyo," I supply.

"Tokyo?" He straight-up cackles like I hadn't already mentioned it two weeks ago. "Shit. She'll definitely forget whatever she's feeling for you right now. Women? Once they're done, they're done." He sounds like he's speaking from personal experience, but I don't know which woman from his past has him stuck. "And we both know Olivia has a strong detachment game."

"So, basically what you're saying is you think I need closure? You do realize your advice is in direct opposition to you betting that I could hold out on sex, right?"

"I'm not dumb," says Zeke, leaning his elbows against the counter. "But unless she's leaving tomorrow, you're going to hurt yourself resisting for no reason and the money isn't worth me dealing with you crying over blue-balls regret that at least you should've dicked her down before she left."

"Wow, so caring of you, cousin." I wipe the fridge handle down once, then again, and Zeke kisses his teeth when he notices. "What? I have no idea when you last washed your hands."

"Stop deflecting with your germophobia shit," Zeke says. "Listen, have confidence that you can handle your heart when it comes to Olivia now. If she wants your body, I see no harm in giving her the business. And who knows . . . the sex might even be bad after all these years."

"After what we did today, I seriously doubt that, and what if I don't want to stop?" I say.

"When Olivia leaves, you won't have a choice," Zeke replies. "But at least you'll have gotten the not knowing what it would've been like part of it out of your system. That's enough to drive any man crazy."

"I hate when you have a point," I say.

He smiles, and I realize I should probably say that more to him. He's insightful, even when his language is vulgar. "But how about you keep this from Vero for at least a few days after you prove me right?" he says.

Chapter 33

Olivia

Now

"THE DATE STARTED OFF PRETTY GOOD," KATRINA SAYS. "Until we pulled out those cards."

As soon as I left Carmello's house, my first instinct was to call Veronica. Way back, she's who I would've dialed after something cute happened with her cousin. But instead I tried Denise and it went straight to voice mail. Laniah answered on the second ring and squealed over the phone, asking if she could bring Kat, then they both rushed over. They've been here for two hours and what started as a kitchen conversation ended with us laid out on the big couch at my rental, the TV on for background noise. Kat's in the middle of us, her head on a pillow propped on Laniah's lap while she fills me in on how the date-night trial experience went.

I tell them about the idea Carmello and I had to pair the deeper questions with certain savory dishes so that people know what they're getting and aren't surprised when the questions feel like prodding. "I hope that keeps them from doing damage on the dates, but do you think it's in Carmello's best interest to not have them at all?"

"Girl, no matter how you decide to do it, keep the cards," Laniah says. "Issac and I were already so solid, but there were things we needed to talk through that neither of us had the courage to bring up. It's been a tough year. Now, I think we're both feeling even closer than we already were." She pokes Kat's forehead. "And thank God for the cards because my bestie here would have certainly wasted her time on that man."

"Shit, I'm about to purchase a deck from you and Debra to keep in my purse," Kat says.

I smile. "At least tell me you remember what question set off the red flags."

Kat scrunches her nose. "The real question is which one didn't raise red flags all over the place." She's a storyteller. She doesn't even have to sit up to do it well. "But I asked this dude . . . *What were you willing to accept in relationships that you're not willing to accept anymore?* And he had the nerve to say, and I quote, 'back talk.' I laughed and told him he joked like my momma. But then he went on about how women *these days* feel free to disrespect men, and he'll never make a wife out of someone with too much to say."

I blink at the audacity. "What the fuck? So some of them don't wait until marriage to start opening their mouths for outlandish stuff, huh?"

"Nope. And he also revealed that he doesn't do a lot of foreplay in bed. He said he doesn't 'eat pussy'—with a straight face." A wave of heat hits me, remembering how good Carmello looked with his face between my legs, and I have to pinch my thigh to focus on Kat's voice. "If we weren't there for a trial experience, I would've walked out on him right there."

"I'd never ever be able to be with a man who doesn't like foreplay," Laniah says. "Issac . . . well, let's just say we had a lot of it that night."

"Bragging-ass bitch," Kat says with a lot of love in her voice. "But for real, because sometimes the foreplay is even better than the sex. Lord knows some of the men I've been with knew how to wield their tongue but had no idea what they were doing with the other tool God bestowed on them. So thank you, girl. Because at first, the man had a lot going for him. Educated, nice to look at, probably makes just as much money as I do, doesn't have kids. What he did have was stinky breath, but I was being delusional: singing *I can fix that* in my head."

This sends me and Laniah into a fit of laughter, and I'm tempted to tell them about what Steven said in the kitchen, how on point he was, except Kat looks a little sad suddenly so I keep it to myself, but it does make me reconsider a match for her with Steven. Until she says, "Dating in my midthirties has been terrifying. It's like shopping on clearance racks and half the men are busted as hell while the other half are already being claimed by other women in the store. I've decided to be celibate for a while. I need a break from looking for love. Especially with all the other stuff I've got going on." Kat briefly retreats into herself, a frown on her face. I have the urge to ask where she went, but I'm not sure it's my place. I watch Laniah run a comforting hand over Kat's hairline, and it relaxes me too. "But anyway," Kat says, smiling again, "enough about me. How do *you* feel about your man having a kid, Livy girl?"

I feel warm at the new nickname. "Carmello's not my man . . . anymore," I say.

"If his heart eyes look anything like yours right now," Laniah says, "I'm positive we'll be having a different conversation soon."

"I'm leaving for Tokyo," I say. "I know y'all remember."

Laniah and Kat shoot each other looks like they've been talking about it privately, then I hear the hope in Laniah's voice when she asks, "Do you really have to?"

"Do you really *want* to? That might be the better question," Kat says, and there's the same sound. My heart flutters. I think I've just made some new close friends.

"I don't know," I say, smiling. "To answer your question, it doesn't bother me that Carmello's a dad. He's a good one. And his son is so cute. But . . . what if he's bugging out already? What if he's regretting what happened, or thinks that an alarm literally going off to stop us from exploring is a sign?"

"Don't freak out about him not texting you," Laniah says, reading my mind. One of the reasons I've been so anxious is because he hasn't reached out since we split earlier, and I don't know if he's having regrets after saying we should talk before rescheduling. "He's probably just thinking deeply about it, same as you. The situation is complicated because of your past."

"Laniah would know. She had to think and think before she secured her man," Kat says.

Laniah picks a pillow up and fakes like she's going to smother her best friend.

"Wait." Kat laughs. "I forgot to add that you had a good reason."

I watch them and realize how happy I am to be here, and suddenly I'm smacked upside the head with a pillow. Laniah's the culprit. She shrugs like she's innocent, and I think she's not the only one who will miss doing friendship in person while I'm in Tokyo. "You zoned out over there, Liv," she says. "But Kat's right. Issac was understanding. I had a lot of heavy shit going on. I can just imagine what a second-chance romance is like in real life. Give Carmello time."

"But," Kat says, "would it be bad if all he did was give you good sex before you leave?"

"If I become addicted again, yes," I say.

"Then simply don't become addicted," Kat says. "Remember, you're the prize. He's the winner. Get you a fine Japanese man and move the hell on."

"Kat doesn't do big feelings like that," Laniah says, reaching over to touch my hand where it's resting at the back of the couch, "but I have to say . . . I don't disagree."

I'M STILL HIGH OFF OF THEIR POSITIVE ENERGY TWENTY MINutes after Laniah and Kat leave, so when I hear the doorbell, part of me hopes they left something here and we'll be able to squeeze one more "and another thing" in before they go. But when I open the door, it's Carmello who's standing on the front porch. My pulse picks up at the sight of him. Just a few hours ago he made me come in a way I haven't in years. I'm flushed in the face when I say, "Hey."

He smiles a little. "Hey."

My eyes flick to his truck. The tint is dark enough that I wouldn't be able to see if someone was inside, but my mind is looking for an innocent reason he'd be here. As it stands, him showing up at my door looking finer than he did earlier in that all-black outfit and assessing me with those dark eyes makes for quick fantasies. "Where's Teddy?" I ask.

"He's watching a movie with my cousin before bed," Carmello says. "I've got an hour before Zeke has to get to a gig, but I hoped that'd be enough time to . . . talk if you wanted to."

I wonder if whatever is going on between us is ending much quicker than it started. History does have a tendency to repeat itself. "And we couldn't do that over the phone?" I say it teasingly, but inside I just want to postpone the inevitable.

"I needed to see you," he says before he lets his gaze wander down my body. "But now that I'm here . . ." Goose bumps break out across my bare arms. I can feel my heart beat. He meets my eyes again, and the want is visible on his face before he takes a step toward me. "I wasn't envisioning you'd be standing in front of me braless. I can see your nipples through your white tank top, Olivia, and I can't remember what I thought we should talk about." He takes another step, locks me in place with his arms at either side of the porch rail. "And there is something I still owe you if you're prepared to receive it."

I steady my breathing while a rush of feelings floods through me, then I push him away and nod to the door. "Come on in, Carmello. This grown woman likes to collect on her debts."

Chapter 34

Carmello

Now

WE FALL INTO EACH OTHER SLOWLY. I KEEP HER CLOSE to my body as we kiss beside the bed. My senses are heightened while we explore each other with lips and tongues and teeth, and I think of how much I've forgotten about her over the years. With as much as I have to do these days, my mind usually lets go of anything it finds unimportant, but I know it's working overtime to process this in an attempt at playing keeps. Memorizing her soft skin, the width of her hips, the dip at the small of her back. Every touch and caress feels like it's pulling on something deep inside of me. She tastes like mint and she's small in my arms. When she sighs against my lips, it signals my brain to move even slower to savor her sounds.

She hooks her arms around my neck, pitches up on her tiptoes to kiss the hollow of my throat. Nips the skin there, sucks with a pressure that has my eyes rolling back.

"Off," she says, tugging at my shirt. Time is lost to me when I'm with her, so I do as I'm told, and I'm swiftly rewarded with the feel of her nails scraping against my skin. She digs them into my back and pleasure shoots straight to my middle. I'm harder than I've ever been, and she reaches between us to touch me through my pants, whining a little and pulling my waistband after she feels it. "I need you, Mello," she whispers. I put my fingers in her hair, tilt her face. With access to her lips, I stroke my tongue over hers and she moans into my mouth.

"So you'll have me," I say, and palm her ass with both hands while pushing her backward toward the bed. Once we reach it, I tug on her pajama bottoms and repeat, "Off."

She smiles into a kiss, then does as she's told. Drops her panties too.

But before I can make my next move, she sits on the bed and gazes up at me with want in her eyes. For the past week, I've fantasized about having her like this, and I hope she can see the want in mine too. I run my thumb over her bottom lip and she takes it into her wet mouth.

Fuck.

When she reaches for my belt, I grow thicker just watching her work to unbuckle it. Once I'm standing in front of her naked and fully erect, she sucks in a breath through her teeth and wraps her hand around my swollen shaft. The tips of her fingers aren't touching when we both examine the view. "Oh damn," she says, and I know that feeling. That was me staring at what I could see of her earlier and realizing she looked even better than I remembered. Or maybe we just weren't looking at each other the same way a decade ago.

She doesn't even have a good grip on me, and it still feels heavenly to throb in her hand. When she places a kiss on the head, I have the urge to thrust myself into her mouth. But I check my watch. Time is already eluding us. I take a breath and touch her shoulder instead.

"As much as I want you to do that," I say, "I want other things more first."

She nods in understanding but still leans forward to encircle me with her mouth. Gives me one good suck. Steals a groan. I'm already seeing stars when I hear her release me with a pop. She smirks and pulls her tank top over her head. I take in every inch of her beautiful body and, while I'm telling her how stunning she is, something pulls at my heart, knowing we're back here and how badly I want it.

I swore she was out of my life. I told myself I wanted nothing to do with her. But when she looks up at me with soft eyes, I think maybe I should stop being ashamed to admit that I'll always be a sucker for this woman. She could tell me all she wanted from me for the next few weeks was my face between her legs and I'd let my tongue go numb if it meant pleasing her.

I bend low to cup her face. Her eyes fall closed, waiting for a kiss, and I realize the answer to Zeke's question earlier is this: I never really did fall out of love, I just learned to live without her.

Chapter 35

Olivia

Now

"WHAT GYM DO YOU GO TO? BECAUSE I'D LIKE TO LEAVE a review," I say, letting my eyes wander his stomach. Carmello has a six-pack and the pectorals of a Greek god. He laughs. "No . . . you're beautiful."

He pushes my legs apart, drawing a finger up my thigh.

"How about we save the reviews and the compliments until after I'm done with you?"

"Ooh. Okay, Mr. Confidence. I like that."

He touches between my legs and draws back to lick his fingers. *Well, shit.* I bite my bottom lip while he lowers himself on the bed, nerves gathering in the base of my belly anticipating what's about to go down. I open my mouth to say something quippy about him looking hungry, and he shuts me the hell up by gliding the flat of his tongue over me. One lick and I'm sure this man has never seen a bad review from anyone. Carmello uses his mouth with a passion I haven't experienced before now.

Not from him when we were inexperienced, and not from the most skilled partners I've had over the years. He sucks and nibbles and nuzzles and spreads me wider to lick everywhere. I grip the sheets, his hair, his shoulders, push off the bed to meet the heat of his tongue. He encourages me while I'm grinding on his face with one hand under the small of my back. Whenever I moan, he mirrors me but with his mouth full.

It sounds like he's devouring something delectable, and I feel lucky that something is me. He doesn't rush it, but he doesn't need to. I feel the crest of my orgasm come quick, and when he sends me over the edge, my body gets the peace it'd been craving in him.

He hovers back over me, kissing my belly, my chest, my neck, my jaw. When he reaches my lips, he presses soft ones there, says, "I like the look of satisfaction on you."

"I wish we had time so that I could satisfy you too," I say, then lean up and lick the taste of me off his lips. Suck his tongue.

"Mm." He moans. "Don't make it harder for me to leave."

I tap his back and heave out a breath, say, "Quick. Pass me my phone."

His brows meet in the center, and a small laugh leaves his throat. "What? Why?"

"Gotta text my friends and ask them to rush back over here so we can squeal into the couch pillows together after I tell them about how good you are with that mouth."

He shakes his head, a big grin on his face, and there's this look in his eyes that my heart wants to interpret as love. "You talked to your friends about us?"

"Shh." I put my fingers on his lips, smiling too. "Forget conversation. Forget my friends. How long do we have? Wouldn't want you to have to run out of here in your boxers. Though my neighbors might enjoy the show."

"You're wild," he says, then rolls onto his back and pulls me toward him. "Don't worry, O. There's enough time for me to hold you for a bit."

Something about that softness from him makes me want to reciprocate. "It's like you've got keys to my brain," I say, throwing a thigh around his middle. Snuggling my face in the crook of his neck, feeling his steady pulse there. "It's scary sometimes."

He raises my hand from his stomach to brush his lips along my knuckles. "What's scary about it?"

I gather all the courage left in my bones and say, "I missed you, Mello, so much. More than just intimately. But I think you already knew that."

He's silent for a second, then he releases a breath. "I've missed you too, O. In all the ways."

My heart starts to race. I don't know what it means that we're both admitting to feelings that are deeper than just sex, but I have the urge to jump us from one moment to the next because maybe that's safer right now. With time running out and heavy questions in the air. And the only way I can think to do that is to say: "Even if this was casual, I still want to be friends."

His fingers go still as they run up my spine. "I don't think we could ever be casual," he says, and it sounds like he's realizing at the same time as he's speaking the words. "Do you?"

I open my mouth to respond and then . . . his alarm goes off. We're quiet for a few seconds and then we both laugh. "Saved by the bell," I say. "Maybe it's a sign we skip the serious talks today and just kiss a couple more times before you go?"

"Or you could answer my question," he says.

"Would you seriously prefer that or do you want my tongue one more time?"

He considers for a second then says, "Come here, you," before pulling me on top of him.

AFTER CARMELLO LEAVES, I'M NOT AS NERVOUS THAT HE HAS regrets but I try not to wonder too much about what it means that he doesn't think what we did was casual either. When I get back in bed, I focus on other things instead. Our shared laughter on the porch when I joked about him actually having time to get dressed and my neighbors missing out on a show. The way he tilted my chin and kissed my lips and said, "Thank you so much for tonight," like I'd given him a gift instead of the other way around. How he turned back to look at me after he reached his truck in the driveway with the biggest smile on his face. Maybe we didn't have the responsible conversation before jumping into sexual acts together, but I think it was the right thing to clear our heads of some of the tension. It will open us up to be more honest with each other later. Or at least, I can hope so. Seeing what we were like together physically again . . . maybe I needed to know before I can make decisions about what I want out of life next.

I can still smell his cologne on my sheets. I concentrate on that too, while remembering his body wrapped around mine. And as the memories of him between my legs come back, I trail my fingers over my breasts. I'm throbbing for all of him when my phone vibrates.

Can't stop thinking of you, Carmello sends. I miss you.

I squeal and do a little happy dance in bed. Feeling seventeen again.

Do you really? I text, trying to play it cool.

I do, he types back. **You're kinda hard to shake.**

I waste not a single second. **So don't,** I reply.

The typing bubbles crop up, then stop. I hold my breath, but his words aren't the kind that make catching it easy: **Maybe I won't,** he says. **Good night, O. Sleep well.**

Chapter 36

Olivia

Now

CARMELLO'S TRUCK IS THE ONLY ONE IN THE PARKING LOT when I pull up at Celia's. I slept like a baby last night, woke up with the high of a teenager who just found out their crush likes them back. But now it's a late-morning-after, with time to process, and I won't lie about being nervous. Especially because I really want to answer that question for Carmello, about whether we could ever be casual, and I'm hoping it goes the way I've been dreaming it can.

He's in the basement, sweeping debris into a pile on the floor. I wait on the stairs so I don't startle him. But he doesn't even look surprised when he hears me say hi. Steven must've snitched about me bribing him to lend me his master key last week so I could make a copy of it. I tell my body to stop being so anxious, but it takes everything not to jump into Carmello's arms and find out how he feels about us one way or the other.

"What time are we opening?" I ask.

"We're not," he says. "And I told everyone they could take

another day off after Steven made a comment in the group chat about how cleaning debris is above his pay grade."

I feel a tug in my chest: a silly little longing to be part of the group chat.

"That tracks," I say. "But I'm sure some of the others would've come in to help."

Carmello shrugs. "I wouldn't want anyone complaining."

I look more closely at the disaster that was left behind by the plumbers. He's right: thick, dirty-looking dust coats everything and there are holes in the ceiling and the walls that are bigger than my head. I stand by what I said, thinking the decision to handle all of this alone was probably more about the way Carmello's big heart worries extra hard for the people he cares about.

He stops sweeping to stare. "What about you, O?"

"What about me?" My face warms during his silence. I clear my throat. "Mello?"

"I think you're happy to be here," he finally says. "Is that true?"

"In Rhode Island?" I ask, heart thrumming. "Or with you?"

One side of his mouth curves up, and I think I can see the nerves on his face now too. "I meant with me, but you don't have to answer either of those questions."

I inhale and take the last step. Knowing I need courage for this conversation too, knowing *he* still needs me to be the one to make the first move. That's fair. Plus, I'm the kind of woman who doesn't mind being the hero. So, once I'm standing in front of him, I tilt my head and say, "Would you believe me if I told you I was already happy with you *and* here in Rhode Island before last night and that the five-star oral sex was an unexpected bonus I hope we can do again and again?"

I love the way he laughs. It always kisses his eyes and reaches for my heart. "I can believe you feel that way, yeah. But what does that mean for us? I know *I* can't just have sex with you until you leave. Casual or not. I care about you too much for that."

"I care about you too," I say.

He scratches the back of his neck. "So . . . what do you think about us continuing to see each other even after you go?"

"You're serious?" I ask, stomach squeezing and throat thick. I want him to be but I need to know. "You forgive me for leaving the first time, just like that? Are you sure you're not hypnotized by having your head between my thighs last night?"

A smile breaks out across his face. "O . . . I forgive you."

"That fast?" I narrow my eyes. "Bullshit. You were so pissed when I first arrived here."

"Well, my mom did give part of my restaurant to someone else, making me question whether she had faith in me . . . or whether she wanted to play matchmaker because that someone was my ex-girlfriend, who waltzed in here like it was normal. And I worked so hard to forget this girl, but there she was making my heart race like it used to." He blows out a breath. "O, these past few weeks have made me feel things I haven't felt for anyone in ten years. You make me laugh, inspire me, you shake things up and challenge me, and we may be different but it feels like we understand each other. When you told me about your endometriosis, I wished I could take it from you and carry it myself so that you don't have to live with it. It's scary how much I care about you, but it feels right. I thought about us all night and the only thing that'd be getting in the way of me telling you that I still want you is ego. I can't afford ego when the truth is I don't want to let you slip through my fingers if there's a chance you feel the same way I do."

I feel myself soften, wanting nothing more than to take another step toward him, wrap my arms around his middle. Tell him I had the same thought about his mom playing matchmaker. But I hold steady and say, "You don't even know the reason I left the way I did, Mello."

"The reason doesn't really matter anymore, O," he says. "We were young. You left, I stayed. Now we're back here. I had a ten-year head start on forgiveness before you busted down my door again. That's why it seems fast."

I ignore the pestering feeling to push him a little harder, to make sure he means what he's saying, but I'm not sure I want to delve into why I left either. Not when I'm aching for him to kiss me and tell me he's as certain about me as I am about him. "I don't think we can date while I'm in Tokyo," I finally say. "That's too long of a distance, even for me. But . . . if you ask me to stay, I might say I still have time to tell my client to find another private chef."

He lowers his brows. "You want to stay *here*? To work in this small city, at this particular restaurant? Are you sure? Because I can't ask you to stay for me. You have to want to stay for yourself. If I'm your only reason, I'm not sure how long your happiness can last. And I have a good life here. I have Teddy. I like the stability. Starting something with you . . . it'd be serious for me, O."

I hear the words he's not saying. He does forgive me. He wants to be with me, but he doesn't fully trust me yet. I'm willing to show him that he can. "This is already serious for me, Mello," I say. "I want to be compensated and treated like an equal, but you should know I still plan on signing my shares of the restaurant over to you if I stay."

He shakes his head and with a firm voice says, "No. If you're here, it's yours too."

"You shouldn't make any promises yet on that front. Though, I wouldn't mind that result in the end." When he smiles back at me, I cup his face. He closes his eyes and leans into my touch. When he finally opens to my gaze again, there's a well of feelings right there for me to sift through. Fear, uncertainty, yearning . . . something deeper? "If you don't think we should take time to be intentional and make sure being together is the right decision," I say, "I'll jump right in with you. But you've gotta believe me when I say I can vacation in Tokyo, I don't need to live there. And I don't think I was ready to hear the words before, but now, I need to know you want me to stay. Because I've spent most of my life scared to tether myself to something, somewhere, someone . . ." I think back on how much I lost at such a young age, and how that loss—and the way my parents reacted to it—shaped my values, made me eager to protect myself and prevent more pain, and how empty I've felt as a result. "I don't want to be scared anymore. I love working with this movie cast of a staff you've hired. I missed Paula's pandesal and, God, her cupcakes. And for the first time in my adult life, I think I'm actually part of a friend group. It's not *just* because I'm still in love with you, Carmello."

I hear it when his breath catches. He blinks and searches my face, but not longer than a second, because if there's one thing that's always been true about Carmello it's this: he might not wear his feelings where everyone can see them, but he'll pour into you as long as he can see where to aim his heart. I feel the reciprocation when he bends down to capture my lips before he says anything at all.

I took the first step, and now he feels safe to take two.

When he breaks the kiss, he bows his forehead against mine.

"I've never stopped loving you, Olivia. It's been a decade without you, so I'm pretty sure I always will."

My eyes are wet, heart stuttering from happiness, butterflies beating their wings in my belly. But there's a part of me that wonders if this is too easy. If we're missing something and rushing the feelings, and then a louder part of me says, *Why shouldn't it be easy? We know each other so well, so deeply. He still loves you and you still love him and you've spent this long apart. You get to stay. Be a chef at this restaurant you love with people you adore. Isn't this how you wanted it to happen? Hasn't Providence always been calling you home?*

So, I swallow and say, "We're really going to try again? Do better this time?"

He pulls my hand from his face to kiss my scarred palm. Memories flash of us sharing our first dance. I didn't have sensation in my skin there then, but tingles spread through my body the same way they do right now. He meets my eyes. "We really are, and I know we'll both do better. I don't want to lose any more time with you."

"Neither do I, but I think life worked out exactly the way it was supposed to," I say.

"I'm glad you think so," he says, then he walks over to the rack on the wall and hands me the second broom. "Because owners don't get paid for extra labor."

"How romantic," I scoff. "What if I told you my throat was already itching from being down here so long just to secure my man?"

"I'd say, lucky for me, my girl isn't my employee."

I squeal and raise my shoulder to my chin. "Say it again."

"You're my girl," he says, then slaps my behind. "Now I need you to be a good one and get your hands dirty so we can go do nasty things before I have to pick my son up from school."

"You know, that might be the sexiest thing you've ever said to me, Rodriguez."

"Just you wait until I hit you with the dad jokes, Jones."

Chapter 37

Carmello

Now

THREE HOURS LATER, OLIVIA AND I ESCAPE TO MY HOUSE and waste no time undressing each other. She moves to the top of my bed and I hover above her, kissing her stomach, licking her sternum, gently taking her nipples between my teeth. She arches into me, body begging for friction while I run my mouth over her breasts. I want everything, all of her. She smells like shea butter, and that alone can drive me crazy. But I'm consumed by her moans and the way she says, "Oh, God. Mello, do that again."

I lower my body and let her writhe against me while we kiss. She's wet, and grinding with her unravels my self-restraint. I'm twitching and aching to be inside of her, but when I push up to a sitting position to put on a condom, and spread her thighs, she grips my forearms. "Are you sure you're ready for this?" I ask, holding eye contact while pushing into her slightly with a smile on my face. I'd rather her think I'm teasing than to feel weird about me asking if she feels okay for a third time. I researched endometriosis after she told me she had it. It says sometimes sex can be painful and your partner might not say anything because they feel too embarrassed or want to please you. Paying close attention to expressions and body language is key. I won't take my eyes off of her today.

She pouts and says, "Mello, you're going to get cussed out real soon with the way . . ."

When I slide in, I steal her words. She digs her nails into my forearms, throws her head back into the pillow, and cries up at the ceiling. "Wait. Wait. It's so damn big."

I pause there and try to focus on her face. Her needs. Whether she feels good. Because just pulsing inside of her while she's clenched around my shaft this tightly tells me I'll be fighting for my life not to come quick. She feels perfect. And this is *her.* My Olivia.

"Okay," she breathes out and I begin moving again, slowly building a rhythm while she adjusts to my size and thickness. Soon, I'm collecting her moans like they're the prize through her open-mouthed kisses. I'm hungry to hear every variation of the way she whimpers when it starts feeling *too good*. And it's enough for me to know I could last all night long if we had more than a couple of hours.

We spend the time we do have so well though, and when Olivia bites my shoulder and grips my ass, urging me deeper, she tells me what she wants. "Harder, faster, more."

I flip her over and a startled laugh vibrates her body. She's quick to get into position, arched perfectly for me. I smack her backside then push into her again. This time, we both cry out. *Shit.* It's so fucking deep. We move in sync: our bodies slamming into each other on a rhythmic beat. But I can't see her face to be sure that, if she experiences any pain, it's slight compared to her pleasure.

I stop, lean my body over the side and tug her chin toward me. "O. Tap on me, give me a safe word, or do something wild, but you have to tell me if it hurts, okay?"

She closes her hand over mine and sighs contentedly. "I promise, Mello."

"Thank you, baby," I say, and then she pushes back into me to give me herself again and again and again. I'm still careful while I stroke. Stopping to throb inside of her and take her whimpers as a sign of when I should start again. When she drops her body to the bed, exhausted but still wanting me, I come down on top of her. Grind against her ass, God, it feels so good, hold her hand, reach for mouth kisses that are hard to get in this position. We're slick against each other, and I love this, but I want to see her face again before we run out of time.

She whimpers as I pull out, but when I tell her to get on top of me, she seems as happy to stare into my eyes as I am hers. She needed to be closer to me like this too. While she rides me, I brush her hair from her face and kiss her collarbone. When her face starts to take the shape for an orgasm, she slows down, but I'm greedy to see it happen. I grab her hips and work her out, listening to the way she sounds coming undone for me. She's so beautiful.

I bring her low to my body and while we're chest to chest, I can feel her heart beating against my heart when I come too.

Afterward, I kiss the crook of her neck, she puts her mouth on my shoulder, and it finally hits me that we're back together. We built separate lives but even time couldn't keep us apart forever and all we needed was to be in the same space before gravity pushed us toward each other.

Chapter 38

Olivia

Now

THE PAST COUPLE OF WEEKS IN THE KITCHEN HAVE BEEN smooth, but now Carmello and I are working in perfect tandem. It's not just about anticipating each other's needs but about how effective our communication is. We're aligned, the tension from weeks ago is gone. And I'm high on the fact that I'm a girlfriend. Carmello's girlfriend again. I came here hopeful, searching for signs, but I didn't let myself believe this would happen. It's hard not to let the happiness show on my face because he's working across the room and each time he looks at me my body turns to liquid. "You two better keep it PG in this place or I'm quitting," Steven says, not bothering to look up as he puts the finishing touches on a meal he just plated.

I add lomi noodles to boiling water. "We have no clue what you're talking about."

Carmello keeps a straight face while he spatchcocks a chicken. "None."

Steven cuts me a look, then slides his headphones over his

ears. He might teach self-defense, but one doesn't have to be skilled at reading body language to see the difference in our demeanor the last couple of days. Around noon, Paula pulls me aside to ask if we're back together, and twenty minutes later Debra has the whole front-of-house gossiping. But as happy as I am, whenever Veronica walks into the kitchen to pick up an order I feel myself shrinking. She hasn't made eye contact with me today, but I did catch a look she exchanged with Carmello. I have a feeling she either blames me for whatever happened in her relationship during the trial experience, or she's upset about me and her cousin. Maybe both.

Denise is another one who has doubts. *I don't know, Olive, in the decade I've known you, something has always pulled your attention somewhere else. But even without your personality traits, I still think spinning the block should only be for sex. This feels fast, and aren't you the one who said people are for seasons and reasons? Maybe you'll remember your own words once the orgasm-filled haze clears and you realize the past has caught up to you.*

Her words made my stomach twist at first, then I decided she was right but not about everything. It's true that my attention gets pulled—maybe because of my ADHD, or maybe how I was raised to follow wherever my path takes me—but there was something about Rhode Island that held it right away. I remember visiting the beach with my parents after we'd gone a long time without being by an ocean, how walkable it was as I wandered through its small cities while they worked, the way it felt like I'd found a piece of my culture that I'd been missing when I ate Celia's food for the first time, how my heart raced when Carmello's eyes caught mine as I sat in a booth as a customer. And falling in love with working as a chef at this very restaurant.

So, I'll sit in the joy I feel knowing life has led me back here.

After we push out a batch of orders, I pull out my phone and text him. **You're across the room, but I miss you.** I see when he gets the notification on his watch. His jaw clenches and he raises his head to meet my gaze. A delicious shiver shoots up my spine from his heated stare.

Because of the gas leak, some regular customers haven't been back. After forty-eight hours, it's already starting to pick up, but it's a negative hit on the business. Still, I don't think we accounted for any positives. When Steven goes to the front-of-house to speak to a customer about specials, Carmello comes up behind me at the stove. Presses his body to my backside. "Can I have a taste?" he asks over my shoulder. I give him a spoonful of sauce, and he groans a little, mouth on my neck. My eyes fall closed and I almost forget where we are, aching for another kiss, for him to keep rocking his erection against me like he's doing right now.

"Meet me out back in twenty minutes," he whispers.

His break time. I'm giddy at the thought that we can take it together, and I try hard not to let it show on my face when Steven comes back with suspicious eyes.

I SET THE PACE SO CARMELLO DOESN'T HAVE TO. I CAN TELL IT bothers him that he doesn't have many moments to steal to spend time with me, but I'm excited every chance we get. It takes five minutes to drive to a secluded lot. Carmello parks under a few trees, even though I've already told him I feel safe enough with his tint. With twenty minutes on the clock, I'm quick to climb over to the driver's side and straddle him. It's tight, but we make it work.

A ripple of warmth spreads through my belly. I bite back a whimper when he pulls my breasts out and sucks my nipple into his mouth. "Wait," I say. "Take off your shirt first."

He doesn't ask why, just pulls it over his head and tosses it to the passenger side, letting me admire his beautiful body in the daylight. With the sun glinting off his shoulders, I run my hands from his wrists to his forearms, showing attention to every vein, tattoo, and sinew along the generous expanse of his brown skin. As much as I'm wanting his tongue on me, I need a second to look at him like this. To merge in my mind the boy I used to know and the man he is now. Heat floods through my chest as I gaze down at the hard lines of his stomach and the dips in his torso. I trace my fingers along the V that disappears beneath his boxers and lean forward to bite his neck. "Mine," I whisper against his skin.

He puts his fingers in my hair, tugs to tilt my chin, marking me with his teeth there too. "And you're mine," he says against my throat while we start to grind. "Mine. Mine. Mine."

Moans steal my breath, make my back arch, but I'm silenced by the view through the clear glass of Carmello's sunroof. Because above my head, the branches of a big oak tree whose dark green leaves have fully budded are swaying in the wind, and right now, I can't think of anywhere in the world I've been that's more beautiful than this. I don't know if Carmello completely believes I'm ready for the commitment, but someday he'll realize I left my heart here and I just needed time before I came to get it.

Chapter 39

Carmello

Now

I KNEW IT WAS GOING TO BE LIKE THIS. THERE WAS NO WAY I could let down my walls and Olivia Jones wouldn't come crashing in. She takes up so much space just with her personality. I want the vision she brings when I see situations as black-and-white and need someone with a more balanced opinion. I love the way our fusion menu is shaping up for the date-night events because we're doing it together. The other day my father stopped in and she got him to soften up by suggesting he be our taste tester for the Dominican dishes. I haven't told him about us yet, but I think he's accepting that whatever happens happens.

I'm glad not to hear his mouth because I want *her* to keep happening to me. But she's not in my bed right now and my body punishes me for it.

It doesn't help that she looks this good over FaceTime.

I tucked Teddy in then cleaned the house before I called her. For the past few nights, we've made it a routine to talk like this. Yesterday, she wasn't feeling great. Had a heating pad on her stomach and requested that I read to her while she curled up. I had to fight the urge to tell her to come over so I could give her a massage and read to her in person. Told myself Teddy's here and it's too soon for that. But she's better tonight, bright-eyed while she tells me about the pictures her parents sent her. They're in Guatemala and the work has been grueling, but the country is beautiful. Volcanoes and waterfalls and amazing food.

"We'll have to get you out of your fear of flying to go there together. Work you up for the long flight to the Philippines," she says, and I find that I want to do that with her.

"As long as you go easy on me," I say, trying to mimic her pouty face. "Hold my hand?"

"I'll do you one better and wear a low-cut shirt to distract you with my breasts," she says.

I breathe through my teeth and let my gaze dart down to them now. "Yeah, that'd work."

She puts her hands over her chest and opens her mouth wide like she's scandalized. "I was kidding. But Rodriguez, are you trying to start phone sex?"

"Would it work, Jones?"

She bites her bottom lip, and my body reacts before she even slides her hand into her tank top. I watch her pinch her nipple and my mouth waters. It's only been a couple days since we've last had sex, and I feel like I have no self-control. So when she tells me to grip myself through my boxers, I don't hesitate. She wants to see, and I'm about to show her how thick it is right now . . . but then, parenthood calls me from inside the house.

Olivia laughs, and covers her mouth with her hand. "Oops." When she sees I'm not laughing, she frowns a little. "I thought you said he sleeps like a brick and your door's locked."

"Both true," I say, but I'm too busy looking over at it to make sure I really did lock it. What I don't say is that my pulse has picked up considerable speed, as if a few walls between us isn't enough privacy. In the span of seconds, my thoughts run wild. Because, even though my son only called me once, I don't want him to think he's alone. Or what if something bad happened to him and he can't call out to me again? "I gotta go, O."

"Good night, babe," she says after a beat. "I'll see you tomorrow."

TEDDY'S SITTING UP, HUGGING HIS GIRAFFE IN FRONT OF HIM when I sit at the end of his bed.

"Did you have a bad dream?" He nods his head. "What was it about?"

"I was drowning," he says. "A big wave got me."

When I first saw him safe in his room, my heart sighed in relief, but it just jumped back to beating fast. I reach for him and he wraps his small arms around me. "But I made it out okay," he says, "because I'm so good at swimming I could be in the Olympics."

I was just thinking about how it's time to kick up the swimming lessons, but since I'll have even less time with him because of the event night, I'll have to add on another bill and get him into classes. Olivia said he's emotionally intelligent and I know that to be true; look at him, comforting himself and probably aware he's comforting me after *he* had a bad dream. Sometimes, it feels like he's the other side of my coin, and he can feel what I feel. And that kind of love is more overwhelming than anything I've ever had, but it's so worth it.

I pull back to smile at him. “Like Mufasa making his way out of the water?”

“Like Mufasa,” Teddy agrees with that toothy grin. “But Daddy . . . can I sleep with you tonight? I’m still a little scared.”

“Of course,” I say, still a little scared too. I don’t know what I’ll do if anything horrible ever happens to him. It’s a constant worry in my mind and sometimes it’s suffocating.

“Who were you talking to?” he asks, and the question genuinely confuses me for a second. “I heard you whispering on the phone. That’s why I only called you once.”

“Oh,” I say, almost forgetting about our FaceTime. “It was . . . Olivia.”

“Sometimes she calls me Theodore like my teacher does. I like her,” Teddy decides.

I let the words hit and, when they make my chest tight, I take a deep, long breath. Then, I decide too. Teddy is my life, and if Olivia’s going to be a part of it, I can’t be scared to let her all the way in.

I squeeze his hand. Say, “Yeah, Theodore. So do I.”

Chapter 40

Olivia

Now

I T'S SATURDAY, WHICH MEANS TEDDY DOESN'T HAVE SCHOOL. He's so excited to be at Celia's and everyone is greedy to spend time with him. He helps Bobby refill the water and the syrup tanks for the soda gun. He greets customers at the door with Debra. Steven takes him for a walk around the block on his lunch break, and they come back with sliders from Harry's. He's downstairs with Paula for hours learning how to ice flowers onto an ube cake that reminds me of the one she made for my birthday years ago. And I can't lie, I want a piece of him too. I think he notices because an hour before closing, I look to my left and find him a few feet away, staring up at me.

"Hi, Theodore," I say. "Are you having fun?"

He nods but he looks like he's in serious need of a nap, so I ask him if he wants the milk carton again. He happily sits down, then scoots it closer to me. That he's comfortable enough to do that makes my eyes sting a little. I'm definitely getting my period any day now. While I cook, he tells me about his favorite things to watch on his tablet: kids doing extreme sports and horror flicks. I'm not too surprised. Sounds like more of Celia's influence.

After a few minutes, I feel Carmello staring from across the room. This time, he smiles at me. My face warms at the idea that he was watching his girlfriend bond with his son.

When Vero comes into the kitchen to tickle Teddy and give him a pop quiz on reef sharks, he shows her a picture of him and One Piece on his tablet screen, and I sneak a peek at it. The two cuties are wearing baseball caps and Carmello's sunglasses.

"That big gray beast doesn't know his own body weight, almost put me in the hospital, knocking me over the other day," Vero says. The timing of the incident makes something chime in my brain.

"I can't believe I still haven't met One Piece after all these weeks," I say.

I didn't realize Teddy would jump on that. "You can see him today. We walk him when we leave here." He stands up from the milk carton and calls over to his dad: "Can Olivy come?"

Veronica tenses beside me, but I can't pay attention to that because I think I just got nicknamed by Carmello's son, and whatever weirdness I felt about not getting to meet One Piece yet disappears when Carmello gives me a sheepish smile. "Did you ask her if she wants to?"

Teddy looks up at me with those Carmello-shaped eyes, but unlike his father, he has a way easier time asking for what he wants. "She definitely wants to, right, Olivy?"

I smile at the mangled words coming from that adorable voice and say, "I sure do. Should we make One Piece a homemade treat before we go?"

Teddy's face lights up. "He loves bacon and French toast."

I'm about to say I could go for some myself, but Veronica clears her throat. "Can I talk to you for a second, *Olivy*?"

SHE PULLS ME INTO THE BATHROOM AND SHUTS THE DOOR behind me. When we were young, she'd come to Celia's after school sometimes just to gossip in here with me. "I told you to be careful with his heart, Olive," she says, and I'm relieved she got straight to the point. "But trying to jump right into stepmommy activities doesn't seem careful. Not for him or for Teddy."

"Oh," I say. "News gets out about me and Carmello and now you're talking to me?"

Her face twists up and I feel like a teenager again. We rarely fought back then but when we did we both could be pretty petty. "I have been talking to you."

"That 'table nine wants extra aioli' doesn't count," I say.

"I've just been . . . busy figuring shit out with my boyfriend after the trial date night," she says.

"And before then?" I ask. "Because when I first got here, I thought we were good, but you've been distant ever since we danced by the pedestrian bridge. A little weird even before that. And I know you have other friends, but I'm not sure if the only reason I have other friends here now too is because you said you forgave me for leaving but you really didn't."

She sighs and sits up on the bathroom sink, swings her legs while I lean against the door. "It's just . . . we were having fun at the food truck event, then you cut it short to chase after Carmello, and I realized he's the only reason you came back here. On top of the fact that I didn't want to be caught in the middle of you two again, I figured once you got whatever brand of excitement you wanted from him, you'd leave again, so there was no reason for me to get used to you being here. And I know I sound jealous, but turns out, I can be very jealous. Resentful too."

Just like Denise, some people are going to take much longer to see how happy I am here. Or . . . just like Carmello, some people might see it, but still need time to trust that I really am. Still, I can't ignore the nagging thought that they all might have a point about me. There's been a strange feeling I can't describe sitting in my chest the past few days; maybe I'm a little worried this thing with Carmello has been too good to be true. I'm trying to shake the nerves but just because I have them doesn't mean I want to leave or that I'm craving excitement elsewhere.

"Listen," I say. "I won't force you and me. I don't have the capacity to prove myself to everyone I care about right now. Especially those who keep their hearts in a fortress surrounded by a barbed-wire fence." She gives me a small smile. "Maybe eventually, you and I will both be at a good enough place as individuals, and we can find a new friendship in each other. For now, just know that I'll be careful for Teddy. But I trust that your cousin will tell me if we're moving too fast. I don't want him to feel like I'm not willing to get to know his son, because I want to."

When I turn for the door handle, she says, "I'm keeping an eye on you two, but for now, just know, I can see how much happier Carmello is with you."

I smile and thank her and then I go.

ONE PIECE IS EXACTLY AS CARMELLO DESCRIBED HIM. WHEN I squat to get on his level, he takes that as permission to knock me over and kiss my face. Teddy laughs, but Carmello tugs softly on his leash and One Piece is quick to release me. I smell like dog drool and my jeans have grass stains but my heart is full. It's dark out, save for the streetlights, and we walk a mile before Teddy gets tired and wants to turn back home. Carmello gives One Piece some slack on the leash so he and Teddy can explore a bit up ahead and—after the talk I had earlier with Veronica—I watch the two childhood best friends with misty eyes.

Damn. Between the excruciating cramps this morning and me crying over everything including dental commercials, I know my period is about to hit hard. They can be brutal because of my endometriosis. I look over at Carmello, who's deep in thought, probably about all the things he has to do. Stocking, paying bills, whatever Dad duties he has tonight. Maybe he's even weighing out how it feels for the four of us to be walking together. He's wearing a fitted hat, so I can't even see his face, but Veronica's words ring through my head because I have no idea if he ever wants to do this again. Meanwhile, I'm fantasizing about baking dog-safe cookies with Teddy in their house tonight.

When he softly bumps my shoulder, I think it's just our magnetic attraction, but then I glance up at him and see his eyes under the low cap. They're definitely teasing, playful eyes.

So, when we hit his street, I reach for his hand. Feeling flutters because he doesn't let mine go when Teddy turns back to look at us. "Owivia." My full name, butchered with a big pointy-teeth smile. "Are you gonna come inside for cookies?"

Carmello laughs. "Are you trying to steal my girlfr . . ."

He never gets to finish that sentence because his face goes slack. When I follow his line of sight, I see someone standing on his front porch. "Mommy!" Teddy calls and breaks out into a run.

Carmello lets go of One Piece's leash and lets him run over to Daniela too. I watch her give the boys her affection while my stomach is in my throat because, even though Carmello hasn't moved away from me, he has let go of my hand.

When we make it over to the porch, Carmello climbs one step, but I stay back a few feet, and her eyes still find mine first. I can see the hurt on her face illuminated by the light over her head. She's still hugging Teddy, and One Piece is licking her ankle, but she doesn't seem to notice.

"Hey," Carmello says. "You're back early."

"I had to talk to you about something." Her voice is tight when she speaks to him. I get that she won't talk in front of me, that's normal. I'm a stranger who was just holding hands with the father of her kid while said kid walked ahead of us with a dog she clearly loves. So, for a flash of a second, I feel like Carmello's mistress. I know that's not what this is, but it's like we were caught.

"Did something happen to you in the Bahamas?" Carmello asks, strain in his voice.

She shakes her head quickly, then glances down at a worried-looking Teddy. Squeezes him tighter. "Actually, it was mostly that I really wanted to see this kid's face. And it wasn't a big deal; there was a flight out a day early for just a small price increase."

My brain latches on to those words and to the smile on her face while she looks at her son. She came early for Teddy. Not for him *and* Carmello. I let go of that other wild thought.

But Carmello clears his throat. "Daniela, this is Olivia. Olivia, this is . . . Teddy's mom."

We both shoot him a look. If it wasn't obvious by him scratching the back of his neck that he's uncomfortable, that last clarification in the introduction proved it.

"It's nice to meet you, Daniela," I say, fidgeting with my fingers. Not sure if I should climb the steps to offer her my hand or keep at this distance. She only gives me a small smile.

Thank God for children and their inability to sit still.

Teddy tugs on her pants. "Mommy, come see my new books!"

Daniela looks at Carmello as if she needs permission, and I get the distinct feeling she's never really had to do that before. The moment is tense before Carmello answers by telling Teddy: "Make sure to give Mommy a slice of the cake you made with Paula, okay?"

"Okay, Daddy," he says, but he doesn't look at either of us. Just goes on his tiptoes to grab the door handle and pull it open for his mom and his best friend to follow.

Carmello stares after them for a few seconds, as if he needs time to process whatever the hell this just was, but I'm already walking backward toward my car. When he snaps out of his thoughts, he takes a few strides with his long legs and he's in front of me.

"O," he whispers. "That was weird. I'm sorry."

I smile and say, "It was very weird, but it's fine. It's not your fault."

"I have to talk to her," he says. "But I want to make sure you're okay first."

"I'm okay," I rush to reassure him, knowing how often he overthinks things.

He tentatively cups my face, then relaxes when I lean into his hand. "Are you sure?"

I tell him I *mostly* am because I'm not upset with him, I know he'll explain why it was weird later. I trust him, but I'm also starting to feel more crampy and I really wanted to go inside and bake some cookies and maybe watch *Mufasa* with Teddy and now I'm sad.

I tiptoe to kiss him, and he gets lost in my lips for a minute, but then he breaks away and puts his mouth against my cheek. "I love you, O," he says.

"I love you too, Mello," I tell him, but the words feel like they come with more complications than they did yesterday.

And halfway on the drive to my Airbnb, I get my period too.

Chapter 41

Carmello

Now

WHILE TEDDY'S GETTING HIS THINGS READY TO GO, I say, "I'm sorry you had to see . . ."

"Carmello," Daniela cuts in. "I don't care that you're back with your ex. It was a bit of a shock to see her with Teddy, sure, but you were right about everything you said when we talked about us. And there are more important things to discuss now."

She takes a long breath and tells me something did happen in the Bahamas. She got an update call from Teddy's therapist and she freaked out about it and booked an early flight home.

My pulse picks up. I lean forward in my chair and ask, "Well, what did she say?"

"She said he's too young for her to feel comfortable diagnosing him with it yet, but she thinks Teddy might be developing OCD," Daniela says, and I'm stunned for a second, thinking of everything I know about the mental health condition and everything I don't. "She wanted to tell me about her suspicions now because the earlier we can work together on any tics or tendencies he has, the better chance he has to overcome any OCD-related obstacles as he ages," Daniela continues. "And maybe he won't even fully develop it when he's an adult, but if he does, he'll have tools to help him not suffer from it."

Suffer. The word rings harsh in my ears. My stomach twists. I sit back in the chair and say, "Why does she think he has OCD? What are the symptoms?"

"She said he has a particular fear of germs and dirty hands, and she notices some compulsions or rituals, small things like the way he anxiously ties his shoes and has to lace them a certain way and how he talks about his fear of drowning and . . ." Daniela trails off for a moment, and I reach out to squeeze her hand, remembering my conversation with Teddy after his bad dream the other day. "She said he hyperfixates on bad stuff. You know? Like he's scared of things a kid his age shouldn't be scared of. And that we should be watchful of repetitive reassurance-seeking, a need for order, and if any of those things produce rituals and behaviors. And . . . if he has any intrusive thoughts about him hurting himself or others." I watch tears fall from Daniela's eyes and feel a knot in my throat. "Our baby."

"Hey," I say, pulling her close to comfort her while I'm still digesting the news.

Teddy might have OCD, but those symptoms feel so familiar.

Daniela pulls away and looks me in the eyes, says, "People grow up and deal with all sorts of things, you know? But if there's anything we can do to make Teddy's future a little easier, we should try our best. You're his family, which means you're my family too and we have a responsibility to each other because of him. So, I'll work on my own mental health, but I need *you* to find time to speak to his therapist this week and maybe get one for yourself too. I never really knew what OCD was. I just always pictured it as people who keep their house extra clean. But Teddy's therapist said that's just a romanticized version of the real thing and that OCD can be genetic and run in families, and that she's noticed you . . . hyperfixate on certain things when she recaps with you too, like over-worrying about Teddy's safety. She said that sometimes hyperfixation can be triggered by trauma. And Carmello, we always joke about how you're the helicopter parent between the two of us, but maybe it's deeper than that. Maybe you have unhealed trauma from your mom being sick the first time."

"Mommy, I'm ready," Teddy says, and I turn to see him standing in the doorway with One Piece. I wonder if he heard any of that. I wonder if he can see how fast I'm breathing.

ORDERLY. FIRST: I TEXT DANIELA TO REASSURE HER THAT I'LL find time to see a therapist and get evaluated because my son takes up the most space in my heart, so making sure he's safe *and* happy is my top priority. Second: I get in the car after Olivia agrees to spend time with me because she also takes up space in my heart and I don't want to lose her.

But when I pull up in her parking lot, I don't text her right away. I zone out scrolling through the information on the California OCD Treatment Center website. According to what I read, hyperfixation is categorized as when a person chooses a certain object, thought, or activity to intensely focus on at any given time. And I realize I do that, mostly when it comes to my fears over Teddy. That I silently seek reassurance and I learned to read body language long ago to get it because my parents weren't the best at communicating with their words and I didn't always know whether they were happy with me as a son. That I seek reassurance in Olivia's smile, just to calm my racing mind about whether she's happy with me as a boyfriend. That maybe my mom had intrusive thoughts that caused rituals too. It might be why she always worried about me going to the mall, saying I might get kidnapped. And why she never wanted me to sleep over at anyone's house because people were creeps. And why she reminded me to pray and then would call me to remind me *again* before she went to bed, and why she always had to tell me to stay safe—just like I have to tell Teddy now or something bad might happen to him too.

I lose track of the time scouring the internet about OCD and Olivia notices I'm outside by peeking through the blinds and seeing me on my phone. She's not mad that I was twenty minutes later than I said I would be. Just kisses me and tells me she wants to go to the pedestrian bridge.

Now here we are, and I'm trying to concentrate on her. This moment, sitting across from her on a bench. But my mind is telling me that I should still be searching the web to make sure *I* don't have rituals that could inadvertently cause damage to our relationship.

"I have to admit," Olivia says, breaking our silence, "I saw the photo strip of you, Teddy, and Daniela in your glove compartment, and I've been trying not to wonder if there's any part of you that wants to be with her and grow a family. But is there?"

I reach to gently tip her face so she can meet my eyes. "No, O. I promise you this: Daniela gave me a beautiful son. I'll always be grateful to her for that, but co-parenting is all we'll ever do. I want you."

She chews her lower lip, then says, "That's good because I would have been devastated if you said otherwise. But I have to be honest with you about something. I told you about my endometriosis. What I didn't tell you was . . . as a result of suffering from this all these years, I've decided I don't want to have children. The endo already took away so much control of my body, and with it, my autonomy. I don't think I can give up any more of that, but even if I did ever change my mind, if something makes me want to try with you . . . in the future . . . the endo might make it more complicated."

"So then we won't have kids," I say simply while stroking her cheek.

"You told me you wanted more," she says. "And I want to be fair to you, Mello."

"I did say that, but I promise it's not something I'd ask you to compromise on. My life is full enough already. I have you and Celia's Place, friends, family, and I already have Teddy."

She smiles. "You sure?"

I smooth my hands down her arms. "I'm sure."

She nods, then stands up to lean over the railing, says, "I'm sad I lost another sunset here tonight, and who knows if I'll ever get to see one because of what time Celia's Place closes. But it's fine. I'd probably still prefer it at this time anyway."

When I join her, she leans into me a little. And I hear what she's saying, but this is the way I focus on her: elbows propped to steady herself on the railing of the bridge, her hair blowing in the wind while she stares across the Providence River. I tell myself that when her attention slips from one thing to the next and then she gets quieter than usual, she's probably thinking of all the things she said she liked about being here this late. Like the way the lights sparkle from the tall buildings and the State House "actually makes it look like magic from a distance." And the dark water against this yellow-lit bridge. Or that there are only a few other people here but they're so far from us it feels like we're alone together.

I hear what she's saying, but my brain is orderly. It might not always focus on the thing that happens first, but it does focus on what's heavier or harder to fix. And sometimes it gets stuck there. If catching sunsets makes Olivia happy, maybe she'll want to catch more of them. And she should. *I* want her to have all the happiness that she wants. But I do wonder how she can do that here with me, working at Celia's Place, in Rhode Island with a routine.

Right now, I don't want to be focused on heavier thoughts. I want to be wrapped up completely in her closeness. I want to be able to feel it fully—the way she seems to when she suddenly reaches up to pull my face down for a kiss. But when she breaks away, humming in satisfaction over the heart feelings as well as the physical ones, before looking back across the water, my mind spins with these thoughts. I feel too slow to catch up. These are the things I hyperfixate on while we spend time together. But the biggest one is how I'm so scared that we won't have enough of it. That our moments won't be exciting enough to keep her here. With me.

WHEN WE CIRCLE BACK AND ARRIVE AT HER AIRBNB'S PARKing spot, Olivia grins in a way that tells me she's got a plan for me on the brain. "Teddy's with his mom. That means you can sleep over?" she says, and everything else falls aside for a second. I lean over the console to kiss her, remembering the wild time we had in my truck the other day. At first, I was nervous someone would see us, but Olivia reassured me my tint was too dark for that. Still, I'll admit I was a little distracted feeling protective of her after she straddled my lap.

Sometimes her personality clashes with mine in a bad way. But I've long realized that much more often, it challenges me to do some of the things I haven't had the balls to. And right now, she's pouting for me to stay, even though she's tried so hard to hide the fact that she's been cramping all day and it's gotten worse. I think she's on her period. But that's not why I'm wondering if sleeping over is the best idea for tonight. I have so much to do back at my place still. Will have to wake up even earlier to go home and shower, feed and walk One Piece, definitely skip my morning run.

"You're thinking about it so hard," Olivia says, faking offense. "Forget it."

I roll my eyes, kiss her forehead, and shut off my engine. Knowing it'll be worth the extra work if I get to sleep beside her tonight. As much as her presence challenges my nervous system, it has equal ability to calm it too. And I can tell my presence does the same for her. When we get in bed, I'll massage her lower back and she'll start telling me a story and then jump to another story and before I know it, she'll fall asleep mid-sentence, and I'll curl my body around her and my brain might just hyperfixate on how good it feels to do that and how I never want to stop. And at least being with her will distract me from spending the night worrying about whether I've passed OCD on to my son and what that'll mean for him.

Chapter 42

Carmello

Now

IT'S TOO BIG TO FIT THERE," OLIVIA GROANS.

"It feels good right here to me, babe," I tease. "Stop fussing."

We're outside of Celia's Place on the patio, and she shoots me a look before pushing herself off the chaise and trying to move it to the left with me still on it. In the past week, we've worked tirelessly with Debra's and Bobby's help to get the patio ready. I cleared trash and clutter from the area and let Bobby handle the bugs. He's from down south and declared himself an expert on getting them gone. I had the pavement patched up and polished, the weeds ripped out. We draped string lights over the tables and hung lanterns on the black birch tree. Debra made centerpieces with floating candles and Olivia thought of lush white curtains for the canopy to create a romantic ambience. And yes, among the comfortable furniture we thrifted for out here, there's a chaise that Olivia's been struggling to find a place for.

I stand up to move it for her two more times, and finally, she looks satisfied. She kisses my cheek and says, "Sorry, I'm just nervous."

I am too. We've blown the last of my mom's emergency fund pulling all of this together, and I'm trying not to worry about no longer having that safety net. Our first official Table for Twos-Day is in a couple of weeks and the ten slots are already filled with high demand for the following one. Other than the vibe, Olivia and I have added both Cape Verdean (from her side) and Dominican (from my side) foods to the small bites menu. For entertainment purposes, the women at Celia's came up with wild names for the card categories that go along with the foods like: "Small Bites: Getting to know you," and "Sweet Treats: Turn up the romance." Zeke spread the word around the city, shouting out what new things we were bringing to the restaurant when he was on stage as the head DJ for a Boston music festival. Olivia's friends helped get the word out too: Laniah telling customers at Wildly Green about the "perfect date" with her husband, and Kat gossiping about the shitty one that saved her from future mistakes (her words, not mine). Men with money to spare have started calling to request the space for a private date night. When I asked Issac if it was he who spread the word to his "rich folk friends," he denied it. But he did give me the number to his therapist and told her to slot me in first on her wait list.

"Don't be sorry. I understand why you're nervous, O." I reach for her left hand and kiss her palm. "This idea *truly* seems like it's going to take us far, but it's going to be a lot of work and mental stress, especially because we already have a reputation to uphold."

She smiles and tilts her head, a twinkle in her eye, calmed by my words. "May I have this dance?"

It's not even a slow song, but we start that way. She puts her cheek against my chest, and I move us to the music, whispering soft reassurances to her while she looks around. *You see how beautiful this is? It's exactly right. Can't you feel what you did here? Trust your instincts, O.*

And once her body relaxes to match mine, I spin her in circles around the patio.

We're out of breath, laughing when we crash on the couch to cuddle. We haven't had much time to sit still with each other, but there have been stolen moments like this. Her fingers in my hair. My lips against her temple. Tired nights together too. I'll bring my clothes and One Piece to her apartment and help her adjust her heating pad when the pain hits hard, distracting her with kisses and conversation. She hasn't had a single bad dream about the fire, and we both like to think that's because I'm sleeping over most nights. In the mornings while I go for a run, she cooks something for One Piece and for me too.

It's inexplicable the way we fit and it feels like no time has passed. Like she carved out a place at my side and all she needed to do was come back to claim it.

She reaches to brush her fingers along my jaw. "You haven't told me how your first appointment went with Issac's therapist this morning."

I've been working to keep *my* worries from her, refusing to hold our past so close to my chest that I can't focus on our present, but I did tell her about Teddy possibly having OCD the other night. We kept the conversation brief, and I've wondered if it's been on her mind.

"It was good," I say, wanting to keep it simple. "She seems great. Easy to talk to."

Olivia nods. "A good therapist can be a lifesaver. I'm glad you're seeing someone. Over the years, I've had times when I felt so lost, directionless, and it's really helped me to have someone to talk to. And I'm not a therapist, but if you ever want to talk to me too, you can."

"I know," I say, but I can't imagine sharing some of my intrusive thoughts with her, knowing how graphic they can get. I exhale and then change the subject. "I have one more idea for date night, but be honest if you think it's corny."

She searches my face like she is expecting me to tell her something, then shrugs and says, "If you and I worried about what's corny or cheesy, we might not have a date night at all."

I smile and pull a pack of markers from my pocket. "Might not be as cool as the bouquet-making station," I say, referring to the stand she and Teddy set up where we'll have fresh flowers for couples to put together during their date if they want to. It warmed my heart to see her engaging one of Teddy's interests, and pulling in something my mom loved too. "But they're for temporary tattoos. I thought maybe we could put them in a jar with a sign just in case people want to imprint on each other before they leave." I wait for her to say something and, fuck, I'm nervous, because most times it's easy to read her expressions, but harder for me to know how the feelings hit her. "I don't know . . . maybe . . . the idea is too *us* to share with anyone else?"

She's quiet for a moment, then she says, "Come here, Carmello."

Her hands find my face, and she gives me the sweetest kiss, pulls back and presses her forehead to mine. "Everything about this place means we're sharing little pieces of ourselves," she says. "And I think that's kind of beautiful. I love that we're sharing the fake tattoos, but I'll for sure claim it was solely your idea if anyone calls it corny."

I laugh. "How magnanimous."

She runs her fingernails along the back of my neck. The feeling of them scraping my skin shoots down my center. She smirks like she knows the power she has over my body. That a simple touch like this can send me over the edge. That I'm hers.

"Now let me tattoo my name on your neck," she says.

"Wherever you want," I breathe.

She arches an eyebrow. "You ain't about that life."

I point to the free spot at the center of my throat. "Right here."

Her eyes catch a spark and then we're kissing and a contented sigh slips from her lips. One of my favorite ways to tell she's happy.

Chapter 43

Olivia

Now

MY PERIOD WAS HEAVY AND RELENTLESS. TOO DAMN long. And since it's been gone, Carmello and I haven't had many chances to be alone. Last night, we got in late and curled up together. I had the thought to start something, but he was playing with my hair and I drifted to sleep before I got the chance. When I woke up this morning, he'd already left to get a head start on paperwork before everyone and everything else pulled at his attention. But there was a text waiting for me. **You deserve rest. When you see this, close your eyes for a few more minutes. I love you.** I smiled and then rushed to get ready because I refused to spend the whole day distracted by my need for him. It's been showing in my efficiency and has messed with my abilities. I oversalted two dishes this week and that rarely happens.

When I show up to Celia's, no one is here except for Carmello. He's in our now *shared* office and his face is all serious as he crunches numbers. He doesn't even look over from the computer until he hears the door click shut, so I know whatever is on his mind is important enough to consume it fully. But just this once while we're at the restaurant, I need him. Especially if he expects us to keep functioning effectively in this space.

Confusion crawls over his features seeing me here so early, but his expression changes quickly when he realizes we're alone and I closed the door. I know he's already twitching below the belt the moment he leans back in his chair. While he watches me walk over to him slowly, he absentmindedly chews his pen cap, and I know he's consumed because . . . well, Carmello and cross contamination.

I push his chair out and drop to my knees in front of him. His breath hitches and he starts to speak, but I put my hands over his mouth. When he's successfully silenced, I run my hands over the erection forming in his pants and my body grows hungry for him. I'm starved.

He watches me while I pull him out and press my lips to the head. Hisses through his teeth when I encircle him down to the middle with my mouth.

"Yes, baby," he breathes, throwing his head back. "Just like that."

The encouragement makes me want to take him as deep as I can. And I'm soaked. So wet because he tastes good and he's moaning, and I love making him feel good. When he calls me his *bad girl*, I work even harder to show him that I'm his. Until his words start slipping in and out of coherence. He's close, but I stop to tease him like he does to me, stroking the bottom half of his shaft while I taste him with my tongue. I shiver when a deep sound spills from his throat, and he pushes my shoulders softly to stand.

He turns me around, pulls down my pants, says, “Hands on the desk. Now.”

I do as I’m told, and he explores my breasts from the back, grabs my hips, tugs me to him. He slides two fingers inside of me from behind, and we both moan. While he builds a rhythm that makes my vision blurry, he tilts my chin with his other hand, nips my ear with his teeth, and then he finally gives me what I’ve been waiting for. The first slide in is slow, torturous, and exhilarating. But then he’s deep, I’m full of him, stretched out and aching for him to thrust into me.

“I know just how you want it,” he says, and then his fingers are in my hair and he’s taking me harder and faster than he usually does and I’m biting down on my lip so that I don’t scream his name. This is risky and I love it and I love him and I’m so fucking happy.

When we finish at the same time, it feels like our bodies were meant to wait for each other. I’m shaking and he drops down over me on the desk to kiss my shoulder blade, to hold me. “Thank you, baby,” he whispers. And we stay like that for a moment, breathing together, the kind of comfort that comes when two souls are undoubtedly connected.

When he pulls out, my legs are jiggly and I’m grinning. I pull my pants up and run my fingers over my lips. His eyes darken again when I lick them a little.

“You should get yourself cleaned up. You know, start your day productive, Rodriguez.”

He smiles and smacks my ass to send me out of our office.

Then I go to the bathroom to take my own advice.

But my skin is still buzzing, and I tell myself to stop smiling or Steven’s body language assessment will read *Just been sexed.*

Carmello and I have been way more proper around him since our first few days as a couple—we hardly even work near each other during business hours, content with cooking across the room—but today might be the day that Steven actually quits if he realizes something went down between us just minutes before he had to clock in for his shift.

Grouchy ass.

Except . . . when I hear his voice at the front-of-house, he sounds like he's smiling? He's talking to someone, but no one else comes in this early. I peek my head out the kitchen door to see who it is, and my stomach grows sick right before Carmello's father notices me and says, "Olivia, would you mind getting my son? The three of us need to talk."

Chapter 44

Carmello

Now

AS SOON AS OLIVIA CAME TO TELL ME MY FATHER WAS here, that tightness that had been easing over time crossed my chest again. Seconds before, I was still reeling from being with her. Now we're sitting at a booth across from my father staring at my mother's will.

I see Olivia's hands shake slightly as she picks it up to examine it again. But a closer inspection won't change what my father has already proven. My mother didn't follow proper protocol. What I failed to notice in this very dense, monotonously written will and testament was that one of her witnesses was named as a beneficiary. Which means they have an interest in my mother's estate. Even though the gift Celia Rodriguez gave this stranger-to-me witness was something small, the entire will is invalid because of that. Which means my mother's previous will is the one that counts. And Olivia Jones isn't on it.

I am the sole owner of this restaurant.

"Don't worry," my father says, "even my lawyer missed it."

Olivia must not like his light tone because she lifts her chin and puts the will on the table.

I clear my throat. "Pa, how did *you* catch this? I thought you were letting me handle it."

He shifts in his seat, folds his fingers together on the table. "I was," he says. "Until I received an email from your mother two days ago. Something she scheduled to send me before she died, the same way she scheduled the email for you containing this . . . fake will."

"Wait," Olivia says. "Fake? Do you mean you think she knew including a witness in her will would make it invalid?"

My father's not a villain, but he's protective of those he loves, and I know my mom is still on his list. "Celia was a perfectionist when it came to the accounts," he says, and he should know. They shared so much with each other toward the end. "I'd say she knew exactly what she was doing. And the email she sent me is the only proof I need."

"What did it say?" I ask.

"She gave me the password to her personal email address and told me she needed me to help her with something." His eyes flick to Olivia's face, then back to mine. "She said she did what she thought was right for you, and now she needed me to do what I think is right. That was my only instruction. When I signed into her account, there was an email there and the name on the address looked familiar. That's when I realized I saw it on the will. The email was from the witness. And you know your mother. She liked her riddles. So I decided to search through the will myself one more time. And there it was. Celia wanted me to find her . . . mistake."

I haven't been able to get my heart to stop racing. Celia Rodriguez. Tricks and games.

Olivia's shoulders slump, and I know she's fighting to keep from crying in front of my father. "Well, then." She sighs, but her voice is steady despite whatever she's feeling inside.

I've only had two sessions with Issac's therapist. She said it's too early for her to feel certain enough to diagnose me with OCD, but it has been nice to talk to someone that's trained to listen to my fears. And she said something about Olivia after I mentioned the fire that made me smile. *Sometimes the things we learn in survival mode can be useful even after we've healed. It sounds to me like your girlfriend has the strength of someone whose parents taught her to pivot.*

Olivia doesn't sound like she knows how to pivot right now though. She fidgets with her fingers. "I guess . . . this was all . . . I don't know what the hell it was, actually."

I cover her hand with mine, and my father's eyes dart down to our fingers. His jaw clenches. "Before you make any reckless decisions with your heart, Carmello, I want you to think hard on what this restaurant can mean for your future, for your son's future."

I will admit, those words send a new wave of fear at me, but I take a deep breath and say, "I understand, Pa, but could you please give us some time alone to discuss this?"

He heaves out a breath. "Fine, but did Olivia tell you she's going to Tokyo for a year? How excited she is about leaving?"

Olivia stiffens beside me, and I narrow my eyes at my dad.

"She's not going anymore," I say. "But how did you even hear about that?"

"Like I said, your mom was a perfectionist, Carmello. That

personal account was free of spam. It only contained emails from two people. The one from the witness and dozens from Olivia." He shifts his gaze to my girlfriend, an apologetic look on his face. "I only read this one." He takes a folded paper from his jacket and pushes it toward us, then stands and says to Olivia, "I just want my son to know what he's getting himself into with you before he makes any decisions."

"Pa, you don't know what you're talking about," I say, but he's already turning his back on me. When my father leaves, staff members start to come in for their shifts and instantly realize they walked in on something serious. But Olivia wastes no time; she shudders out a breath and doesn't so much as glance at me before she's heading for the door too.

I'm finally fast enough. I snatch the folded paper off the table, so the staff doesn't snoop and go after her. When I catch up, I tell her to wait and reach for her hand. She turns around, and I try not to focus on the fact that she's crying now. Instead, I focus on what I can control: my own feelings.

"So, you're just going to walk out of here without us having a conversation?"

"What kind of conversation should we have right now, Carmello? The restaurant is yours, and I need to get my mind right."

"It's yours too," I say. "We've done all this together. And . . ."

"That," Olivia says, scrunching up her nose. "That's why I need some space to think and why you should take some space too. You're so quick to try to solve everything because you think I'm going to leave if you don't. Like your father said, you don't even have all the facts." Olivia nods to the paper in my hand. "Go on, read it. And read the rest of my emails too."

I crumple the paper up and cup her face with my other hand.

"Hey. That's not necessary. He's overprotective, but he crossed the line and invaded your privacy by reading them. I'm sorry."

Olivia puts one hand over mine and looks me dead in the eyes. Then, her words steal air straight from my lungs. "Carmello, I haven't told my client that I'm not going to Tokyo yet. I still have another week before I can't contractually cancel on her anymore."

A beat of silence. Two. I take a step back, letting my hands fall to my sides. "Were you . . . waiting so you could have some sort of escape hatch in case you changed your mind about us?"

She shakes her head. "I've been planning to tell her, I have . . . but something keeps stopping me from sending the message."

My mind tries to slip to the past, to dark thoughts and how horrible it felt when she left the first time, but I force myself to remain in the present. "I *know* how happy you are with me," I say, the confidence coming from how connected we've felt these past few weeks. "I feel it. So, what is this about, O?"

She gives me a small smile and then she starts to sob. "I'm glad you know." A breath. One more. "And I'm happy here too, but Mello . . . it's like your heart and mine are linked and I can feel how scared you are to trust *that* part completely."

I reach for her face again, gently stroking her jaw with my thumb. "Why do you say that, babe? Please don't run scared because you're assuming something about me or because you're worried this isn't going to work between us for things that may not even come to pass in the future. You can have the shares you think you lost. You don't have to pivot. I'm in this. Have confidence in me."

"I don't want to break up, Carmello," she says. "But it's hard to have confidence in us. One moment you want kids, the next you don't care. I love how attentive you are, but sometimes I feel like you're quick to compromise your own comfort. You tell me you might have OCD, but you avoid conversations about it, and I feel like that's because you don't want me to fully *see* you because you think there might be something in you that I don't like. An excuse for me not to commit all the way. And I . . . I've been avoiding this feeling that maybe we're moving too fast, that maybe I jumped into this because I lost a home a long time ago and I find a steadiness in you that I crave. My parents told me I'm my own home but I've been thinking home can be a place too. And now I find out that your mom might not have had the confidence in me that I thought she did. Maybe she didn't believe I could build a home here. And maybe I need to tell you why I left the way I did a decade ago, not for you, but because I want you to see *me* fully. I'm not perfect, I'm just a person, and I don't want to be the bad guy and hurt you again in the future if I can't show you who I am." I open my mouth to respond but she breaks away from me. "No, Carmello. You're going to stand there and listen to what I remember from the day I left."

She releases a breath, then she begins.

Chapter 45

THE PANDESAL I LEFT BEHIND

Olivia

10 Years Ago

MY PARENTS TAUGHT ME TO BE PRAGMATIC WITH TRAVEL plans. A car could break down on a random road in the country: *Know how to change a tire.* A storm could delay a flight: *Have a backup plan and never be scared to rent a car instead.* You could think you have everything accounted for, but realize that's not true: *Hope for the best but always be prepared for the worst.* Before leaving me in Rhode Island when I was seventeen, my father sat me down and said, *I know you love him, but be careful with attachments. Love is fickle. Always choose yourself.*

His love didn't seem fickle with my mother, but how was I to know all they'd experienced? They'd been together longer than I'd been alive. I just assumed he was worried I was staying in Rhode Island only because Carmello wanted me to, but at the time it wasn't true. I loved Celia and cooking and I loved having friends and knowing the names of my teachers at school. And just because I was staying for now, didn't mean it'd be forever.

I still wanted to see the world after graduation, and Carmello said he'd see it with me.

But then seventeen quickly turned to eighteen and suddenly Celia had breast cancer. Carmello found her on the floor at home one day and swore she was already gone. I could see how hard it hit him, but then she had treatments and she was "fine."

So, when twenty seemed like it was fast approaching and our roles at Celia's Place only became bigger, I got nervous that our previous dreams to travel were just that. But after I expressed my worries to Carmello and told him how badly I wanted to go, he hugged me and said, "So, we will."

We bought train tickets to New York: the place we planned to start our journey as prep cooks, hitting as many kitchens as we could in the States. We'd saved enough for three months of living, had backup funds just in case, and most importantly, we had each other and our beating hearts. But two weeks before we were set to leave Rhode Island, I had this burning feeling in my belly. I thought Carmello was acting strange, but he never complained. And I take my share of the blame: I wanted to ask him if he was sad to leave his home to be with me, but I was scared he'd say yes and I'd want to go regardless.

Carmello worked earlier shifts than I did, but I went to Celia's early that day to help Paula bake pandesal in the basement. Filipino bread rolls were soft and airy, slightly sweet, my favorite to watch rise. But when I went back upstairs to get something for Paula from the fridge, I heard Carmello's voice coming from Celia's office. I almost made my presence known, but that feeling in my stomach was happening again and I found myself listening outside the door instead.

"Just tell her that you don't want to go," Celia said.

"I can't," Carmello said. "She's so excited about it and . . ."

"You're going to sacrifice your happiness for her?" Celia cut in, her voice sharp and stern. Unlike my mother's when I'd tell her about one of my impulsive ideas.

"I don't want to be without her," Carmello said.

"But you want to be here, no?" Celia pressed. "Answer me, Carmello."

"Yes."

The words echoed in my ears. I leaned up against the wall, mind racing.

"You're too young," Celia said. "You're supposed to graduate from business school. And relationships require hard work. Sometimes love is not enough."

Carmello said something I couldn't hear, then Celia answered back in Tagalog, tongue quick, tone biting. I found myself wishing I'd learned more of the language while I was around her.

"I shouldn't have told you," Carmello muttered. "I just wanted to talk, but . . ."

"Don't talk to me if you expect my silence," Celia said. "You're my son and I don't want you to be a fool and regret chasing her around the world while she's looking for something she can get right here. Has she even asked what you want?"

Something about the formal way Celia said *she* stung. The woman was rarely vocal with her emotions, but I felt like she considered me family. Carmello said something else, but I couldn't bring myself to listen any longer. I could hear how heavy his voice sounded. His mom was making sense and that would weigh on him. She was making sense to me too, but I couldn't let it weigh on me. I was going to choose myself, just like I'd been taught to. So . . . I quietly grabbed my jacket, left Paula and the pandesal waiting for me in the basement, and went back to their place to pack. I knew he'd resent me for leaving, but I couldn't pretend not to know how he truly felt, and I was sure he might resent me more in the end if I asked *him* not to choose himself, his mother, Celia's Place.

The truth is, part of me did prepare for Carmello not wanting to leave, but what I did not prepare for was what it would feel like to have to live without him.

Chapter 46

Carmello

Now

"WOW," I SAY, MY CHEST RISING AND FALLING IN REACtion to Olivia's confession. It feels like I got the wind knocked out of me. I wasn't expecting her reason to be *that* at all. "Wow."

"Are you going to say anything else?"

I clear my throat and say, "I can't imagine how it felt being on the other side of the wall and hearing that conversation. The truth is . . . I loved my life here and I was scared of leaving my mom. What if something bad had happened to her while we were gone? She was only in remission for a year. But I should've told you I didn't want to go. I'm sorry. I just . . ."

"Carmello, I don't blame you for that," Olivia says. "But I need you to see why you can't just rush to solve this for us. I don't want you to be so scared of losing me that you don't even take a moment to consider *yourself*. I want to consider *myself*. I dealt with the fallout from Michael being resentful of me. And that was okay because I know I was never in love with him. But I learned a lot about myself being with him. I know I was partly to blame for my marriage failing because I wasn't intentional about how it began. I'm solid in my decision to be with you. I'm glad I've been able to open up and show you that, but you said you want to be intentional too, and I don't know if you've grown past your fears. Maybe you're too blinded by your love for me and you don't want to face them. I'm afraid you're not opening up to me completely because you fear that I won't stay, but if you don't trust me to see you fully, what does that mean for us? And aside from our personal problems, aren't you afraid to dishonor your parents? Because I am. This shit is heavy, and I'm hesitant to say, *Oh, his parents are just overprotective, they'll get over it*. They worked really fucking hard to give you this life. I've been around the world, Carmello. To do what your mom did here with Celia's Place? It had to be an incredible feat, and just because she cared about me doesn't mean I should be included in her legacy. Tricks or not. I respected her wishes back then, and I still want to now."

I know what she's saying. When I was a teenager, I had a hard time understanding why my parents were so strict, why all they did was work, why they were so protective. But I've long come to terms with it. And after this week working with Daniela to make time for therapists where there was none in order to give Teddy his best shot in the future, I respect my parents a hell of a lot more than I did. Because they might not have always shown their love in warm ways, but they both came to this country with nothing and had to work twice as hard to give me an easier life than they had, and along the way they taught me the drive to reach for some of the same opportunities as my peers.

I don't know what's more loving than that.

But the determination they taught me is why I clear my throat and say, "I do respect them and want to honor their wishes, but we don't know that my mom didn't want this for me *and* you." She frowns and my eyes prick knowing my words aren't enough right now. She reaches up to brush my cheek with the raised skin of her palm, and I find comfort there. And then, my face is wet and I'm hearing myself admit: "I do have fears. But I'm just so in love with you, Olivia."

"I know you are, Carmello," she says with a small smile. "But it's up to you to decide what to make of it, because what I've decided is that I work too damn hard. I'm an incredible chef, and these past few weeks have taught me that I make just as good of a boss as you. I'm smart and talented and the event night we created together is going to fucking shine, and you're right, a large part of that is from me giving it my all. I love Rhode Island and Celia's Place but I never want to give up my agency or any of my other desires either. And Carmello, I *know* you love me enough to give me the shares that your mom didn't." She taps her fingers to her chest. "I can feel it right here. You'd give me a place in this business that I feel I'm owed if I'm here, but I need you to be certain that it's not just because you're scared to lose me. I need to know we can start fresh for real, and that you believe I've grown enough not to call it quits when things get hard. Because if I lose all of this, Mello, I don't know if I'm elastic enough not to break. So, I think we should both take a breath and decide what our future can look like while seeing each other fully. Read the emails in your mom's inbox. Feel your feelings. They're important."

My stomach is in knots. It's hard to breathe. But I reach and wrap my arms around her. Hold her close. "All right, O," I say. She buries her face in my chest and cries, kisses me there. And then, she goes.

I watch her walk down the block until I can't see her any longer, and when I turn around four sets of eyes are staring at me through the windows of Celia's Place. I lose track of time and space whenever it's me and Olivia. That's something I can admit to being scared of. Because as beautiful as it can be, there are other things that take up space in my heart, other people that need my love and attention.

My staff at the restaurant is one of them.

Once I'm inside, they try to act like they weren't paying attention, but no one has started getting us ready for the morning. Then, Paula claps her hands; she looks like she was just crying. "All right, nosy gang," she says, "this ship still has to run without its captain sometimes."

"I like that analogy," Debra says, squeezing Bobby's shoulder. "Don't you, Bob?"

He smiles, and I notice he finally looks refreshed after a few bad weeks of dealing with his family drama. "I like it too," he says.

Steven snorts. "That analogy is played out and cringe, Debbie girl. But . . . I guess you have a point." He looks at me, says, "I can get the kitchen ready on my own today."

WHEN I SHUT MY OFFICE DOOR FOR PRIVACY, MY HEART IS even fuller—to the point of discomfort. But I think I know a way I can make more space. I stop in front of my dusty bookshelf and pick up the only framed photo on it. It's of my mom teaching Teddy how to cook something on the stove. I don't remember what she showed him or how I felt about Teddy's first time near the fire, because all I was focused on that day was that two parts of my heart felt like they were finally meeting in the same place.

And every day since my mom died, I've secretly come to this spot to stand in front of this frame and pray for my mom's spirit. But if the only thing I did was pray, that would be okay. Instead, I spend so much time stressing while I stand here too. My brain swirls with dark stuff that makes my chest hurt. Reliving her most painful days when I could do nothing more than squeeze her hand while she suffered through it. I think of ways I could've done better by her. I think maybe she'd still be here if I wasn't so distracted with my life that I didn't notice she was getting sick again. But that's so much to put on a person.

Memories come of me finding my mom on the bathroom floor years ago, and I think of how when I was a child she used to say the same kinds of things about me being emotionally intelligent that everyone now says about my son. I think of how Teddy rushes to comfort me, and how I take comfort in the fact that he does it, but how that's so much to put on a child.

And then I bring the frame with me to the desk I share with Olivia to search through my mom's personal inbox. She left me access to it months ago, but I never could bring myself to open it up and see *her* fully. She must've known that I wouldn't. That's why she scheduled the email for my dad to do her dirty work.

Just like he said, there are only emails from Olivia and the one with the will attachment from the witness. But since my father sat me and Olivia down at the booth to tell us what he found, I've been thinking of the email my mom scheduled for me to receive weeks ago with the weird one-line note she left me above the illegitimate will.

I hover the cursor over her drafts folder, take a breath, then click on it.

There are so many emails sitting in this folder. All addressed to me.

But there's one in particular that catches my attention. It sends a quick shiver up my spine. I look over at her face framed in the photo beside me and feel her presence in my bones. My dad was right. She never made any decisions without purpose.

And I want to be intentional too.

Olivia needed to know that I would take my time.

But I have faith hers are not the emails that *I* need to read.

Chapter 47

*F**OR CARMELLO. THIS ISN'T A DRAFT.***

My Dearest Son,

You might notice that my other emails are mostly photos throughout the years and think that this one was written by an impostor. But a friend helped me write it, so no tricks here, sadly. And I know you'll wish to tell me my English is strong enough that I could've done it myself, but I don't have the time to waste trying to make it sound like I want it to, so please stop shaking that damn head you should always remember I had to push out of my own body. Lately, you're so annoying. Always telling me something. Like to focus on drinking these nasty smoothies, and not to focus on what the doctors are telling me. But I know you hear what I hear.

I beat cancer once, but they're saying sometimes it rebounds.

For me, it came back to win this time.

That being said, I'm sorry if I'm making too much light out of this whole situation we're in. I know how much it hurts you, my son, but I love to hear you laugh. And I'm going to miss you equally, if not more. That's the only reason I let you come over and use my blender for these gross smoothies you make me, God dammit. (I just said a prayer by the way, so I should also confess that I flush them down the toilet when you leave.) Before your brows get to meeting in the middle of your face, I do it because they might help someone less close to the afterlife than I am, but it's too late for them to help me. Therefore, I refuse to suffer. And I wish I had the heart to tell you that if you want an excuse to sit at my side, feed me a damn burger instead. Steven eats them all the time and you don't say anything to him about red meat and empty carbs.

But Carmello, you are my greatest gift. Your father and I agreed the other day we raised such a fine man. And your strong love for me has motivated me since the moment you came into my life. I am a better chef, and I believe I am a fairly decent human, because of that. In fact, I know I should be telling you what else I have to confess in person, but I have a hard time getting my words out when they feel this big in my chest. And I don't have many days left to waste trying. I just want to hear you laugh and pretend I can make sense out of the theories you've heard about spider lilies and whatever else you think might cure me. If you're reading this, you may have found out about the little stunt I pulled with the will. My friend here helped me get someone random to be a witness and pull it all together too. You might know her. She's at our restaurant all the time and eats the same thing for lunch every single day. So boring. She paused her typing to stare at me just now. Okay, here we go.

The present you that is reading this letter is probably anxious for me to get to the point, but please cut me a damn break. I deal with your nonsense. Past you is probably going to show up for me in the present any moment to make sure I'm okay, even after I told you that I already am over the telephone.

Anyway, this woman, my friend, told me recently that you used to come to her very nervous sometimes after school when you got a bad grade. And maybe that's because I put too much pressure on you to help at the restaurant while also maintaining your studies. I didn't want to hear it at first. She's not a parent, so what the hell does she know? But she had parents that did the same thing to her, and if there's anyone I trust to tell me about myself, to tell me about you, it's her.

Carmello, I haven't been tough on you at the restaurant because you're a great help for me (sometimes, you're annoying there too). It's because I need you in a different way.

Years ago, you were on a plane with your father and experienced bad turbulence. While you were telling me what happened, it felt like my heart was being ripped out of my body, it felt like I was suddenly on the plane with you and we were both falling. And after that, I wanted to keep you close to me so I never felt that kind of fear ever again. I've been anxious about your well-being since you've been born, but that day it was worse, and that's why I did this to you and Olivia. My friend here wants to remind me that I also meddled in getting Olivia's parents to agree for her to stay with us the first time. I don't regret that one. It was nice having you both around together. And Olivia seemed happy to me until I realized she wasn't anymore. But that is where my mistake began.

I know I am leaving my restaurant in the best of hands with you. But my reason for creating this elaborate will situation is even more selfish. Many years ago, I met a man who gave me butterflies and now I've come to realize they never left. That man is your father, but we were both too focused on building the best chance for us and for you in America that we didn't try hard enough to overcome any obstacles we faced to make our relationship work. It was easier for us to get along and be the best parents we could be with some type of distance. But now I know he still has butterflies for me too because when you leave me here with a disgusting smoothie, your father comes over and brings me pastelón or Dominican spaghetti or whatever else my heart desires. Even though he hates cooking for himself, he cooks for me.

And I think you've already had someone that meets you where you're at that way too. Because you haven't moved on, Son. I can tell in the way you can't even talk about her. Olivia hasn't let you go either. I see that in the way she tries to subtly get me to mention you when we email sometimes.

But back when she turned eighteen and wanted to show you around the world, I was too tired from my first fight with this disease to not have you near me. So, when I realized she was snooping outside of the door while you were telling me how scared you were to leave this place, I didn't tell you what I should have: that if it makes you happy to go, you should try, because I will always have a stove waiting for you at my side whenever you're ready to come home.

I'm sorry, my son.

I hope you can both forgive me for the years I may have stolen with my actions, and I hope my meddling brings you two back together like I can only have faith that it may. I'm not that much of a genius though, and I'm definitely not a perfect person because I thought of making the will official at first and forcing you two together long-term by giving Olivia some of my shares as I planned. She has grown up to be a fine chef and an even finer woman. But she doesn't seem happy living her life *only* traveling anymore. I think she'd be happier having a home with you. Still, my friend here told me to make the will as convincing as I'm hoping it was but that I should give you two the chance to make your own choices in the end.

Okay, well. I know I don't have to ask you to take good care of my Teddy Bear because I already know you will. But Carmello, I do ask that you honor me by living a little more than I did.

All my love,
Your darling, hilarious, beautiful, kindhearted mother,
Celia Rodriguez

PS: You might have guessed that the friend typing this is Paula. She knew of my plan all along, but please forgive her for it. I think she loves me a little more than she loves you.

Chapter 48

Olivia

Now

IT'S ONLY BEEN TEN HOURS SINCE I LEFT CARMELLO OUTSIDE of Celia's, but my bones are really trying to make me believe it's been thirty-four years. I'm at the pedestrian bridge, waiting for the sun to set, and I wish he were here to see it for the first time with me. I stand by what I said about us being certain, but I already miss him and I'm so scared to lose him. By 7 p.m., I'm sick of checking my phone for a message from him so I scroll to my high school email account. It's the address Celia had when we first emailed ten years ago, and I've kept it open just for her. Maybe this is the perfect moment to tell her that I still have fears too. That I'm afraid she didn't believe in me, that she didn't miss me like I hoped she did. But as soon as I click into the account, I get overwhelmed. It has so much spam that I'd never check it if it wasn't for—

My mind gets snatched and held hostage for a moment.

Because between Aéropostale and Tumblr is a new email from Celia.

Goose bumps break out all over my body. I swear even my left pinky finger tingles.

"Celia, what the hell? I told you to haunt Carmello, not me," I say, but I'm really wondering if she scheduled an email for me like she did for her son and his dad.

And then suddenly my belly warms like it knows Carmello is behind me before he says, "When did you tell her to haunt me?"

I whip around to face him, pulse racing before it settles to a rhythm that makes me feel safe. I wished for it, and he came. He hesitates before he takes a seat. But he's not close enough.

"At the cemetery one day," I confess. Then: "You're looking at me like I might bite."

"You can if you want to," he says.

I bite back a smile, and ask, "Why are you here?"

He nods his head to my phone. "Read for yourself."

I inhale once and then open Celia's email, which is when I notice it's really addressed to the person sitting beside me. He cc'd me in it when he sent it to himself.

"I don't feel comfortable reading something meant for you."

"How do you think I felt when you tried getting me to read the emails you two sent each other?" he replies. "Just scroll to the bottom, Jones."

I lift the phone again. "Fine, Rodriguez, but I don't know why—"

I'm silenced for the second time today because underneath Celia's superlong signature to her son and a wordy PS, there's a short message from Carmello.

O,

After you read this, do you think we can meet to talk at the pedestrian bridge? I'd pick you up, but I want you to have the freedom to get there on your own, or not. Still, you should know that I had already been solid and decided in my decision to keep you in my life. Even if it's just through a computer screen.

—Mello

"I'm here because I waited all day for you to message me after reading my mom's email, then I realized maybe you didn't, but something told me you might already be here anyway." I raise my head, confused about what this all means. "I'll explain everything, but first, I need you to read it. Please," he says.

I agree, then he scoots closer. With his thigh pressed up to mine, I take my time with it.

Minutes later, there are tears in my throat and my nose is running and I can barely breathe. Celia Rodriguez loved her son, and she loved me too. She picked me for her restaurant and to be family for Carmello after she was gone, and she wanted to give me the choice to accept. Carmello wipes my nose with his shirtsleeve, even though he definitely has germophobia, and I lean my head against him while I read the letter again.

"Paula," I say with a smile.

"The deceit," Carmello says, and I hear him smiling too.

"How dare they," I say right as another email hits my inbox. It's from Carmello.

I stare at the pdf file attached in the body of the email, then my head snaps up to look at him. He leans in to kiss one of my eyebrows, says, "I need you to read through this one too."

My face tingles and I want him to do that again, but I nod and do as he asked.

What I learn while I'm scrolling: the document was dated a week ago and drawn up by Carmello's new lawyer. With his e-signature attached in various boxes, he gave me 25 percent of his shares, which would have caused him to lose controlling interest in the restaurant. Had Celia's second will and testament not been discovered obsolete today, Carmello Rodriguez would've been giving me more than just a partnership. Fifty percent of the restaurant would have belonged to *me*.

I work on my breathing until it slows, I get my heart to steady, and then I meet Carmello's eyes and say, "How dare you, Mello."

"You wanted me to take my time," he says, "but I've spent so many years overthinking when it came to you, O. And I've learned more about myself and the way my stuff clashes up against your stuff and makes things hard for us faster in these few weeks than I did in a decade." He brushes a strand of fallen hair from my face. "But I know exactly what I want and that's *you* in my life, in whatever form you see fit. However close you want to be to me. I do have fears, but I don't think they're those same fears anymore. I won't ask you to stay in the way I want you to stay, but I will ask that you always find a place for me in your life. I can't lose you again."

"You came here with a pdf file in hand, smelling as good as you do, sitting as close as you are, and you think you're losing me?" I ask. "I'm confused as to why we're not kissing yet."

"You're making that face that you know makes me weak, Jones," he says.

"So be weak, Rodriguez," I say.

He gets close enough to barely skim his lips against mine and things happen to my body that shouldn't be happening on the bridge with this many people waiting on the sun to set.

"I can't just yet," Carmello says, pulling back with a smirk. "We should talk. You know, take our time. Be certain." I call him a tease, and he shrugs. "Olivia Jones, this is serious. You say I'm quick to try to fix things, but you didn't even finish reading the pdf file to know the terms in which I'm giving you my shares before you got impatient."

"All right," I say, "you might have a point that I'm impatient. But knowing that, if you can be so kind and explain the boring language to me so that I can stare at your beautiful face and hear your voice while I listen, that would be much appreciated."

"You're such a princess," he says with a laugh that makes my stomach somersault. "Fine, but you should sit down with my lawyer later to talk about anything you don't agree with. And we have to adjust some of it anyway, because in order for you to be an equal partner with me, I need to give you 50 percent of my shares, instead of 25 percent, since my mom stole hers back from you." My pulse quickens. Carmello really wants me to be an equal partner. I open my mouth to speak on it, but he gives me a stern look. "No, Olivia. You're going to sit here and listen to me now."

"Sheesh," I say. "Did I sound this sexy being strict earlier?"

He attempts to raise a brow at me, and it's cute, even though he's bad at it. "Anyway, as of right now, I had my lawyer include terms that say you don't have to officially live in Rhode Island. You can travel as a private chef if you want to. But I'll need you to contribute, which I stipulate needs to include that friendly attitude of yours and your big brain. You can work on the accounts if you're not here, make sure our event nights are running smoothly when you're in town. Come up with new ideas too. Celia's Place wouldn't be what it is right now without your input. And you're currently looking like you want to jump out of your skin, but if you're worried that my contribution to the workload will weigh more than yours, don't. I want to spend more time with Teddy and other people that I love without feeling so stressed about it, so I think we should figure out the funds to hire a couple station chefs. I'm certain the date-night event will help with that."

His eyes start to flick away like he just said a little too much, but I tug his shirtsleeve.

"Tell me more," I say. "Please. Your story is getting to the good parts."

He smiles. "I want you to make the decisions that feel best for your nervous system," he says, and those words alone do the work, but he keeps them coming. "I promise you, O, I am not trying to keep you in Rhode Island against your will, and I promise it's not because I don't trust that you're happy here when you tell me that you are, I just want us to be fair to each other. And being fair means we should consider all parts of you, including the ones that itch to get up and go search for new adventures. All you're required to do is communicate with me. If something changes with your availability or anything else, I need you to slow down a little and explain it to me, give me the time to process. And I promise to be better at communicating what the restaurant needs too. What *I* need from you."

"I have a feeling this offer of freedom is for more than just us as business partners," I say.

"First," he says, "do you *know* that you belong to Celia's Place and it belongs to you?"

Damn. He's good at this. "I'm grinning like I know, aren't I?"

I say. "Now tell me about the second thing. The *us* stuff. I'm getting rather impatient again."

"Fine, fine," he says. "I'll start with this: my mom told me a long time ago that relationships require more than love, they're hard work. And being close to you, cracking jokes with you, cooking with you, craving you, that's the easy part. But neither of us is perfect, Olivia. I think I do have OCD, and you should know for me that means I have these dark, intrusive thoughts that are hard to shake. I fear the worst for the people that I love, I constantly have voices in my head that try to throw me off. If you want to see me fully, you need to know how scary that is for me and how scary it might be to tell you my thoughts, but I want to try if you do." I reach for his hand, lace our fingers, tears pricking at my eyes. "Sometimes I'll worry, O, sometimes you'll jump, and we'll keep crashing into each other unexpectedly, but there's no one else I'd rather pick up the pieces with. You balance me out, Jones, and I'd like to think I do the same thing for you. So I'm asking you to do the hard work of a relationship with me. We can go as slow as you want. We can keep our choices, and should you choose to wake up and work at this with me, then I'll be there every single day, smiling at you from the other pillow—even at times when we're on different continents."

"Carmello," I say, swatting at my eyes. "I love you so much, and I understand why you'd be afraid to let me in all the way, but I'm grateful you're opening up to me about your OCD. I know it's different, but I've spent years working through my ADHD diagnosis and recognizing where my thoughts and desires stem from . . . and, well, I hope you know that I understand what you're working through. We can be open about how our brains work, together. I'm here for you, Mello. Just like I know you're here for me."

"Always," he says, and brushes hair from my face. "Now come here."

When our mouths meet, there's no other word I can think of to describe it but magic. Carmello's kisses call me home. Time after time. And I think I'll have that feeling from him for the rest of my life. We break away and he presses his forehead to mine so that we can breathe together.

While our faces are touching, I take his hand and put it right beneath my breastbone.

"Do you feel how fast my heart is beating?"

"Here," he says, putting my hand on his chest too. "You're not alone."

"This is all so crazy," I say. "Your mom was . . ."

"The original swindler," he says.

"I was going to say an innocent little angel, but she was definitely a well-rounded woman," I say, and with us connected, both of our bodies vibrate when he laughs.

He pulls back and says, "Did you know there were dozens of emails for me unsent in her drafts folder? Pictures of my report cards, of her and me, of Teddy cooking in the kitchen, of our staff having fun, and dishes I made for her when she was sick. One-liners like: *I'm proud of you.* I wonder why she never sent them."

I smile and say, "I remember years ago she told me that she wanted to feel closer to you. I didn't understand what she meant, but then I realized you both kinda floated around each other with heart eyes instead of saying the words. So, I shared with her something that me and my parents have always done since even before the fire when they'd travel for work."

"What's that?"

"Send each other out-of-context pictures through email of

whatever was going on that day, just to know that we were thinking of each other even when we felt far away. She never responded to my idea to do that with you, but months after I left she checked in with me for the first time over email. Like a fairly typical electronically deficient human being of her generation, she didn't write much in the body of it, just asked how I was doing and sent me a picture of her rolled lumpia. And my heart still leaped that she cared about me enough to do that and to remember what emails like that meant to me. But Carmello, you were always right by her side; maybe that's why she never sent the emails to you. Maybe she thought you already knew how much she loved you."

"I did know," he says, and I can hear how thick his throat is. "That's why I always wanted to be by her side too."

I wrap my arms around him and we brush faces with each other. "Like lions," he whispers, and I have images of us curled up on the couch together, watching movies with Teddy.

When golden hour starts to give way to pink skies, Carmello reaches for my hand and pulls me toward the railings so we can watch the view over the water.

"I hope we'll get to see more sunsets together," I say, tilting my head up to look at him. "Do you think while we're working to spend our lives together, we can work on that too?"

"Oh, I'll shut down the whole restaurant early all the time if that's what would make you happy, Jones," Carmello says. "Don't you know how much I love you?"

"We probably can't afford to do that just yet," I say, smiling. "But I think we can find a balance. And I knew you loved me down bad way before you made me a partner. Probably the first time you saw me sitting in a booth at the restaurant. I was eating so damn good because life wasn't as complicated yet and there you were trying to be mean, but I was just too cute."

"You're so cocky," he says, then he spins me around and bends low to kiss me.

"And you like it," I say, reaching for another. "You're captivated by me, Rodriguez."

When I suck his bottom lip into my mouth, he makes a delicious sound before his eyes flick to something behind me. He releases a heavy breath and pulls me closer, wrapping his arms around me and hiding me against his broad chest. "Oh, completely," he says. "And I'd like nothing more than to make out with you on this bridge, but we get carried away when we do that, and I didn't even notice that we have company kind of close. I'm pretty sure they're doing shrooms but they're also staring at us. Wouldn't want us to risk public indecency and not be able to come here after this."

I get on my tiptoes and kiss his chin, whisper, "Let's go to the truck after this."

"Deal," he says, then we turn back toward the water and I get to watch the sky transition to night at my favorite place with my favorite person.

But I don't forget about the other people in my heart. Balance.

While Carmello's elbow touches mine on the railing, I smile at the single text from Denise: **Girl, at least tell me he's still got some good . . .** I see what she's putting down and lean against Carmello, his body supporting me like the trunk of a tree while I send Denise emojis that'll definitely give her the vision of what my life has been like, in and out of bed.

Then, I realize for the first time in a while it's not that hard to focus my attention on more than one thing at a time as long as it feels right.

Epilogue
HALO-HALO

Carmello

Two Years Later

CRUSHED ICE AND EVAPORATED MILK MIXED TOGETHER with an assortment of fresh fruit and a variation of other ingredients. I chose jackfruit, ube, coconut strips, and bananas as my mix-ins. My tito ordered the same thing minus the bananas and added green jellies and sugar on top. It's the first dessert I've tried since arriving in the Philippines last night, and it doesn't disappoint.

It feels surreal to be in my mom's country with her family. I got to see the home she grew up in and meet her mother and nieces, people I've only seen in pictures and video chats. My tito could be her twin brother; they've both got the same eyes that crinkle around the edges and the same boisterous big-bellied laugh. And he has the best stories of her playing pranks during her school days that I've been eating up.

But as happy as I am to be here, I'm already dreading the day we have to leave. It took twenty-one hours to get here by plane, and my brain is calculating the risks of my anxiety meds wearing off too quickly again along with every other possible scenario that could go wrong on the way back home. Earlier I made a joke to my therapist about canceling my return flight and living here. But I've been thinking all day, truly, does it have to be a joke?

I've got a lot of what I need right on this beach anyway.

Up ahead, Olivia is filling a bucket with the clearest blue water I've ever seen and still she's the most stunning thing in view. Her hair is longer, big, loose honey-colored curls down her back, and her sun-kissed skin is glowing. Below her red sunglasses, there's a huge smile on her face. She's wearing flowy white shorts and a cropped tank top. From here, I can see the fox tattoo on her hip, and I smile to myself remembering the day she said it was her first and her last because the pain was *ridiculous, unbearable, downright ugly.* A few months later she was scheduling an appointment for another one. In the past couple of years, we've both had firsts and lasts together that ended that way. Table for Twos-Days took off, and it's been everything we've dreamed up and more. But the first time we tried speed dating with the card game, it was a bit of a catastrophe. We said it would be the last, but instead we worked out the kinks and we're now offering it every month. The first time we spent weeks without each other as a couple was when Olivia joined her parents in Cape Verde. When we finally saw each other again, she threw herself into my arms at the airport and said she was homesick. But each time she travels it gets easier on both of us. And each time I travel with her, it gets easier on me. After our turbulent flight taking the full-time staff to the Dominican Republic last year as a bonus, I vowed I'd never get on a plane again. Three weeks later, I was giving Olivia my credit card info to book four flights to the Philippines. Now here we are.

I watch her bring the bucket of water back to where Teddy is burying his grandfather in the sand. My usually very serious dad is covered from the neck down, a straw hat on his head, warning Teddy not to get more sand in his mouth. But soon Olivia is helping Teddy compact said sand with water so they can cement my dad in place better and they're all laughing and I'm letting my halo-halo melt because I'm too busy concentrating on them. *That's the trick, Carmello,* I can almost hear my therapist saying. *Concentrate on how good it feels to live in the moment with those you love and give less of yourself over to the fears of not having them in the future.*

Olivia blows me a kiss from across the sand, and I feel a rush of peace wash over me.

I turn to my uncle with a smile. "I'm ready for another story," I say. "Tell me more?"

Author's Note

Dearest reader,

This book didn't pour out of me the same way my last one did. In fact, I worked on another book before this that wasn't the right one for the moment. Instead, *The Bridge Back to You* came to me slowly, starting with a vague idea for a shared restaurant and a second-chance romance between two people who never stopped loving each other. The scenes came in bits and pieces, passion and pining, yearning, dialogue, and banter, and characters who felt lost at times the same way I felt while writing it. I think that's because this book was one that I had to dig deep for, confronting things I hadn't over the years to get to the heart of the story I was trying to tell.

While this is a book about love and not trauma, the mental health representation in its pages was important to me. Though the portrayal is intentionally gentle and maybe even subtle at times, Olivia, Carmello, Celia, and Teddy have all struggled in some form with their mental health.

In my early twenties, I was diagnosed with ADHD as well as OCD, but back then I didn't have the tools that would have made it a little easier to live with these conditions. And right after I turned in the first draft of this book, I had the kind of mental breakdown I hope I'll never ever have again. I'm mentioning this because, since then, I am better at taking care of myself by having a good routine which, for me, consists of adequate sleep, daily exercise, medication, and consistent therapy. This, in turn, has made me more conscious of the ways in which I could unintentionally affect those in my life when I'm not doing the work of taking care of myself mentally.

It's incredibly scary to talk about these things publicly. I feel vulnerable knowing this book is out in the world and people will be able to see me more fully after reading this note. But I think it's important for any reader who is struggling or has struggled with their mental health to know that they aren't alone. I hope meeting Olivia and Carmello may have helped with that, even a little. Regardless, I see you. We are deserving of love and happiness and peace, just like Carmello and Olivia. And I truly hope you found joy in their love story. So many things about them speak to my heart and always will. Thank you for reading my work and allowing me to be vulnerable with you.

With love,
Riss M. Neilson

ACKNOWLEDGMENTS

The Bridge Back to You wouldn't exist without my talented editor, Amanda Bergeron, who felt a spark in Carmello and Olivia's story when they were still new in my mind, and I was working through the details of how they'd make their way back to each other. I can't thank you enough for your patience and brilliant insight, and for believing in me and this book.

I have Jess Regel to thank for being such a rock in the process of me getting a second adult book done when I wasn't sure if anything would feel right. Thank you, thank you, for all of the phone calls and plotting and the encouragement. Our relationship has meant more to me than you'll ever know. You're a gem of an agent and a person, Jess!

Theresa Tran. Thank you for being another pair of eyes and for loving Carmello and Olivia. You've helped with the dreaded impostor syndrome so much. Especially when I needed it most. <3

I can't thank my wonderful team at Berkley enough. Jessica Mangicaro, Hillary Tacuri, Tara O'Connor, Yazmine Hassan, Megha Jain, Christine Legon, and copy editor Marianne Aguiar. You're all so amazing, and I'm grateful for your time, talents, and everything each one of you has done for me and this book.

I'm beyond grateful to each author who took the time to read and blurb this book. Hugs and love to you all. I know how much work it takes, and I hope it was a good time, at least.

My heart is full just typing this, but thank you to each reader, reviewer, bookseller, and librarian who has picked up *The Bridge Back to You* or has helped it find an audience.

To my family. My'ah and Jada Abreu, my babies, who are both teenagers now and were incredibly patient and understanding and caring while I was getting words on the page. Thank you so much. Your hugs are an absolute gift. To my parents, Angelique and Antonio Gagnon: thank you for your strength, empathy, and unwavering love for me during one of the toughest stretches of my life. I couldn't have done it without you. Just like I couldn't have done it without my brothers, Jadin Gagnon and Carlos Cruz, and the father of my kids, Nilson Abreu. I love you all so much.

To Shirlene Obuobi. I'll never forget all you did for me and the solid ground you gave me when I was trying to get the first draft done with a lot of highly stressful things happening in my life. I can't even begin to describe how much I appreciate you and will always love you for that.

I'm incredibly thankful for everyone who's made a difference in my life before, during, and after writing this book. Yolanda Rodrigo, Kathy Reyes, Lolita Villanueva, Carmelita Bisignani, Constance Neilson, Shylene Lopez, Jennifer Ramirez, Mindaluz

Lacap, Rochelle Baker, Diana Bonilla, Rachel Menard, Addie Wallace, Isha Abreu, Carissa Broadbent, Ali Rosen, Jenny Howe, Danica Nava, Iyanna Paniagua, Elsa Varela, Kamilah Cole, Kelly Andrew, Jas Hammonds, and Philip M. Johnson. I want each of you to know how much you mean to me.

To Em North. We've been friends for a decade, reading and editing each other's work, but I can't thank you enough for being a light in the dark for me this year. For sitting beside me quietly and for pushing me loudly when I needed it and for being consistent in the way you care for me.

It wouldn't feel right not to mention my late aunties Debra, Denise, and Paula, and my late uncle Bobby. Adding your names to this book gave me and Celia's Place a sense of family, and I pray you all are resting peacefully.

Thank you, God. Another year, another book out in the world. And more life and insight and lessons. I love you.

Laura Beth de Baker, Diana Bonilla, Rachel Menard, Addie Wallace, Jana Abreu, Carissa Broadbent, Ali Rowe, Jenny Howe, Danica Nava, Leanne [illegible], [illegible] Varela, Kamilah Cole, Kelly Andrew, [illegible], and Philip M. Johnson. I want each of you to know how much you mean to me.

To [illegible]: We've been friends for a decade, reading and editing each other's work, and I can't thank you enough for being a light in the dark. For [illegible], for sitting beside me, and for pushing me [illegible] and for being constant in the way you care for me.

It wouldn't feel right not to mention my late aunties: Debra, [illegible], and Faith, and my late uncle. Holding your names in this book gave me and [illegible] a sense of family, and I miss you all more than I can say.

Thank you, God. Another year, another book out in the world. All my love and thanks. Thank you.

The Bridge Back to You

RISS M. NEILSON

READERS GUIDE

Discussion Questions

1. Do you believe in second chances? Or are they solely for romance novels? What's your favorite second-chance romance novel?

2. With Daniela and Carmello's relationship, I wanted to showcase what healthy co-parenting could look like. Do you have any examples of healthy co-parenting in your life? Do you feel like the way Daniela and Carmello do it is realistic?

3. Olivia takes risks and is willing to put her heart out there to win Carmello back. Some of my favorite books portray women who are like this, such as Susan Lee's novel *Seoulmates.* How do you feel about women being the "hero" in romance novels?

4. Do you prefer having dual POVs in romance novels or do you enjoy the surprises that come from having only one?

5. What's your favorite memory involving food?

6. If you could travel anywhere in the world, where would it be and why?

7. Carmello's OCD shows up in small ways throughout the novel. Do you or anyone you know have OCD? How do you think it affects relationships, if at all?

8. Is there a first-time experience you'd relive the same way all over again?

Books That I've Read and Loved Recently

The Very Secret Society of Irregular Witches by Sangu Mandanna

Promise Me Sunshine by Cara Bastone

Love Is a War Song by Danica Nava

No Ordinary Love by Myah Ariel

The Romance Rivalry by Susan Lee

Love at Full Tilt by Jenny L. Howe

Can't Get Enough by Kennedy Ryan

Phantasma by Kaylie Smith

One Summer in Savannah by Terah Shelton Harris

Blood Over Bright Haven by M. L. Wang

In Universes by Emet North

Author photo by Jadin Gagnon

Riss M. Neilson is a magna cum laude graduate of Rhode Island College, where she won the English department's Jean Garrigue Award for creative writing. Her debut young adult novel, *Deep in Providence,* was a 2022 finalist for the New England Book Awards. She lives in Rhode Island with her two daughters and four fur babies, including a bunny named Michael Myers. *A Love Like the Sun* was her debut adult novel.

VISIT RISS M. NEILSON ONLINE

RissMNeilson.com
RissMNeilson